Friday Nights

Friday Nights

JOANNA TROLLOPE

BLOOMSBURY

First published 2008

Copyright © 2008 by Joanna Trollope

The moral right of the author has been asserted

Bloomsbury Publishing Plc, 36 Soho Square,
London W1D 3QY

ISBN 978–0–7475–9593–9

10 9 8 7 6 5 4 3 2 1

Typeset by Hewer Text UK Ltd, Edinburgh
Printed by Clays Ltd, St Ives plc

The paper this book is printed on is certified by the © 1996 Forest Stewardship
Council A.C. (FSC). It is ancient-forest friendly. The printer holds
FSC chain of custody SGS-COC-2061

FSC
Mixed Sources
Product group from well-managed
forests and other controlled sources
Cert no. SGS-COC-2061
www.fsc.org
© 1996 Forest Stewardship Council

CHAPTER ONE

Toby's mother said that when Eleanor came he'd have to go down to the ground floor and help her with the lift.

Toby said – sulkily, because he was angry with her for something he couldn't quite put his finger on – 'She doesn't need help.'

His mother was standing in front of the mirror she had propped on top of a chest in her bedroom. She was arranging her hair in a complicated kind of knot, and she had a hairclip between her teeth.

Through it she said without looking at him, 'Toby, this isn't about need. It's about manners.'

Toby kicked one foot clumsily against the other. Then he went out of his mother's bedroom and banged the door shut and leaned against it. This door, his mother's bedroom door, was one of only a few doors in the flat. There was just that door, and the front door and the door on the bathroom. The rest was just space. Upwards, outwards, sideways. Just space.

'I live in a loft,' Toby said to someone when he'd started his new school.

Several boys had stared at him, elaborately uninterested. 'Whatever,' they'd said.

'I do,' Toby had said to himself silently all that day. 'I do.' And then, 'My father bought it.'

He had. Toby's father had bought the loft two years ago, and had given it to Paula and Toby.

'Conscience money,' Paula's friend, Lindsay, said.

Paula hadn't replied. She put the photograph of Toby's father on the black rattan chest between two of the huge high windows. It was a photograph taken on a boat, and Toby's father was sitting on the roof of the cabin, and he was smiling. His feet were bare. The photograph did not, however, include Toby's father's wife and children who were, Toby knew, the reason why he and his mother lived in the loft on their own.

'At least,' Paula said sometimes to Toby, when she got very loving and then very angry, 'at least you know who your father *is*.'

What she meant by that Toby hadn't the faintest idea. And he certainly wasn't asking. Occasionally, if he was alone in the flat while Paula went to buy a newspaper, or to collect the dry-cleaning, he would pick up his father's photograph and lay it face down on the black rattan chest.

'You just stay there, Gavin,' he'd say. 'You just do as you're told.'

He sighed now. He wanted to be back in his mother's bedroom, but he had made that impossible. He sighed again. The loft looked enormous in the gathering gloom, as if the walls and ceiling were quietly dissolving into the darkness, just melting away so that the night could pour in. Paula had lit her lamps, the lamps that threw light up into the dusky spaces, the lamps that let light fall on to her orange cushions and the rug striped like a zebra. She had put glasses on the low table between the sofas because people were coming, glasses and bowls of varnished Japanese rice crackers. People were coming. Eleanor was coming.

Toby pushed himself away from the door and stood up. He liked Eleanor. She walked unevenly with the help of a stick, and her hair was a white fuzz, and she talked to him as if he might have an opinion worth hearing. He also liked how his mother was with Eleanor, how she was calm and able to think about things that weren't automatically going to upset her. Eleanor once said to Toby that the older she got the more she preferred the universal to the individual and personal. Toby had wondered if she was talking about galaxies.

He went slowly across the living space, avoiding, as usual, actually treading on the zebra rug. On the far side, a metal staircase resembling a ladder with perforated treads rose up in the dimness to the platform where Toby's bed was, and his computer, and the toy theatre for which he collected puppets. He climbed the ladder slowly, a deliberate tread at a time, until he was out of the glow of the lamps and into the privacy of darkness. Then he sat down on the top step of the ladder and leaned forward, until his chin was on his knees, and he sighed again. Friday nights.

It was Eleanor who had started these Friday nights some years back, after observing from the bay window of her front room two young women endlessly trailing up and down that low-built street in Fulham. One had a baby and one had a small boy. They were never together, and they were never, as far as Eleanor could see, accompanied by a man.

Eleanor had seldom been accompanied by a man herself, but then she had never had a baby or a small boy either. Watching the young women, she had seen what she had so often seen during her long working years as an administrator in the National Health Service – manifestations of those brave coping mechanisms devised by people concerned not to be pitied for being alone. Being alone, Eleanor knew, was not in itself undesirable: it was the circumstances of aloneness that made it either a friend or a foe. And being alone with a small dependent child, and thus in a situation considered by the conventional world to be ideally a matter of partnership, was not a situation for the faint-hearted. Some-times, Eleanor thought, watching them over the top of her reading glasses, the set of those young women's shoulders indicated that their hearts, for all the outward show of managing, were very faint indeed.

One day, seeing them both approaching from opposite ends of the street, she had limped out on her stick into a sharp spring wind and offered to babysit. Both had been extremely startled, and both had demurred. The girl with the baby said she couldn't leave him. The young woman with the small boy said she had no money. Eleanor said she didn't want money. The young woman said, somewhat desperately, that she couldn't handle obligation.

Eleanor leaned on her stick. She took off her reading glasses and let them hang round her neck on the scarlet cord she had attached in the hope of not losing them.

'Then do *me* a favour,' Eleanor said.

The girls waited, sniffing the wind.

'Let me be the obliged one,' Eleanor said. 'Come and see me. Bring the children. Come on Friday night.'

They came, mute with awkwardness. The baby slept in his pram. Toby, aged almost three, squirmed on the sofa under a crocheted blanket and threaded his fingers endlessly in and out of the holes. Eleanor opened a bottle of Chianti, and poured out large glasses. She learned, with patience and difficulty, that Paula, Toby's mother, could not, for some reason, live with Toby's father. She learned that Lindsay, mother of baby Noah, had been widowed when her husband, a construction worker, had been crushed by a cement slab.

'It was a year and three months ago,' Lindsay said. She looked across at the pram. 'I didn't even know I was pregnant.'

'Nobody should be required to bear that,' Eleanor said.

4

Lindsay said quickly, still looking at the pram, 'I'm not bearing it.'

They did not, either of them, seem to know how to arrange themselves, nor when to leave. At ten o'clock, Eleanor got stiffly to her feet and said that she was afraid it was her bedtime. They went out together, with the pram and the pushchair, hardly looking at her as they said goodbye. Eleanor, beginning on the nightly ritual of closing and locking and bolting, thought how often it was the case that a small good intention was snatched out of one's hands by human conduct and inflated into something much larger and much less manageable. She regarded herself dispassionately in the looking glass let into the art deco coat stand in her hall.

'Persevere,' Eleanor told herself. 'Keep going.'

Three Fridays later, they came again. Eleanor had seen Lindsay in the newsagent's on the corner of the street, and Paula comforting Toby who had fallen out of his pushchair while struggling against being strapped in. They had not accepted with enthusiasm, but they had not refused either. Eleanor made pâté, and bought French bread, and chocolate, and juice for Toby in a small waxed carton with a straw. Lindsay brought six mauve chrysanthemums in a cone of cellophane printed to resemble lace. Toby climbed out of the crocheted blanket and drank his juice on his mother's knee and stared at Eleanor's hair. They had stayed until ten-fifteen, and Paula had been able to look straight at Eleanor for a few seconds and say uncertainly, 'That was kind of you.'

Eleanor took her glasses off.

'If kindness isn't just a form of self-interest, thank you.'

A few weeks later, Lindsay asked if she could bring her younger sister. She looked at a point just past Eleanor's left ear while she asked this, and the request became entangled in a long and confused explanation of how Lindsay's parents' inability to parent in any sustained way had left Lindsay as the only person in her sister's life who could provide any mothering. It was an anxious task, Lindsay implied, since her sister seemed to have inherited her parents' taste for a wild and irresponsible life. She was working in a club in Ladbroke Grove as a warm-up disc jockey when she could get the work, and Lindsay was worried about the ways in which she was spending her free time.

'What is her name?' Eleanor said.

'Julia,' Lindsay said.

'Jules,' Jules said, when she came. She had red-and-yellow striped hair and was wearing a flowered tea dress over thick black leggings and heavy laced-up boots. She had on purple lipstick. Toby stopped staring at Eleanor's hair and stared at Jules instead. She stared back, her bitten-nailed hands wrapped round a mug of tea, which was all she would drink. She spoke to no one except to say, her eyes roving over the incoherent contents of Eleanor's sitting room, 'Cool room.'

Lindsay had come round to Eleanor's house the next morning. She had a baby cyclamen in a plastic pot in her hand.

'It's a bit awkward,' Lindsay said.

Eleanor smiled at Noah. He was lying in his pram, wearing a yellow knitted hat that made him resemble an egg in a cosy.

'Oh?'

'Jules, well, Jules doesn't live in a world where people say please and thank you much.'

'I'm used to that,' Eleanor said.

'I didn't want you to think –' Lindsay stopped.

'I didn't.'

Lindsay held out the cyclamen.

'Please . . .'

Eleanor transferred her stick from one hand to the other.

'I like cyclamen. But I don't need an apology.'

'Bah,' Noah said from his pram.

Lindsay looked down at him.

'Jules never pays him any attention. It's as if she hasn't seen him.'

Eleanor took the cyclamen out of Lindsay's hand.

'She's seen him all right. Thank you for this.'

'I don't expect she'll come again –'

'No.'

'I'm sorry –'

'Do you know,' Eleanor said, 'these days, I seem to save getting upset for the big things.'

Almost two months later, Jules did come again. She wore a pink baby-doll chiffon top and a leather waistcoat and a miniskirt over jeans. She thrust a parcel wrapped in newspaper at Eleanor and went wordlessly off to the kitchen to make tea. In the newspaper parcel was a battered hand mirror made of black papier mâché inlaid with mother-of-pearl.

'Thank you,' Eleanor said, surveying herself in the clouded glass. 'I am very touched.'

Jules shrugged. She looked round Eleanor's determinedly unmodernised kitchen.

'Yeah,' she said approvingly.

It was that same evening that Toby slid down from Paula's knee and went to stand two feet in front of Jules so that he could examine her properly. It was that same evening that Eleanor described her childhood, growing up in a tall redbrick house down the southern end of the Munster Road. Her bedroom had looked out on to the railway, and her world, she said, had been a linear one, defined by the number 14 bus route, with school in Putney at one end, and infrequent snatches of bright-lights life in Piccadilly at the other. It was that evening that Lindsay had broken down completely and out of the blue, and Jules had fled to the stairs where Eleanor found her steadily banging her head against the wall while chanting, 'Shit, shit, shit,' like a mantra. It was also the evening when, escorting them all out of her front door and down the negligible path to the pavement, Eleanor had seen her neighbour of two doors away, a well-dressed woman invariably in a professional-looking suit, pause in the process of unlocking her own front door to look at them all with more than passing interest, with, in fact, considerable curiosity. Eleanor looked back. The woman gave an irresolute smile. Eleanor nodded.

'Who's she?' Paula said.

'A Miss Campbell, I believe.'

'Shush,' Lindsay said. 'She can hear you.'

Miss Campbell got her door open and pulled her key free.

'She can,' she said, and stepped inside.

The door closed. Jules was standing on the pavement, her fingers in her mouth.

'Ask her too,' she said.

'I think,' Eleanor said, 'Miss Campbell doesn't lack for a social life.'

'I dare you,' Jules said.

Blaise Campbell arrived some Fridays later, with a bottle of Riesling and a bunch of violets. Noah was complaining in his pram and Toby had taken the crocheted blanket under the table and was lying with his thumb in his mouth and his free hand grasping his mother's foot. Lindsay and Paula watched Blaise enter Eleanor's sitting room as if she were embarking on the unknown tests of an initiation rite.

'We are not used,' Eleanor said, 'to wine as superior as this. Thank you.'

Blaise made a little deprecating gesture. Perhaps she was thirty-five, Paula thought, perhaps older. She had the polish of someone older but that might be because she was a lawyer or an accountant or one of those professionals who have to look older than they really are in order to look as if they know what they are doing. She watched Blaise step round Toby's protruding foot in its blue-and-red slipper sock, and take a chair with the neatness of someone used to doing it in public. Paula looked at Blaise's hands. Well cared for. Ringless. She had folded them on the table, as if she were in a meeting. Perhaps she was also used to meetings.

'It's very kind of you,' Blaise said, 'to include me.'

Eleanor smiled as her.

'I expected you to turn me down.'

'Oh no.'

Noah's voice rose to a wail.

'He's hungry,' Lindsay said. She went over to the pram, her skirt rucked up from where she had been sitting. 'He's always hungry.'

Blaise said politely, 'How old is he?'

'Eight months.'

Under the table, Toby's hand left his mother's foot and walked, crabwise, across the floor to one of Blaise's feet. It was shod in a patent-leather pump. The hand considered the patent leather for a moment and tried a few experimental taps, and then it crept up Blaise's foot and grasped her ankle.

'Oh!' Blaise said. Her eyes widened.

Paula glanced under the table.

'Stop it, Toby.'

Toby, his thumb still in, paid no attention.

'Let go!' Paula said.

Blaise said hastily, 'I don't mind . . .'

'Don't you?'

'No.'

Paula sat back. It was another tiny test.

'Oh well then –'

Blaise looked round at them all. She cleared her throat.

9

Paula tried to catch Lindsay's eye, to mouth at her, 'She thinks we're a meeting!'

'I probably shouldn't ask this,' Blaise said, 'especially on my first visit, but – but can anyone join?'

Eleanor put a handful of old-fashioned hock glasses with green stems down on the table.

'Within reason –'

'It's just,' Blaise said, 'it's just that I've got a friend, I mean a colleague, someone I work with, who was terribly envious of me when I said where I was coming tonight. She says she almost never gets to talk to women, except at work, she's just too busy.' She looked round the circle. She said, a little louder, 'She's the breadwinner, you see. Her husband is an artist. They have two little girls. She simply made me promise I'd ask. So I have.'

Eleanor drew the bottle towards her. Nobody spoke. Toby let his hand slide down Blaise's foot to her shoe. His hand was warm and slightly damp. He found he could stick it and unstick it to her shoe.

Eleanor pulled the cork out of the Riesling. She looked at Blaise. Blaise was looking at Lindsay and Lindsay was looking at Noah.

'Well, bring her,' Eleanor said. 'Why not?'

It was nice, Toby thought now, jiggling his feet on the metal ladder, when they used to go to Eleanor's house. Once they went all the time, from the flat that had been home before they moved to the loft, the flat that Toby could still remember, especially in terms of texture and smell, in every detail. It was on the first floor of a house like Eleanor's, a two-storey Edwardian house with a heavy frieze around the solid bay windows. The frieze was punctured with quatrefoils and painted with thick pink paint. Eleanor's house, which Toby could see from their sitting-room window, was painted cream and the paint was flaking off. Their flat only had a sitting room and a bedroom and a kitchen and a bathroom like a cupboard that filled with steam in seconds. Paula hated it with a passion. Toby loved it, especially the decorative blisters on the wallpaper that you could pop with a fingernail and the china doorknobs that rattled in their base rings like loose teeth.

They lived in that flat for six years. It was the flat that Toby started school from. It was the flat that Paula went to her part-time job from, her job in a shop further east up the Fulham Road that specialised in uncompromising dark furniture from Indonesia. It was the flat that Gavin, Toby's father, came to sometimes and, after minutes of supreme tension in the sitting room with Paula, removed Toby from to take him to a pizza place.

On some of these occasions, Toby had talked as if he'd had a dose of laughing gas. On others, he said almost nothing, cutting his pizza into an unnecessary number of little strips, and waiting for Gavin to say, as he always uselessly said, 'Well, where would you like to go now?'

Toby never knew. He would take gulps of his Coca-Cola and make don't-know faces. The contrast between the anticipation and the reality of Gavin's visits left him bereft of ideas, let alone the means of expressing them. Usually Gavin would watch him in an unpractised way for a while and then say, 'If I was a member at Stamford Bridge, at least we could go there. But as I'm not, we can't,' and he'd give a little bark of laughter. Toby didn't join in. He knew Gavin had three other children, three daughters, and they somehow joined in those outings with Gavin in a shadowy, insistent way, like moths pattering against a hot lampshade. They had names that Toby took care not to remember in any easily accessible parts of his mind. They were obviously the ones that Gavin was in tune with, the ones who never got asked where they would like to go, because it was never necessary.

Usually, they walked. They walked the streets so familiar to Toby, past shops he saw every day, the manicurist, and the ironmonger where, on weekdays, the ladders and buckets on display on the pavement were chained together like a convict gang, the antique shop full of dusty Far Eastern idols and a pearl-lined shell as big as a small canoe, the herbalist who offered acupuncture. Gavin didn't try to take Toby's hand on these walks, although he put his on Toby's shoulder as they crossed streets, and so Toby would walk sufficiently apart from him in order to make hand-holding out of the question. On the way back – Gavin was always checking his watch, always saying, 'We must stick by the arrangement, mustn't we?' in a way that made Toby despair – they always passed Eleanor's house, and if he could see her fuzz of white hair through the sitting-room window a drop of cool comfort fell into the hot bile engendered by the afternoon. Sometimes she looked up and saw him and she would take one hand away from the book or paper she was reading and raise it in a kind of salute.

'Do odd jobs for her, do you?' Gavin said, his voice a shade too hearty.

'No,' Toby said. Eleanor was not somehow for sharing. 'No, she does them herself.'

Since they came to live in the loft, however, things had changed. The loft was a change in itself, of course, the result of something happening to Gavin's job that meant he could buy them the loft and be photographed on a boat and give Toby a computer. But the loft had changed Paula too, had meant that she had found the courage to apply for, and get, the job of managing the Indonesian furniture shop, and that she now found excuses not to spend too much time in Eleanor's sitting room.

'I want to look after her now,' she said to Toby. 'I want to pay her back a bit.'

Toby thought Eleanor liked being in her own house. There was something about the way she looked round the loft, whenever she came, that made him think she found it faintly – well, funny really. And the sofas were too low. You could see that. It needed Toby and Paula together to get Eleanor out of the sofas.

Paula came out of her bedroom. Her dark hair was pinned up in a spiky ball behind her head and she was wearing shoes Toby hadn't seen before. Black with red heels. He regarded them with disapproval.

'Toby?'

He said nothing. Paula picked up a box of long matches and began to light the scattering of tea-light candles across the low table.

'I don't think Noah's coming tonight,' Paula said. 'Only Poppy. So there'll just be you two children.'

Toby stared at the little flotilla of tiny flames.

'But that's OK, isn't it? Poppy likes your theatre.'

Privately Toby quite liked Poppy. At six, she was two years younger than he was, and spoke in an intense whisper. Her mother, Blaise's friend Karen, said that this was because her infinitely competent older sister was always shushing her. But Poppy was not the kind of child who would ever have taken kindly to being shushed, for whatever reason. Poppy talked all the time, and if she did so in a whisper there was no point or logic in telling her to shut up.

'OK,' Toby said.

Paula walked away towards the kitchen part of the loft. The red heels were quite high and she didn't walk very steadily. Toby watched her open the door of the big new fridge and stand looking inside as if she was considering something.

She glanced towards him.

'I even bought you and Poppy some Coke,' Paula said. 'As a treat.'

Toby began to inch down the steps, arching his back and balancing on his hands and feet.

'OK.'

'That's not a very gracious response to a treat, is it?'

Toby reached the floor with his feet.

'Why is it a treat?'

'Because it's Friday night –'

'You don't usually –'

'Toby,' Paula said, 'I don't know what's eating you, but don't take it out on *me*.'

Toby got to his feet.

'Why can't we go round to Eleanor's?'

'Because it's my turn. Because I like having everyone here. Because Lindsay is coming early.'

Toby began to walk along one of the lines between the floor-planking as if it was a tightrope.

'Is Jules coming?'

'I don't know. You never do know, with Jules.'

She took a bottle out of the fridge and began hunting in a drawer for a corkscrew. Toby watched his grey-trainered feet flip down in a moving line, one foot after the other. The line ended up a short distance away from Paula. She held the corkscrew out.

'You should learn to do this.'

'I'm not allowed wine,' Toby said babyishly.

'Yes, you are. With water. If I say so. Anyway, taking corks out of bottles is something you have to learn to do. Come and try.'

Toby wanted to try. He hung back, his feet still arranged toe to heel.

'Come on.'

'I'm coming.'

'It's no big deal,' Paula said. 'It's just useful.'

Toby put his arms out to balance his position.

'OK.'

'Do you behave like this at school? If so, I wonder why Miss Wingate, or whatever she's called, doesn't want to throttle you.'

Toby unjammed his feet.

'I expect she does.'

'Do you like her?'

Toby looked agonised.

'I dunno –'

'What does she look like?'

Toby's expression changed from agonised to appalled.

'*What?*'

'What does Miss Wingate look like? Tall? Short? Fat? Thin? Short hair? Long hair?'

Toby took the corkscrew and flapped its metal arms up and down.

'I didn't look.'

Paula took the hand that was holding the corkscrew and held it above the bottle.

'I've taken the foil off. That plug in there, dumbo, is the cork. What do you think *I* look like?'

Toby jabbed the corkscrew down at the bottle and missed.

He shouted, 'Don't *ask* me this stuff!'

He heard Paula catch her breath, a long, slow intake. Never a good sign. She took his hand again and held it, painfully hard.

'To think I have all adolescence to get through and you haven't even got there yet. Put your left hand on the bottle.'

Toby didn't move.

'Do as you are told!' Paula said loudly.

Toby put his hand on the bottle, very slowly. It was cold and hard and wet.

'Ugh,' he said.

'Now, centre the screw on the cork. Carefully.'

She pushed his right hand downwards. Her nails dug into the skin of his hand.

'Ow –'

'In the middle. The absolute middle. Now push. To get the tip in, before you turn.'

Toby pushed, the tip of the screw skidded sideways and knocked the bottle over.

'Dear God –' Paula said.

The doorbell rang. The bottle rolled slowly to the edge of the kitchen table and Toby caught it, using a reflex he had had no intention of employing. Paula said nothing to him. She ran unevenly across to the intercom in her red heels and pressed the buzzer that released the street door.

'Come on up,' she said into the intercom, 'before I murder Toby.'

Toby set the bottle upright on the table, inserted the corkscrew, twisted it down, flipped the metal levers and pulled the cork out. Paula came back to the kitchen.

She looked at the extracted cork.

'You little sod.'

Toby shrugged.

'What was all that about?'

Toby shrugged again. Paula took him by the shoulders and bent to look in his face.

'Answer me. What was all that about?'

Toby said truthfully, 'I don't know.'

'Is it school? Has anyone upset you? Are you being bullied?'

The front doorbell rang.

'We'll talk about this,' Paula said. 'We'll talk about this tomorrow. In the meantime, just try and behave. Just try. OK?'

Toby gave the smallest of nods. Paula let go of his shoulders and ran across to the front door. Lindsay was standing there in her beige hooded coat with a carrier in her hand.

She said, kissing Paula, laughing, 'What's he done?'

Paula didn't look at Toby.

She said, 'I asked him to describe what I looked like and he couldn't. I could wear orange-peel teeth and a green fright wig and he wouldn't notice.'

'I would,' Toby said, under his breath.

Lindsay took her coat off. She looked round her.

'This is so great. I love coming here.' She held out the carrier bag. 'These are for you. I know you like big candles.' She looked towards the kitchen and she called, 'Hi, Toby. Noah says to say hi too,' and then she looked down at Paula's feet and she said, 'Wow. Hot *shoes*.'

Paula was looking in the carrier bag.

'These are lovely. Just what I like.' She glanced at her feet and gave a little giggle. 'I know.'

Lindsay bent closer.

'Come on, then.'

Paula bent her head too.

'Well . . .'

'Come on,' Lindsay said, 'come *on*. You said come early, so I've come. Tell me –'

Paula shifted a little on her red heels.

There was a pause, and then she said, in quite a low voice, but with a pride and a thrill in it that made Toby, standing by the kitchen table, feel suddenly sick, 'He's called Jackson.'

CHAPTER TWO

Paula's father had never wanted her to come to London. After her mother left him – to live with a man who worked on the oil rigs out of Aberdeen – he had summoned up heroic energies to gain custody of his daughter, and he had succeeded. But the effort, the sustained and focused exertion of persuading the authorities to go against their habitual favouring of mothers in such cases, seemed, Paula thought later, to have drained him dry. All that commitment, all that vigour and enterprise and resolve, was not, it appeared, a latent and unexplored quality in a mild-seeming man. It was more like a reserve he had in case of emergency, and Paula had turned out to be that emergency and the reserve had been entirely used up. It was a life supply, and she had taken it. Once the courts had decided finally in his favour, and Paula had, for the umpteenth time, made the disorientating journey from Scotland to Somerset and the bedroom of her childhood – the only thing, she sometimes thought, that remained a constant – the fires that had blazed so magnificently during the struggle had died back to ashes. Warm ashes, to be sure, but ashes all the same.

He looked after her most conscientiously. He was an accountant in a firm in a market town and he kept regular hours and was in every sense to be relied upon. He applied the attention to detail that his work required to fatherhood.

He strove, not just to be a good provider and protector, but a good companion too. Schoolfriends of Paula's, envious of a parental situation less orthodox than their own, even saw a man in him, where she could only see a father.

'He talks to you,' her friend Elaine said, 'doesn't he? Doesn't just tell you where to get off. He talks to you.'

Paula supposed he did. There was, after all, no one else to talk to, except work colleagues and fellow members of the local tennis club. There were certainly no other women. Paula kept a sharp eye out for them, but her father's apparent indifference seemed to be far more effective at keeping them at bay than her watchfulness. His pleasure, his satisfaction, came from her company, from knowing he was doing well by her, that he was allowing her to grow and develop in a way that fulfilled both her desires and her capacities. Until she said, aged almost eighteen, that she didn't want to go to university, she wanted to go to London.

It was January. Her father was up a ladder in the small garden behind the house she had known all her life, pruning the apple tree. She stood at the bottom of the tree and looked up at his familiar shape, bulked out by winter clothes, and delivered her announcement.

Her father made two or three more precise snips and let the gnarled grey twigs fall to the grass.

He said, 'There are excellent colleges in London.'

Paula said, 'I know.'

Her father said, 'I imagine it's harder to make friends when you aren't in a place devoted to a student community, but it can't be impossible.'

Paula hunched her shoulders up, and her chin down into her scarf.

'I don't want to go to university.'

Her father said nothing. He stopped snipping, and held a twig and stared at it.

Paula said, 'I want to get a job and earn money and live in a flat. I want to *live*.'

'What do you imagine you are doing now?'

'Getting by. Waiting.'

'Waiting for what?'

'Waiting for something to happen.'

Her father put the secateurs into the pocket of his padded jacket and began to descend the ladder.

'Define that thing.'

'I can't,' Paula said. 'I just know I can't go on marking time.'

'Most people,' her father said, not looking at her, 'feel like that at the end of secondary education. It's natural. You want to stop being told things and get going on something of your own.'

'Exactly.'

'But going to London and working in a shop will only be a short-term solution to that. It won't deal with the long term. It won't help your future.'

'I didn't say I wanted to work in a shop.'

Her father glanced at her. He gave her a quick, tired little smile.

He said, 'Who else would have you?'

Paula blew into her scarf until it was warm and damp against her chin.

Her father said, 'The point of continuing your education is to provide you with the tools for a satisfying life later on. Nobody notices their twenties and thirties going by because there's so much going on.' He stopped and then he said sadly, 'It's the forties and fifties you have to worry about. It's when it all starts slowing down.'

'I can't think about that,' Paula said.

'Well, you should.'

'If I think about that, I'll waste *now*. I feel I'm wasting now already. I feel there's something happening out there without me and I want to join in.'

Her father looked up at the tree. The branches he had trimmed looked neat but somehow rather startled.

He said, 'I can't stop you. I can advise you not to, I could even tell you not to, but I can't stop you.' He gave a long, tired sigh. 'I do want you to go to university. I don't want you to go to London. But I won't stop you.'

She did find work in a shop. She found a room in a house belonging to a cousin of her social-studies teacher at school, and a job in an artists' materials shop in the Fulham Road. It was a remarkable shop, fashioned to look as if it had been there for a hundred years instead of just ten, and the customers shopped with the purposefulness of people in pursuit of something they need, rather than simply drifting about in the vague hope of finding something they might like. When Paula's father came up from Somerset to see her, she showed him the shop with a kind of defiant pride, as if willing him to acknowledge that, even if she was working in a shop, it was a cultured, almost academic shop. He stood in the middle of the floor, his hands in the pockets of the outdated overcoat he had worn as long as Paula could remember, and looked about at the shelves of handmade paper, the racks of sketchbooks, the silvery lines of oil-paint tubes, the piles of neat tins of expensive German pencils, and said, 'You could always have made art a hobby, you know.'

Paula started a portfolio. She enrolled for life-drawing classes at the local college. She enrolled for flower-arranging classes and classes on photography and book-binding. She obtained a prospectus from Cordwainers College about shoe-making and one from Queen Mary's College about Renaissance studies. She went to two or three classes of everything, but no more. The prospectuses lay in their torn-open envelopes unread. The portfolio got pushed under the carpet. When the shop closed in the evening, Paula went looking for distractions that had nothing to do with improving her mind or her future, distractions that were the only way she could dissipate the enormous energies rising up in her, all the time, like lava.

There were men, inevitably. Not many of them, according to some of the girls Paula was mixing with, but enough to make her think uneasily sometimes about her father. There were certainly none she wanted to take to Somerset, not because they were second-rate, but because there could be no story attached to them, no settled present, no anticipated future. She couldn't, she felt, take someone down to meet her father and say, 'This is Jake, Dad. I met him on Thursday and I expect we'll see each other for about three weeks.' So she went home alone now and then, and when her father said – never looking at her – 'And how about boyfriends?' she always said, 'Nothing to tell, Dad,' and changed the subject.

Until she met Gavin. And when she met Gavin, there was suddenly, and simultaneously, a great deal to tell and most of it impossible to confess to. How was she to tell her father that she, at eighteen years old, on an income of just over eleven thousand a year with no identifiable prospects and not much to offer beyond the dynamism of her age, was deeply involved with a married man of thirty-two with a child at home and another baby on the way? How could she explain that this man, for all the obvious drawbacks – and in her obsessed eyes, they seemed neither real drawbacks nor glaringly obvious – had given her exactly what she had been meandering about looking for, that he was, at once, both the point and the purpose of her life, that he was, gloriously, it seemed to her, the *answer*? How could she possibly tell her father all this when her father, going about his methodical life in Somerset, simply did not have the language to comprehend what had happened to her?

Gavin, a lawyer in a large insurance company, was making a reasonable living. That living provided him with a four-bedroomed house in Clapham and a subscription to a smart gym north of the river. When he met Paula, he was going to the gym four times a week on his way home. After he met her, he went to the gym once a week and the other, supposed, times he spent with Paula. He was perfectly open, proud even, about showing her a photograph of his small daughter, scowling under her fringe with a blue-towelling rabbit clamped in her arms. He was equally open about admitting that the second baby was unplanned and too soon after the first, for both him and his wife. His wife had just started back at work, as a physiotherapist. She was, Gavin said, as fed up about this pregnancy as he was. She didn't want him anywhere near her. He told Paula this quite candidly, fixing her with his guileless hazel gaze and deftly transferring any responsibility for his actions from his shoulders to hers.

'I don't know what I'd have done if I hadn't met you,' he said. 'I'm not really exaggerating when I say you've saved me.'

It would have been such luxury to reciprocate, to tell him that he'd saved her in return. But some small instinct for prudence and self-preservation held her back, some notion that to tell a man he'd saved you from nothingness, from a kind of violent vertical existence, might not be what he wanted to hear. In any case, he didn't need to hear it. He seemed completely confident of her feelings, an absolute stranger to any anxiety about her eyes straying to a man who was younger, who was single, who did not have almost two children. It was stunning, Paula thought, his confidence.

The manager of the shop, a brisk Glaswegian who had married her English husband almost entirely, she said, because he wasn't Scots, saw Paula's situation levelly.

'Men aren't a career, you know. A man isn't your life's work, however much he'd like to be.'

Paula was shuffling classy birthday cards on a spinner. She moved so that Margie couldn't see her face.

She said, 'Can't a man give you something to believe in?'

'No.'

'Margie –'

'I'll amend that,' Margie said. 'The answer's yes, if it's yourself.'

But Paula didn't want that. Paula wanted to believe in Gavin, in his ability to transform her life for her, corral all those wild yearnings in her into something less wasteful, give her not just an appetite for the future, but an exciting idea of it. He not only dominated her life – the meetings, the phone calls, the unbearable, negligent silences – but he found her a better place to live, a part-time evening job in a wine bar cum art gallery, a bicycle, to save her money and make her exercise.

'Nothing sexier,' Gavin said, buckling her helmet on, as if she was a six-year-old, 'than a good-looking girl freewheeling through traffic on a bike.'

After the second baby was born – another girl, about which Gavin expressed pleasure to Paula, but not rapture – Paula discovered that she had, quite without intending to, fallen into a role and a pattern. She could talk about 'my boyfriend' to other people, she could mentally decorate each week ahead with the little glowing candles of seeing Gavin, but she could not, somehow, convince herself that the composition of her life had anything much to do with her own volition. When Gavin was free, she obliged. When Gavin was not free, she waited.

'It's called collusion,' Margie said. 'It's what you do when you think it's the only way to get what you want.' She glanced at Paula. 'What do you want?'

'More,' Paula said.

Margie looked back at the stock lists in her hands.

'More what?'

'More Gavin.'

But somehow, there was no more Gavin. Or at least, there was no more Gavin available. Paula put blonde stripes in her hair and joined a tango class, but there was still no more Gavin and nothing that seemed to do instead of Gavin. She might be growing increasingly frustrated at his evasiveness about the future hardening into a refusal to talk about it at all, but she still could not bring herself to walk away, to step bravely out into a life without him for the simple reason that such a life seemed too bleak and pointless even to contemplate. Her teens melted into her twenties, her job into Margie's job when Margie abruptly left both it and her English husband to go back to Glasgow, her flat into another flat and then another, and the feeling of being on the edge of a dance in which she could not join, that feeling she had tried to express standing under the apple tree with her father, returned like an old haunting.

Then Gavin told her, with the air of one who in no way should be held responsible, that his wife was pregnant again. Paula was woken, as if by a sharp slap. This physiotherapist wife had never represented an intractable problem for Paula. She had never seemed a threat, because of the way Gavin described their relationship. She was just there, someone who had to be accommodated until those two little girls were older. Just a little older. And now she was – again – pregnant. Paula, galvanised by something irresistible and ungovernable, bought a large jar of folic acid tablets and threw her contraception pills down the lavatory. Three months later, at twenty-two and three months, she was pregnant herself. Filled with a renewed conviction that life was only there to be lived to the full, and then some, as she had been under that apple tree, she announced her pregnancy, with a kind of glowing triumph, to her lover and to her father.

Both were completely dismayed. They were very different men in character, but their reaction to this unexpected baby was almost identical.

They both said:

'How could you let this happen?'

'What are you going to do?'

'Will you keep it?'

Only Gavin added, with a chill, angry misery, 'Have you tricked me?'

Paula was stunned. And furious. She was the one who'd been tricked, she yelled at Gavin, she was the one who'd been led to believe she was crucial, vital. The One. Why should she take any more responsibility for contraception than he did? Who was the single one, after all, who was the one who was not committing adultery or whatever stupid phrase out of the Ark he'd just used? Why was this baby her problem anyway? Why was it any less his problem than his wife's babies? How dare he, dare he, *dare* he ask her if she was going to keep it?

She did not yell at her father. He came up from Somerset and she looked at him across a café table in the Sainsbury Wing of the National Gallery – had he chosen that as a rendezvous because there were so many paintings around him of the Madonna and Child? – and decided to be as unhelpful as possible. He asked her about Gavin, and Gavin's circumstances, and about her plans and her financial situation and every brief answer she gave seemed to drive him deeper into gloom. He pulled a notebook out of his jacket pocket and wrote some neat figures inside.

Then he said, 'I can make you an allowance.'

She opened her mouth to say, 'I don't want one,' and nothing happened.

'I'm not reproaching you.'

You are, she wanted to say; you are, by just sitting there, by doing sums, by offering me money.

Her father looked up. He had disappointment stamped all over him.

'Will he look after you?'

Paula nodded.

'I'd like to,' her father said, 'all the same.'

'I can't pretend,' Paula said in a hoarse whisper, 'that I don't need it.'

'No.'

'I want this baby.'

'Yes.'

'I want Gavin's baby.'

'Um.'

'I love him.'

Her father looked at his cold coffee and pushed the cup aside.

'I think,' he said, 'we'll leave love out of this.'

'I can't.'

Her father shut his notebook.

'I know,' he said, sadly, resignedly, 'I know. That's why you want to keep it, I imagine.'

Paula was very well during her pregnancy. She gained the right amount of weight, every scan and test was satisfactory and she was congratulated a good deal on being pregnant at twenty-two rather than at forty-two. Emotionally, however, the pregnancy was another matter. Gavin, entirely out of his depth in a situation he had started without giving the smallest of thoughts as to how he might sustain it, let alone finish it, flung himself recklessly upon his wife's mercies. She did not feel very merciful, and, while not melodramatically insisting that he cut Paula and her child out of his life for ever, declined, with some force, to discuss the matter further in any shape or form. Gavin went back to Paula, and lay on her bed with his head against her swelling belly, and waited for her to tell him what to do.

She had hoped he would look after her. She had imagined, once the first fireworks of shocked surprise were over, that he would revert to the tender, adoring older man who had buckled her cycling helmet on for her. To see him, instead, lying against her almost defeated by the turn his careless life had taken was, quite simply, frightening. She was not sure how she was going to take care of herself, and this baby, let alone Gavin too. Yet the thought of him getting off that bed and trailing out of the door and back to his wife and children filled her with something close to panic. A teacher at her old school, who was a great advocate of the blessing of free will, used to recite the glories of choice with shining eyes. Well, Paula thought, lying with one hand on her belly and one hand on her child's father's unhappy head, choice was all very well until you coupled it with its consequences. And then, of course, it wasn't choice any more at all.

She gave birth to Toby alone, in the maternity ward of the Chelsea and Westminster Hospital. Her father came the next day, and sat in a plastic-covered armchair beside her bed, and was visibly moved at the sight of his grandson. He held Paula's hand wordlessly for some minutes, and when she put Toby's stiffly wrapped little white form into his arms, he held him with delight and confidence.

He said, 'I've let your mother know.'

'She won't come.'

Her father gazed down at Toby.

'No.'

'I don't – care. Really.'

Her father glanced up.

'Has – he been?'

'Not yet.'

Her father grunted. He ran a fingertip over Toby's clenched knuckles.

'Big hands.'

'Gavin,' Paula said, 'has big hands.'

Gavin came on the third day when she was crying. When he saw Toby, he cried too. He held his son, standing up, and cried into the white cellular blanket that swaddled him. Part of Paula, through a heaving turmoil of hormones, watched her lover and their baby together and succumbed to a fierce, sudden fantasy of hope. The other part, the weary, realistic part now shaped by experience, watched and saw Gavin saying hello and goodbye to his son in the same wretched moment. When it was over, Gavin put Toby into her arms and went, almost at a stumbling run, out of the ward.

He didn't come again. He sent flowers and a cheque for five hundred pounds and a letter. The letter had plainly been dictated by someone else and explained, in formal and not quite grammatical language, that Gavin accepted financial responsibility for his son and was also prepared to pay for a modest roof over Paula's head. He would also like to see his son now and then and would be grateful if these arrangements could be made without recourse to legal intervention. The letter was signed 'Yours ever'.

There were times, later, when Paula wondered how she had managed. Not just with the business of getting used to a baby and the infinite responsibility of it, never mind finding somewhere to live and the means to live in it, but with the agony of loss. There was the loss of Gavin himself, and then, rippling out from that, the loss of a companion, the loss of a future, the loss of a kind of optimism she realised she had relied upon in every decision she had made since she met him. The intensity of her feeling about this new – and mostly very obliging – baby only seemed to emphasise the yawning emptiness of almost everything else around her, but somehow, inch by painful inch, she found the flat in Fulham, and she found a part-time job and she found a childminder three streets away for whom Toby, even at six months, made his enthusiasm plain.

It was a strange life, a kind of half-life while waiting, at some subconscious level, for something more to happen, but at least, as her father pointed out, it had a focus. It was kind of him, Paula thought sometimes, not to point out as well that Paula had never been required to focus on anything but herself, and so Toby was growing her up as well as saving her sanity. She adored him but she found, at the same time and all the time, that life on her own with him was hard. It was hard because there was no respite, no sharing and no support. It was hard because she was twenty-three and had, with her eyes wide open, gambled, lost, and not yet recovered her equilibrium. It was hard because, as time went on and her broken heart began to heal, she couldn't help asking herself if Gavin was less of a true and great love in her life and more a waste of space, and thus a gnawing regret.

Pushing Toby in his buggy along the street, on those endless, contrived errands for a pint of milk or a box of cereal, Paula had noticed Eleanor. There were several houses in the street like Eleanor's, battered and firmly unimproved, whose occupants had plainly lived there since long before Fulham became a target for domestic styling. These houses had thick net curtains, ornaments on the windowsills and serviceable shrubs in the tiny front gardens. At Christmas, they sported multi-coloured fairy lights and, when Chelsea Football Club were playing at home, blue-and-white pennants in upstairs windows. There were no cars parked outside, unless they had visitors, and no satellite dishes. They looked to Paula not so much old-fashioned as simply biding their time until all this makeover nonsense was over, at which point the occupants would revert to the habits of forty years ago and throw a street party with sausage rolls.

Eleanor's house only differed because there were no visible ornaments and no fairy lights. There were net curtains at her upper windows, but none at the downstairs ones, which enabled Paula to see that the sitting room contained an upright piano, a very small television, full bookshelves and a considerable number of piles of papers and magazines. It looked like a man's room, except no man was ever visible, only an elderly woman, imposing of figure if slightly stooped, with a halo of thick white hair and a walking stick she never seemed to be without. It wasn't a National Health walking stick, Paula observed, not a light tubular-metal adjustable affair, but a stout wooden one with an old-fashioned hooked handle and a fat rubber bung on the end. If Eleanor was standing by her table or leaning against her bookshelves, the stick was hooked over her arm. Perhaps she hooked it on to her bedpost at night. Perhaps she gave it a name. Whatever she did, she had a permanent air of self-sufficiency that made Paula ache with envy. Glimpsing her in her sitting room, reading a newspaper with her head thrown back in order to keep her spectacles far enough up her nose to see through, aroused in Paula, irrespective of Eleanor's age or physical condition or solitariness, a sharp jealousy of her complete absorption. Eleanor never looked as if she was yearning. She never looked as if she was raging at life for not feeding her with more than measly morsels.

Unlike the girl Paula sometimes saw in the grocer and newsagent's on the corner. She was a thin girl with sharp features and large eyes who wore her poker-straight hair tied back in a high ponytail. The things that Paula noticed about her were the bruise-coloured shadows under her eyes, the fact that she was never without a baby in a pram and her air of desperation. She didn't look to Paula like someone who was longing for life to bloom into something rich and rare, but more like someone who was unable to see that life could possibly offer such potential. Their eyes met briefly occasionally, as they paid for their small and unremarkable purchases, but they managed never actually to say anything to one another. And as the habit of silence is as engrossing, in the end, as the habit of speaking, their not speaking wasn't even an embarrassment.

It might, Paula thought later, have gone on for ever, meeting in the shop, passing on the street without speaking, if Eleanor hadn't intervened. Paula had been in the street some yards away, conscious of the thin girl's approach but no more, when Eleanor, with the kind of obliviousness she applied to her newspaper reading, emerged unsteadily from her front door and limped to the middle of the street. When she actually spoke to them, neither girl had the social poise to do any more than stop and be spoken to. They stood either side of her while the wind made their eyes water, and waited.

It took a while to take in what Eleanor was saying. She was offering to babysit. She was offering to look after their children so that they, Paula and the ponytail girl, could go out and enjoy themselves.

The thin girl recovered first.

In a voice that wasn't much more than a whisper, she said, 'I never leave him. I never go out. I can't leave him.'

Eleanor turned slowly on her stick and regarded Paula. Paula felt her face flush.

She said, too loudly, too abruptly, 'I haven't got the money.'

'Money,' Eleanor said, in a completely unoffended voice, 'hadn't crossed my mind.'

'I can't,' Paula said, her voice edgy with some kind of frenzy, 'I can't owe you anything. I don't know you. I can't do it. I can't accept favours.'

Eleanor looked at them both.

She said, 'Then do *me* a favour.'

They waited again, sniffing slightly.

'I've watched you,' Eleanor said. 'I've watched you going up and down this street with all the cares of the world on your backs. I quite see about feeling obliged. Well, let *me* be the obliged one. Come and see *me*.' She glanced at the pram and the buggy. 'Bring the children. Come on Friday night.'

They watched her limp back inside her house and close the door.

'D'you think she's cracked?' the thin girl said.

Paula shook her head.

'Will you go?'

Paula hesitated. There was something about Eleanor that called to her, something about individuality, about certainty, about making something of what was on offer, however odd. She glanced at the thin girl. The shadows under her eyes were grotesquely dark today.

'Yeah,' Paula said, trying to sound careless, 'if you will.'

CHAPTER THREE

'I'd like to suggest,' Blaise Campbell said to her meeting – a small group of middle management in a global consultancy firm – 'that you are suffering, maybe collectively, from what I term a workplace disease.'

One of the men, mid-thirties with carefully gelled spiked hair, looked elaborately at the ceiling. The other man present looked at the tabletop. The three women looked at Blaise. The oldest of them, in her late forties, with a practical haircut and no make-up, seemed mildly interested. The other two, younger and sharper in both appearance and manner, wore appraising expressions, as if more concerned with working out the cost – and origin – of her suit and the implication of her ringless hands.

Blaise sat up a fraction straighter. She kept her hands, loosely linked on the table in front of her, completely still. She glanced, briefly but directly, at all five of them in turn.

'Striving to conform to a company's culture,' Blaise said in the level tone she had cultivated to deal with possible recalcitrance, 'delivers unquestioned results in terms of promotion. Work can be an enriching experience. Commitment to work can bring out the best in us.'

The man with the spiked hair yawned cavernously. He had taken his BlackBerry out of his inside pocket several times at the beginning of the session and looked at it longingly. When

Blaise asked him to turn it off, he obeyed as if suffering excruciating physical pain in so doing. He was plainly thinking about it now with a kind of craving. His hand fluttered up involuntarily towards his pocket. His eyes were slightly glazed.

'Trouble starts,' Blaise said, 'and that is the reason why I am here, why I have been called in, when the very elements that motivated you and enriched you and made you valuable to the company begin to undermine your effectiveness because your commitment to them is so great that they are beginning to make you' – small pause – 'unhappy.'

The room was suddenly very still. The man staring at the table glanced furiously at Blaise and flung himself back in his chair. The BlackBerry man's straying hand froze against his jacket. The two younger women seemed abruptly to focus.

'Not *unhappy*,' the older woman said sweetly.

Blaise looked at her. She smiled at her. She did not move her hands.

'I have assigned colours,' Blaise said, raising her voice slightly and regarding the BlackBerry man, 'to various workplace cultures that I see. In this way, we can all picture what I'm describing. It may seem childish, but I can promise you that it works. In my system, a yellow culture is a people-focused one, in which consensus and discussion are central. A blue culture is one that values professional skills above everything, and is suspicious of anything that isn't driven by reason. A red culture – and I think we are in the presence of one now – is one that emphasises drive and commitment and, above all, achievement.'

The older woman smiled back at Blaise.

'Achievement,' she said clearly, 'is what makes us happy. That is why we are here. We are all achievers.'

Blaise glanced at the man slumped in his chair.

'Are you?'

He glared at her. The two younger women exchanged lightning looks.

'Isn't this exactly why we are here?' Blaise said. 'Might it not be the case that the company culture to achieve is so strong, so powerful, that anyone who cannot conform to every detail of that culture feels themselves rejected?'

'Not at all,' the older woman said. Her smile had fixed itself into an expression that in no way involved her eyes. 'Not at all. In this company, we pride ourselves on our appraisal processes. Appraisal processes make sure that no one is ever left out. No one.'

Blaise let a beat fall. Then she turned to the man with the BlackBerry.

'Appraisal processes?'

'Yes,' he said.

'Describe them to me.'

He leaned forward.

He said, with a rush of relief at being diverted from his BlackBerry for a moment, 'Well. There are a hundred and fourteen.'

'A hundred and fourteen? A hundred and fourteen *what*?'

'Competencies,' he said. 'Areas of competence in which management is assessed.'

'Continually?'

He nodded.

'Yes.'

'My father –' one of the younger women said suddenly. And then stopped.

Blaise turned.

'Your father?'

'My father calls it FISO.'

'Does he?'

'FISO. Fit in or shove off.' She shrugged. 'He's self-employed, of course.'

Blaise leaned forward a little and regarded her resolutely composed, interlinked hands.

'Does it not strike you,' she said to no one in particular, 'that such a strong culture as the one you're in, one that resists diversity and therefore change, is in danger of failing to adapt to changing markets?'

The older woman snorted. The slumped man had stopped looking furious and now seemed simply miserable. The two younger women were writing busily on company notepads as if various significant things had urgently occurred to them. Only the BlackBerry man was still leaning forward, looking at Blaise for the first time.

'How can you not adapt,' he said, 'if there's a hundred and fourteen ways you might get it wrong? All the time?'

She put her hands flat on the table.

'Precisely.'

'I can't,' he said aggrievedly, 'change the company culture. Can I?'

'You can help,' Blaise said. 'Plenty of companies *are* changing. That is, if they want to innovate.'

The woman snorted again.

'And,' Blaise said, 'if they want to avoid a negative impact on clients.'

The man took his BlackBerry out of his pocket and put it on the table. He tapped it, authoritatively.

He said, 'Clients can reach me any hour of the day or night.'

Blaise looked at him.

'Precisely,' she said again.

In the ladies' washroom – plastered with brightly expressed instructions not to waste water, or time, or offend fellow employees by not leaving the facilities as you would wish to find them – Blaise soaped her hands thoroughly and tried not to look at herself in the wall of mirror ahead of her. If a meeting had gone well, she didn't mind her own reflection. If it had gone badly – as this one had – she was afraid of the unsettling sense of failure this always induced in her being visible in her face. She had been the last to leave the meeting room, and saw that the older woman had ostentatiously left Blaise's company literature on the table. When she'd walked down the corridor to the washroom, she'd passed the entrance to an open-plan area of office and heard one of the younger women describing Blaise's colour-coding method to an unseen colleague.

'So we are too *red*, she says, and we need to be more *yellow* with touches of *blue*. Honestly. What does she think we are, stupid cow? First year of a primary school?'

Blaise balanced her bag on the basin surround and extracted a lipstick out of a black make-up pouch. She put it on deftly, without looking. All those years of training – linguistics, psychology, a dissertation on workplace behaviourial patterns – never quite, it appeared, anaesthetised her against sheer human nastiness, however small and slight its manifestations. You could try to understand, it seemed, why people behaved the way they did until you were blue in the face, but it still didn't prevent you from being cast down, almost diminished, when those same people chose to interpret your efforts to assist them as a gross interference, only to be punished by malevolence. And when it came to malevolence, Blaise thought, women were often the worst. Women could be both subtle and ingenious in their spite. She put her bag on the floor, took an envelope out of her briefcase and inserted the literature that had been left on the meeting-room table. Then she addressed it to the older woman, prefacing her name with 'Ms'.

At the reception desk, an alert girl in a telephonist's headset looked up at Blaise and gave her a wide, white smile.

'Everything OK for you then?'

'Yes,' Blaise said, 'thank you.'

She put the envelope down on the reception desk.

'Could you see that Ms Fuller gets this, please?'

The girl looked at the envelope. Then she looked back at Blaise, plainly aware that her smile was the shining first face of the company.

'Right away,' she said.

Blaise Campbell's company, Workwell, had been founded five years previously in partnership with someone she had met while attending a course at the Center for Advanced Study in the Behavioral Sciences in Stanford, California. Blaise was in her early thirties, single, with a degree in psychology and an interest in linguistics. Karen Spicer was a year or two older, married to an abstract painter ten years her senior by whom she had two small girls, and possessed of an idea that people would like working more if the way they worked was improved. As the only two Englishwomen on the course, they naturally gravitated towards each other and derived schoolgirlish pleasure from the cultural differences between them and their fellow students. Over the length of the course, and over countless plates of waffles and giant salads and Cajun chicken, the notion of persuading organisations to change in the way that they worked crystallised into a definite project called Workwell. In fact, the more that they considered the proposition – no capital required to set it up, no premises needed, flexible hours for Karen, autonomy for Blaise – and the more encouraging Merlot they drank the better it became. They flew home, exhilarated and determined. Britain's workforce – most claiming, if recent surveys were to be believed, that they would stop work altogether if they won the lottery – was to be transformed into ranks of cheerful individuals able to think alone and work collectively and – this was key – maintain a healthy work–life balance. They landed at Heathrow as new-minted zealots.

The reality, of course, was very different. Blaise found she couldn't work without an office. Karen found that working at home meant hours on the helpline to her computer company and an inability not to listen out for the washing machine stopping washing. Devising a company strategy, and a working method, and a professional relationship, and a promotional scheme seemed painfully difficult to achieve without the Merlot, and the time out of life provided by Stanford. They argued and sulked and, on three occasions, decided the whole scheme was unworkable and refused to speak to one another for days. Blaise felt Karen was only partially committed to the project because she was mostly committed to her family; and Karen considered Blaise sensationally unimaginative and unsympathetic about her situation as both mother and breadwinner. They were only saved by an unexpected and tentative request from a small insurance company trying to specialise in women drivers as clients, with whom Blaise had had some dealings in the past, asking for help in harmonising a mixed-gender workforce. Blaise found herself saying yes, on the telephone, even before she consulted Karen.

And yet it was Karen who said that they needed an office, at least to begin with. It was Karen who said they needed a small bank loan to launch themselves with professional promotional material. It was Karen who said she would like to run the business and leave most of the public performance to Blaise.

It was Karen who said, 'If we don't get this off the ground, and I have to go back to working for someone else, I will probably kill Lucas. No. I will certainly kill Lucas.'

Blaise said, 'But I thought he was a wonderful father.'

'He *is* a wonderful father.'

'Then –'

'Blaise,' Karen said, 'let's change the subject.'

After that, it was quite easy to make a business plan. In fact, everything was easier once there was an office, a physical representation of their fledgling partnership. An address somehow conferred both reality and possibility on the scheme, even if the address represented a room above a dry-cleaner's on Fulham Broadway, with a kettle in a cupboard and a shared lavatory two floors above.

'It's a good postcode,' Blaise said.

Karen, painting the walls with a shade of white paint chosen from twenty-three different white options, said would they be able to remember the postcode when weeks of fumes from the dry-cleaner's had rubbished their memories? And Blaise knew, from the determined crossness of her tone, that Karen was very happy.

She was at their shared desk in front of the computer when Blaise walked in from her meeting. Blaise worked in business suits: Karen mostly worked in tracksuits with her hair pinned up carelessly and her feet in running shoes. Every so often, she appeared in a dress and high heels and earrings, and it was almost as if she took on another gender then, as well as another look. When she unpinned her hair, it fell halfway down her back in a heavy brown curtain, the colour of Indian tea.

She didn't turn from the computer.

'How'd it go?'

'Resistant,' Blaise said, 'highly resistant. Answered back and made fun of my colour codes.'

'They *are* funny.'

'Only to the Brits. Americans wouldn't think so.'

'We aren't in America,' Karen said. She took her hands off the keyboard and turned round. 'I like resistance.'

Blaise dropped her case on the floor.

'Why?'

'Nice long contract,' Karen said. 'Takes weeks to win them round. Like those organic-food people who were so holier than thou and couldn't see why their attitude was reflected in their sales figures.'

Blaise sat down in the second office chair and took her shoes off.

'I got a bit dispirited this morning. There was one tricky woman –'

'There usually is one tricky woman.'

'But only if there's men there too. And men and women hear things so differently. What a woman hears as diplomatic a man hears as dishonest. And if they're together, they hear everything as some sort of challenge. Today's challenge was not to let me put them down in any way even though that was the last thing I was trying to do.'

Karen swung back again.

'Well, you're easier to resent than the senior management who called you in.'

'True.'

Karen tapped some keys.

'Let me cheer you up. Good monthly figures. Better quarterly ones. And I have all the reports up to date and seven new enquiries this week of which at least two look promising.'

Blaise looked out of the small high window that gave a view of a section of wall, and gutter and roof, and a satellite dish usually garnished with a pigeon or two.

'Should we expand?'

'You say that every week.'

'I think it every week.'

'To support another employee,' Karen said, staring at her screen, 'would mean doubling the business to pay another person and for larger premises. It would dilute the control we both have and alter the essence of our service. I seem to have said this several times before.'

Blaise stretched.

'I don't like standing still.'

'We're hardly doing that.'

'But I want us to move on before we get to that point. I'm trying to apply my own principles.'

'I can't,' Karen said in a tightly controlled voice, 'afford your gambles.'

Blaise said nothing.

'You know how things are for me,' Karen said. 'You *know*. I'm at a stage where I am at last just balancing, just juggling.' She paused and then she said, 'Lucas last sold a picture fifteen months ago.'

'I know.'

'For eight hundred pounds.'

'I know.'

'He is a seriously good painter,' Karen said, 'and he doesn't resent my working at all. But he doesn't seem to see the urgency himself to work at anything at all except paintings that don't sell.'

Blaise got up and perched on the edge of Karen's desk, so that she could see her face.

'What's happened?'

'Nothing.'

'What's happened to bring this tirade on? I know all this stuff. Why do you need to tell me again?'

Karen typed something rapidly.

'Lucas has rented a studio.'

'I thought he had a studio. In the house.'

'He does.'

Blaise waited.

'He says that he can't work with the unspoken domestic pressure at home. He's found a studio just behind Fulham Cross School. Besides the rent, it takes him away from home. It takes him away from being there for the girls after school. He'll be there half the night, smoking joints and staring at his canvas.' Karen gave Blaise a quick look. There were tears in her eyes. She said bitterly, 'He's an artist.'

Blaise said gently, 'That's why you fell for him.'

'Yes.'

'Are you sure he doesn't resent what you're doing?'

'Sure,' Karen said. 'He's propelled by creative impulse. I'm propelled by practical necessity. Drives me nuts.'

'And the girls?'

'They adore him. They fly at me if I criticise him over the smallest thing.'

Blaise looked at the ceiling.

'What would you like me to do?'

'Nothing,' Karen said.

'Nothing?'

'Nothing. No changes, no expansion, no new partners, no change of premises.'

'All right,' Blaise said cautiously, 'but not for ever.'

Karen muttered something.

'What?'

Karen said, 'I said nothing's for ever.'

Blaise got off the desk.

'My mother used to say tiredly that only parenthood was.'

Karen began typing again.

'I'll tell you in due course. Especially when Poppy and Rose are teenagers and tell me they wish I wasn't their mother.'

'Do you want to bring them tomorrow?'

'Tomorrow,' Karen said without inflection.

'Friday night,' Blaise said. 'My place.'

'Can't.'

'You haven't been for weeks.'

'Too complicated.'

'Why?'

'Because of Paula.'

'What about Paula? There's always something about Paula.'

'She's bringing this man. It's like an episode from *Sex and the City*. We all get to have a look at him. This Jackson man.'

Blaise gave a little glimmering smile.

'Ah,' she said, 'this Jackson.'

*　　*　　*

43

Rose and Poppy shared a bedroom at the top of their house. It was a tall, thin house with a steep stair that zigzagged up through a series of small rooms at front and back, and the girls' room was the highest of all. Their father had painted a landscape round the walls – forests and a castle and jungle beasts and a unicorn – and a starry sky on the ceiling. When they were older, he said, he would replace the unicorn and the tigers with rock stars and cover the night sky with psychedelic patterns. Rose said what was psychedelic and Lucas said intoxicating and narcotic, and Rose said what was intoxicating and narcotic, and Lucas said drunk and drugged and both girls fell on the floor squealing and rolled their eyes.

Lucas, who was a marvel to his daughters, had also made wind chimes out of glass beads and metal discs and hung them at their window, and decorated their beds with snakes and creepers. He read to them at night with wonderful animation and let them do spatter paintings on the kitchen floor and taught them to salsa. Poppy, especially, was good at the salsa roll. When they were in their bedroom, and they knew Lucas was on the floor below in his studio, whose chaos they found exciting, they both felt, unspoken though it was, a kind of exhilarated happiness. When Karen came in, and they heard the street door slam all those floors below, a sense of security was added to the happiness but also, perversely, a tension.

Rose, being older than Poppy, also knew a particular anxiety. Even at nine, she felt a responsibility for Karen's evident and frequent tiredness, and for a level of frustration that simmered just below the surface, like the water seething in the frying pan when Lucas was teaching them to poach eggs. When the front door slammed in the late afternoon, or early evening, and Karen shouted up the stairs, 'Hi, guys!' Rose felt her stomach tighten very slightly, as it did at school when a teacher was asking the class to admit to some crime, and the culprit wouldn't own up. She wanted, very badly, to thunder down the stairs and fling her arms round her mother, but she also felt that she *had* to. Poppy plainly didn't feel like this and Rose didn't think she should have to. Rose just knew, for no reason she could put her finger on, that somehow she was bound in conscience to her mother in a way that nobody else was, that she was implicated in the circumstances of Karen's life.

Both Rose and Poppy had been to Karen's office, and had played games with the graphics programme on the computer. They knew Blaise almost as well as they knew their own parents, and relied on her as the only adult in their lives to give them money at Christmas and on their birthdays, real paper money that she rolled up and tied with ribbon and put in Indian jewellery bags that came from the accessories shop near the tube station. They understood that between them Karen and Blaise and the computer in the office produced something called business, which in turn produced money – in a different form, obviously, from the ribboned rolls – that you needed if you were going to have a house and food and school trips and a telephone. Poppy had thought telephones were free because they were only about talking and talking was free, after all. But Lucas had drawn her a picture of how telephones worked, even complicated ones with satellites (he made the satellite look like a little spinning firework), and explained how all this had to be paid for. And then Karen said that you couldn't get money to pay for it unless you worked, and people paid you for working.

'So,' Poppy said, 'where does money come from in the first place? Out of a cave?'

And Karen looked at Lucas and said in a voice that went straight to Rose's stomach, 'You tell them.'

It was clear to Rose that this money thing was a burden to her mother but also that it gave her a kind of power. She might be out for most of most days, and it was their father who was there after school, spreading peanut butter on crackers and hearing their French vocabulary and beguiling all their friends whose fathers did not have hair to their shoulders and purple shirts. But all the same, it was Karen who decided things, Karen whose often absent hands still held the reins of domestic control. The girls learned, without being instructed, that final decisions about anything bigger than who got the plastic gremlin in the cereal box had to be referred to Karen. And this state of affairs made Rose sorry for both her parents, for different reasons, and envious of Poppy because Poppy didn't care. In Poppy's eyes Karen wasn't burdened by having too much power and responsibility and Lucas wasn't diminished by not having enough of either because Poppy saw her parents as being conveniently obliged to her, their child, rather than the other way about. Rose thought Poppy was spoilt. Sometimes she said so to her father, and he would agree with her.

'Probably is, Rosie. Some people just manage things that way. All their lives.'

All she said to Karen was once, greatly daring, 'I can't always be the good one, you know,' and Karen gave her a long hard look and said, 'You may have to be, Rosie. You may just have to be.' And something in her tone, instead of being upsetting, made Rose feel marvellously, significantly complicit.

They were all in the kitchen when the street door slammed, cutting random shapes out of biscuit dough.

Poppy hurtled off her stool at once and screamed, 'Mummy, Mummy, Mummy!'

Rose glanced at her father. He was cutting out an elongated diamond and he went on cutting, head bent.

Karen appeared in the doorway with Poppy in her arms. Poppy was hissing in her ear. Karen looked at Rose.

'Hi, Rosie.'

Rose got off her stool. Karen dumped Poppy on the floor

and gave Rose a hug and then she went over to Lucas and gave him the kind of kiss that was more just a quick collision of faces.

Lucas said, 'How's things?'

'Good,' Karen said. She went across to the counter by the sink and flicked through a pile of post. 'All in order.'

'Bravo,' Lucas said. He finished his diamond and laid it carefully on a baking tray.

Poppy got back on her stool and began to whisper urgently at the biscuit dough. Rose leaned on the table and watched her parents.

'I'd like to go round to Blaise's tomorrow night,' Karen said, still flicking.

There was a beat and then Lucas said, 'Sorry, babe. I'm working. I get the studio tomorrow. I want to start setting up.'

'In the evening?'

'In the evening.'

Rose did not at all like the feeling in the room.

'Shush,' she said to the whispering Poppy.

Poppy took no notice.

'I haven't been to a Friday night for weeks.'

'I'm sorry,' Lucas said. He began on something that looked like a squashed figure of eight.

'Luke –'

'Sorry,' Lucas said, 'but tomorrow night I am not at home.'

Rose took a deep breath.

'Can't we come?'

Karen seemed to rouse herself from some way away.

'Come?'

'Come to Blaise's with you.'

'It – it was going to be my grown-up time –'

'Mine too,' Lucas said.

Rose held her breath.

47

Poppy stopped whispering and said out loud, 'We often go.'

'You do,' Karen said, 'but tomorrow is a little bit different.'

'Why?'

'Because there is – a new friend to meet.'

Rose watched her father lift a lovely, fluid, nameless shape of dough on to the baking tray.

'Does she have children?'

'It's a friend of Paula's,' Karen said. 'A new friend. A man.'

Lucas raised his head and gave Karen a long look.

'Take them,' he said evenly.

'Yes,' Poppy said. 'Yes, yes, yes.'

Karen came across and stood close to Lucas.

She bent until her mouth was close to his face and then she said, 'Who's going to be there is not the point.'

'Sorry, babe,' Lucas said firmly.

Karen suddenly looked extremely alarming. Rose shut her eyes.

Karen took a breath and said, 'OK, girls, you can come.'

Poppy kicked against her stool.

'Wicked,' she said.

CHAPTER FOUR

E leanor had been an only child. Sometimes she thought that this fact concentrated both the disappointment her mother felt because her only daughter wasn't pretty and her father felt because his only daughter wasn't a son. Eleanor did her best to compensate her father by being athletic and clever, but there was nothing to be done about the absence of prettiness, and both she and her mother knew it. If they happened to catch their reflections side by side in a mirror, they both, automatically and without comment, looked at Eleanor's mother. It wasn't that Eleanor minded looking at herself; it was more that she couldn't see the point. She knew what she looked like, and no amount of examination was going to make any difference.

She was tall like her father, and lean like her father, but she had inherited, from long-ago grandparents, big features and nondescript colouring and frizzy hair. She wore spectacles to correct severe myopia, from an early age, which she tied behind her head with an uncompromising piece of elastic when she played games. She played games vigorously and accurately, and derived enough satisfaction from that, and from classroom successes, not to waste herself in wishing she looked otherwise. In any case, it was evident that her mother's face – unquestionably pretty – had not brought its possessor much satisfaction. On the contrary it seemed to

have created endless opportunities for frustration and dis-
illusion. What, her mother's expression and demeanour
often said quite plainly, was a woman as good-looking as
she was doing in an unremarkable house in the Munster
Road, living with a small-time engineer with a passion for
cricket and a daughter with whom she could share no
intimacies? There was an episode once, Eleanor remembered, involving a well-built man with a Rover and a
membership of the Hurlingham Club, but Eleanor had taken
care not to include herself in that, and to discourage any
confidence. It was an early lesson in the perils of surrendering to too much expectation.

After her schooldays, both parents seemed at a loss as to
what to do with her. Eleanor solved the problem by doing
something for herself. She found a job in a local solicitor's
office, and from that position – dull, but it produced the first
money of her own she had ever seen – she applied to several
London colleges that offered courses in management and
administration. At twenty-two she left home for a small
and discouraging flat in Ealing and her first lowly adminis-
trative post in a hospital on the Fulham Palace Road. By the
age of thirty-four she had bought a house in Fulham, and was
a senior administrator for the health services of her borough.
Her life was settled and, as it included promotion and travel
and, over time, a couple of distinct romantic possibilities, she
saw absolutely no reason to change it. It was, after all, what
she had chosen. Her mother flitting disconsolately through a
life apparently not of her choosing in any way, and seeming to
lack any capacity to control anything more significant than
her appearance, had been the most effective of examples.

Just as she had not given way to lamenting her looks,
Eleanor resolved – by stages, over the years – not to give way
to regrets in any other direction, either. The two romantic
possibilities, one an ear, nose and throat consultant, the
other a fellow member of a mental-health tribunal, in the end

melted back into their previous lives and relationships leaving Eleanor firm about not regretting that they had happened, or come to nothing. The same was true of children. She had chosen a career, she had chosen a single life. She would never stop being interested in children and families, but she would equally never seek sympathy for not having had either. Her life, grounded in varied and responsible work and enhanced by friends and outings and walking holidays in the Pyrenees, was what she had made of it because that is what she wanted. At her mother's funeral, attended by seventeen people in All Saints' Church in all its Victorian Gothic gloom, Eleanor felt the weight of her mother's lifelong blighted hopes lift from her own shoulders and blend into the air like smoke. She went back to her house after the service and closed the front door behind her with relief and gratitude. When, a few weeks later, a senior colleague (male) described her – in her hearing, quite deliberately – as being 'admirably well adjusted', she had not felt remotely patronised, but rather that she had been given full, and cherished, membership of the grown-ups' club.

Over the years that followed she had increasingly been turned to for advice. She sat on numerous boards, attended tribunals and conferences both in England and abroad, chaired important advisory bodies, especially in the field of mental health. Her work on special schools for children with emotional or behavioural difficulties was seminal. It was also completely absorbing, so that the house in Fulham became a place she returned to, rather than a home, and she could almost congratulate herself on not needing to identify herself by any of the personal or domestic details that seemed such a preoccupation with most women. The walking holidays, the visits to the Wigmore Hall, the dinners with fellow professionals in well-established restaurants were all, to her mind, entirely complementary to her working life. She looked complete to outsiders for the very simple reason that she felt it.

And then retirement came. She had thought about retirement, and planned for it, for some time, and expected the transition to be uneasy but perfectly manageable. It was indeed uneasy, acutely so, but managing it was far, far harder than she had anticipated. It wasn't just that a crucial structure had gone, and that it had taken almost everybody she relied upon knowing with it, but also that, having neglected domestic life for so long, it simply wasn't there to fall back on. Professional friendships proved distressingly expedient and the interests that had been such a wonderful counterpoint to work looked strangely unsatisfactory when required to stand up by themselves. Eleanor was shocked. She was shocked at the threadbare nature of her personal life and doubly shocked that she had let it slide into such a condition. She looked round her house – quite comfortable but with all the decorative allure of a provincial dentist's waiting room – and realised that it wasn't in her to make something of it. Many women – most women, even – would seize the day and the scrubbing brush and hang new curtains. Eleanor was not such a woman. New curtains would do nothing for her except cause great irritation. No, she realised, looking at her high old-fashioned bed, and the piles of books that sat on every step of the staircase, the adjustment to this new stage of life was not going to come from without. It was going to have to come from within. She was going to have to look at life quite differently; she was going to have to look at people, at *types* of people, she had never looked at before. She was going to have to – as a human being without the restful authenticity conferred by an acknowledged professional position – go out there and make friends – quite naked, as it were.

Looking in the mirror, at this juncture, was not encouraging. The briefcase of office, she realised, had been a magical accessory, and had conferred a distinction on her appearance, irrespective of what she actually looked like.

Without it, she was just a woman, rather bulkier now than she would have liked, who looked every minute of her sixty-five years, with a fuzz of iron-grey hair and the beginnings of an arthritic hip. She had her height – though even that seemed to be lessening – and she had her firm features: otherwise, she looked like any old extra in any old crowd. I do not long for beauty, she told herself resolutely in the glass in the hall coat stand, but I do require some significance. I am not in any way ready or prepared to be rubbed out. I do not agree – or submit – to being invisible merely because my outward self, lacking the required drama for contemporary life, gives no indication of what is going on inside.

Both her parents – one admiringly, one fretfully – had told her she was stubborn.

'I like to see a bit of grit,' her father said.

'Nobody,' her mother wailed, 'was ever so determined they were right about everything, all the time, as you are!'

For herself, Eleanor had felt that she could not, in truth, risk being anything other than stubborn. If she didn't hold fast to certain certainties – her ambition, her good sense, her undoubted talents – she might be swept away in a flood of destructive regrets and longings. If you started wanting to change the basics – who you were, how you looked – who knows where that terrifying careering ride would land you. So the thing was, the thing had always been, since she was a young adolescent, to accept the unchangeable situation cheerfully, and set it aside. Indeed, that method had worked admirably for decades, and the fact that it wasn't working now because the accoutrements of a professional life had been swept away and replaced by a blank brought all Eleanor's habitual stubbornness to the surface. She would not change, just to satisfy a shallow clamour from the modern world. She would not have her hair dyed and pluck her eyebrows and dress in fuchsia pink. She would not, in short, assert her significance in the world in any other way than the way in which she always had, namely the application of her good mind and steady heart to the life around her. And that life, although encompassing books and music and news, for which she had a passion, was not about cushions and lipstick: it was about people.

In Eleanor's street, there were a good many people she knew. She had lived there for over thirty years and had seen the relentless conveyor belt of family life turn working people into pensioners and babies into dropouts and young executives. But street living had its decencies. It had intimacy, for sure, in terms of mutual help and consideration, but that intimacy was expected to refrain from becoming a burden of psychological complication or need. A neighbour would gladly save you from a burning house but should not be expected to mend your broken heart. A dignity was expected to be displayed and observed, and to push the habits of neighbourliness into something deeper would upset the dynamic of the community and possibly cause rejection. Eleanor liked her street, liked her neighbours, liked her corner shop, but they were figures in her landscape that could not realistically be summoned into the foreground. If she was going to people her life in a way that was both new to match her new status and old to match her old habits, she was going to have to look outside the street. And she was going to have to look outside all the categories she had known so far.

The eureka moment came on a spring day, after weeks of watching Paula and Lindsay, and their children. She had watched these young women, she had wondered about them, she had considered how the sexual freedoms of their time had also seemed to abandon them to a terrible isolation, and then she had thought, abruptly and without warning, 'I am fascinated by them because they are so *young*.'

Young. She had written the word down, forcefully, in capital letters, in the margin of the newspaper in which she was doing the crossword. *Young.* They looked twenty-five at the most. Over forty years her junior. As young as she had been, while living in that dismal flat in Ealing and working at the hospital in the Fulham Palace Road. *Young.* But discouraged in a way she could not recollect feeling at that age, and yet they both had what she had never had, which was children, which in turn meant having been close enough to someone, however fleetingly, to have conceived those children. And suddenly, sitting there in the bay window of her front room, staring at the crossword but not seeing it, Eleanor had felt a surge of energy, a sensation that, after years of working diligently at being a grown-up, there might now have come a time to reconnect, to everyone's advantage, with the non-grown-ups, with the young, with her own youthful self. She heaved herself out of her chair and looked up and down the street. It was mid-afternoon and quite empty. Next time she saw them, Eleanor told herself, she would speak. Next time.

That impulse had brought her Paula and Toby, Lindsay and Noah. Then it had brought her Jules. Jules! Then Blaise. Then Karen and Rose and Poppy and the shadowy figure of Lucas, who came by every so often to accomplish something deftly among the broken things in her house and went again, leaving behind him, like Peter Pan, a kind of indescribable echo. None of them – except Lucas – was yet forty. Jules was twenty-two or -three. Noah, the youngest, was six. She had known Noah since he was a baby. She had watched them all like each other, and not like each other, and get used to each other with the acceptance born of custom. She had watched Paula's restlessness and Jules' capriciousness and Blaise's determination hold sway in turn and be defeated. She had watched couples form and separate, she had watched children divide and rule, she had watched men, puzzled or challenged, circling round Lindsay's apparent vulnerability, Jules' unorthodoxy, Blaise's seeming competence. But something central had held, something at the core of this random collection of women had been worth holding on to, and proved too sturdy to be easily dismantled. It was a ramshackle arrangement, a sort of mad happening that had metamorphosed into something that offered value and identity, however impossible to define, and Eleanor, when she closed the door on her own Friday nights, came as close to giving ardent thanks to someone or something as she ever had in her life. 'Define friendship,' she once said to herself, hunting for fuses for a defunct table lamp, and then, 'Don't be idiotic. If you can't recognise it when you have it, then you don't deserve it.'

It had all changed, of course, when Paula's good fortune arrived.

'My Lottery win,' she said to Eleanor.

'No!'

'Gavin,' Paula said. Her eyes were shining. 'Gavin's company has been bought by some other company and he's got shares and a huge bonus, and he's buying us a luxury flat!'

Eleanor looked out of the window.

'And you want that?'

'Of course!'

'Why of course?'

'So Toby and I can move out of the dump and Toby can –' She stopped.

Eleanor transferred her gaze to Paula.

'Go to a better school?'

'Yes,' Paula said. 'What's wrong with that?'

'Nothing.'

'Then why –'

'It's simply,' Eleanor said, 'that I – stuffily probably – prefer to earn things rather than be given them.'

'I have earned this.'

'Ah,' Eleanor said, 'the martyr's robe of single motherhood. You don't often wear it.'

'He's been such a –'

'He's weak,' Eleanor said. 'That's all. Weak.'

'That's enough.'

'I quite agree. It's more than enough to explain a life like his.'

Paula leaned forward.

'What are you worried about? What d'you think will change?'

'You will.'

'No, I won't. I'll just be happier, in a cool flat with nice things. I'll still come here.'

'Too good of you, dear.'

'I didn't mean it like that.'

'What you meant is that there will be a shift of power. You will have more.'

'Don't you want me to have that?'

'Oh I do,' Eleanor said. 'I shall be so interested to see how you use it.'

'I'm not jealous,' Lindsay said to Eleanor a few days later.

'Of Paula?'

'Yes. I'm not jealous. Of her flat and money and stuff. It's blood money, after all.'

'Is it?'

'Yes,' Lindsay said. She was drinking tea, holding the mug in both hands, the way her sister did. 'He's felt bad all these years and he thinks that by shelling out the dough he'll feel better.'

'In her place, would you take it?'

Lindsay looked into her tea.

'I might. But I wouldn't be in her place. I'd never have had the nerve to get involved with someone like him. He'd never have noticed me anyway. D'you think Paula will be different?'

'Yes. But so will you be. So will I.'

Lindsay glanced at her.

'I don't want you different.'

'I don't mean unrecognisable,' Eleanor said. 'I just mean that with Paula and Toby not on the street we will be different with one another. We will move round the dance.'

Lindsay grinned.

'On a stick, in your case.'

'Certainly,' Eleanor said. 'Still on my stick.'

The first few months had been unsettling. Paula had found a flat almost at once, buying, off-plan, a new loft conversion down by the river and speaking in property developers' jargon. Karen and Jules had taken no notice of her; Blaise and Lindsay, in different ways, had seemed threatened, and both had retreated, but not together. And then the flat had been finished, and Paula had set aside her metaphorical clipboard, and had with her usual appeal and energy asked for help, for interest, for reassurance that this large, sophisticated industrialised space could be made into something that was recognisably hers and a home for Toby.

'It's like a school trip,' Toby said to Eleanor. 'It's like being in the Science Museum.'

'Lucky you.'

'I like our old flat.'

'One always does. One likes what one knows. You'll get to know this.'

'There aren't any doors.'

'I have too many doors.'

Toby said obstinately, 'I like doors.'

'When you have your own house, you can have as many doors as you like.'

Toby kicked irritably at the leg of Eleanor's chair.

'Why can't I have what I like now?'

When Paula and Toby moved in to the new flat, Paula threw a Friday Night Extra. There was champagne and balloons and lit candles fringing every sill and step. The group moved round each other as if they had hardly met, talking gratefully, to or through the children, not catching each other's eyes. Eleanor, beached upon a new low sofa against piles of orange silk cushions, was a point of reassurance, something fixed and recognisable, clutching her champagne glass in one hand and her stick, like a token of flight or escape, in the other. One by one, adults and children alike, they came and sat down next to her as if they were hoping that she would, like the director of a treasure hunt, hand them the next vital clue. She found that she was much amused. She was amused by the flat, amused by Paula's wound-up pride in it, amused by everyone's being so disconcerted by this change of environment and its effect on all of them. Then, when she got home, she found she was not amused at all. Apprehensive is the word, she said to herself, locking and bolting. Apprehensive is what I feel. Apprehensive at things slipping away. Again.

Since then she had held her breath, and waited. She had watched while Lindsay, like someone opening an unfamiliarly exotic present, gradually slid from suspicion to delight about Paula's flat. She had watched while Blaise, taking her cue from Karen, had put on a show of elaborate indifference to Paula's changed circumstances. She had watched while Jules, who came to more Friday nights than she would have cared anyone to comment on, somehow never appeared when it was Paula's turn, despite an evident liking for Toby. And she had watched with admiration while Paula applied for her manageress job, and got it.

'You see?' Paula said. 'I told you I'd be different.'

'Yes.'

'And happier!'

'Yes.'

'Do you begrudge me?'

'I congratulate you. From my heart, I congratulate you.'

And then, slowly, like feathers coming lightly to rest, it seemed to settle. The meetings resumed something of their old nonchalance, Paula's high-octane exuberance steadied, Blaise and Karen abandoned their positions. Even Jules came to Paula's flat one week and sat cross-legged on the zebra rug, drinking tea, before climbing up to Toby's platform and falling asleep on his bed. Toby didn't like to say how disappointed he was when Lindsay woke Jules up to take her home. He sniffed his pillow hopefully, but she had left no trace, except crumples in his duvet.

Eleanor had breathed again. She had been slightly ashamed of herself about her anxiety, ashamed that she had allowed herself to be defenceless, to fear – even if barely admitted – that Paula's good fortune might alter the balance of this unconventional friendship to such a point that it might fragment and leave Eleanor – well, that was the part she did not want to contemplate. That was the shaming part. She had never, ever, thought like that in the past and she didn't want to start now. Even when her romantic relationships had ended, her first thought had been, quite genuinely, she remembered, sadness that it was over but an overriding relief at recovering her freedom. That was what she had always prized, above everything. Freedom. And it was uncomfortable – no, it was closer to intolerable – to have to admit, even with only a corner of one's mind, that freedom didn't look quite like it used to. It had a bleak appearance these days, as if it had lost its purpose. She had always robustly refuted the gloomily romantic notion that freedom was just another name for nothing left to lose – but now she didn't feel quite so robust. She felt relieved and thankful that Paula's flat and all that it signified was settling down into an element – however inorganic to them all – that could be confidently accommodated.

Then Blaise came to see her. It was a Saturday morning. Blaise's weekday uniform of business suits gave way on Saturdays to pressed jeans and shirts with, sometimes, a sweater tied over her shoulders. She was holding a small square cellophane packet. She never came, despite Eleanor's objections, empty-handed.

'Shortbread,' Blaise said, holding out the packet. 'With stem ginger.'

'Fatal,' Eleanor said. 'If you insist on bringing me things, why can't you bring me something I detest?'

'Like what?'

'Pilchards in tomato sauce.'

'I'll try,' Blaise said.

She stepped inside. She was as tall as Eleanor and her hair had a sleek bounce that never, mysteriously, seemed diminished by fatigue or being out in the rain.

'I'll make you coffee,' Eleanor said.

Blaise followed her to the kitchen.

'You didn't,' Eleanor said, 'come last night.'

'To Paula's? No. I was working. I was writing a report. I have an intractable new account. Karen is very pleased because she thinks they'll take months to persuade and that's lucrative.'

Eleanor propped her stick against the kitchen counter and reached into a cupboard for coffee.

'Quite the other way about in the public sector.'

'Yes. Do you miss it?'

'No,' Eleanor said. She rummaged in a drawer for a spoon. 'Yes.'

'I think about work so much,' Blaise said. 'I *plan* for it. I plan all the time. I can't seem to help it.'

'Why should you help it?'

Blaise pulled out a kitchen chair from the littered table, and sat down.

'I spend my working life trying to get people to balance their work–life ratio, and then I reflect on how unbalanced mine is.'

Eleanor measured coffee unsteadily. Blaise watched a

small shower of grounds patter to the floor and resisted, with difficulty, the urge to spring up and find a cloth.

Eleanor said, 'I think you have to burn the fuel while you have it.'

'Does it stop?'

'It turns into a different fuel. Slower-burning.' She turned round. 'Something was burning last night. Paula and Lindsay. Some secret.'

Blaise looked at her hands.

'Yes.'

'Well,' Eleanor said, turning back to her coffee making, 'I'm not interested in girls' dorm behaviour.'

'No.'

'And now you're here.'

'It's my turn on Friday,' Blaise said.

'Yes.'

'And – well, Paula's asked me something.'

Eleanor pressed the start button on the kettle and stood, her back turned to Blaise, watching it boil.

Blaise said, 'She's met someone.'

There was a pause and then Eleanor said, 'A man.'

'Yes.'

'Well?'

'She –' Blaise stopped. And then she said, 'She wants us to meet him.'

'I expect we will.'

'No, I mean she wants it to be a sort of introduction. To all of us. On a Friday night. She wants to bring him to my house on Friday.'

Eleanor gave a small snort of laughter.

'Exhibit A.'

'Sort of.'

'What a bizarre notion.'

'I know. I think – I think she –'

'Is showing off?'

62

'A bit. Maybe. But I think she wants us to approve.'

Eleanor said nothing. She poured water into the coffee pot, and stirred the contents.

She said, 'Does he need approving of?'

'I have no idea,' Blaise said.

'Haven't you?'

'No. All I know is that he came into Paula's shop and placed a huge order. That he's about forty and single and called Jackson.'

'And he's to be paraded before us.'

'Yes.'

Eleanor put the coffee pot on the table, on top of a garden catalogue. Blaise got up to find mugs.

'Sit.'

'I can do it. I'd like to –'

Eleanor lowered herself into a chair.

'So you were deputed to come and warn me of this great happening.'

Blaise put two mugs on the table.

'I just came. I thought you'd like to know. I thought you'd like to be prepared.'

'Don't you think Paula might tell me herself?'

Blaise shrugged. She picked up the cuffs of the sweater tied round her shoulders and inspected them.

'Or,' Eleanor said, 'do you want me to react? For the sake of your own reaction?'

'Yes, please.'

Eleanor poured coffee.

'He's a natural progression, isn't he? First a new flat, then a new job. He was what was lacking.'

'He may be lovely,' Blaise said.

'Indeed.'

'We may be jealous.'

'Only – if we need to be.' She pushed a mug towards Blaise.

Blaise said, 'You'll come, won't you?'

'Naturally.'

'I think you'll – sort of steady it.'

'I think you are verging on the melodramatic. Paula has got overexcited again and met a personable man she wishes to display to us.'

'It – it, well, it feels like more.'

Eleanor looked at her.

'Does it?'

Blaise leaned forward.

'Don't you ever have feelings of foreboding? Don't you ever worry that people you've come to rely on mightn't be reliable? Mightn't even be there any more?'

There was a tiny beat. Eleanor met her eye.

'Never,' Eleanor said firmly.

CHAPTER FIVE

If there was one place in the world that could be guaranteed to lift Jules' spirits – apart from a club – it was D'Arblay Street. D'Arblay Street, Soho, London, W1. She went every week, saving the visits as a kind of insurance policy against all the frustrations and disappointments that she seemed to bang into all the time. When things went wrong, she'd think to herself that on Thursday there'd be D'Arblay Street, and if things – seldom – went OK or a little bit better, she'd tell herself that she could go on Monday too, and celebrate.

She'd been going to D'Arblay Street since she was twenty. A boy in a club, a thin, dark boy called Benny, told her he worked in a record shop in D'Arblay Street and suggested she drop in. He told her the shop was frequented by disc jockeys who bought their vinyls there, to mix on their own decks at home.

'It's the core of the scene,' Benny said to her. He bought her a Red Bull and vodka. 'It's the underground.'

The shop itself had a narrow entrance, painted black. Inside it was narrow too, lined on one side with a long counter. There were three playing decks along the counter, and a double deck on the L-shape at the end, and all the vinyls, in their bright jackets, were on racks behind the counter, so arresting that you didn't bother to look up and notice that the ceiling tiles were all about to fall off. Those racks were the thing. Those racks of talent and energy were what gave Jules a thrill every time she went in, all that red and yellow and pink and blue, all those punchy band names – Fanatix, Hardsoul, Fridayloop, Code Red – all the knowledge that the guys playing this stuff played *live*, with real instruments.

Benny had been too serious about the music in the shop to seem overtly pleased to see her. When she told him that all she wanted was to be a DJ he hadn't scoffed at her, he'd just said, 'You'll have to fight your corner.'

'Because I'm a girl?'

'You'll have to assert yourself. It'll have to be the only thing you want to do.'

'It is,' Jules said.

Benny had told her she had to specialise her music. Why not try house, he said, that's what he was into, in fact had been into it since he was thirteen.

'It's coming up,' he said. 'Hip-hop and R & B have been the choice for kids for so long, but house is coming up. Watch out for funky house.'

Jules loved it, loved house music. She loved the fact that it had an uplifting, positive message, that the four-four beat – that beat that felt like the pump in her blood – always gave way to a breakdown, when everyone on the dance floor stopped dancing and started swaying, slowly, hands in the air, eyes fixed on the DJ, waiting, waiting, waiting for the beat to pick up, the pump to start up again. She loved the fact that it had no dress-code image, that it had originated in a gay club in Chicago – how cool was that? – that it had a strong European profile. She loved the fact that when she was playing it she had a conviction so strong – she wanted to cry sometimes at the relief of being so certain – that this music, playing this music, was all she wanted to do.

Benny sold her her first vinyls. He also found, through a friend, her first decks, which she carried round all the places she was dossing, the floors of friends' flats, the sofa in Lindsay's sitting room. And he took her to Soundproof, the club where she was first allowed to DJ, he took her and pointed her at the manager's closed office door and said, 'Sell yourself.'

That's what it had been about, the last three years: selling herself. She'd thought the music would do the communicating but that wasn't what the clubs wanted. Sure, they wanted the music, the music was key, but the music had to be worthy of being on the dance floor, and only a DJ could keep it that way. Only a good DJ could keep the dance floor full, push the boundaries, keep the beat moving, keep the mood alive. If she wanted to impress the dance promoters, she had to know, to learn, how to keep that floor full, and moving. She had to develop her name.

Miss Jools, she called herself. She might like Benny and his shop the best, but she had to go round all the shops, all the clubs, she had to listen to all the music, all the big DJs, to read what they, the DJ stars, the Norman Cooks and the Pete Tongs, said and thought.

She had a quote from DJ Pierre pasted on the side of one of her decks: 'The DJ's power is like a parent. It's like a president. The DJ has a responsibility, like any person in power. When you have an audience, you better do the right thing and make sure you educate.'

And on the other deck was a battered magazine picture of Francis Grasso, the Italian-American born in Brooklyn, who was the first DJ to mix records, the man regarded as the godfather of beat-mixing, the man who started all the amazing stuff back in the late sixties, which felt like prehistory to Jules. His picture – big, soft face framed with long, curly dark hair – was an inspiration and comfort to Jules. Francis Grasso proved that music, this music, didn't need you to be rich or beautiful or especially educated, it just needed you to love it and understand it and want to share it. And that, Jules told Alan Hayes, the manager of Soundproof, was how she was. All she wanted was to have a connection with the crowd and put the best energy through her mix. Alan Hayes, who looked, Jules thought, more like a bank manager than a club boss, said he'd heard all that before but he'd give her a try, he'd let her do a warm-up.

That had been the beginning, that warm-up. She was given two hours, till ten-thirty, and she was so excited and so nervous she thought she might faint. The club had been empty at first, then there'd been the first handful, then a few more and then, just before the real DJ took over, a line of boys in front of her watching, taking her in, not sneering, just looking to see if she was any good, assessing.

When the session was over, she'd been wired to the ceiling. She'd bought a few Es for a tenner and danced till daybreak and then slept on someone's floor till Lindsay woke her by ringing to ask how it had all gone. She cried then, cried because she was so excited and tired and relieved and longing to be back in that booth with the decks and the strobe lighting and those treble and bass controls that you could ride the crowd with.

'Did they pay you?' Lindsay said.

'Yeah –'

'How much?'

Jules rolled over. She was in someone else's sleeping bag and there were, well, garments of some kind at the bottom. She pulled her feet up.

'Two hundred.'

'Two hundred what?'

'Quid,' Jules said.

'Two hundred quid for playing records for two hours?' Lindsay said incredulously.

'Yeah.'

'Jules –'

'A top DJ,' Jules said, proud of the mountain peaks of her new profession, 'gets thousands. Ten, maybe.'

'You're joking.'

Jules said nothing. She lay on the dirty carpet with her phone to her ear and her eyes closed and smiled. It didn't matter. Two hundred quid didn't matter. Nothing mattered. She had done two hours and she had done good.

Since, she had not so much done bad as found it hard. There were more rival girls than she had bargained for, more competition for promoters' attention, for radio plays of original mixes, more antagonism from the men. It wasn't so hard to be tomboyish and assertive, but it was hard to have to push twice as much, to prove yourself eternally, to start anew with every club, every audience, just because girls had to go twice the distance to establish themselves.

'Show me,' promoters kept saying. 'OK. I know you did it last time. But show me again.'

That was where D'Arblay Street came in. She only had to go back there, and talk to Benny, and pick out some new vinyls, to remember why she was doing this, why this struggle had to be worth it, what had got her started. Benny always had someone new for her to listen to – a couple of rising producers from Croydon, a Frenchman singing in English who was going to take the summer club scene by storm – and always reminded her that, in the end, this was about the music, and nothing else.

'You'll get there,' Benny said. 'You'll mix something that catches on.'

It was Lindsay's suggestion that she start a blog, on the web. Lindsay had done a computer course when Noah started school, and it was one of the few things that she and Jules didn't argue over.

'MySpace,' Lindsay said. 'That's what you want. You need a site on MySpace.'

They set it up on Lindsay's computer. Miss Jools. Miss Jools – Soundproof. Miss Jools – Soundproof – Ask Me!

The first message came the first day.

'Yo, Jules! Ow R ya? Hey, luv ur stuff. Spreadin the word.'

Then two more.

'Good to see a female reppin!'

'You smacked it on Thursday! Keep doin your thing, sister!'

'There,' Lindsay said.

The messages began to pour in, ten, twenty, forty, too many to count.

'You throw down one hard beat.'

'Heavy, heavy.'

'Mad respect.'

'Big up to you, peeps!'

She did three warm-ups on three successive nights and, by the third night, the floor was full by ten-thirty.

When the main DJ took over he said, 'Wicked set, honey,' and then he winked. 'There's nothing like it, is there?'

Going to the manager's office to collect her wages, Jules knew she was grinning, grinning like an idiot.

Alan Hayes was on the telephone. When she came in, he didn't look at her, but he went across to the filing cabinet where he kept the wages and opened a drawer. Then he turned back to Jules and handed her her envelope. She was still grinning. She took her envelope and made for the door.

'Won't do,' Alan Hayes said into his phone. 'Won't wash. Stop there, Jules.'

She stopped, her hand on the door.

'Think again,' Alan Hayes said to his caller. 'Call me when you've thought. You can have a Thursday.'

'What?'

'I said, call me when you've got another idea. You can have a Thursday.'

'Me?'

'Not for a while. But you can try. I'd want to see minimum 450 through those doors.'

'D'you mean it?'

'Yes.'

'Two sets?'

'Yes.'

'I want to die,' Jules said.

Alan Hayes began to dial another number.

'I'll give you a date some time next week.'

'Thank you –'

He waved a hand at her.

'Scoot.'

'*Thank* you.'

He turned his back.

She went into the corridor that led to the dance floor and sat down, leaning against the wall, hugging her knees. He was going to give her a set, a proper set, on a Thursday. He was going to hand four hours to her! Four hours! When she'd be in complete control of what the mood was out there, what happened to the energy. She put her eye sockets against her knees and pressed until the blackness behind her lids exploded with random stars. She had to tell Benny. She had to go to D'Arblay Street the next day, and tell Benny.

Benny wasn't in. Adam, his manager, who was always grumpy round Jules, said Benny had called in sick and wouldn't be coming in.

'What's the matter with him?'

Adam put his earphones on and began flicking discs on to the decks along the counter.

'Wouldn't know. He didn't say.'

'He's never sick,' Jules said, almost accusing.

Adam shrugged. Jules stared at him for a moment and then turned and went out into the street. A thin, irritating drizzle was falling. She flipped her phone open and dialled.

'Lin?'

'I'm at work,' Lindsay said in a whisper. 'You know I'm at work. Are you OK?'

Jules pictured Lindsay, in her blue polyester suit, in the back office of the building society where she worked, visible but inaudible to the public behind a glass wall.

'I've got something to tell you.'

'Are you OK?'

'It's a good thing –'

'Can't it wait?'

Jules put her face up into the soft dampness. She sighed. 'Meet me at lunchtime,' Lindsay said.

Jules sighed again.

'I'm in the West End –'

'What?'

'I'm in Soho.'

'Jules,' Lindsay said, 'I've got to go. Call me later.'

Jules snapped her phone shut and gripped it. She closed her eyes, and counted. She counted backwards from twenty, then up again. Then she opened her eyes and began walking, slowly, up towards Oxford Street. She had open-toed shoes on, and in a while, with the rain, there'd be black, gritty splashes of damp in her shoes. Why did Benny have to get sick?

In a coffee bar on Oxford Street, she ordered a tea, *grande* size, and took it to a high stool in the window. There were a couple of schoolgirls on the next stools, wearing personally customised versions of their uniforms, and they gave Jules long, insolent looks – the holey leggings, the minidress, the pinstriped jacket with gold braid on the sleeves and shoulders, the pink plastic peep-toes – before collapsing in giggles together. Jules hitched herself on to her stool, and put both hands round her tea mug, and stared out into the rain. People were putting up umbrellas and resting carrier bags and newspapers on their heads. One man had pulled up the back of his T-shirt, right over his head, so his skinny pale spine was exposed, and his arms hung grotesquely forward, dangling like a puppet's.

If it wasn't for Lindsay, Jules knew – she *knew* – she'd probably be dead. She wouldn't be dead for any particularly dramatic reason, but more that she'd have let herself be shoved here and pushed there and abandoned somewhere else until neglect and aimlessness just spun her life out into nothing. Literally nothing. Her childhood had made this sort of drifting familiar, sometimes with one parent, sometimes with both, sometimes in a bed-and-breakfast place, or a broken-down flat, even, for a week, with her father in a burnt-out bus in a demolition yard. But always, even in the most chaotic times, there was Lindsay. Even if she didn't live with them – and she took care not to, as soon as she could – she was around, tense with anxiety but also insistent on some kind of structure, some kind of consistency. When she was sixteen, she'd gone to live with her boyfriend's family, but she would, somehow, find Jules every week, bringing bananas and clean underwear and reading books. Jules couldn't remember her smiling. She was too worried to smile. And although Jules knew she had always given Lindsay plenty to worry about, and had often taken very little trouble about minimising the causes of that worry, she also knew that without Lindsay's anxiety she'd be lost.

She looked down into her tea. Half of it remained, but the heat had gone out of it. The two schoolgirls, no doubt compounding their evident truanting, had hitched up their skirts and their sweater sleeves and sashayed out into the rain. Jules got off her stool. She stood for a moment, thinking about the chance Alan Hayes had offered her, about Benny at home in bed in his mother's flat in Tulse Hill, where he had lived all his life. She looked out of the window. She would get on the tube and make the annoyingly complicated journey down to Fulham Broadway and meet Lindsay for lunch.

*   *   *

'Don't eat that rubbish,' Lindsay said pleadingly. 'I've got you a proper sandwich. Chicken salad.'

Jules looked down at the bag in her hand. Cinnamon-sugar pretzels from Auntie Ann's in the Fulham Broadway Centre.

'I like them.'

Lindsay took the bag out of her hand.

'I can't stand the muck you put in yourself.'

'Don't start –'

Lindsay put down a tray with sandwiches and yoghurt and juice on it.

'I want you to eat decent stuff, Jules.'

'I came to see you,' Jules said. 'I came. Oxford Circus, I was –'

Lindsay sat down opposite her and dropped her bag between her feet.

'I know. I'm sorry. It's just –' She looked at her sister. 'You know.'

'I've been offered my first gig.'

Lindsay pushed a sandwich towards her.

'But I thought you already –'

'That was just warm-ups. This is the real deal. My night.'

Lindsay looked straight at her.

'Well done.'

'Yeah.'

'Can you do it?'

Jules peeled back the plastic film from the sandwich.

'Hope so.'

'How many hours?'

'Four or five –'

'Four or five hours of music?'

Jules took a bite.

'I'll have to work on it.'

'Well done,' Lindsay said again. She looked Jules up and down and grinned. 'He booked you, even looking like that.'

'He booked me because I'm good,' Jules said. She didn't glance at Lindsay. 'I can talk signal-to-noise ratio with the best of them.'

'Why can't you get a flat, then?'

'Don't want a flat.'

'Why not?'

'Don't want the hassle.'

'What about the hassle of never knowing where you're going to sleep?'

'I do know where I'm going to sleep.'

'Do you?'

Jules carefully extracted the tomato slices from her sandwich and dropped them into the discarded wrapping.

'Yep.'

'Tonight, for example?'

Jules didn't look up.

'Yours.'

'Really?'

'Uh-huh.'

'I'm out tonight. It's Friday.'

Jules licked the mayonnaise off her fingers.

'I know. I'm coming.'

'I thought you were –'

'Not tonight,' Jules said with emphasis. 'I may have been offered a gig, but I haven't been offered a *Friday*.'

'Don't you want to sleep?'

'I'll sleep tomorrow.' She put down the half-chewed sandwich and looked at Lindsay. 'Don't you want me to come?'

'It's at Blaise's.'

'So?'

'I thought Blaise –'

'Blaise is OK. I'm cool with Blaise. Who got Eleanor to ask her in the first place, anyway?'

Lindsay opened her own sandwich packet and neatly extracted half the contents.

'I never thought you'd come, you know. When I asked Eleanor, when Noah was a baby, when I asked her if I could bring you, I never thought you'd come.'

Jules didn't care for these kind of conversations. She knew of old where they would lead, with Lindsay expecting her to say something soft, and explain what it was about having a sister, or knowing Eleanor or liking Paula's Toby that kept her coming back, however irregularly. She also didn't want to talk about the time when Noah was a baby, when she'd been living nominally with her mother, but actually nowhere much, and she'd been so excited and terrified and out of it most of the time that she couldn't go near Noah, she daren't, in case, like the bad fairy at Sleeping Beauty's christening, she cast some terrible blight on him without meaning to, which only she would know about and would never be able to share. And she would always know that, when Lindsay had been widowed at that same period in her life, she'd been no support, no help, no consolation. In fact, she couldn't yet look at those memories. She couldn't look at them because they made her flinch and cringe, not just because of what had happened, but because of the way she'd behaved. There had been no excuse for behaviour like that, and never would be. And Lindsay, although for years looking as if a dimension had been sucked out of her, had never reproached her, had never required her to imagine what it was like to lose your young husband, let alone in such a terrible way. All Lindsay had done was to redouble her efforts to stop Jules, if she possibly could, from leaving her as well.

Jules picked at some chicken stuck in her teeth with a fingernail.

'I'm coming tonight, Lin.'

Lindsay looked down at her sandwich.

'Then you'll meet Paula's new man.'

'Yeah?'

'She looks amazing,' Lindsay said. 'She's so happy.'

'That OK by you?'

'Why shouldn't it be –'

Jules regarded her.

'You know.'

Lindsay put her sandwich down.

'I'm fine,' Lindsay said. 'I'm fine on my own. I'm fine.'

'But you wouldn't turn a man down.'

'Not the right one.'

Jules gave a little snort.

'If they're hot, they're hopeless. And if they're not hot, who cares?'

'We wouldn't want the same ones,' Lindsay said primly.

'Right.'

'And I like seeing Paula happy. I like seeing her all lit up like this, new shoes, haircut –'

Jules reached across the table and helped herself to Lindsay's second sandwich.

'You don't like tuna,' Lindsay said.

Jules bit into the sandwich and said through it, 'What about Toby?'

'What about him?'

'What about Toby and this new man?'

Lindsay gave Jules a quick smile.

'He's a season-ticket holder at Stamford Bridge.'

Jules shrugged.

'Toby coming tonight?'

'Shouldn't think so,' Lindsay said, and then added in a rush, 'unless they, unless Paula –'

'Wants to play happy families.'

'Don't say that.'

'You're soft,' Jules said to Lindsay. 'You're just soft.'

Lindsay began to gather up the sandwich wrappings.

'I've got to go back to work.'

'I'll get Noah from school.'

'Jules –'

'What?'

'Can I,' Lindsay said, her brow creasing, 'can I *trust* you to do that?'

'OK,' Jules said, staring elaborately past her, 'don't.'

'I didn't mean –'

Jules stood up.

'Why don't you come and check on me?'

Lindsay said nothing. She gave a resigned small shrug and picked up her bag.

'Trouble is,' Jules said, looking down on her, 'you don't trust anyone, do you?'

Lindsay stayed silent, holding her bag on her knee.

'Not me, not any man who's ever been anywhere near you, not Noah to stay safe, not even the girlfriends. No one. Do you?'

Lindsay stood up. She gave Jules a quick fierce glance.

'No,' she said, and then she turned and began to walk away.

Outside Noah's school, Jules established herself in a prime position by the gates so he couldn't possibly miss her. There were a handful of mothers, some with babies in buggies, and a man who might have been a father or just might have been a creep. In the bag slung over her shoulder, Jules had a packet of chocolate beans for Noah and a CD of some of her music. She planned to put this on for him when they got back to Lindsay's flat, and dance with him. Noah liked dancing. He was a silent little boy, an observer, not a participator, his teacher said, but he liked dancing. When Jules played her music he would quietly stop doing whatever he was doing and come and dance. He danced like a lot of people in the club danced, with that look of inward concentration that makes a partner irrelevant, and he would dance as long as the music was playing.

He came out of school on the edge of his group as usual, not exactly on his own, but not talking to anyone either. Jules crouched down so that her face would be level with his.

'Hi, Noah.'

He looked at her. He gave a small smile.

'We did music,' Noah said.

'I've got more,' Jules said. 'I've got more music for you.' She straightened up and took his hand.

'We're going to play music. And dance.'

'OK,' Noah said. He was wearing a small backpack, shaped like a panda, and it had pulled his anorak away from his neck so that it looked particularly vulnerable. Jules gave his clothes a rough twitch. He didn't object. Jules couldn't remember him ever objecting to anything much. Not like Toby. Toby had always had a mind of his own.

She began to walk along the pavement, Noah's hand in hers. He was so used to having his hand held that he never tried to pull away. He didn't look up at her, but occasionally he said something so that she had to stoop to hear him.

'What?'

'Where's Mum?'

'She's coming,' Jules said. 'She's at work. She's coming.'

And then a bit further on, 'What?'

'I've got a recorder.'

'Can you play it?'

Pause.

'Noah?'

Silence.

'Noah?'

'Yes?'

'Can you play your recorder?'

Pause.

'No.'

She looked down at him. Funny little boy. He had Lindsay's narrow features and his father's thick dark hair. There was a picture of his father in Noah's bedroom, in the uniform of a naval rating. He'd thought he wanted to be a sailor but it had only lasted two years. Then he joined the construction industry. He'd been married a year when it happened. He didn't even know he was going to be a father. Fathers! Jules tightened her grip on Noah's hand.

'I've got chocolate for you,' Jules said. 'And we're going to do dancing.'

CHAPTER SIX

L ucas had made a small pile in the hall of things he was taking round to his new studio. Lucas's old studio, up near the top of the house under the girls' bedroom, made disorder seem a description of tidiness, but this pile was very neat: a portfolio of boards and paper, scrupulously tied, a trim canvas roll of brushes, an unfamiliar (newly purchased?) plastic toolbox full of paint tubes graded by colour. Looking at the pile gave Karen the distinct impression that both its presence and its nature were deeply deliberate on Lucas's part.

He came down the stairs, apparently absorbed in texting something on his mobile phone. He was wearing familiar old black jeans and an unfamiliar russet linen shirt and he had tied his hair back, something he had stopped doing in the last few years. Having it tied back became him, showed off his excellent bone structure, and even that, to Karen, standing below him in her work tracksuit with a bulging work bag over her right shoulder, was a signal. He didn't exactly look as if he was going out on a date, but he certainly looked as if he was removing himself from familial responsibility.

Karen indicated the pile on the floor.

'Very organised.'

Lucas finished his text. Then he raised his eyes very slowly and looked at Karen.

'I wish you'd come and see it.'

'Luke –'

'What?'

She let her bag slide off her shoulder and hit the floor with a thud.

'To be absolutely frank with you, I'd just stand there and think, This is costing six hundred and fifty quid a month, which means earning almost twice that to pay for it. So it's better I stay away just now.'

'Just now?'

'Yes.'

'Until I have justified it by selling something I've painted in it?'

Karen looked down.

'Well – yes.'

Lucas walked past her.

'At least that's clear.'

She put a hand out and caught clumsily at his sleeve.

'Luke, I don't want to be like this. I don't want to be a mean-spirited killjoy. But I can't work any harder, I can't –'

He moved very slightly so that his sleeve slipped from her hand.

'Kay, babe, we've had this conversation.' He bent and picked up the portfolio. He said, 'You used to believe in me.'

She looked directly at the wall ahead of her.

'That,' she said in as neutral a voice as she could manage, 'is a deeply unfair thing to say. I still believe in you.'

Lucas said nothing. He wedged the roll of brushes under the arm that held the portfolio, and picked up the toolbox.

'I haven't changed,' Karen said. 'I still believe in your talent. You are a very good painter and a truly wonderful father. But something in you has changed. You've sort of – sort of stopped trying.'

Lucas indicated the front door with his head.

'Could you? I'm a bit burdened –'

She reached past him and unlatched the door. He put a foot through to lever it open, and then he turned to look at her.

'Not trying,' he said. 'Not trying. So what do you think this new studio is all about?' He continued to regard her for a few seconds and then he said, 'The girls are fed and Rosie's done her homework. All yours. Have fun,' and then he went out into the street and the door swung shut behind him.

Karen turned. Poppy was standing on the stairs wearing a party dress of two winters ago, so short now it barely covered her knickers, and embellished with a feather boa and glitter knee socks.

'OK,' Karen said.

Poppy leaned forward. On closer inspection, she was also wearing eye shadow and large pearl earrings.

'I think,' Poppy said, 'you'd better change.'

'Come early,' Blaise had said to Karen. 'Eleanor's always on time and I need you to be, too. I need the room full. Well, not full, but not empty either. Not just me.'

It was strange, she thought, looking round her sitting room, how unpractised she felt at having people in it. She was so used to public entertaining, to the rituals of restaurants and bars and boardrooms, but doing it at home, where she bore sole responsibility and had to fulfil every role that she normally paid other people to do, was faintly alarming. She had grown used to having just the girls there – though she had been careful to visit all their houses before she surrendered her own – but tonight was different, tonight she felt more on display and it was disconcerting.

Her sitting room was normally her leisure place. The deep sofas, the large television, the top-of-the-range music system were all there to provide the alternative to work that she endeavoured to design as conscientiously as she devised everything else in her life. There were even, upstairs in her wardrobe, clothes purchased specifically to be leisured in, to convey somehow that this space and time were as valuable and nourishing to her as the work times were. She had asked Eleanor once if, while she was working, she had filled her house at weekends with friends and colleagues and Eleanor had paused and then said, with a shade too much emphasis, 'Heavens, no,' and then she had said, 'But of course, I am not very interested in houses. And you, I think, are.'

Blaise considered that she was interested in her house, at least.

'Not really,' Karen said.

'What do you mean?'

'I mean you like it as a place to have, but not, fully, to live in.'

'Is this another jibe at the single life?'

'I expect so,' Karen said, 'but houses aren't just settings, you know.'

Perhaps, Blaise thought, looking round now at her calm, pale room, they were more manifestations than settings. Perhaps people like her, who consciously chose linen blinds and restful pictures, wanted to complement themselves, rather than strive for something that they weren't, but would like to be. Maybe the room was her, just as Karen's more ethnic sitting room was her and Lindsay's neat, pastel one was her and Eleanor's bookish muddle was – oh, stop this, Blaise thought, stop analysing this. What's different about tonight except that a man is coming?

The letterbox banged a few times unevenly.

Poppy shouted through it, 'We're here! We're here!'

Blaise went out to the hall and opened the door. Eleanor, Karen, Rosie and Poppy were outside, Karen holding a bottle and Poppy a large, slightly creased sheet of paper.

She thrust it at Blaise.

'I did you a picture!'

Rosie stepped forward.

'I'm afraid,' she said confidingly, 'it isn't very good. Poppy can do much better than that.'

'Are you coming like that?' Lindsay asked.

Jules didn't even glance down at what she was wearing. She had taken off the pinstriped jacket while she was dancing with Noah, revealing a green-lace long-sleeved T-shirt under her minidress.

She said defiantly, 'Yeah.'

'Haven't you got –'

'No,' Jules said, interrupting, 'I haven't got anything except a toothbrush. Try and like it that I've even got a toothbrush.'

'OK,' Lindsay said.

She had put on her beige hooded coat over black trousers and a neat red sweater with a V-neck. Noah had on a tracksuit and his school anorak over his dinosaur pyjamas. When he was dancing with Jules, his cheeks had briefly pinkened, but they were pale again now. He stood by the door, obediently ready to go, clutching his panda backpack with his slippers in it.

'Sorry,' Lindsay said, 'I'm a bit nervous.'

'Why?'

'S'pose – s'pose I don't like him –?'

'Why does that matter? He's Paula's bloke, not yours.'

'It drives a wedge. In friendships. If you don't like some-one's partner. You know it does.'

'Why don't you think you'll like him?'

'I don't. I just think, s'pose I –'

'It'll be worse,' Jules said, 'if you fancy him.'

Lindsay looked shocked.

'Oh, I wouldn't do that!'

Jules grinned. She picked up her jacket.

'I'm only into fancying people,' Jules said. 'I don't care about *like*.'

Lindsay steered Noah out into the hall.

'Stupid talk.'

Noah said something.

Lindsay stooped.

'What?'

'Can I take my recorder?' Noah said.

Well, Eleanor thought, deep in one of Blaise's armchairs, with a glass of wine in her hand and Mozart tastefully on the sound system, the stage is admirably set. Here we all are, even Jules, the candles are lit, the children are supplying an important element of unselfconsciousness – I think Noah may even be asleep – and we have had enough wine to embolden us and not so much as to make us careless. We are, I think, ready for all exhibits. The question is: is the poor exhibit, after this extraordinary build-up, ready for us?

She looked at the floor. Jules was sprawled on it on her stomach, playing some kind of paper game with Rosie. Rosie was lying on her stomach too, her hair falling on to the paper she was writing on. Round them, shuffling unsteadily, was Poppy in her party dress and Jules' peep-toe shoes. Every so often, she bumped into Rosie and Rosie said, 'Ow!' elaborately and piercingly, and Karen, talking to Lindsay, took no notice.

Blaise, Eleanor observed, was in the kitchen. She wasn't, presumably, cooking although, through the arch that divided the sitting room from the kitchen, Eleanor could see her opening the oven door, and sliding baking trays in and out. It was an unspoken rule for Friday nights that you could make a small effort about food and drink, but not a large one, on account of a fatal female propensity to hospitable competitiveness. The night Paula produced champagne had been proof of that. It wasn't simply that it might not be fair, but more that it might unbalance things. Supermarket wine, cheese on crackers kept things level, kept things manageable.

But it looked to Eleanor, from her armchair, as if Blaise had temporarily forgotten this tacit regulation. She put her wine glass down on the ledge of a nearby bookcase, and heaved herself out of her chair. Then, carefully negotiating the bodies on the floor, she limped out to the kitchen.

The kitchen table bore several gleaming boxes with photographs of perfect little canapés printed on them.

'What are you doing?' Eleanor said.

'Just heating things. Bought stuff, as you can see. Nothing special.'

Eleanor bent over the table and scrutinised the boxes.

'I consider king prawns and smoked salmon reasonably special.'

Blaise put a tray of tartlets the size of fifty-pence pieces on the table and began to lever them off carefully with a palette knife.

'It's for Paula, really. A bit of a celebration –'

'Is she,' Eleanor said, 'engaged to be married to this man?'

Blaise stopped levering and looked across the table.

'No, I just –'

'Aren't you rather overdoing things?'

Blaise gestured at the table.

'A few little quiches? Hardly.'

Eleanor grunted. She straightened up a little, still leaning on the edge of the table.

'At least the children are being normal. Noah is being excessively normal by being prudently fast asleep.'

The front doorbell rang.

Blaise gave a little start.

'Come with me –'

'Certainly not,' Eleanor said. 'It's your house.'

Blaise dropped the knife on to the tray of tartlets and almost ran towards the front door. Eleanor went slowly back to the sitting room. Jules and Rosie were still on the floor, Karen and Lindsay were sitting as before but silently, staring towards the door, and Poppy, unevenly balanced in Jules' shoes, was standing with her arms out in a stagey, touching gesture of welcome.

The front door opened. There were voices – Blaise, Paula, even Toby – and a man's voice. Poppy raised her arms to a kind of salute and then Paula was in the room.

'Hi, everyone!'

They all stood up, except Jules, who remained where she was.

'Oh!' Paula said. 'Lovely! Oh, *great*! Great to see you all!'

They converged on her, young women and children, as if she had come through some great ordeal, as if they had somehow thought they would never see her again. She was laughing, they were all laughing, Poppy was squealing. Eleanor watched them from where she had halted by her armchair, and then her gaze travelled steadily behind them to the man who was standing in the doorway. He was not looking at Paula and the young women. He was looking at Eleanor. He gave her a brief, grave nod.

Paula broke away from the group and ran across the room.

'Eleanor –' She put her arms round Eleanor. 'I meant to come and see you. I wanted to –'

Eleanor held on to the chair back with one hand and patted Paula's back with the other.

'Do you remember my saying to you once that I reserved getting upset for the big things?'

Paula pulled away.

She said, 'This just might be a big thing!'

Eleanor looked past her. The man was pleasant-looking enough, well built, what she would privately deem personable. She turned back to Paula.

'I was afraid you were going to produce a god for us.'

'A god!'

'All the build-up. Where is Toby?'

Paula turned round.

'There.'

Toby had cast himself down on the floor next to Jules. She was whispering to him.

'How is Toby?' Eleanor said.

'Impossible,' Paula said. 'Adorable. You know Toby. I'm going to get a drink.'

She spun away from Eleanor.

'Drink, babe?'

The man looked across at her. He smiled. Then he moved towards them, still smiling.

'Love one.' He turned to Eleanor and held his hand out. 'Jackson Miller.'

His handshake was firm and warm. He was not handsome, certainly, but there was something about him, something physically confident, that made Eleanor want to withdraw her hand in self-defence.

'I am Eleanor.'

'I know,' Jackson said. 'I know who you all are.'

'You are an exception to our rule, Mr Miller.'

She saw him hesitate. Had he been about to say, 'I like being an exception,' and thought better of it? She waited a moment, watching him, and then she took pity and said, 'Could you pass me my stick?'

He was plainly glad to. He assisted her competently back into her armchair, propping her stick so she could reach it.

'Is your mother still alive?'

'No, she passed away ten years ago.'

'You seem practised. You seem good at heaving old ladies about.'

'My pleasure.'

Eleanor looked at the floor. She caught Toby's eye and beckoned. He got up clumsily and came over. He did not look at Jackson.

'The trouble about these new living arrangements,' Eleanor said, 'is that we hardly see each other. We used, you see, to live on the same street. This street.'

'You have an amazing place now,' Jackson said to Toby. His tone was not at all cajoling.

'I liked it here,' Toby said to Eleanor.

Paula came spinning back, holding two glasses of wine. 'Oops, at last! Did you think I'd forgotten?'

Jackson looked at her.

'No.'

Eleanor said to Toby, 'You could fill mine, if you like.'

Toby looked at her glass on the bookcase.

'There's some in it –'

'But not enough,' Eleanor said. 'Not enough to be encouraging.'

'OK,' Toby said. He picked the glass up and sniffed the contents.

'Toby!' Paula said, remonstrating.

'What do you think it smells of?' Eleanor asked.

'Vinegar,' Toby said. 'Pee.'

Paula groaned. She bent her head as if about to rest it, in theatrical despair at Toby's conduct, on Jackson's shoulder.

Toby wandered off, holding the wine glass at an exaggerated distance from himself.

Jackson didn't look at Eleanor. He simply stood, his eyes on Paula, waiting for her to recover.

'Boys,' Jackson said easily. He glanced at Eleanor, smiling. 'Boys.'

Jules made a picnic on the floor for the children. She put a selection of all the weird little things Blaise had bought on a plate, emptied a bag of crisps over everything and put the plate on the carpet. Then she arranged a ring of cans of drink round the plate, and sat down cross-legged, her bare feet with their chipped crimson toenails well on display.

Rosie came and sat beside her. She had taken the feather boa away from Poppy because she thought Poppy was getting too overexcited and had wound it round her own neck instead. She sat down carefully with her back to Poppy because Poppy was doing some kind of dance not very far away from Paula's man friend, and it was, frankly, embarrassing. She picked up a crisp.

'Is this normal food?'

Jules had her mouth full.

She licked the fingers of one hand and said indistinctly, 'No way.'

'I like Daddy's food,' Rosie said.

'I like all the gross stuff,' Jules said. 'Burgers and chips and doughnuts.'

Toby materialised beside her. She gave the nearest leg of his jeans a quick tug.

'Sit down.'

He slumped beside her. He reached into the pile on the plate and extracted a small pastry triangle.

'Is this a samosa?'

'Try it.'

Toby bit. He put the rest of the triangle back on the plate.

'What's the matter?'

His eyes strayed to Blaise's giant plasma television.

'I want to turn that on.'

'You just want to be annoying,' Jules said. 'Eat the crisps. They aren't scary.'

'Daddy's got a new studio,' Rosie said. 'He's going to paint a picture as big as a wall.'

'Cool.'

'We're going to see it. We can paint in it. He's going to let us do oil paints and mixing.'

Jules popped the ring pull on a can of lemonade.

'I do mixing. With music.'

Toby inspected a crisp.

'Is the red stuff peppery?'

Rosie looked across at him. She adjusted her boa.

'Do you still play with your theatre?'

Toby studied the crisp. He had played with his theatre only two hours ago. He didn't mind Rosie, but there was something about life just now that was preventing him from being able to be helpful, even in conversation. He flicked the crisp on to Blaise's pale, clean carpet.

'Not now,' he said.

'Wait and see,' Karen said to Lindsay, 'how long it is before Blaise notices that crisp.'

Lindsay was holding a plate with two small things on it. She looked at the carpet.

'I'll pick it up –'

'No,' Karen said, 'just wait. It's amusing.'

'Not if it fusses Blaise. It'd fuss me.'

'I shouldn't have pointed it out.'

Lindsay made an effort and surveyed the room.

'Look at Poppy.'

'I'd rather not.'

'She's such a flirt –'

Karen took a swallow of wine.

'At least she's got taste. He's pretty gorgeous.'

Lindsay picked up a tiny vol-au-vent and put it down again.

'D'you think so?'

'Oh yes!'

'I think –' Lindsay said, and stopped.

'What?'

'I think he's a bit – well, *animal*-looking.'

'Yes. So?'

'I don't like that.'

'You know,' Karen said, 'one of the comforting things about being married is that you can look at gorgeous men quite objectively. You can look at them the way you'd look at a sculpture or a painting. You can just think to yourself that the room looks better for having them in it.'

'I wouldn't know,' Lindsay said. 'I wasn't married long enough.'

There was a beat, and then Karen said, not looking at Lindsay, 'Sorry. That was careless.'

'Paula looks wonderful,' Lindsay said. 'So happy.'

'It's a good stage, this early in-love stage. It makes you like everyone and everything much more than usual.'

Lindsay put her plate on the floor.

She said suddenly, 'D'you think Eleanor's ever been in love?'

Karen glanced across the room. Jackson Miller had pulled an upright chair up close to Eleanor, and was leaning towards her almost deferentially.

'Heavens, no,' Karen said. 'Far too much good sense.'

'Bit sad, that?'

Karen turned to look at her.

'I don't want to be tactless a second time,' Karen said, 'but I'd have thought you'd had too much pain to justify any pleasure there'd been.'

Lindsay pushed her hair behind her ears.

'Then you'd be wrong.'

'Thank you,' Paula said.

Blaise took the last baking sheet out of the oven.

'For what?'

'All this,' Paula said. 'Making it special.'

'Eleanor ticked me off.'

'That's what Eleanor's for, to tick us off. But I like it, I like it that you made it special.' She looked back through the arch to the sitting room. 'What do you think?'

Blaise slid the contents of the tray on to a plate.

'I think he's conducting himself admirably.'

93

'Talking to Eleanor?'

'Talking to Eleanor and sizing us all up.'

'He wasn't at all fazed,' Paula said, perching on a tall black stool. 'He just said, "Good idea," when I suggested it and when I said, "Won't it be a bit of an ordeal?" he said, "Why?"'

'Good for him.'

'He's so confident,' Paula said. She took a swallow of wine. 'I wish I was –'

'About him?'

'Oh no. About myself.'

'Is he married?'

Paula took another swallow.

'Why do you ask?'

'So many men are –'

'Well, he has been. Twice, in fact. But not now.'

Blaise picked up her own wine glass.

'What does he do?'

Paula grinned at her.

'Typical you. Lindsay asked me if he had children. He's a businessman. He runs a company providing mobile technical support. Computer geeks on motorbikes.'

Blaise looked at Jackson with some interest.

'Good idea.'

'He's full of good ideas. You'll see when you talk to him. Come and talk to him.'

'Not now.'

'Why not now?'

Blaise looked past Paula to the sitting room.

'Don't force the pace, Paula.'

'I'm not!'

'Even this evening,' Blaise said, 'is forcing the pace a bit.'

'But it's lovely! Look at them! Listen!'

Blaise put out her free hand and took hold of Paula's arm.

'It's fine. But it's – not like we usually are.'

'Of course not –'

'And we can't make him an honorary member.'

'I never said –'

'Paula,' Blaise said, holding her arm, 'if this relationship turns out to be very important, fine. But it's your relationship. You can't share it. That's all.'

Paula stared at her.

'What are you on about?'

Blaise let her arm go. Paula slid off the stool.

'Nothing. Forget it.'

'D'you think I can't be in love and still stay friends with you all at the same time?'

'I said forget it. I'm being clumsy. I just meant –' She stopped.

Paula pushed her face close to Blaise's.

'I'll show you.'

Blaise said nothing.

'I was first in this group,' Paula said. She took another gulp of wine. 'I practically started it. You only –'

'I know,' Blaise said. 'I'm sorry.'

Paula moved away. She picked up the plate of canapés. From the archway, she turned and looked back at Blaise.

'I don't know why you seem to begrudge me,' Paula said. 'I didn't think that's what friends were for.'

Lindsay sat down on the edge of one of Blaise's deep sofas and looked at Noah's back. He had lain down and rolled himself over almost as soon as they had arrived, and had stayed there, steadily sleeping, for over two hours. It seemed criminal to wake him, but she had to so that they could go home. Not far, to be sure, and she could still just carry him, but when she looked at his back, and the back of his oblivious dark head, her heart smote her. It felt, at this end of the evening, unbelievably selfish to have come out and dragged Noah with her. Noah should have been tucked up peacefully in his own bed with Shamila, from the flat downstairs, babysitting him for pocket money, while she did her citizenship homework.

'Your son?' Jackson said. He was crouching down by the sofa so that his face was on a level with Lindsay's.

She gave him a fleeting glance.

'Yes.'

'I'm not very good at ages,' Jackson said. 'Maybe he's five?'

'Six,' Lindsay said.

'Not a party animal –'

'He's very at home here,' Lindsay said, staring at Noah. 'He's lived round here all his life. He knows this house.'

'And you are Lindsay.'

Lindsay nodded.

'Paula's told me about you.'

'She's a good friend –'

'I'm sure,' Jackson said easily. He straightened up. 'Want me to lift him?'

Lindsay shook her head.

'I'll do it. It might scare him –'

'A stranger –'

'Yes.'

'OK,' Jackson said. 'Nice to meet you.'

Lindsay didn't look up.

'You too.'

'I like your friend Eleanor.'

Lindsay nodded again.

Jackson bent.

'Have I done something wrong?'

'Oh no –'

'You just seemed –' He stopped.

Lindsay took a breath.

'I'm really happy for Paula. Really happy.'

'Good.'

'It's just – that I have to see to Noah.'

Jackson waited a moment. Lindsay felt he was smiling but couldn't look to see.

'OK,' Jackson said.

'Daddy's back!' Poppy squealed.

She went racing into the kitchen ahead of Karen and Rosie. Lucas was sitting at the kitchen table, eating eggs.

He looked up as they came in.

'Good evening?'

Karen made an equivocal gesture with one hand. Rosie had smudges of fatigue under her eyes.

'Good evening, Pops?' Lucas said to Poppy.

She reached up and stuck a finger in the egg.

'Poppy!'

'Let her,' Lucas said. He scooped Poppy up in one arm and set her on his knee. 'So nothing to report; all rather disappointing?'

Rosie leaned against the table, yawning.

'It was really boring.'

'Was it?' Lucas looked at Karen. 'Was it?'

'Not exactly –'

'I wasn't bored,' Lucas said to Poppy. 'I had a lovely evening. My studio has a cat. I'll take you to meet him in the morning.'

Poppy went on sticking her finger in the egg, and then licking it.

Rosie said, 'I've been *longing* for a cat.'

'Long no further,' Lucas said. He kissed the top of Poppy's head. He said, not looking at Karen, 'Didn't you like the guy?'

'Hardly spoke to him –'

'That wasn't very friendly.'

'It just didn't kind of happen.'

'What about you, Rosie?'

Rosie blinked.

'What did you think of Paula's boyfriend?'

'Was he a boyfriend?'

Lucas began to laugh.

'I think so –'

Poppy said in a whisper, 'He was nice.'

'She means,' Karen said, switching on the kettle, 'he was worth flirting with.'

Lucas looked up.

'Was he?'

Karen opened a cupboard and found a mug.

'No.'

'Well, that makes things simpler, doesn't it?'

'Daddy,' Rosie said.

'Yes, poppet?'

'Daddy,' Rosie said. Her eyes were enormous with fatigue. 'Daddy –' She glanced at Karen, and then she said tiredly, 'Daddy, I wish we'd come with you.'

CHAPTER SEVEN

The shop that Paula now managed was situated in the New King's Road. On one side of it was a large lighting emporium and on the other an antique shop that specialised in gilded furniture and only ever displayed a single, dramatically lit piece in its window. Paula's shop, by contrast, had room sets behind its vast sheet of plate glass, a bedroom, or a sitting room with cushions and curtains in white linen to show off the dark wood of the furniture, and tropical ferns and grasses sprouting brilliantly out of pots that might, just might, have once graced a Balinese temple.

The wood that made the furniture in the shop was carefully sourced. Some of it was teak from Indonesia or South Africa and some of it was acacia from Vietnam. It was stored in a warehouse in a disused gasworks not far from Paula's loft, every kind of furniture imaginable, from four-poster beds (to be draped, Far Eastern style, in white muslin) through partners' desks and dining tables, to lamps shaped like obelisks, and frames for mirrors. This furniture, grouped invitingly in the shop's gleaming but shadowy spaces, was accessorised with silk and linen cushions and smooth pale objects carved out of soapstone. Paula prided herself on knowing where everything had been sourced and how it had been made. She liked to give the impression to customers that she had actually squatted in the bazaar at Siem Reap and watched the copper linings being hammered into the pewter bowls, and the opalescent silks stretched across the lampshade frames. Even Jackson had been briefly taken in. He'd stood, hands in pockets, surveying the studs and hinges on the campaign chair of which he had just ordered six and said, 'So you've seen them make this stuff?'

Paula hesitated a little. She was very much in manageress mode, order pad at the ready, telephone in hand to see if the warehouse could make an exception, just this once, to its usual delivery time and oblige this particular customer in two weeks rather than six.

'It's mostly made in the Far East, in Vietnam and Cambodia –'

'Where you've been?'

Paula considered saying, 'Not actually,' and discarded it as unprofessional. She looked intently at her order pad.

'No,' she said.

He glanced at her. She thought he looked amused.

She said, 'Delivery time will of course depend upon our shipments.'

He went out of the shop fifteen minutes later, having ordered six chairs, a table and a wood-and-seagrass wine rack. He came back the next day, ordered the most expensive bed in the shop and a panelled wardrobe, and asked Paula to have a drink with him. She declined, against every instinct. A week later, he returned, cancelled the second order and renewed his invitation. Paula, surrendering naturally to her inclination this time, agreed.

When he had gone, Joel, her deputy manager, paused by her desk long enough to say, 'I knew he'd be back. I knew the second order was just a ruse. Hope he takes you somewhere nice.'

Paula shrugged.

'It's only a drink.'

'Nice-looking guy,' Joel said. 'Nice shoes.'

'Oh?'

'Patrick Cox,' Joel said. 'Or maybe Tod's. Nice, though. Expensive.'

Paula focused on her computer screen.

'I don't notice men's shoes.'

'Well, you should. Tell you a lot, shoes do.'

'I'll try and remember,' Paula said.

She stared at the screen, waiting for Joel to move.

She said, 'At least he didn't cancel both orders –'

'Couldn't have asked you out then, could he?' Joel said. 'Wouldn't have had the nerve.'

'It was his nerve,' Paula said, looking straight ahead, 'that I liked.'

Joel bent briefly over her shoulder.

'That,' he said, 'is what gets you into trouble.'

It was odd, Paula thought with more pleasure than dismay, how much more attracted she was to men with a sulphurous whiff of danger about them than to safe men. Over the years since Gavin – not so many really, though it sometimes felt like a lifetime – there'd been dates and brief affairs and more dates, but none of them had amounted to more than a hope followed by a possibility followed by a decided withdrawal. Paula knew herself well enough to know that, in a sense, she was looking all the time, looking at men in the street, on the tube, in bars, not avidly and indiscriminately, but with a keen curiosity to see if a face, an attitude, a voice could rekindle in her what she had felt for Gavin, that surrendering, out-of-her-depth feeling that had rendered all decisiveness pointless because there were no choices to be made. And there was no doubt that, if ever she felt a flicker of interest, it was the bold men who aroused it, the men who dared, the men with nerve.

'It's your dad,' Lindsay said.

'What's my dad?'

'It's your dad who gave you your nerve around men. He gave you the confidence.'

Paula thought about her father, of his regular, uneventful visits to London to see Toby and her, of his habits and his familiar clothes, of his apparent lack of appetite or ambition for any development or difference in his life.

'I don't think so –'

'He gave you security,' Lindsay said. 'That's what girls need from their fathers. He made you feel safe enough to be daring.'

'Suppose,' Paula said, 'that I just am daring? Jules is, after all, and she's got the same father as you.'

Lindsay sighed.

'Jules isn't daring. She's just wild. She's like you are when you overdo it.'

Paula looked at her.

'D'you talk about your father? You and Jules?'

'Not if I can help it.'

'Why not?'

'Because,' Lindsay said with uncharacteristic energy, 'he's a waste of space.'

'He's still your father –'

'That,' Lindsay said, 'was just an accident.'

An accident. It occurred to Paula sometimes, especially when she and Toby had met, head-on, about something, that almost everything in her life – apart from her father – had been an accident. Or, if not precisely an accident, then something random and unexpected. She had fallen for Gavin, fallen into motherhood, fallen for her line of work. She had never had, as she suspected Blaise had had, or Eleanor, or Karen even, a planned purpose, a goal requiring focus and discipline, a self-knowledge sufficient to be able to prioritise. She had known, instead, this extraordinary energy, this life force, this urge to throw herself into things even at the risk of drowning.

'I engage with life,' she'd once announced dramatically to her father when he was demurring about yet another impulse, yet another chance taken. 'I take up the challenge.'

Her father was eating toast. He spread marmalade, thinly and evenly, right to the edges, and then he said, without heat, 'You take up challenges, all right! No! You take them up before they've even been offered.'

Once she'd asked him if she was like her mother.

'No,' he said, 'not in any way. You're not like anyone in the family.'

'Does that bother you?'

'No,' he said again and then, maddeningly, 'but I don't make judgements about you. Never have. You are as you are.'

'I am as I am,' Paula said sometimes to Toby.

He sighed when she said that. He sighed like someone resignedly accepting the unacceptable. But, if she pressed him further, he stopped sighing and climbed up to his bed platform, away from her.

'I don't blame you for not liking what I am,' she'd say. 'How would you like me to be different?'

He looked appalled then. He'd back away from her, averting his gaze, as if she'd asked him something completely outrageous, something no normal boy should ever, ever be asked to contemplate. And then he'd climb his ladder and turn his computer on and flee thankfully from reality into fantasy. Here be dragons, Paula thought, but at least the dragons weren't mother dragons and didn't ask questions.

But the questions almost asked themselves. If she didn't ask, didn't try and get Toby to tell her what he didn't like, what he felt he was missing, what he was afraid of, how would she ever know how she was doing? Looking at other parents – Karen, Lucas, Lindsay – was no help because they were not parents to Toby, and it was Toby who concerned her so deeply, Toby who looked so much as if he needed and longed for a father, yet simultaneously seemed to shy away from any real engagement with his own father, with hers. Toby often gave the impression that he was driven mad by her being female while at the same time pulling back from other males. His grandfather, after all, while hardly an example of raw and rampant masculinity, was a perfectly reasonable one of decent manhood. He was a professional, he still played tennis, he was knowledgeable about jazz and cricket and American thrillers. He understood the internal combustion engine and could wield an axe and erect a tent. He should have done, Paula often thought, as a role model for Toby, a specimen of trustworthy, capable fatherly maleness, someone who could see Toby through childhood and adolescence until he had the maturity to choose and emulate his own heroes. But Toby – and it was a characteristic that reminded her very much of herself – gave every indication of impatience with what was on offer, of an almost exasperated dismissal of any potential role model available to him while he waited, with ill-concealed discontent, for something – someone – truly worthy of his admiration. And that situation, that apparent state of Toby's mind and feelings, was often very, very hard for her to bear alone.

Lindsay would, of course, let her talk about it all she liked. Lindsay was never too tired or too bored or too impatient to talk about bringing up a boy on one's own. But Lindsay, having Noah, having the unfair but undeniable orthodoxy of widowhood to arm herself with, was not in the same situation as Paula. She had been through violent and brutal tragedy, and had been left with this small, quiet child in consequence. But she had not instigated her tragedy in any way, had done nothing in her life except try and make some structure out of the chaos of her childhood, and the injustice of what had happened to her had, even if she hadn't sought it and didn't want it, burnished her reputation. Whereas Paula – well, Paula deserved everything she got, Paula had been impulsive and reckless and abandoned in her conduct. And Paula had ended up not with a small, quiet child but with a medium-sized, impenetrable one, who seemed to be making it plain that she couldn't possibly give him what he longed for. To talk to Lindsay about that got neither of them anywhere.

'He loves you,' Lindsay said. 'You're his mum.'

'I know.'

'He's got no one else to go for.'

'I know.'

'He's a bit like you. Maybe that's why you fight.'

'Yes,' Paula said, 'I know.'

There had been times in the past – though not recently – when Paula had confided in Eleanor. Eleanor, after all, made no exception for children. Children were just more people for her, and she displayed all the genuinely disinterested interest in them that she displayed in the rest of humanity. Paula had always found her lack of overt maternal feeling refreshing. Eleanor had not wanted children and did not apparently regret not having had them. And this situation gave her an objectivity in the matter that Paula had found soothing and consoling in the past. Quite what had happened recently between them Paula couldn't quite work out, but the attitude that she had once found reassuringly neutral now seemed to her less sympathetic, and more – more judgemental. She felt, for the first time in their friendship, that Eleanor wasn't liking what she saw, that Eleanor, while pleased to see her progress, felt that that progress was changing Paula in some way, and not for the better.

She had noticed it first in Eleanor's conduct towards Toby. They had always got on comfortably together – Eleanor adopting no traditional role, Toby accepting what was on offer – but there had been, overtly at least, no special bond, no identifiably particular relationship. But recently, Paula noticed, Eleanor had begun to look out for Toby, to summon him to her, to talk to him as if she had, however small and lightly expressed, a distinct concern for him. It was as if, Paula thought, Eleanor was sorry for him.

The moment – it had been this way all Toby's life – anyone looked as if they might pity Toby, something in Paula fell to pieces. She could take being disapproved of, or despised, or even disliked, but she could not bear to be pitied and even less could she bear pity for Toby. If anyone pitied Toby, it immediately made her feel that she was not enough for him, that she was responsible for giving him an existence that was somehow inadequate and unfair, that she had been selfish in the most profoundly selfish way any human being was ever capable of, in relation to an innocent child.

'Don't be so hard on yourself,' Lindsay said.

'Aren't you?'

'I wish Noah had his dad,' Lindsay said, 'of course I do. I wish he had brothers and sisters. But I don't think I'm doing a bad job. It's hard, but I don't think I'm doing badly. Nor are you.'

'Eleanor thinks so.'

'No, she doesn't.'

'She isn't,' Paula said, 'the same with me any more.'

'Talk to her.'

'I can't.'

Lindsay looked away. She was wearing the expression Paula often saw her wear when unhappy at yet another exploit of Jules'.

'You mean you don't want to.'

And Paula didn't want to. She told herself that there was nothing to apologise to Eleanor about, nothing that needed explanation or justification. Eleanor might not like – 'approve of' was the phrase Paula used to herself – the new flat, but that was her problem. Paula felt herself to be moving onwards at last, to be propelled by a new momentum, and nobody's disapproval was going to cloud her prospects or her optimism. Nobody was going to suggest to her that the choices she was making – or even the offers she was accepting – weren't as good for Toby as they were for her. Especially not Eleanor.

Sitting in the shop now, staring at her computer screen just as she had done the day she accepted Jackson's first invitation, she felt, resentfully, unsettled when she thought of Eleanor. The other evening, at Blaise's house, had been as fraught with inner tension as it had been crowned with outward success. Jackson had behaved admirably, her friends had seemed to her impressively diverse and interesting, the children had been no trouble. And yet the evening had not been – well, very *happy*. She had sensed, despite all the apparent ease, that Eleanor felt about Jackson as she did about the flat, that he was some shiny new acquisition that was diverting Paula from the path of integrity and industry; that was diverting her, more dangerously, from putting Toby first. And if Paula, rearing up defensively, had pointed out that, in order to be a good mother, she had to have a life of her own and that included, *thank* you, a relationship with a man, she had a feeling that Eleanor would simply have looked at her over her reading glasses and said that the two selves, maternal and personal, were not incompatible as far as she could see: they merely had to be kept in balance.

Paula gave an impatient, involuntary little gesture. Why should she bother what Eleanor thought? Jackson had liked her, after all, said she reminded him of his father's sister who had been an officer in the WRNS and led a purposeful, practical life.

'She couldn't stand my mother,' Jackson said. 'Thought she was an idiot. Treated her as if she was a half-wit, only interested in parties.'

'Did you like her?'

'Who?'

'Your aunt.'

'I suppose so.'

'Did you want her good opinion?'

Jackson yawned.

'Heavens, no. Why should I?'

Why should I want Eleanor's? Paula thought. Why should I care? Why should I let her make me feel I'm not making Toby happy? But – and it's a huge but – even if I don't admit it to anyone but myself, Toby isn't happy. Toby hasn't been happy for ages and it isn't getting better.

The telephone rang. Paula collected herself, sat straighter, picked up the receiver.

'Temple Trading Company. How may I help you?'

'Hi, there,' Jackson said.

'Oh!'

'You're smiling –'

'That's guesswork –'

'You're smiling,' Jackson said.

'Yes,' Paula said, smiling.

'Quick call,' Jackson said. 'On my way to a meeting. Toby.'

'What about him?'

'You said he wasn't very keen on football.'

'No, I didn't, I just said that he hadn't had much opportunity, that he didn't know much about it, that I wasn't much help –'

'Well, I'm taking him.'

'What?'

'I'm taking him. In two weeks. I've decided. Home game against Portsmouth.'

'He'll – he'll be thrilled, he'll be absolutely –'

'Good,' Jackson said.

'You're so kind. He never does anything like that, he never has time doing boy things with a man, he –'

'Gotta go,' Jackson said and then he said, 'Wait for me,' and rang off.

Paula put the telephone down slowly and unsteadily. She put her hands over her face and mouthed into her palms some kind of undirected thank you. Then she surrendered for a moment to an intense and extraordinary joy.

Joel paused behind her. He was carrying a pile of black silk cushions balanced precisely one on top of the other.

'Good news?'

'Go away.'

'Look at your face.'

Paula pushed her hair back.

'Jackson is taking Toby to a Chelsea game.'

Joel took a step away.

He said, over his shoulder, 'So, he's serious then.'

Eleanor opened the door six inches. She left the safety chain stretched across the gap.

'It's only me,' Paula said.

Eleanor fumbled with the chain.

'Halloween,' she said. 'It starts earlier every year. Fireworks through the letterbox are one thing. Rapacious little ghouls on the doorstep are quite another.'

'Do they bother you?'

Eleanor opened the door wider.

'Irritate, yes. Frighten, no.'

Paula stepped inside.

'What does frighten you?'

The hall was dark. Paula couldn't see Eleanor's face clearly, but there was a distinct pause before Eleanor said firmly, 'None of your business.'

'OK,' Paula said.

She followed Eleanor through to the kitchen. There was a bowl of huge bananas on the table, and piles of pamphlets and brochures and a hammer and a newspaper folded open at the crossword.

'I thought you were at work,' Eleanor said.

'I am. It's my lunch hour. I've left Joel in charge with an avocado-salad wrap and the promise of leaving at five.'

Eleanor leaned on the table. She indicated the cooker with her head.

'I was about to heat some soup –'

'Lovely,' Paula said. 'I'll do it.'

'I'm not an invalid –'

'No,' Paula said, 'but I'll still do it.'

She crossed the kitchen to the cooker and turned on the gas under the soup pan.

She said, 'You're not an invalid, but you're pretty cross. Would you like to tell me why?'

Eleanor lowered herself into a chair and folded her arms on the newspaper.

'I don't think I'm cross.'

Paula turned to look at her.

'I feel disapproved of,' Paula said.

'You shouldn't.'

'I didn't have to come here,' Paula said. 'I didn't have to make the effort. But I have because I feel we've got ourselves at cross purposes and I don't like that. And I feel that you feel I've done something wrong and I'd like to know what it is.'

Eleanor put on her glasses and studied the paper.

'I appreciate your coming.'

'Thank you,' Paula said.

There was a silence. Paula turned back to the stove and gave the soup a stir with a wooden spoon.

She said, 'And?'

Eleanor took off her spectacles.

'I liked your friend.'

'Jackson?'

'Yes. I admired the way he coped with us all. He has good manners.'

Paula smiled, privately, down at the soup.

'Yes.'

'But I don't think Toby likes him.'

Paula waited a moment and then she said carefully, 'Toby doesn't like anything new. Not people, not places. He isn't good at change.'

'No,' Eleanor said, 'I expect that's true of most children. Do you think he sees a change in you?'

'In me?'

'In you. Because of – Mr Miller.'

Paula turned the gas out and opened a cupboard in search of bowls.

'Well,' she said, 'I'm happier. Do you think it bothers Toby that I'm happier?'

'It might,' Eleanor said, 'bother Toby that the effect happiness has on you is not to his advantage.'

Paula straightened up. She put the soup bowls down on the table with some force.

'What do you mean?'

'That Toby feels he has been pushed aside.'

'For God's *sake*!' Paula shouted.

Eleanor said nothing.

'Look,' Paula said, '*look*. After years on my own, not impossible years but not easy years either, I suddenly come into two pieces of great good fortune. I am given a wonderful place to live and I meet a wonderful man. Of *course* I'm happy, of *course* I'm excited and thrilled and relieved and – and grateful. But nothing changes my feelings about Toby, *nothing* could alter his position as the most important person in my life. *Nothing*.'

Eleanor looked up at her.

'Good.'

'You don't sound as if you believe me.'

'It doesn't matter whether I believe you or not. It only matters that you believe yourself.'

Paula took a sharp intake of breath.

'You know, Eleanor, don't you, that this is none of your business?'

'Then why have you come?'

Paula turned back to the stove.

'It – it bothered me that you seem sorry for Toby.'

'I am sorry for Toby. I'm glad for you but that is not, I'm afraid, incompatible with feeling sorry for Toby.'

Paula lifted the pan up and began to pour the soup into bowls.

'Jackson rang me this morning.'

Eleanor grunted.

'He rang to tell me he was taking Toby to a Chelsea game in a couple of weeks.'

'What is your point?'

'That he is trying to forge a relationship with Toby. That he is trying to include Toby, make Toby *feel* special.'

'Will Toby want to go?'

Paula stared at her.

'What is the *matter* with you, Eleanor? What on earth do you want me to do, him to do?'

'I simply want to see you at your best.'

Paula gave an exasperated sigh.

'What would you know, anyway. You've never had children –'

'No.'

'You've never been a mother. For heaven's sake, you aren't *my* mother, Eleanor, you aren't anybody's mother. What right do you think you have to talk to me like this?'

Eleanor put on her glasses.

'You asked me,' she said reasonably. 'You asked me and then you didn't like the answers.'

'What *are* the answers?'

'No,' Eleanor said, 'no. No more. Drink your soup.'

Paula waited. She stood for a moment staring down at the disordered table and the two bowls of orange-coloured soup.

She said, 'Where would you be if you didn't have us all?'

When she returned to the office, Joel had taken an order for a coffee table, rung three suppliers, checked the week's invoices and served two women who had come in for cushions and gone out with tablemats. Paula put a tall takeaway coffee mug down in front of him.

'Reward.'

'No carrot cake?'

'That would have required you to sell the cushions as well as the tablemats.'

'Nice lunch?'

Paula didn't look at him.

'No.'

She slung her jacket on the back of her chair and sat down at the computer again.

'I've got half an hour to do here, then I'll be on the shop floor. Call me if you need me.'

'Yes, *ma'am*,' Joel said.

Paula typed three rapid words and deleted them. Then she looked at her mobile to see if there were any text messages. Then she scrolled to the spreadsheet she had started earlier that day with a summary of monthly figures. She stared at it unseeingly. From the shop floor she could hear Joel explaining something to a customer. When he spoke to customers, he managed, by raising his voice slightly at the end of every statement, to turn everything he said, pointlessly, into a question. Paula clenched her teeth, just slightly. It was a supremely irritating habit, but not one she would be justified really in pointing out to him.

'Damn,' Paula said aloud, and reached for the telephone.

'Yes?' Eleanor said, as she always did when answering the telephone.

'It's me.'

'Ah.'

'Eleanor, I'm sorry.'

'It struck me,' Eleanor said, 'after you'd gone, that if you really are as happy as you claim it's difficult to account for your sounding, sometimes, so unpleasant.'

'I am happy.'

'Did you hear me?'

'I shouldn't have said what I said to you –'

'I have a hide like a rhino,' Eleanor said.

'I shouldn't have said it and I didn't mean it. The debt isn't that way round.'

'Sometimes,' Eleanor said, 'I share Toby's dislike of these kind of conversations. You were good to ring but I think you have work to do.'

'On myself?'

'No. In your place of business.'

'Eleanor, could I just say something to you?'

There was a small silence. Paula pictured Eleanor in her armchair by the sitting-room window, crossword on her knee, telephone in hand, looking out, over her reading glasses, at the sky above the rooftops across the street.

'Of course,' Eleanor said at last.

'I know you're right about Toby. I know he isn't happy at the moment. I know he doesn't like changes. And I really am trying, Eleanor, I really am trying not to go too fast or force things on him or make him like Jackson before he's ready to. But I'm a person, too. I come into the equation as well as Toby and if I get a bit carried away by the changes that have happened that's me, that's how I *am*. I don't want you to think I'm not trying. I don't want you to think I don't realise that the changes are difficult at the moment, for everyone, but they'll get better, I know they will, they'll sort themselves out and everything will calm down.'

'Changes –'

'Yes,' Paula said, '*yes*. There are changes now but they won't last, we'll become used to them. Even Toby.'

There was another silence and then Eleanor said, almost sadly, 'I doubt we will. Not for a long time anyway. Because, you see, they've only just begun.'

CHAPTER EIGHT

'F ollow me,' Jackson said.

He had parked his car – a silver Mercedes with leather seats – in a school yard off the Fulham Road. Toby had sat beside him in the deep passenger seat and watched the moving map on the satellite navigation system. Jackson didn't say much so there wasn't any need to say anything back, once it had been established that Toby knew, something at least, about football.

'You play?'

Toby nodded.

'At school?'

Toby nodded again.

'What position?'

Toby sighed.

'I'm a defender.'

'Centre back? Full back?'

'I stand in front of the goalie.'

Jackson glanced at him.

'I wouldn't have thought you were big enough for a centre back.'

Toby looked at the travelling yellow arrow on the satellite map. He could not, obviously, say that he didn't much like football. Nor could he say that he was only sitting in this car on a Saturday afternoon because the announcement that he was going to sit, on a padded seat, just above the centre line in the East Stand at Stamford Bridge on Saturday had caused such shock and awe at school that he had realised that complying with his mother's and Jackson's wishes was very much to the advantage of his image and his popularity. There were boys whose fathers and, in two cases, older brothers, had taken them to sit in the Matthew Harding Stand on very rare and remarkable occasions, but nobody had had seats just above the benches.

'You jammy little fucker,' Darren Wicks said.

Darren was half a head taller than everyone else in Toby's class, but Toby had never learned to be intimidated by him.

'I didn't ask,' Toby said, 'I never asked. It just happened. They just told me.'

Paula had, in fact, handed him a plastic bag. It was a blue-and-white bag and inside was a blue T-shirt with 'Lampard' and an '8' stamped on the back in white. Toby looked at it.

'I bought it at the Chelsea Megastore,' Paula said.

'Is it for me?'

'I stopped at Stamford Bridge on the way home,' Paula said. 'Guess why.'

Toby looked harder at his T-shirt.

'Well, I like Lampard better than Terry –'

'You're going,' Paula cried.

'Going where?'

'To a game! With Jackson! He's asked you, you're going on Saturday week, to Chelsea with Jackson!'

Toby put the T-shirt down.

'Oh,' he said.

Paula leaned forward.

'Did you hear what I said?'

Toby nodded.

'Most boys,' Paula said, 'would be over the moon. Most boys wouldn't be able to believe their ears. Most boys would be cartwheeling round the room if they'd heard what you just heard.'

Toby looked up at her.

'Will you be coming?'

Later, she had made him ring Jackson. He made a tremendous fuss about doing so and was rewarded by getting Jackson's answering machine. Into it he said, 'ThisisToby-thankyouverymuchaboutthefootball,' as if it was all one word and then he took his Lampard shirt into the bathroom and tried it on and tried, equally, not to feel thrilled at wearing it. It was immensely, almost impossibly, difficult to be given something one might have liked very, very much in exactly the wrong way and precisely for all the wrong reasons.

When he came out of the bathroom, he shouted at Paula.

'Don't stand there waiting for me to be pleased!'

Jackson was rather easier to handle. He had never touched Toby, except accidentally while passing something, and seemed very good indeed at leaving him alone.

'OK,' he said, when Toby went into his awkward, Paula-rehearsed gratitude routine. 'OK. Glad you can come.' And then he added, imposing another layer of alarm for Toby, 'We'll have lunch there.'

'Lunch!' Paula said.

'It's good. Three courses. Sit-down, and pretty waitresses.'

'Not too pretty, I hope –'

'Very pretty,' Jackson said, grinning.

And now, here they were, Toby in his Lampard shirt under a blue fleece and Jackson in cords and a tweed jacket, saying, 'Follow me,' and setting off, fast, down the Fulham Road.

Toby had passed Stamford Bridge hundreds of times in his life. The huge forecourt and vast glass and steel and brick buildings were as familiar to him as the Town Hall or the tube station. But walking among them was different, walking in with thousands and thousands of other people, some women, but mostly men, made him feel at once extremely important and extremely insignificant.

'This way,' Jackson said.

He put an arm out and made an arc with it, behind Toby's back. They entered a new building and crossed a carpeted space and found themselves in front of a pair of silver-coloured lifts. A man in uniform checked Jackson's tickets and said, 'Enjoy the game, sir. Your first time, young man?' and Toby nodded and followed Jackson into the lift and was followed in turn by an old woman and an old man and the old woman was saying, 'I'm telling you, if we don't win by two clear goals, I'll get a headache.' Then she looked at Toby and said, 'Hope you haven't come to cheer Portsmouth.'

'He wouldn't dare,' Jackson said.

She gave a cackling laugh. She had frizzy orange-coloured hair and lots of diamonds.

'Matthew Harding's grandson's the mascot today,' she said. 'He's even smaller than you are.'

Toby nodded. He couldn't think what she was talking about. Mascots were things like his lucky-dice key-ring that he put in his pocket for maths lessons to ward off unanswerable questions.

'I'll need a double gin and lime,' the old woman said. 'I need to be in good voice.'

The lift doors slid open. A huge, clattering dining room stretched ahead, filled with tables covered in white cloths and flowers and glasses and name cards in tall metal stands.

Jackson strode forward, Toby pattering at his heels.

'Gianni Vialli,' Jackson said, gesturing at a name card. 'One of my heroes.'

He pulled a chair out from a table by the window.

'Sit here. Coke?'

'Well, I –'

'Diet or full cream?'

'Sorry?'

'You don't need Diet Coke,' Jackson said. 'Diet Coke is for girls. I'll get you the big stuff. Do you like steak?'

Toby hovered above his chair.

'Yes, I –'

'Look out,' Jackson said, 'look out there.'

Toby turned to the window. He had never seen a space so enormous, so green, so blue-and-white. It was so big it made the bits of sky hiding behind the glass canopies look small. It made him, obscurely, suddenly both pleased and proud to be wearing his Lampard shirt.

'What do you think?'

'Brilliant,' Toby breathed.

'Steak, then? And chips?'

'Yes,' Toby said. He couldn't look at Jackson's face, so he looked at his tweed sleeve instead. 'Please,' Toby said.

Their seats were, as Jackson had promised, right above the centre line. Across the pitch, in the middle of the West Stand, was a long line of glass directors' boxes. In the centre of this line, a figure in jeans and a brown leather bomber jacket was leaning against the glass, arms and ankles crossed, alone and concentrating.

Jackson handed Toby his field glasses.

'Roman Abramovich.'

Toby fiddled with the focus.

'He owns all this,' Jackson said.

'He –'

'He owns this whole thing, the place, the players . . . He's Russian.'

'You can't own people,' Toby said.

'Not literally. But you earn so much money here, the players want to stay, they want him to own them, to buy them. If you want glamour in football, Chelsea will give it to you. Roman Abramovich has given it glamour. Now the players have given it glamour too.'

Toby had never heard Jackson say so much in one breath. He held the field glasses half an inch away from his face, and slid his eyes sideways so that he could look at Jackson furtively. Jackson was leaning forward, elbows on his knees, looking with great intentness at the players warming up nonchalantly on the field. He was sitting still, but all the same he looked energetic. It began to dawn on Toby slowly that football, that Chelsea, was very important indeed to Jackson, and that being asked to share in this importance must mean that – well, that – heavens, Toby thought, he must sort of want me to be here, he must have kind of decided to ask me because, well, he wanted me to be with him. Toby felt his face grow hot. The resentment about Jackson he had been nurturing so comfortably suddenly began to feel as if it wasn't in any way the right response, that it wasn't relevant, even, maybe, a bit silly. He shifted in his seat and brought the field glasses close to his face again.

'Is Ashley Cole a striker?' Toby said.

At half time – no score – Jackson took Toby back to the dining room. The lunch tables had been cleared and were now set for tea, oval plates of tiny sandwiches, round ones of cakes. Jackson, without asking Toby, ordered him a second Coke. Toby considered revealing that he had never been allowed two in the space of a few hours, and decided against it. He sat down and looked hopefully at the cakes.

'Enjoying it?' Jackson said.

Toby went on looking at the cakes.

'It's brilliant,' Toby said seriously.

Jackson picked up the nearest plate and deftly slid a couple of cakes on to the plate in front of Toby.

'We're warming up,' Jackson said. 'That's Chelsea's way. Watch and wait and then give it to them in the second half.'

Toby picked up a cake and took a bite.

'They're so fast.'

'Some of them are. And some of them can get the ball. And some of them can keep it.'

'I didn't,' Toby said, almost looking at Jackson, 'know it would be like this.'

'It isn't, on telly.'

'If we don't win,' Toby said, 'I'll go ballistic.'

'We'll win.'

The phone in Jackson's pocket beeped twice. He took it out, pressed a button, glanced at it and held it out over the table. Toby peered at the screen.

'Are you having fun?' Paula had texted. 'Are you missing me? Xxx'

Toby took another bite of cake.

'What'll you say?'

Jackson dropped the phone back in his pocket.

'Nothing.'

'Why not?'

Jackson gave him a brief smile.

'No need. She knows the answer. We're having fun.'

Toby looked down at his plate. He was. They were. And he wasn't missing her.

When the final whistle went, Toby screamed. He hadn't meant to scream, even though everyone else in the stadium seemed to have been yelling their lungs out for an hour and a half, but the relief and pride and excitement had built up in him to such a pitch that it seemed far more natural to scream than to hold it in. So he screamed. Chelsea had won 2–1 – there had been a wonderful moment when they were up 2–0 – and there was a kind of mad joy in him that had to come out somewhere. And while he was screaming, and whirling his fleece round his head like a banner, he was conscious that Jackson was looking at him, and laughing, and it was, for some reason, a very gratifying situation to find himself in.

When they went back through the dining room, one of the pretty waitresses stopped Toby and gave him a white box. He stared at her. She smiled, and then she smiled at Jackson.

Then she stooped and said in a loud whisper to Toby, a whisper with a foreign accent, 'Some cakes to take to your sister!'

Toby looked at the box.

'I haven't got a sister –'

'But you have a friend! A friend who is like a sister!'

Toby glanced up at her. He was beginning to get the hang of all this.

'Can't *I* eat them?'

She laughed.

'Of course you can! But it's more fun to share.'

'Only some things,' Toby said and then, remembering the courtesies out of sheer gratitude for the afternoon, 'Thank you. Thank you very much.'

The girl looked at Jackson again.

'Stops me eating them!'

Jackson said nothing. He just smiled, and then he nodded at the girl and steered Toby towards the lifts, his hand between Toby's shoulders.

'Was she right?'

'What?'

'Do you have a friend like a sister?'

Toby considered. Maybe Poppy . . .

'Well, sort of –'

'Yes,' Jackson said, 'thought so.' He pushed Toby into the lift. 'Shall we go?'

'Go where?'

'Go to Poppy's. Give her the cakes.'

Toby looked at the box. He thought, abruptly, how much he didn't want the afternoon to end, and become ordinary.

'Now?'

The lift doors slid shut. Jackson leaned against the wall. He glanced down at Toby.

'Why not?'

'Just remind me,' Jackson said, 'what Poppy's mother is called.'

Toby was looking at his programme. He had been given it at the beginning of the afternoon, when it meant nothing, and now he wanted to read every word and pore over every picture. There was a photograph of Lampard, standing behind his father, once a footballer himself, with his arms linked around his father's shoulders and chest, which seemed to Toby an image of exceptional beauty. Something about it made him feel tearful but in a way that wasn't, for some reason, alarming.

'Hello,' Jackson said. 'Base to Zulu One.'

Toby looked up.

'What?'

'Poppy's mother. Her name.'

'Lindsay,' Toby said absently. 'No. Karen.'

'Dark?'

'I don't know –'

'Good-looking?'

Toby was practised at this question. Years of living with Paula had trained him.

'She's a mother,' Toby said firmly.

Jackson laughed. He laughed with the kind of ease that Gavin never seemed able to display. Toby had been trying not to think about Gavin, in an uncomfortably comparative way, all afternoon and he didn't want to start now. He hunched down inside his fleece and held his programme close to his face.

'D'you think Lampard likes being a midfielder?'

Jackson looked at his navigation map.

'I think all players like being the best in their area of the field.'

'I'd want to be a striker.'

'You'll learn,' Jackson said. 'Is this the street?'

Toby peered over his programme.

'What number?' Jackson said.

'It's over there. With the red door.' He glanced at Jackson. 'Will they mind?'

'Why should they? Two males and a box of cakes. What's to mind?'

Toby sniggered. It was the noise he reserved for dirty jokes at school and not one ever, ever worth making in Paula's hearing. But it seemed OK to indulge himself, alone with Jackson, and when Jackson said, 'Now, now,' he knew he was right. Two males. He looked at the picture of Frank Lampard with his father again, and felt, with a new sensation of pride, that he was somehow part of an alliance, an alliance that had, well, something rather heroic about it. He sniggered again, just faintly, and said with studied non-chalance, 'Search *me*.'

Jackson parked the car smoothly just down the street from Poppy's house. He got out, and swung his door shut and then came round to Toby's side, and waited while he scrambled out, clutching the box of cakes. Then he put a hand, firmly but impersonally, on Toby's shoulder.

'You'll have to introduce me again. I've forgotten who everyone is.'

Toby looked resolutely straight ahead. His heart was lifting a little.

'OK.'

Jackson took his hand off Toby's shoulder. There was a small but important glow where it had rested. They crossed the street to the red front door.

'You ring,' Jackson said.

'OK.'

He pressed the bell. There was, almost at once, the sound of soft footsteps inside.

'Here we go,' Jackson said quietly in his ear.

'Wow,' Karen said.

She stood, holding the door open, dressed in a grey velvet tracksuit thing, with bare feet. Toby looked up at her. She was looking at Jackson.

Jackson gave him a nudge.

'Go on –'

Toby held the cake box up.

'We brought these.'

Karen glanced down at him.

'Toby –'

'We've been to the football, to Chelsea. I got given these. They're for sharing.'

'Cake,' Jackson said.

'Excuse me –'

'We've been to the Chelsea–Portsmouth game,' Jackson said. 'The waitress in the dining room gave Toby a box of cake.'

Poppy's head, wearing a green glitter hairband with swivelling-eyed antennae attached to it, appeared round her mother.

'What kind of cake?' Poppy said.

Karen stepped back and held the door wide.

'Come in –'

'I thought you'd never ask,' Jackson said.

'We've already got cake,' Poppy said to Toby. 'We made it. With Daddy. Now we're eating it. It's *amazing*.'

Toby held the box firmly.

'These are football cakes.'

'Oh well,' Poppy said, adjusting her antennae, 'oh well, *football*.' She began to skip ahead of him, down the narrow hall to the kitchen. '*Football* cake. You *would*.'

In the kitchen, there were lit candles on the central table.

There were also mugs and plastic beakers and a teapot and a big, half-eaten cake with bright icing patterns on it. Blaise was sitting at the table with a silk scarf tied round the neck of her sweater, and her hands round a tea mug. Jackson didn't recognise her with her hair on her shoulders.

'You remember Blaise?'

Jackson held his hand out. Blaise half rose and stretched hers out across the table.

'No –'

'You came to my house,' Blaise said.

'Oh God.' Jackson smacked his hand against his forehead.

Rosie, engaged in tidying cake crumbs into neat small piles said, to no one in particular, 'It was dark.'

'Thank you,' Jackson said.

Karen and Blaise laughed. Toby put his cake box on the table.

'I was given these at the football –'

Blaise looked at the box respectfully.

'Was it wonderful?'

'Yes,' Toby said. He wanted to say it very firmly and, preferably, while Jackson was standing next to him. But Jackson was taking off his jacket and hanging it over a chairback and was not, apparently, as aware of Toby as he had been a few minutes before.

'Tea?' Karen said. 'Cake?' She picked up a long smeared breadknife. 'Jackson Pollock cake, created by Lucas and the girls only this morning.'

Jackson sat down.

'I'd love tea,' he said. Then he looked at Toby. He winked. 'But I only eat football cake.'

'Time for wine,' Karen said.

She was sitting on one kitchen chair with her feet up on another. The box of football cakes, now empty except for crumbs, was on the floor against the wall, and Toby and

Poppy, sitting against the opposite wall, were throwing corks into the box from a huge glass jar where Lucas liked to keep them, Karen said, for no reason that she could see. The Jackson Pollock cake sat on the side.

Jackson was leaning back in his chair. Blaise was leaning forward in hers, her arms folded on the table, her head bent. Between them Rosie was colouring in a very small picture she had drawn, with ferocious neatness, of a girl leading a cat on a ribbon. She looked very much as if she was concentrating, but she was actually keeping an eye on both her mother and her sister.

'Do you mean,' Blaise said to Karen, not looking at her, 'that women don't identify themselves by work, the way men do?'

'I thought,' Karen said, 'I thought I said it was time for wine.'

'Before that,' Blaise said patiently.

Jackson stood up slowly. He did most things, both Karen and Blaise had noticed, with apparent slowness.

'I'll get it. Man's work.'

Karen spun a knife on the table.

'I think men identify that way more completely than women do. That's all. I think women identify themselves mostly by their relationships.'

Rosie added a minute bell to the cat's collar. If Karen was going to start on the wine then she, Rosie, would like Lucas to be there too. It wasn't that Karen got drunk – Rosie had a horror of people getting drunk, getting embarrassing and noisy and thinking they were funny when they completely were not – but more that, if one parent was going to have wine, it was better, somehow, if the other one was there to have it too. And Lucas was at his studio. He had gone there after they had finished making the cake and he had not, for some reason, wanted her and Poppy to come too.

'What about Daddy?' Rosie said loudly, but to her drawing.

'What about him?' Karen said. Rosie didn't like her tone of voice.

'In the fridge?' Jackson said.

Blaise drew an invisible circle on the table with her forefinger.

'I wouldn't agree with you,' Blaise said. 'It doesn't apply to all women. It's perfectly possible to have a very healthy view of relationships and a huge commitment to work as well.'

'If you say so,' Karen said.

Rosie gave the cat exaggerated eyelashes. Karen sounded to her as if she was showing off. A bit at least.

'Or red in that rack beside the cooker,' Karen said.

Rosie looked up. At the same moment, Poppy got to her feet and threw a cork at her mother.

'Daddy would like wine,' Poppy said.

Karen turned to look at her.

'Did you throw a cork at me?'

'Only a bit,' Poppy said. She pulled her hairband down so that the antennae looked like her own eyes, on stalks.

Jackson was laughing. Karen glanced at him.

'Not funny.'

'Sorry,' he said, not sounding it, 'but funny.'

Rosie put down her crayon and got off her chair. She crossed the kitchen to the side table that served as the household desk, and came back with Karen's mobile.

'I'll ring him.'

Karen regarded her.

'You do that.'

'I'll tell him to come back.'

Jackson put a bottle of red wine on the table.

'Corkscrew?'

Toby pushed himself upright against the wall. The appearance of a wine bottle always meant that things were about to get really, really dull. He thought of the television upstairs in Karen and Lucas's sitting room. He thought of the football results. He thought of how the football results had never before occurred to him on a Saturday afternoon and he wondered how he could have managed without them. He looked at Jackson. Jackson had rolled his shirtsleeves up to just above his wrists and he was inserting the corkscrew into the wine bottle.

'I can do that,' Toby said.

Jackson took his hands away from the bottle.

'Do it then.'

Rosie put the mobile on the table.

'His phone's off. He's not answering.'

'He'll be concentrating,' Karen said, 'don't you think?'

Rosie leaned against the table.

'I don't want him to be left out.'

Toby pulled the cork smoothly out of the bottle.

'Good,' Jackson said. 'Good man.'

Blaise stood up.

'I'll go and get him,' she said. 'Shall I?'

'Get Luke?'

'Well, yes. If Rosie's troubled –'

'Are you, Rose?'

'Yes,' Rosie said. 'I don't want there to be a party without him.'

'He might not want to stop.'

'I'll ask him,' Rosie said. She looked at Blaise. 'I'll come with you.'

Toby thought suddenly of Paula. He gave Jackson a quick glance. Was Jackson going to suggest ringing Paula?

He opened his mouth to ask and said instead, 'Can I watch television? Can I see the results?'

Karen laughed. She looked very relaxed, sitting there draped across two chairs.

'Of course,' she said. 'D'you want to ring Mum too?'

Toby shrugged. He didn't want it to be his idea, he didn't

want to go back to being just Paula and him, not just yet, anyway.

'I'll ring,' Jackson said. 'In a minute.' He took his telephone out of his pocket and laid it on the table. 'I'll just have a squint at the results, with Toby.'

'I see,' Karen said, 'I see. You'll all push off and leave me with no one to talk to –'

'There's me,' Poppy said.

'That's right,' Jackson said. 'Abandoned for the footie. Classic female fate.' He put his hand on Toby's shoulder again. 'Lead on.'

They went out of the room and up the stairs.

'She's lucky,' Karen said.

Blaise was pulling on a leather jacket.

'Who is?'

'Paula. He's cool.'

Blaise glanced at Rosie.

'So nice for Toby –'

'Yes. Blaise, don't get me wrong –'

'About what?'

Karen swung her feet to the floor and sat straighter.

She said to Rosie, 'Maybe get a fleece, darling?'

'About what?' Blaise said.

Karen spun the knife again.

'About me and women and work.'

Poppy came to lean against her mother. She had taken off the hairband and had one of the antennae eyeballs in her mouth. Karen put an arm round her.

'I didn't mean you can't have both,' Karen said. 'I didn't mean you aren't a complete woman if you don't have both, either. I just mean that women seem able to identify themselves more broadly. That's all.'

Rosie came back into the room, struggling into a twisted fleece. Blaise held out her hands to help.

'I know what you think,' Blaise said. 'We've had this conversation a hundred times before. It was just that tonight you sounded different.'

'Different?'

Blaise inserted her hands inside Rosie's collar, and flipped out her hair.

'Yes,' she said, 'different. In front of him.'

CHAPTER NINE

Noah had made a construction, and left it on the sitting-room carpet. It comprised a chopping board, some plastic cups linked together with a length of string, a few uneven towers of Lego and two small knights on horseback, their plumes and caparisons meticulously moulded and coloured.

Lindsay stood and looked at it, the brush section of the vacuum cleaner in her hand. Her instinct – her perpetual instinct – was to tidy it up, restoring the board to the kitchen, the knights to their cardboard castle in Noah's bedroom, the cups and the string (rolled up) to the appropriate drawers. But Noah never made anything. He played, quietly and almost solemnly, with his cars and his knights and, to Lindsay's mild distress, with a Barbie doll someone had once left behind, arranging them and pushing them about, but he never constructed anything, he never attempted to put anything together except in the form in which it had arrived.

Lindsay put the hoover brush down and knelt on the carpet. The plastic cups were upended, and the string had been attached to their bases with nuggets of blue gum. The crooked towers of plastic bricks were placed randomly around the cups and the knights were either end of the board, facing outwards. Were they defending a castle? Had they just ridden around the cups and towers, weaving in and out as a kind of test of horsemanship? Were they about to leave something ruined? Lindsay put a finger out, and touched one knight on his tiny, plumed, helmeted head, and he at once fell over.

When had Noah made this? He certainly hadn't made it the day before, as Lindsay never went to bed without leaving the sitting room orderly for the following day. And when she had gone in to wake him for school, he had been lying in bed with his thumb in, flicking his comfort rag about with his free hand and watching the shadows it made on the wall, in the light cast by his bedside lamp. He must have got up in the night, or the dawn, and collected all these strange little items, and knelt there in his pyjamas and built it, whatever it was. And why would he have done that?

Lindsay picked the knight up and set his horse on its hooves. She couldn't clear it all away. She would have to leave it there, disturbing though it was, and ask Noah about it later. And of course, he might not tell her. He might not be able to tell her. He might have no idea why he was impelled to get out of bed and go into the kitchen and collect a chopping board and plastic mugs and string and make a – a something out of them. And when she thought about it, she remembered that there had been no sign of disturbance in the kitchen, no drawers pulled out or cupboards left open. And she would have noticed when she went in first thing to put the kettle on. She noticed everything.

Paula used to tease her about it. She would accuse Lindsay of not taking in something vital someone was saying because she was so distracted by a fallen hair on their collar or a missing button on their cardigan. She told Lindsay that she lived as if she was playing a permanent Kim's Game, memorising trayfuls of random objects, as if her life, almost, depended upon it. When they were out together, Paula would suddenly say, 'Go on then, how many Asian men have we passed since Feldom Street, how many tomato slices did I eat at lunch, what were the odds on a white Christmas in the betting-shop window?' and she'd always know. It was as if something in her brain told her that if she recorded everything – everything – then there'd be nothing left to catch her unawares.

That, really, was why Paula meant so much to her. Of course Paula was attractive and energetic and openly, engagingly, emotional, but the quality Lindsay really valued was her lack of carefulness. She spun round blind corners without checking to see what might be waiting, she took chances, obeyed impulses, flung herself into the business of being alive. And although Lindsay couldn't emulate her, not in a million years, she felt that some of Paula's impulsive vitality rubbed off on her, loosened her white-knuckled grip on things. In ordinary circumstances – the circumstances that had prevailed for the last five years, at any rate – Lindsay would have telephoned Paula and told her about Noah's creative achievement and Paula would have suggested they take it straight over to the White Cube Gallery. And when Lindsay said, 'But d'you think he's upset about something and doesn't know how to tell me?' Paula would say, 'Are you crazy? This is called *development*. Noah's learning to *do* something, without being told –'

Lindsay got to her feet and picked up the hoover brush again. Ordinary circumstances were not, however, currently prevailing. Paula had something else on her mind which seemed to mean that there was no space left for much else. She had always been self-absorbed – it was a quality Lindsay recognised from all those involved in her ramshackle childhood – but that had sharpened into something closer to a complete abstraction since she'd met Jackson. If Lindsay rang Paula now, Paula would listen for twenty seconds and then she'd start on again about why Jackson hadn't rung her from Karen's house the previous Saturday, when he'd been there with Toby, after the football.

When Paula first met Jackson, Lindsay had been included. In fact, she hadn't been so much included as vital to the exhilarating opening scene of this drama, the only person who knew, the only person Paula wanted to know, the only person who could be relied upon to rejoice and say go for it, girl, go for it, in that crucially supportive way required of the true sisterhood. She had been the audience for the new shoes, the new underwear ('I'm a cliché,' Paula said, 'aren't I?' But she was laughing), the text messages, the account of that first drink and every syllable he'd uttered, every gesture, every look. And if Lindsay had felt, on occasion, pangs of envy so keen they were almost physical, she would never have admitted them. After all, it wasn't Jackson, whoever he was, that she was envious of: it was seeing Paula feeling like that, just blown away, completely liberated from all the little guy ropes of anxiety and self-discipline that kept Lindsay tethered to the self-imposed orderliness of her life.

But now things were different. They were different because Paula was deeper in, and wanted more of Jackson, wanted Jackson to move to fill the confidential space Lindsay had once occupied. And of course, she knew Jackson better. At least, she knew as much as he'd let her, as much as he seemed, tantalisingly, to be inclined to show. She knew enough, Lindsay could see, to make her realise how much she didn't know and to begin to fear how vulnerable that ignorance, and her growing dependency, might make her.

Lindsay stooped to unplug the hoover from the wall, and to press the button that caused the cable to shoot itself back into the interior of the machine. When she'd been left alone with Noah, as a baby, she remembered she'd had a feeling that the whole world had just gone away and left her, that whatever she looked at had dwindled to a miniature distance, like something seen through the wrong end of a telescope. She remembered saying, when Eleanor gently asked her how she was bearing her situation, 'Well, I'm not bearing it,' and meaning it, meaning that she had a permanent sensation of being about to fall into a pit of something fatal, which she supposed was despair. But she hadn't fallen. She was still here and she had a job and a flat and friends and a sister and a little boy who had made something original and unfathomable and left it on the sitting-room carpet.

She opened the hall cupboard and stowed the vacuum cleaner in its usual place beside the ironing board. If she mooned about any longer, she'd be late for work.

'Someone to see you,' Joel said.

Paula looked up, bright with anticipation. It was a Thursday, a lunchtime, just the kind of moment, surprise occasion that he . . .

'It's Lindsay's sister,' Joel said. 'She was lying on one of the sofas. I told her. I told her last time.'

'Oh God,' Paula said. She got to her feet. 'D'you think there's a crisis?'

'Couldn't say,' Joel said. Although his private life – heavily hinted at – had its wild side, his appearance and personal habits were intensely fastidious. Jules' random life and personal dishevelment were distinctly not to his taste.

'What a pain,' Paula said. 'Is she high or anything?'

Joel shrugged. He might be able to write a dissertation on party highs but he declined to associate himself with the cheap rubbish kids like Jules sustained their dancing with. 'I told her not to move till you came.'

Paula went down the steps on to the shop floor. Jules, in a floor-length knitted coat of sagging purple wool over a tartan minidress and scuffed gold pixie boots, was standing, slouched on one hip, beside a leather sofa, picking plum-red varnish off her nails. She didn't look up at the sound of Paula's heels on the waxed floorboards.

'What's up?' Paula said.

'Your little fairy friend –'

'This isn't a doss house,' Paula said. 'This sofa is for sale. It's not for kipping on after a hard night just because your sister is a friend of the manager's.'

Jules sighed.

She said, 'I wanted to have lunch with Lindsay. But she said she was working through lunch. Said she was late in this morning, or something.'

'Are you OK?'

Jules yawned.

'Shattered.'

'Apart from that.'

'Yeah,' Jules said. 'Fine.'

'Aren't you staying at Lindsay's?'

Jules eyed her.

'Not for ages.'

'Oh –'

'Didn't you know that? I thought you and Lin –'

'I miss some things,' Paula said, 'even me. D'you want some lunch? I could do twenty minutes.'

'OK.'

'I've been busy,' Paula said. 'So busy.'

Jules put her hands into her purple knitted pockets.

'I know.'

Paula looked away. She looked as if she wanted to smile at something private. Then she looked back at Jules.

'Come on then. Quick pasta fix. I'll tell Joel.'

'I haven't seen you,' Paula said, 'since that Friday. At Blaise's.' She pushed the chrome-lidded jar of grated Parmesan across the café table towards Jules. 'That Friday.'

Jules stirred the sauce into her pasta in big, slow circles with her fork.

'I've had three gigs since then,' Jules said, 'and a day job.'

'A day job!'

Jules gestured at the noisy little café with her fork.

'This crap. Waitressing. Five twenty an hour plus tips. Same as a kitchen porter.'

'Does Lindsay know?'

'I told you,' Jules said, 'I tried to see her.'

'There are telephones –'

'Maybe.'

'Three gigs. That's great.'

'Yes,' Jules said seriously, 'it is. We have a DJ residency this month and I warm up for him. He plays soulful house. I get them ready for him. I'm getting good at it.'

Paula took a swallow of water.

'I should come. We should come.'

'You should,' Jules said. She took a bite of pasta and then said casually through it, 'He did.'

'What?'

'He came. Last Thursday.'

'Who did? Who came?'

Jules speared more pasta.

'Your fella.'

'Jackson?'

Jules nodded.

Paula said, 'Jackson came to your *club*?'

'He was the oldest there by about a hundred years.'

'Why,' Paula said, leaning across the table, 'did Jackson come to your *club*?'

'I suppose he wanted to –'

'How did he know about it?'

Jules put in another mouthful.

'He asked me.'

'He *asked* you?'

'Mmm.'

'When?'

'That night,' Jules said, 'at Blaise's.'

'But you didn't even speak to each other –'

'He said so you're the disc jockey and I said yeah and he said where's your club and I said you wouldn't know and he said I might and I told him and he turned up.'

Paula looked directly at Jules.

'Alone?'

Jules grinned at her.

'Four blokes. Four old blokes.'

'Did they dance?'

'Are you joking?' Jules said. 'They drank. The bar was well pleased.'

'At Blaise's,' Paula said carefully, 'when did this conversation happen?'

'Does it matter?'

'Yes,' Paula said. 'No. I want to know when because I thought –'

'I was putting Poppy's coat on,' Jules said. 'I was kneeling on the floor, putting her coat on.'

'What d'you think of him?'

Jules bent over her plate.

'I don't think anything.'

'D'you like him?'

'Does it matter?'

'I don't know,' Paula said. 'It just feels so strange –'

'What does?'

'When things happen, and I don't know about them. What I don't know –' She stopped and then she looked at Jules. 'Why did you tell me?'

Jules looked at her. Then she tore a piece of bread in two, and used one piece to wipe the remaining sauce from her pasta bowl.

'Why not?'

'Well –'

'We know each other,' Jules said. 'Because of Lin, we're part of the same group. Women. And groups like ours, well, we tell each other stuff. Don't we?'

Paula screwed her paper napkin into a ball, and dropped it into the remains of her pappardelle.

'Why do we?' Paula said.

'You look awful,' Lindsay said.

Jules was kneeling on Lindsay's sitting-room floor looking respectfully at Noah's construction.

'So Paula said.'

'Paula?'

'I had lunch with her.'

Lindsay put her chin up a fraction.

'I know.'

'What's this?'

'He won't tell me.'

Jules looked up.

'What d'you mean?'

'I asked him. I brought him in here after school and I said, "What's that, Noah?" and he said, "It's what I made."'

Jules looked back at it.

'Did he want to play with it?'

'No. But he didn't want me to clear it up either.'

Jules grinned.

'No. I bet not. Is he in bed?'

'I think his light's still on –'

Jules got to her feet and shrugged her purple coat off on to the floor. She put a hand out to Lindsay. 'I'll pick it up in a minute. In a *minute*.'

She went out of the room and across the tiny hallway to Noah's bedroom door. He was lying on his side with his thumb in his mouth, listening to a voice telling a story very animatedly on a brightly coloured plastic tape machine on the floor. His expression didn't change when Jules came in. She closed the door and sat down so that she was leaning against his bed.

'What's this?'

Noah took his thumb out to say, *Horrid Henry*, and put it back again.

'Can I turn it off a sec?'

Noah nodded.

Jules pressed the off button.

She said, 'I saw what you made.'

Noah sucked on.

'What is it?'

Noah rolled on to his back.

'Is it a castle? Is it a fort?'

Noah took his thumb out and said, 'It's not anything.'

'Why don't you want Mum to clear it away?'

'Just don't,' Noah said. 'I made it.'

'That seems a good enough reason.'

Noah rolled back. He reached his free arm down and started *Horrid Henry* playing again.

'D'you want me to go?'

Noah nodded once more.

Jules got up and bent to kiss him.

'You're a little weirdo, but I like you.'

He closed his eyes. He was learning, Jules thought, small as he was, to do that male thing of taking back control by switching off.

'Horrid Henry,' Jules said. 'Naughty Noah.'

Noah said, round his thumb, 'I'm not naughty.'

'No,' Jules said, 'you're not. I wish you would be sometimes. Sleep tight.'

Lindsay was in one of the armchairs in the sitting room, reading a gossip magazine.

She said, 'I suppose you want to stay?'

Jules hooked a foot into her purple coat and kicked it clumsily aside.

'Why are you pissed at me?'

'I'm not –'

'OK,' Jules said. She sat heavily into the second armchair

and pulled off her gold boots. Two toes, their nails roughly painted green, pushed through holes in the feet of her tights.

'Do you *have* to dress like that?' Lindsay said.

Jules lay back.

'Actually I'm thinking of changing. I think I'll get more respect if I change my look a bit.'

'*Respect*?'

'At the club. I'll look more professional.'

'Oh,' Lindsay said faintly, 'I see.' She put the magazine down on a small table at her elbow, and made to get up. 'I'll get us something to eat.'

'Lin,' Jules said, 'I only had lunch with Paula because you said you were busy. I was going to see her sometime, but there wasn't any hurry.'

'She rang me,' Lindsay said, 'at work.' She pulled herself forward in her chair. 'She doesn't ring for weeks and then she rings me.'

Jules said nothing. She lay back in the armchair and watched her sister.

Lindsay looked into the fireplace, which had been filled in with faintly pearlised beige tiles.

She said, 'What did you say to her?'

Jules moved her green-painted toes slightly.

'I told her.'

'What did you tell her?'

'I told her about her fella. That he'd been to the club.'

Lindsay looked at her.

'Was that true?'

Jules looked back.

'Why would I make it up?'

'I don't know –'

'I didn't make it up,' Jules said. 'He came with some others and they had some drinks and tried to chat up some girls and then they went. That's all.'

'Did he chat you up?'

Jules' gaze didn't waver.

'I was working. It was a Thursday.'

Lindsay said, 'Paula's really cut up. That's the second thing.'

'What second thing?'

'That he hasn't told her.'

Jules said nothing.

Lindsay got slowly to her feet.

Looking down at Jules, she said, 'It upset her, knowing.'

'Yes,' Jules said.

'So you knew. You knew it would upset her.'

'Uh-huh.'

'Then why did you do it? Why did you let her take you out to lunch and then deliberately tell her something that would upset her?'

'Because,' Jules said.

'Because what?'

'Because,' Jules said, 'she's just about dumped you in the last few weeks. Since she got back into men.'

'Jules –'

'You're my sister,' Jules said.

'And you think behaving with petty spite towards Paula makes you a good sister to me?'

'That's how it works.'

'Not in my book,' Lindsay said. 'Not to my way of thinking. It just makes you look like a jealous little kid.'

Jules looked away for a moment. Then she heaved herself to an upright sitting position and thrust her feet back into her boots.

'Fine.'

'What's fine?'

'Put Paula first,' Jules said, 'if that's what you want.'

'Oh don't be so silly. You're my *sister*.'

'When it suits you.'

'Jules,' Lindsay said, 'I don't want to fight about this.'

Jules went across the room and picked up her purple coat. She began to turn it round, hunting for the sleeves.

'You don't get it, do you?'

'What don't I get?'

Jules shoved an arm down a sleeve, realised it was the wrong one, and yanked it out again.

'I can't give you anything,' Jules said. 'One day I hope I can but at the moment I can't. All I can do is stand up for you.'

'It isn't standing up for me to upset Paula. Paula's my best friend.'

'OK,' Jules said, 'OK.' She settled the coat roughly across her shoulders. 'I look awful, I don't eat my greens, I don't wash enough, I pop pills and I smoke dope and I earn money in a club you'd rather not think about. No wonder I upset your friends.'

She bent and picked up a battered black-and-gold carrier bag.

'Where are you going?'

'Doesn't matter.'

'It does. I don't want you to go. I want you to stop here and have some supper and a shower.'

'Yes,' said Jules, 'but I don't want that.'

'Jules, *please* –'

Jules paused and looked down at Noah's construction. Then she looked at Lindsay.

'That's two of us today won't do what suits you. Tell you anything?'

When Eleanor's phone rang, she couldn't immediately find it. Blaise had organised for her to have a modern cordless telephone which had the immense advantage of mobility, but a compensating disadvantage of being both easy to lose and hard to locate when lost, as the main ring tone appeared to come from the base unit and not from the handset. There was going to come a time – a time she preferred not to think about too much – when she would find it inconsequentially left in the saucepan cupboard or under the sofa cushions. Or in the fridge. On this occasion, she knew it was somewhere under the papers on the sitting-room table, the newspapers and the journals and the myriad bureaucratic forms, requiring infinitely detailed filling in, forms which had made perfect and acceptable sense to her in her working life, and which now seemed, in equal measure, exasperating and unacceptably intrusive. In the course of shuffling through all this most of it cascaded in chaos to the floor.

'Yes?' Eleanor said irritably into the handset.

'I'm outside,' Jules said.

'Who –'

'It's Jules,' Jules said. 'I'm outside.'

'Outside what?'

'Your door.'

'My door?'

'I'm standing outside your door. I thought I'd ring so's you'd be OK about opening it. You'd know it was me.'

Eleanor dropped the telephone, and Jules' continuing voice, back on to the table, and limped out to the hall. She switched on the outside light and could see, dimly through the coloured glass panels, which everyone wanted her to replace with something less vulnerable, a figure outside.

She took the chain off the door, unbolted it, and opened it wide.

'Has something happened?'

'No.'

'It's ten o'clock –'

'Your bedtime.'

'I'm not such a creature of habit as that,' Eleanor said, 'but ten o'clock is late for an unannounced visit.'

Jules stepped inside, and watched while Eleanor went through her security ritual.

'I had a bit of a row with Lindsay.'

'Ah.' Eleanor looked at her. 'Have you eaten?'

'No.'

'Tea and toast then.'

Jules followed her to the kitchen.

'I'm going to sit here,' Eleanor said, 'and you can make tea for both of us.' She lowered herself into a chair by the table. 'You know where everything is.'

'I don't want to talk about Lindsay,' Jules said.

'Fine by me. Tell me what you've been doing.'

Jules ran water into the kettle.

'Good work and bad work.'

'Bad work?'

'Waitressing. I need the money. It's crap but it isn't the worst job I've ever done.'

'Ah,' Eleanor said. She made a space among the books and objects on the table, and reached into the cupboard behind her for plates. 'What was the worst?'

'Bar work,' Jules said. 'You wouldn't have liked it.'

'Oh?'

'It was in a hotel. The club lounge of a hip hotel. Early evenings it was all women, then couples. Later it was all men. In packs. I had to wear a cocktail dress.'

Eleanor looked at Jules' feet.

'I can't quite picture that.'

'It was gross,' Jules said. 'Bare arms. Bare shoulders. They wanted me to wear high heels but I wouldn't. I wore trainers. I mean, I had to have some control over those animals late at night, didn't I?'

Eleanor leaned to open a drawer for knives.

'Why were you there?'

Jules was taking slices of bread out of a packet. Eleanor could be relied upon for unapologetic soft sliced white.

'A guy,' Jules said.

'Yes.'

146

'The usual. Just everything. Just fucking everything.'

She paused and waited for Eleanor to comment on her language. Eleanor was retrieving the butter dish from under a crumpled tea towel on the table and said nothing.

Jules said, 'D'you know?'

'Know what?'

'What it feels like to be so hung up on some guy it's all that matters?'

Eleanor paused. She took the lid off the butter dish, then put it back again.

She said, 'No.'

'Lucky you.'

There was another pause. Jules pressed the toaster button down and stared at it.

Eleanor added courteously, 'No. Actually.'

Jules went on looking at the toaster.

'It may not have occurred to you,' Eleanor said calmly, folding her forearms on the table, 'but the same – how should I say it – pulses beat in me as in you. Age is a trial and a test, but it is not a muffler. Nothing visceral is diminished. Altered, yes, but not noticeably diminished.'

Jules said nothing. She took mugs out of one cupboard and a box of tea bags out of another.

'Everything,' Eleanor said, 'that gives life its value is in place. There is enough time now, however, to reflect upon what more opportunity might have meant, despite having no regrets about the choices taken.'

Jules bent over the tea mugs.

There was a short silence and then she said, in quite a different voice, 'Sorry.'

Lindsay stood in her small kitchen, holding her mobile phone. She had typed in text messages to both Jules and Paula, and been dissatisfied with both of them, and had deleted them before sending. She had also plumped up the cushions in the sitting room, ironed Noah's clean school shirt and put out cereals and bowls ready for the morning. There was, somehow, nothing else to be done instead of going to bed.

She went out of the kitchen, turning off both the lights there, and the one in the hallway. In the darkness, a glowing line still showed under Noah's door. She opened it, expecting to find him, as usual, asleep with the bedside lamp on and his comfort rag on the floor. But he was awake, his eyes large and unfocused, as if he had not been awake long.

'Hi, darling,' Lindsay said. 'You OK?'

Noah didn't speak.

She knelt beside his bed.

'Did you just wake up?'

Noah nodded.

'Did you have a dream?'

Noah considered.

He said, 'Did you touch what I made?'

'No,' Lindsay said.

'Well, don't,' Noah said. 'Don't touch it,' and closed his eyes.

CHAPTER TEN

'I have always been very ambitious,' Blaise typed. 'I was brought up to believe that I should set my mind to my goals, and that I would be able to achieve them. I knew quite early on that I wanted to build a business, which is why what I do now is such a good fit for me.'

She stopped and surveyed the screen. She was, as Karen was constantly pointing out, a much poorer typist than Karen was, and could still not fully concentrate on what she was typing and, at the same time, how she typed it.

'Be friendly,' the editor of the business magazine had said on the telephone. 'I want the tone accessible. You're not writing a briefing paper, you're writing about employee satisfaction, what women want from work. I asked you because if anyone knows, you ought to.'

The editor of the business magazine was a man. The magazine was running a survey of the top twenty-five places – or environments – where women wanted to work.

'I'm not asking you for anything on workforce diversity, or accountability or networking opportunities. I want you to focus on what keeps women happy.'

'I'd rather,' Blaise said, 'write about work–life balance – what I teach is work–life balance.'

'OK,' the editor said. He sounded abstracted, as if he was engaged in something else while talking to her. 'You can have half a page on work–life balance or a whole page on employee satisfaction. This is a business magazine, not some lifestyle nonsense. You want to promote your company or don't you?'

'My company,' Blaise typed, 'is called Workwell. It was founded five years ago with my business partner, Karen Spicer, and our purpose is to help companies to improve their output by showing the people who work for them how to work in a way that improves their lives rather than just gets them by.'

She stopped. 'Gets them by' didn't look right. She tried 'allows them just to get by'. It wasn't right either but it was better. It would do for now.

'And one of the things I have learned in the course of the last five years is that women like working for employers who ask them what they want.'

She stopped and took her hands off the keyboard. The magazine would pay five hundred pounds for the article, which would include a photograph of Blaise and Karen, and details of their company.

'Suppose,' Karen had said, 'people want to work for us as a result of this, rather than employ us?'

Blaise didn't look at her.

'We should consider it. At least.'

'A bit of thin-end-of-wedging then, on your part.'

'Nothing stands still.'

'Shut up,' Karen said, and then louder, 'Shut up, will you?' and then, 'Sorry, Bea.'

'Recent surveys suggest,' Blaise typed, 'that, given the right treatment, women are liable to be more satisfied with work than men. I would even go so far as to suggest that women's ability to get more out of working than men is partly due to their general make-up, but also because they are more likely to take advantage of flexible working opportunities. Women have to take decisions about careers and families that might require considerable juggling, and with support, that juggling is possible –'

She stopped, and took her hands off the keyboard. 'With support', she had written. 'With support, juggling of motherhood and a satisfying career is perfectly possible,' she had been going to write. But Karen had come into her mind, of course, and she had halted. She could not go on with Karen planted in her mind like that and saying, as she was increasingly saying, 'What would you know?'

What Blaise did know uncomfortably was that she couldn't make Karen a simple and shining example of what women can achieve, given enough help, enough sympathetic accommodation. If you looked at Karen on paper – her aims, her abilities, her children, her family-centred husband, her income group, her house – you saw all you needed to see for the purposes of illustration. But, if you looked at what was actually happening in the Spicer household, at the day-to-day moods and tensions and frustrations, Karen was not in any way suitable as an example of this encouraging theory. In fact, after the other evening, Karen looked more like someone barely holding things together than someone smoothly spinning plates.

Blaise and Rosie had gone round to Lucas's studio together largely because Rosie had been palpably anxious and Karen had, in a way Blaise might normally have admired for being sensibly laid-back about irrational fears, declined to indulge her. But Blaise, annoyed on this occasion by Karen's affected nonchalance around Jackson Miller, had taken Rosie's part, and they had set off in the dark, Rosie's hand in Blaise's, and in, in Blaise's case, a mild glow of indignation.

Lucas's studio was in a short terrace of late-Victorian houses plainly put up to accommodate artist followers of the pre-Raphaelite brotherhood. The second floor of each house boasted an enormous north-facing window, the glazing bars curving about in an art-deco manner, which gave the façades a blank and startled look. Some of these huge windows were dark, one had evidently been divided to make a double storey inside and another, at one end, was a rectangle of yellow light.

'That's Daddy's,' Rosie said.

She stood on the pavement, looking up, her hand still in Blaise's. Below the lit window, there were other, curtained, ones and the sound of a very loud television.

'That's Mr Carpenter,' Rosie said. 'He's deaf and Daddy likes him. He's got a cat.'

'The famous cat –'

'He comes into the studio and watches Daddy.'

'Mr Carpenter?'

'No,' Rosie said, 'the cat. We give him sardines, the ones in olive oil.'

Blaise gazed up at the window. She could see objects up there, maybe furniture, but no easel, no Lucas.

'Will he mind being interrupted?'

'No,' Rosie said, 'he'll be pleased, if it's me.'

She extracted her hand politely and went up the broken-tiled path to the door. There were three bells in a line, and beside the top one Lucas had pinned a card on which he had written in his graceful calligraphy, 'Studio'. Rosie pressed the bell and stood waiting, her head bent.

'Nothing,' Blaise said.

'He has to come down. There isn't an intercom. He has to come down the stairs and sometimes the light bulb is broken.'

Blaise looked at Rosie's concentrating head. Then she looked at the coloured-glass flowers set into the door and Lucas's clean white card pinned to the flaking frame. She had a sudden sense of the complexity of it all, this child, this man, this separate studio, Karen at home with another child, and a friend's child, and the friend's new boyfriend. She gave a little shiver and then a shape loomed up in the dim light behind the glass flowers and the door opened.

'Rosie!' Lucas said. He looked almost as if he had been asleep. His gaze moved beyond his daughter. 'Blaise – has anything – is something the matter?'

Rosie said, 'I wanted you to be there.'

'What –'

'We were having tea,' Blaise said, 'and then Toby appeared, with Paula's Jackson, after the football, and tea turned into a bit of a party, and Rosie thought you should be asked to join in.'

Lucas looked at her. Then he bent and put an arm round Rosie.

'My kind Rosie.'

'It wasn't a party,' Rosie said. 'It just stopped being tea. It stopped being just our cake and stuff.'

Lucas looked at Blaise across Rosie's head.

'Anything I should know?'

She shook her head.

'Nothing to know. Rosie has described it beautifully.'

'Why did they come?'

'I don't know. Impulse, I suppose –'

'Toby was carried away,' Rosie said. 'He was just besotted about the football.'

'Nice for him though,' Lucas said. 'Don't you think?' He glanced at Blaise again. 'Like to come up?'

'Well, I – if you –'

'I do,' Lucas said. 'I'd like to show you. Rosie'll show you.'

'Is Fred there?'

'No,' Lucas said, 'he's watching *Strictly Come Dancing* with Mr Carpenter.' He stood back and indicated that Blaise should come in. 'All the way up to the top.'

The stairs were half lit and carpeted with grubby drugget. The walls were stained, with random gouges out of the plaster, and there were smells. Blaise took a breath, and held it, and followed Rosie up, past closed doors painted crudely to resemble wood grain and a rusting wrought-iron plant stand burdened with dusty cacti. At the top of the stairs, a door stood open to a steady flood of light.

Rosie ran into the studio and spun round, arms out.

'Look!'

Blaise looked.

'Wonderful –'

'Shabby,' Lucas said. 'Less dusty than it was but dusty. Improved by the lights I've rigged up, but not improved enough yet. But mine.'

Rosie ran about, her feet thudding on the boards of the floor.

'This is where Fred sleeps. And this is his sardine plate. And he can sit here and watch the birds and gnash his teeth.'

In the far corner, away from the great window and behind Lucas's easel and a table covered in tubes of paint and paint rollers and brushes in jars, was a divan bed with a jumbled pile of cushions on it. Blaise looked at Lucas.

'And is that where Lucas sleeps sometimes?'

He looked straight back at her.

'Sometimes, yes.'

'And was just now sometimes?'

'Yes,' Lucas said. 'It's wonderful. I sleep there without dreaming.'

Blaise looked about her. There were very few canvases propped against the wall and nothing on the easel. The only sign of recent creativity was one of Lucas's recognisable abstracts, mildly architectural, lying on the floor on a neatly arranged carpet of old newspapers.

'Is it – good for painting?'

He nodded.

'It will be.'

She said, 'It's a marvellous space –'

He sighed.

He said, 'It's almost exactly what I hoped for. Private, without being secret.'

'But you're not painting now –'

He glanced at the picture on the floor.

'I'm getting to know this place.' He indicated. Rosie, at the far end of the studio, was arranging the old sweaters and towels that formed the cat's nest. He said, 'I'm – convalescing a bit.'

'Heavens –'

'Maybe catching my breath would be a better description.'

Blaise said, 'Are you OK?'

'How nice of you to ask.'

'Of course I'd ask. Of course, I hope –'

'D'you know,' Lucas said, 'd'you know, I can't remember when anyone last asked me if I was OK.'

'And what's the answer –?'

He smiled at her.

'You know how you get into a state of being . . . a state of being a bit tired, a bit sad, a bit hopeless, and you get so used to being like that that you begin to think that that's normal, that that's how you are, how life just is?'

She said nothing. She simply stood and looked at him and thought how he had never seemed so much a painter to her as he seemed now, standing in this high, bright, bare room with nothing on the easel.

'I'm not having a whinge,' Lucas said, 'I'm just describing. You do this in life and then you do that, and suddenly you're in a place that you are fairly sure you didn't exactly elect to be in, and getting out of it is difficult at best and impossible at worst. I'm just getting used to this. To what I've done. I jumped, and I didn't break my legs, but I did wind myself a bit.'

'You *jumped*?'

He smiled at her again.

'It's not fair to talk to you like this, is it? You're Kay's business partner. You shouldn't have asked me if I was OK.'

'I'm your friend too. We've known each other almost as long as Karen and I've known each other. I – I didn't realise it was that bad.'

'It isn't.'

'Then why this place?'

'OK,' Lucas said, 'it is. But I'm fixing it. This studio is part of fixing it.'

'Fixing you –'

'Well,' Lucas said, still smiling but lifting his face towards the high, peaked ceiling, 'I'm the only bit I can fix, aren't I? Can you imagine trying to fix Karen?'

At the far end of the room, Rosie had picked up a tin plate from the floor and was waving it. 'Can I wash this?'

'Sure,' Lucas said. He stayed staring at the ceiling. He said to Blaise, 'Have I shocked you?'

She shook her head.

'Surprised you?'

She said, 'I don't want to sound stuffy, but I can't have this conversation. You know I can't.'

Lucas stopped looking at the ceiling.

He said easily, 'OK.'

Rosie called from the sink under the eaves at one side of the room, 'It still smells fishy.'

'Fred likes fishy.'

'If you don't come back with us,' Blaise said, 'it'll be hard on Rosie –'

'Of course I'm coming back. Who said I wasn't coming back?' He put a hand out and held her forearm inside its neat leather-jacketed sleeve. 'I'm just working things out, Blaise. I'm not going off the deep end, I'm just being here to do some thinking. Or rather, being here because this is a place where I can let thoughts happen.'

She nodded. His grasp on her arm was not at all urgent.

She said, 'Oh, I know –'

'I know you do.'

'But I can't –'

'Of course you can't,' Lucas said, and then he took his hand off her arm and looked across at Rosie, still earnestly scrubbing at Fred's sardine plate.

'Home, poppet!'

'Well,' Karen said, 'that was weird, wasn't it?'

Lucas was inserting mugs and glasses into the crowded top rack of the dishwasher with great ingenuity.

'Was it?'

'Wasn't it?'

'D'you mean Paula's man?'

'No,' Karen said. 'Why should I mean him?'

Lucas put a hand either side of the dishwasher rack and slid it carefully back into the machine.

'I have no idea. Except that he was the only element that wasn't familiar.'

'We've never had Toby without Paula –'

'Where was Paula?'

'At home, I suppose.'

'Why,' Lucas said, 'didn't you ring her?'

Karen was standing by the desk, rifling through household papers. She didn't look up.

'It wasn't up to me.'

Lucas dropped a soap tablet into the dishwasher door and snapped the compartment shut.

'That's an odd thing to say –'

'Why?'

'Well,' Lucas said, 'Paula's your friend. You had her son and her boyfriend, unannounced, in the house for quite a long time, and she might have liked to join in.'

There was a silence and then Karen said, 'Toby was so happy.'

'That was the football. It wasn't being without his mother.'

Karen muttered something.

'What?'

'Nothing.'

'What?'

'I said,' Karen said, 'I said she exhausts him.'

Lucas started the dishwasher and stood back. He gave a little bark of laughter.

'Charming.'

Karen picked her bundle of papers up in both hands and dumped them on the table.

'I'm going to sort these.'

Lucas glanced at the clock. It was ten to midnight.

'Really?'

'Yes,' Karen said, 'the house is quiet.'

'Wouldn't you rather sleep now and get up early to do it tomorrow?'

'No thank you.'

Karen sat down at the table.

As Lucas passed her, she said, 'Did you have a good afternoon? *Did* Rosie interrupt you?'

There was a beat.

'No,' Lucas said, 'she didn't.'

'Is it working, Luke?'

He paused in the doorway.

He said lightly, 'Looking for a return on your investment?'

Karen was looking straight ahead.

'It was a civil enquiry.'

'Then in the same spirit of civility, could I ask you to give me time?'

'Of course.'

'Thank you. Don't be long.'

She didn't turn her head.

'Half an hour.'

She listened while his tread – light still, energetic – went upstairs towards their bedroom. She glanced at the clock.

Five to twelve. Paula would still be out, and possibly dancing. Jackson had said in his offhand way that he would probably take her out later, if Toby would take himself and his sleeping bag to Eleanor or Lindsay's sofa, and Toby had shrugged and said, 'Fine,' in a careless manner that he would never have employed had Paula been there.

Karen shuffled her papers, pulling out the invoices and the fussily expressed information sheets from the girls' school. There was something about picturing Paula dancing, Paula getting into Jackson's Mercedes, Paula accepting a drink, looking at Jackson over the rim of it, that was unsettling. While Toby and Jackson had been in the house there had been a dynamism in the air, something more vigorous than even Toby's euphoria could account for. It had something to do with Jackson's completely male confidence, with his relaxed ease, with his clothes and his haircut and that big silver car parked across the street. Oh damn, and damn again, Karen thought, picking up the invoices and flinging them down again, it had – has – something, everything even, to do with money. Hasn't it?

From the first tentative months of Workwell, Karen had known that Blaise had wider horizons than she did. When she was tired and therefore inclined to be cross, she told herself – and often Blaise too – that it was all very well for Blaise to think big, to budget rather than to housekeep, even to gamble. Blaise might be – indeed was – generous by nature but, being on her own, she could exercise a reassuring control over all aspects of her life that was, quite simply, denied to Karen. And while Karen knew, in her heart of hearts, that she could never be a kept wife, could never surrender the independence, even the power of earning, there was still an element of family life, of family responsibility, however much one adored that family, that represented a shackle.

'I am not free to choose,' Karen would say to Blaise when the subject of possibly expanding Workwell came up yet again, and sometimes Blaise would say, 'I know,' and some-times she would say, 'But you have chosen, and these are the consequences,' and there would be a brief, dangerous silence while they both weighed up the risks of taking the conversation further.

When she wasn't tired – or was, at least, less tired than usual – Karen knew that she and Blaise fitted well together, that Blaise drove her on while she reined Blaise in, that Blaise made her think about work as a career and she forced Blaise to think about work as something that couldn't happen with complete independence from family life. She knew, too, that Blaise needed something from her and Lucas and their children, something she would probably never acknowledge, and certainly never articulate, but which definitely added a dimension to her life. The closest she got to it was saying once, as if the thought had just idly occurred to her, 'I wonder if Eleanor ever had another family she was really close to?'

Karen got up and went across to the kitchen window. It had a blind made of embroidered Indian cotton which somehow never seemed to be pulled down, so that the glass reflected blackly at night, like a mirror. Karen stood and looked at her dark silhouette and behind her the lit kitchen, the cupboards Lucas had painted as if they were frescoed, the children's paintings on curling sheets of paper, anchored haphazardly to the fridge door with magnets, the hanging rack of pans and colanders, the clock that had been salvaged from a defunct railway-station waiting room. She tried to look at it positively, to see it as something they had made, had achieved together, as they had achieved Rosie and Poppy. She tried very hard, and without success, to look at the kitchen and all it represented with pride. I hate whingers, Karen said to herself, I hate spoilt, dissatisfied women who have so much. And I do have so much, I do, and it's in my power to have more, and give more. It's just – it's just that I'd give anything right now to have the shine back on things, the excitement, the feeling that round the corner there might be something that's other than just more of the same.

She put her hands into her hair and piled it roughly on top of her head, holding it there. Standing like that elongated her outline, pulled her waist in, defined her neck. When they first met, all Lucas had wanted to do was look at her. Being a painter and a capable photographer, he had naturally looked at her with a discerning concentration, which had been quite extraordinary and had given her an entirely new perception of herself. She had posed for him for hours, Bob Dylan on the music system, both of them entirely absorbed in her skin, her hair, her body. She grew bored with herself long before he did, yet if there were times when he seemed to be engrossed in something else, she restlessly sought his attention again. She remembered it quite clearly, and without shame, sauntering nonchalantly through his apparent field of vision, draped inadequately in a towel, or only wearing shoes.

She let her hair fall. She wouldn't want that now. She certainly wouldn't want to behave like that now. She couldn't even visualise such a scenario, any more than she could visualise being without the children. She turned and looked at their paintings on the fridge door, at Rosie's tight, neat little pictures and Poppy's random splashes. She thought of them upstairs in their painted forest, asleep under the watchful gaze of their painted unicorn, and felt a pang of almost tearful longing. What was it about motherhood that could put marriage in the shade? What was it about oneself that made one still not want motherhood to be the only identifying mark? What was it about money that seemed – seductively – to promise a taunting vision of freedom even within the confines of these relationships?

She went back to the table and tidied the undealt-with paperwork into a rectangle. Perhaps this was just a stage, perhaps she was merely being dictated to by her physiology, and these complex and warring feelings would pass and leave her in a more serene landscape, like the one Eleanor seemed to inhabit. Perhaps she should talk to Eleanor, or at least talk her way through the confusion of her thoughts in Eleanor's presence.

She moved round the kitchen, putting cereal boxes on the table as a gesture towards breakfast, switching off lights, picking Poppy's antennae hairband off the floor. Then she went out of the room, leaving the dishwasher humming away to itself in the darkness, and climbed the stairs.

Lucas was in bed, wearing a faded green T-shirt and reading Ian Rankin. He lay on his side, holding the book close to his admirable profile, with his hair spread behind him on the pillow, like a woman.

'Have you looked at the girls?'

He didn't move.

He said, 'Of course. Dead to all worlds.'

Karen pulled off her grey velour top and tossed it on to a nearby chair.

'Get your paperwork done?' Lucas said.

Karen stopped stepping out of her trousers.

'*My* paperwork?'

His eyes swivelled sideways towards her.

'Yes,' he said, 'that's how you like it.'

'Oh Luke,' Karen said tiredly, 'stop it.'

'OK,' he said.

Karen went round to his side of the bed and stood looking down at him. He read on, steadily.

'Luke –'

There was a small silence. Then he looked up at her, his expression open and friendly.

'Yes?'

'I –' Karen said, and then she stopped.

'Yes?'

'Nothing,' she said. 'I'm going to brush my teeth.'

CHAPTER ELEVEN

Toby was converting Eleanor to football. Ever since the Saturday evening he had spent in his sleeping bag on her sofa, and in the course of which he had induced her to watch *Match of the Day* with him, he had obviously decided she was ripe for indoctrination, and then transformation, into someone on whom he could practise serious opinions about questionable tackles and contested goals.

He had touchingly given her a slim paperback called *The Girl Bluffer's Guide to Football*. It had a remarkable photograph on the cover, featuring two hefty men in football kit, pictured from waist to knee with their huge hands coyly cupped in front of them. Eleanor had been required to admire the photograph and to acknowledge that the list of contents – including what to wear and how to behave at a football match, such as allowing the men to reign supreme when chanting – were admirably comprehensive and clear.

'I'll probably test you,' Toby said.

Eleanor looked at the open page in her hand. 'If your team scores,' it said, 'go mad!'

'Will I get a prize?'

'No,' Toby said, 'of course not. But I'll be able to talk to you, won't I?'

Most days Eleanor diligently did her homework. This consisted of reading the sports pages of her newspaper and keeping abreast of movement in the league tables. When Toby rang to check on her progress – using a newly acquired mobile phone – she was able, quite often, to hold her own and sometimes even to score a small triumph. One Sunday, she had read that the Chelsea striker, Didier Drogba, had almost qualified as an accountant in France. The revelation of this fact had produced a small but significant silence on the telephone.

'I expect,' Toby said at last, 'that I would have known that sometime.'

'Yes,' Eleanor said kindly, 'I expect you would.'

In all their football discussions, Eleanor noticed that Toby did not mention Jackson. There was nothing either angry or awkward about the omission but rather an impression that this relationship was important, private and not up for discussion. Whatever it was, it certainly was giving Toby confidence and a small stature in his own eyes, qualities that his father seemed singularly unable to supply. Indeed Paula, being Paula, had openly said as much, describing Gavin's latest dutiful Saturday excursion with Toby as a disaster since all Toby wanted to do was find a television with Sky Plus on it in order to watch Chelsea play West Ham and Gavin had been unenterprisingly at a loss about finding such a thing.

'Gavin knows nothing about football,' Paula said. 'I suppose you wouldn't, if you only have daughters.'

Eleanor, who had met Gavin several times when Paula and Toby lived across the street, and had privately decided that he was a man able to get a firm handle on every aspect of his life except – disastrously – the private one, decided not to encourage Paula. She merely said, 'I like seeing Toby fired up like this,' and silently dared Paula to give Jackson the credit. But all Paula said simply was, 'I know,' and her voice had been full of relief.

Eleanor felt relief, too. It would have been perverse not to, not to feel thankfulness at Toby's new appetite for the life circumstances which, only weeks before, had seemed to be everything he didn't like or want. But Eleanor's relief was slightly checked by wariness, a wariness that she sometimes told herself was merely the irritation of being older, and slightly lame, and disinclined to look too far into the future. When she couldn't persuade herself that any of those reasons were valid, and the wariness persisted, she found that her mind reverted to, quite simply, the abiding enigma of Jackson.

The trouble was, Eleanor thought, setting aside the daily newspaper Sudoku puzzle to apply herself to later, that you couldn't precisely identify what was disturbing about Jackson. He was personable, solvent, not obviously encumbered by his personal past, and making curiously imaginative efforts about Paula and her son and her friends. He wasn't especially talkative – a plus, possibly – and he certainly showed no inclination to be confidential – definitely a plus – and he had done and said nothing that indicated that his intentions, as far as they could be gleaned, were other than trustworthy. He seemed to want to make Paula happy; he seemed to want to forge a companionable relationship with Toby; he seemed to want to get to know Paula's friends in an easy, undemanding way. But there was still something opaque about him, something puzzling, something Eleanor could not quite put her finger on, which made her feel that matters could turn out not to be as straightforward as they presently looked. And to cap it all, there seemed to be no opportunity to air these mild anxieties, because Jackson, by giving so little away, seemed somehow to be infecting them all with the same alluring reticence.

Eleanor heaved herself out of her chair and limped to the window. There was a delivery van in the street, and two men in jeans were dragging a series of big flat cardboard cartons out of the back, no doubt containing a wardrobe or a desk, flat-packed in sections, which some hapless man was going to have to assemble later on. Jackson was not the kind of man to assemble flat-packs. Jackson would employ all his own casual competence in employing someone else to do it. Jules had said that, when he came to the club, he'd brought with him several of the men who worked for him as mobile technical support for computers. She said they were geeks, and they had clustered round him drinking vodka shots and looking completely pathetic.

'Did he look pathetic?' Eleanor had asked.

'No,' Jules said.

'Well?'

'He's old,' Jules said, 'but he's quite cool.'

The men in the street carried the boxes into the house diagonally opposite. A white van drove up the street behind the parked van, failed to get past, and sat there, the driver leaning relaxedly back in his seat, the heel of his hand on the horn. Eleanor waited. Shortly a small predictable drama would unfold and there'd be shouting and abuse and the delivery men would elaborately take their time about moving on, and everyone would finally drive off with the agreeably heightened sense of involvement, in a little gender-affirming episode. Men, Eleanor thought, men. Perhaps I know nothing about them. Perhaps I know a great deal. Or perhaps I know just enough to fear their incapacity, sometimes, to see things through. Things that other people have, unfortunately, come to rely on.

Blaise waited on Eleanor's doorstep. She held in her hand a miniature white poinsettia in a plastic pot moulded to resemble china. Blaise was uncertain about the poinsettia, but sometimes bringing flowers seemed too girlish for Eleanor, and anything to eat or drink not, somehow, very flattering. Anyway, it was the time of year for poinsettias, glaring scarlet in every supermarket and greengrocer.

Blaise's father, who had been to northern Burma on business as a timber importer, had reported poinsettias growing in huge hedges, quite wild, and looking as natural and appropriate as rhododendrons did in the Himalayas. And didn't in Surrey, where Blaise had grown up. She looked down at the poinsettia's pale greenish leaves. She wondered why she had brought anything at all. Eleanor would doubtless only be cross.

A light came on above Blaise's head, and a chain clattered inside.

'Well,' Eleanor said, opening the door, 'how very nice.'

She looked at the poinsettia.

'Poor little thing. What do you suppose they did to it to stunt it like that?'

'Shall I take it away?'

'No,' Eleanor said. 'At least I can give it a good life, however brief.'

'Have you ever had a cat or anything?'

Eleanor stood back so that Blaise could enter.

'Something to look after, I mean –' She held out the poinsettia.

'My work was looking after,' Eleanor said, 'even at arm's length. You could argue that yours is too.' She poked a finger into the compost under the leaves. 'It needs a drink, poor little object. I expect you do, as well.'

Blaise took off her coat and hung it on Eleanor's hall stand.

'It's been a long day, but a good one. Some days, you know how it is, you just seem to hold the floodwaters at bay. Other days, you make progress.'

'I remember,' Eleanor said. 'Oh, I remember.'

She indicated the open sitting-room door.

'Go and sit down. I'll give this some water and get us a drink. They are now putting perfectly nice wine into screw-top bottles and my life is transformed.'

Eleanor's sitting room was warm and dim. A couple of unmatched lamps with fringed shades glowed in corners, and beside Eleanor's accustomed chair, an angular metal floor lamp threw a sharp, bright circle of light. There were the usual piles of papers and books, a scattering of pens and mugs and tumblers, a magnifying glass and, on top of the most obvious pile, a surprising-looking paperback called *The Girl Bluffer's Guide to Football*. Blaise picked it up and studied the cover. It was, amateurishly, a page-three picture for women and produced in Blaise a sensation she did not feel very relaxed about. She put the book down carefully, as if afraid of provoking it, and moved one of Eleanor's cumbersome armchairs to the edge of the circle of light.

Eleanor came unsteadily back into the room with two glasses of wine on a tray.

Blaise took them from her.

'Can I ask you something?'

'Of course.'

'A football book?'

Eleanor settled herself slowly in her chair.

'A present from Toby.'

'Really?'

'He has decided that I might make a good football conversationalist if I apply myself to studying the game and its culture.'

Blaise cleared a space on the small cluttered table at Eleanor's elbow, and set down the wine glass.

'Are you enjoying it?'

'Very much,' Eleanor said. 'In fact, I'm wondering about choosing a team other than Chelsea to support, in order to have good arguments. I'm considering Fulham, being London's oldest club, but I think Manchester United or Liverpool would give me more ammunition.'

Blaise sat down in the armchair and picked up the second glass of wine.

'I expect you miss arguments. I would. I dislike personal arguments but really enjoy professional ones.'

Eleanor took a sip of wine.

'The lifeblood of working life. Moving opinion forward, persuading, converting. The mind is engaged and nothing of self need be given away.'

'Unless you choose.'

'Yes,' Eleanor said, 'unless you choose.' She looked across at Blaise, still in her work suit, still with her hair tied smoothly behind her head. 'It's very nice to see you but I sense you are not here to discuss the satisfactions of professional negotiation.'

'No.'

'I may not get out much, but it's extraordinary what I sense, even when I can't see it.'

'Eleanor,' Blaise said, 'this Friday. It's your turn.'

'Technically, yes.'

'Why do you say that?'

'Because I know that, in theory, this particular Friday, you and Karen and Paula and Jules and Lindsay are due to come here for the evening.'

'And?'

'And,' Eleanor said, 'that is not actually what will happen.'

'I'm afraid not,' Blaise said. 'That's really what I came to say.'

'And I appreciate you saying it in person and not on the telephone. But I am not surprised.' She looked at Blaise. 'Why don't you tell me what is going to happen instead?'

Blaise interlaced her fingers and spread them across her knees.

'I don't know about Paula –'

'No.'

'But I think she may be doing something with Jackson because she asked Karen to have Toby and Karen can't because there's an art exhibition that Lucas really wants her to go to with him, and she feels she should, and she has asked me to go along too as moral support, and as they are not – well, things being a bit difficult for them at the moment, and everyone needing support of some kind, I felt I must say yes.'

'Of course,' Eleanor said.

'I'm so sorry.'

Eleanor said nothing. She picked up her wine glass and regarded it and put it down again.

She said, 'Well, that's kind of you, but it doesn't matter.'

'I think it does.'

'Try not to pity me,' Eleanor said. 'There are few things I find unendurable, but being pitied is definitely one of them.'

'I didn't mean to sound pitying. I meant to sound just sorry. About Friday night. Because I am sorry.'

'What about Rosie and Poppy?'

'What about them?'

'Who will look after Poppy and Rosie?'

'I think Lucas wants them to come too. To the exhibition.'

Eleanor turned to look at Blaise.

'Yes. I see that.'

'He needs to show them –'

'Yes.'

'He's a good painter.'

'Abstraction,' Eleanor said. 'Such an interesting idea. Something separated from actual instances, something that exists only, really, as a mental concept. I imagine he can draw?'

'Oh yes, certainly, he draws beautifully –'

'Then one rather wonders why he doesn't. But then, I am not creative. I don't feel the urge to push the boundaries of self-expression.'

'I really am sorry,' Blaise said, 'about Friday night.'

Eleanor picked up her glass again and took another sip.

'Things move on. Things change.'

'I don't like it,' Blaise said.

Eleanor looked at her sharply.

'What don't you like?'

'I don't like what's happened recently. I don't like what we – we've become. There's a difference between being energetic and being restless, and we've become restless.'

There was a pause, and then Eleanor said, 'Are you lonely?'

Blaise gave a small shrug.

'I don't know.'

'No,' Eleanor said, 'nor do I. What *isn't* lonely about being alive, one wonders.'

'I can talk to you,' Blaise said, 'because you did my kind of life, in your time. Because I know you understand that I want to be good at something, I want acknowledgement. I want a job title and I want to make money – not huge amounts, but enough.' She stopped and then she said, smiling, 'Except for the not huge amounts of money, I sound like a man, don't I?'

'I'm glad to hear it.'

'Are you?'

'Oh yes,' Eleanor said. 'I was born at the end of what the tabloid press would regard as the golden age of female caring, the mid-nineteenth to the mid-twentieth century, when, because of the lack of educational and professional opportunities, the most brilliant women gave their talents for free in what might loosely be termed the caring sector. I was lucky to be born late enough to be *paid*.'

Blaise leaned forward a little.

'And children?'

'Ah,' Eleanor said, 'the social glow of motherhood.'

'Yes.'

'What do you think?'

'I think,' Blaise said, 'that we shouldn't be so narrow about families. That the idea of family, even the word family, is often used to be extremely exclusionary. To the rest of us.'

'Which is why you will go with Karen's family to an art exhibition on Friday?'

'Yes.'

'And Karen?'

'What about Karen?'

'Tell me, except for the inevitable exhaustion resulting from a life like hers, what is particularly difficult just now for Karen?'

Blaise unlocked her fingers and laid her hands carefully on her chair arms. Then she leaned back.

'She'd best tell you that herself –'

'Very well.'

'But all I will say is that, for women like us, brought up with the highest expectations, it can be quite easy, I think, to find yourself inconsolable.'

Eleanor told Lindsay that she would, on Friday night, come round to Lindsay's flat. The local minicab firm named Murphy's and staffed entirely by drivers and administrators from Pakistan were well used to taking Eleanor on outings, and it would do her good to get out of the house.

'In any case, you have two small boys to look after and I only have to transport myself.'

Lindsay's flat was in a small seventies block down towards Parsons Green. It was built of brick and whoever had designed it had been thinking of its utilitarian, rather than aesthetic, merit. It sat four square in a small space of asphalt paths and shabby grass, flat-fronted, flat-roofed and blank-windowed. Lindsay's flat, on the second floor, was approached by an internal staircase covered in scratched vinyl. It had a communal lift, but Eleanor distrusted it.

'It never feels reliable, and anyway, it's good for me to climb stairs, even if it takes me for ever.'

Lindsay was waiting at the top, half in and half out of her open front door. She looked anxious.

'Don't look anxious,' Eleanor said breathlessly, pausing before the final half-flight. 'Just go in and don't watch me.'

Lindsay retreated a foot. She waited, listening to the effort of Eleanor's climb.

She called, 'I feel awful, making you do this.'

Eleanor reached the top, and stopped, holding the handrail.

'You didn't,' she said. 'I chose to. I'm glad to be here. I should climb stairs more often and give up eating.'

Toby appeared beside Lindsay. He was wearing his football shirt over his school uniform with grey-wool sleeves protruding from the royal-blue nylon. He went out on to the landing, without being urged, and grasped Eleanor's arm.

'When I have my breath back,' Eleanor said to him.

Toby waited.

He said, 'It wasn't their fault that they lost on Saturday.'

Eleanor extracted her arm from his grip and laid it instead across his shoulders.

'I would agree that it must be hard, psychologically, to play without your captain. I'm going to lean on you, so don't move too fast.'

Solemnly, Toby guided her past Lindsay and into the flat. He took her across the narrow hallway and into the sitting room, in the middle of which lay an upside-down plastic laundry basket.

Toby steered her round it.

'Don't kick that.'

'I won't,' Eleanor said, 'but why not?'

'It's Noah's contraption,' Toby said.

'What is it?'

'I dunno,' Toby said. 'It's just this thing he made. He goes spare if you touch it.'

'Where is Noah?'

'He's in bed,' Lindsay said. 'I think he's got a temperature. They made him lie down at school today, but I can't find anything that hurts him.'

Eleanor looked at her.

'Are you worried?'

'You know me,' Lindsay said. 'I'm always worried.'

Toby stood by a chair, indicating that Eleanor should sit down. She began to extricate herself from her coat.

'What's that?'

'Oh,' Lindsay said, glancing at the laundry basket, 'I don't know. It's just something Noah made one day, and he seems very attached to it. He doesn't play with it, he just wants it left there. He doesn't really play with things and he's never made anything before, so I don't like to touch it.'

Eleanor gave her coat to Toby. He held it bundled awkwardly in his arms, a sleeve hanging.

She said, 'May I see it?'

Lindsay lifted the laundry basket. They all looked at the board and the cups and the string and the plastic knights.

Toby said, 'I don't see why the knights are backwards.'

'No,' Eleanor said, 'I'm not sure I see anything.'

Lindsay replaced the laundry basket.

'Nor do I.' She looked at Toby. 'I promised Mum you'd be in bed by eight-thirty.'

'I'd rather be here.'

'Mum –'

'I'll lie down,' Toby said. 'I won't talk. I'll lie there and just breathe and stuff.'

Lindsay looked at Eleanor.

Eleanor said, 'I think that sounds reasonable, don't you?'

'Pyjamas, then,' Lindsay said. 'Teeth –'

Toby ambled towards the door, still clutching the coat.

At the doorway, he turned and said, 'Jackson says they haven't enough uninjured six-footers.'

Eleanor paused, lowering herself into the chair.

'And he may well be right.'

'He usually is.'

'Teeth –' Lindsay said.

When he had gone, Lindsay came back across the room to Eleanor.

'I'll get you another cushion –'

'No.'

'And there's a footstool –'

'No.'

'I hope that chair isn't too low.'

'Lindsay,' Eleanor said, 'it's perfect. I'm glad to be here. I'm glad to see you. And it's very nice of you to have me and very nice of you to have Toby.'

Lindsay perched on the arm of the sofa, opposite Eleanor.

'She was in a dress,' Lindsay said, 'with her hair up. He was taking her out to dinner.'

'Paula?'

'Yes.'

'They came –'

'She came. She was meeting him at the restaurant. She had a taxi waiting.'

'So she couldn't stay.'

'No. She looked wonderful.'

'I'm sure she did.'

Lindsay looked at the tiled fireplace and then at the picture above it – a Scottish landscape featuring a small loch and a heather-clad slope – and then she said, 'I hardly see her now.'

Eleanor moved a little in her chair, settling herself more comfortably. Lindsay, always thin, was looking very thin. Her dark hair was pulled back in part behind her head, and the rest sat on her shoulders, emphasising the bones in her face, her collarbone, the bones of her shoulders under her neat grey sweater.

'I'm afraid none of us do.'

'I want her to be happy –'

'We all want that.'

'But –' Lindsay said, and stopped.

Eleanor folded her hands in her lap.

She said gently, 'Why don't you make some coffee?'
Lindsay stood up.
'Noah wouldn't eat his supper.'
'No? Did he drink?'
'Oh yes,' Lindsay said. 'He drank.'
'Well then,' Eleanor said, 'why manufacture worry?'
Lindsay smiled at her. She stood up.
She said, 'I just needed someone to come in and make me feel normal.'
'I can see that,' Eleanor said. 'I can understand.'
Lindsay looked at the laundry basket.
'You don't have to understand everything about Noah,' Eleanor said. 'I don't expect he does, either.'

Later, much later, Paula telephoned. Toby, his football shirt firmly in place over his pyjamas, was asleep on the sofa under a duvet he had failed to notice was patterned with sprigs of girlish lavender. Eleanor and Lindsay had drunk a pot of coffee and half a bottle of New Zealand Sauvignon Blanc and eaten peanuts and shortbread.

'Hi there!' Lindsay said into the telephone, her voice full of enthusiasm.

Eleanor looked at Toby's sleeping form, at an outflung blue arm among the lavender sprigs.

'Oh,' Lindsay said, 'oh,' and then, her voice dimming a little, 'oh OK. Yes, it is a bit late, Eleanor's still here – yes, that's fine, that's fine. I'll keep him. OK. You'll call, will you? No, nothing special but I've got quite a lot of bits and pieces to do, you know how it – OK then. Have – yes, I'll tell him. Have fun.'

She clicked the phone off and put it down carefully on the coffee table.

'They haven't finished dinner.'
Eleanor looked at her watch.
'No.'

'What time is it?'

'Ten-past eleven.'

Lindsay looked away.

'Imagine. Candles, flowers, still eating at ten-past eleven –'

'I wouldn't imagine, if I were you.'

'The thing with me,' Lindsay said, 'is I wouldn't trust it, even if I had it. I'm like that. I'd be sitting there in my posh frock thinking, When will this go wrong?'

'My mother would have loved it. All she wanted was posh frocks and places to wear them to. What *would* she have made of me now?'

Lindsay turned her head back.

She said, encouraged by the wine, 'You're the real deal, Eleanor.'

'Well,' Eleanor said, 'thank you –'

'You are,' Lindsay said. 'You are. My mother – well, all you could do was be sorry for her. She couldn't cope, not with anything. I used to dread finding her going through wastebins or something, seeing her by mistake. I used to imagine that happening and get goosebumps. It's an awful thing to say, but I was so relieved when she went away.'

'My dear,' Eleanor said, 'I assumed she'd died –'

'No,' Lindsay said, 'no. She went to Canada. When Noah was a baby. Someone offered her a job. Last seen in Vancouver.' She reached up and took the clip out of her hair. 'When I was a kid, I was terrified of losing her, I was always in a panic about losing my family. Still am, about Jules. But when it came to my mother, I couldn't cope. She was too big a worry, even for me.'

Eleanor waited a moment, watching her, and then she said, 'Jules turned up the other night. At my front door.'

Lindsay shook her hair out.

She said, 'We'd had a row.'

'I know.'

'About Paula.'

'I know.'

Lindsay got up.

'I expect we'll have another. I expect I'll have a row with Paula herself, if this goes on.'

'This goes on?'

'This forgetting,' Lindsay said, 'this forgetting her friends.'

'She hasn't forgotten –'

'Well, what d'you call this? What d'you call never phoning except to ask me to do things for her, to look after Toby? What d'you call only needing me so she can talk about herself, never thinking about me, never asking a single question, never asking about Noah?'

'Is it as bad as that?'

Lindsay was pink with indignation, her narrow face glowing.

'Yes!' she almost shouted. 'No. Yes. Yes, sometimes it is.'

On the sofa, Toby stirred and rolled over.

Lindsay put her hand to her mouth.

'Look what I've done –'

'You should tell her,' Eleanor said. 'If you feel like that, you should tell her.'

'I can't, I couldn't –'

'It's friendship.'

'It'd look as if I begrudged her, as if I was jealous, as if I didn't want her to be happy –'

Slowly, on the sofa, Toby rose up from his duvet. His hair was tousled and his eyes were hardly focused. His gaze travelled blankly round the room, across Lindsay and Eleanor and the coffee pot and the wine glasses. He put an arm up, as if to shield his eyes from something alarmingly unfamiliar, and then, from behind it, he said in a voice of real apprehension, 'Where's Mum?'

CHAPTER TWELVE

Paula dressed with care. She'd lost weight recently – and effortlessly – and found that she could slide into twenty-eight-inch jeans. They were what the shop assistant had described as a snug fit, and she was wearing them with a ribbon-edged, tight little cardigan and the kind of boots she would have considered, only weeks ago, exclusively appropriate to bold girls under thirty.

Toby, leaning in the doorway of her bedroom, was watching her brush her hair.

'Where you going?'

'Nowhere,' Paula said.

'You look like you are –'

'No,' Paula said, 'you're the one going somewhere. Dad's coming for you in ten minutes. Had you forgotten?'

Toby kicked at the door frame.

'Don't say, "Does he have to," ' said Paula, smoothing her hair back into a ponytail, 'because he does, and so do you.'

'I wasn't going to.'

Paula wound the ponytail into a neat bun, and secured it with a pin. Then she added hoop earrings.

'You look different,' Toby said.

'Good.'

'Not normal.'

Paula took a breath.

'What's normal? Trackie bottoms and trainers?'

Toby looked at her feet.

'Not those.'

Paula glanced down.

'What's wrong with them?'

Toby didn't reply. He peeled himself away from the doorway, and disappeared.

Paula called after him, 'I'll take them off if you want!' but he didn't answer.

She turned round, and bent to smooth the duvet cover, conscious of the way heels as high as these pulled pleasurably at her hamstrings. She ran a hand over the left-hand pillow. Jackson's head had been there, Jackson's body had been under that duvet, Jackson's feet had been where she was now standing. She would have liked there to be more evidence of Jackson than mere recollections, but he seemed quietly resistant to the idea. He wouldn't leave so much as a toothbrush in the flat, instead arriving, for the nights he stayed over, with a clean shirt and a few admirably organised shaving things stowed in the back pocket of his laptop case. He wouldn't accept a key, he wouldn't agree to the dressing gown – kimono-style navy-blue linen – that Paula had sourced through one of her Asian suppliers. He didn't reject anything outright, he just calmly, pleasantly declined to be in receipt of anything more than Paula's company.

She would have loved him to have taken the dressing gown, and worn it, and left it hanging reassuringly behind her bedroom door in his absences. She would have loved him to have crowded her bathroom shelf with his toothpaste and razors and seductive masculine bottles and jars. She would have loved to have discovered his kicked-off shoes, a pulled-off sweater lying about the flat. But he didn't do that. Despite the strong atmosphere he generated when he was in the flat, and the resonant echo of himself that he left behind in it, he was physically as self-contained and lightly moving as a cat.

Looking at the bed now, it was very hard indeed to see where six foot of him had been only a few hours before.

Well, Paula thought, regarding herself in the long mirror set into her cupboard doors, I can't fuss about that, I can't complain. He is wonderful to me, wonderful to Toby and as a result Toby and I are both much happier and getting on much better. I mustn't be so conventional, I mustn't long for stupid girl-mag evidence of his interest. He's an unusual man and he behaves in unusual ways and mostly I can't fault him. Mostly.

She went out into the living-room space of the flat. Toby was standing looking at the front door.

'The bell went.'

'Is it Dad?'

Toby went over and peered at the tiny television screen on the intercom.

'Yes.'

'Let him in then.'

Toby picked up the intercom's receiver.

'Hi,' he said into it, without animation. He pressed the door connection and stood back. He was wearing, as usual, his Chelsea strip shirt.

Paula waited at a distance. She was conscious of standing differently, taller, better, corseted slightly by the new jeans. She looked at Toby's back with affection.

'You'll have a great time.'

Toby didn't speak. There were days when he looked almost adolescent, and days when he looked like a contemporary of Noah's. Today was a Noah day. She had induced him to wash his hair in the shower, the previous night, and he had slept on it before it had dried and there was a poignant tuft sticking up on one side, like a crooked cockade.

'Really,' Paula said, 'it'll be great. He really wants to see you.'

The doorbell rang. Toby went forward and opened the door. Paula rearranged herself very slightly, where she stood, aware that this time – no need to look far for the reason – she felt, after all these years, quite confident about seeing Gavin, quite certain that for once he was not going to be the one holding all the personal advantages. She raised her chin a fraction and felt a welcome sensation of control run smoothly down from her shoulders to her feet.

Gavin, in his usual uniform of weekend jeans and a corduroy jacket, bent to embrace Toby. It was habitually a moment of considerable awkwardness on both sides, but this time Gavin seemed to hold Toby, albeit briefly, with conviction. Then he straightened up. He seemed to stand up with particular erectness.

He glanced directly over Toby's head at Paula and his expression wasn't in the least defensive.

'You look well.'

She inclined her head a little.

'Thank you.'

'Very well,' Gavin said with emphasis.

Paula shifted a little on her heels.

'Where are you two going today?'

'Well,' Gavin said, 'anywhere Toby likes. In a minute, that is. In just a minute.' He looked down at Toby. 'Could you amuse yourself for five minutes, while I have a word with Mum?'

Paula put a hand out towards Toby. There was something about Gavin's manner today that was not only different, but also definitely not what she had been expecting.

'Can't he –'

'Five minutes,' Gavin said. He moved a few steps further into the flat. 'And then we'll go and find a widescreen television and all the football you want.'

Toby looked from one parent to the other.

Paula said, 'Just five minutes,' to him. He hesitated. Gavin went on looking at Paula. She said to Toby, 'Honestly. Five minutes. I'll call you.'

He looked away. Then he shuffled across the floor, avoiding the zebra rug, and very slowly climbed the ladder to his platform and vanished into the dimness.

'What's all this about?' Paula said.

Gavin indicated the kitchen, in an attempt to get out of Toby's hearing. Paula moved reluctantly ahead of him and leaned against the refrigerator door, her arms crossed.

'Well?'

Gavin positioned himself behind the breakfast bar. He leaned on it, on his knuckles, spreading his shoulders.

'What's going on?'

Paula uncrossed her arms and examined the cuticles of one hand.

'Nothing.'

'Really?'

'Nothing to do with you.'

'I agree, in a sense, that whoever you sleep with has nothing to do with me. But if the person you sleep with starts playing daddies with my son, then that is very much to do with me and I don't like it.'

Paula stopped looking at her cuticles and folded her arms again. She looked at the floor beyond her boot toes.

'Did Toby tell you?'

'No,' Gavin said, 'he did not. Though I might have guessed, with all this sudden passion for football. But it wasn't Toby. He has never said a word. A friend of mine saw them together at Stamford Bridge. Another friend saw you having dinner, still at the table at midnight. It's typical of you to think you can get away with anything. It's typical of you to try and have your cake and eat it. I don't mind you having this flat, but I'm damned if some other man is going to play happy families in it with my son.'

Paula held her breath. She badly wanted to sit down.

'He doesn't.'

'Are you telling me he doesn't spend the night here?'

'Well, he –'

'And takes Toby to school sometimes in a Mercedes SL?' Paula shouted, 'Why are you spying on me?'

Gavin gestured theatrically in the direction of Toby's bedroom.

'Shush.'

Paula said in a fierce whisper, 'I've never interfered with your family! How dare you try and run my life?'

Gavin stood straighter. He spread his hands out and balanced, consideringly, on his fingertips.

'I may not have been the perfect father –'

'Huh!'

'But Toby is getting older, Toby needs male input in a way he didn't, so much, when he was younger. I don't want that input to be from some tosser of yours in a Mercedes. I want it to be from me.' He paused, and then he said loftily, 'Fiona agrees.'

Paula's head whipped to one side. There had been times, years, when the mention of Gavin's wife Fiona had caused her a pain so exquisite she could remember it still.

'How dare you.'

'I could say the same to you.'

'I've been on my own,' Paula said, 'for years. I've been on my own and had to watch you devote ninety-nine per cent of your time to your wife and your other children. I've never asked for anything, I've never criticised the kind of father you were to Toby, though heaven knows I've had good reason. I've never had one-night stands, I've never subjected Toby to seeing me with anyone other than Jackson, I've never made it difficult for you to see your son. How you have the nerve, the effrontery, the sheer – sheer *shamelessness* to try and lay down the law now, I cannot imagine.' She took a step towards him. 'I'd like to kill you. I'd like to bloody *kill* you.'

Gavin didn't flinch. He regarded her impassively.

He said, 'We have to deal with what is, and not be influenced by the past. My sole concern is with the situation as it now is, and how that affects Toby.'

Paula had reached the breakfast bar. She was less than three feet from him. She gripped the edge.

'There's no dealing to be done. You deal with your pathetic male jealousies as best you can, but I'm making no changes to a situation that makes Toby and me both happy.'

'You always were a fantasist.'

Paula let go of the edge of the breakfast bar, leaned across it, and slapped Gavin stingingly across his left cheek. He let out a yelp, like a dog that's been trodden on.

'You bastard –' Paula said.

He took a step backwards.

'You may be older,' Gavin said, 'but your manners and maturity haven't improved with time.'

Toby said, from ten feet away, 'What happened?'

Paula spun round. From behind her, Gavin leaned forward and gripped her shoulders.

'Do not involve Toby.'

'I hit your sodding father,' Paula said.

'Paula!'

'Why?' Toby said.

'Because he was –'

'Paula!' Gavin shouted.

Toby looked pale and small.

'Don't be like this –'

Paula tried to extricate herself from Gavin's grasp.

'Oh, darling –'

'Don't move,' Gavin said. 'Don't *move*. You brought all this on yourself, behaving like a slut.'

Toby took a step back.

Paula held her arms out to him.

'Darling, please –'

'Don't worry,' Gavin said to Toby, his voice perfectly normal, his fingers digging deep into Paula's shoulders, 'don't worry. We're fine. We really are. We had a bit of an argument but it's over now. We'll go out now, Toby, you and me. Just you and me.'

'No,' Toby said.

Gavin abruptly let Paula go. He came round the breakfast bar and made for Toby.

'I'm really sorry we upset you. I really am. But we'll go and have a nice afternoon and put it all behind –'

'I'm not going out!' Toby shouted. 'Not with you!'

Paula slipped past Gavin and tried to put her arms round Toby.

'Darling, you don't have to go anywhere. You can stay with me.'

Toby didn't look at her. He stood rigidly in the circle of her embrace.

'No.'

'But –'

'I'm not going with him. I'm not staying with you.'

'But –'

'I'm going to Poppy's house,' Toby said.

'He didn't want to stay with me,' Paula said. 'He didn't want to go with Gavin. He didn't want to be alone with either of us.'

Karen was leaning back in her chair, the other side of her kitchen table from Paula. Toby was in the upstairs sitting room, lying on his stomach on the rug in front of the television and a match involving Bolton Wanderers. Poppy and Rosie were out at a birthday party, and he had not reacted at all when he learned this. Nor had he wanted a drink or a biscuit. He had simply bolted up to the sitting room and closed the door.

'OK,' Karen said, as if she was waiting for Paula to tell her considerably more.

'He said he just wanted to come here. He wouldn't say why. He wouldn't really speak to me. He sat in the car and looked sideways out of the window and not at me and didn't reply when I asked him anything.'

'What did you ask him?'

Paula pushed her tea mug about, in a zigzag.

'I asked him if he wanted to come here because you were a family.'

Karen stretched in her chair. She had been having an afternoon's domestic administration in a quiet house when Paula turned up, and part of her mind was still turning over a letter she was composing to the bank about adjustments it had made, without consultation, to her overdraft arrangements.

'No wonder he wouldn't reply,' Karen said. 'What a thing to ask him. Even if it's the case, he'd never have thought it through like that.'

'I got so worked up. Gavin made me so furious –'

'There's none so pompous and self-righteous as those in the wrong.'

Paula said, 'He manages to make me feel that I'm in the wrong.'

'Well, you're not.'

'He called me a slut.'

'That's rich,' Karen said.

'And a fantasist.'

'Paula,' Karen said, 'ignore him. Rise above him. Press the delete button on him –'

Paula leaned forward.

'But he upset Toby. He really upset Toby. And Toby hasn't been upset for ages, you know he hasn't. Not like he used to be. I was just beginning to feel better, I was just allowing myself a little breather, a little holiday, from feeling so guilty about Toby all the time, because of not having a father living with him, because of me working full-time.'

'Can I tell you something?' Karen said, interrupting.

Paula looked mildly affronted.

'Of course.'

Karen got up and transferred a teapot, shaped like a cottage, from the kitchen counter to the table.

'You don't have a prerogative on that guilt.'

Paula stared at the tabletop.

She waited while Karen refilled their mugs and then she said, 'You aren't bringing the girls up on your own.'

'No,' Karen said, 'but I am paying for them, virtually, on my own. I pay the mortage, I pay the insurance, I pay the utility bills, I pay for clothes, food and holidays.'

'I pay the insurance and the utility bills,' Paula said in a tone of childish defiance.

Karen appeared to take no notice. She returned to her seat, picked up her tea and leaned back in her chair again.

She said, 'There's a website I was looking at. It's about part-time work for full-time mothers. There's a new section on this site suggesting potential careers for full-time mothers, careers in publishing and sales and marketing, and journalism. Things like that. And it's all very bright and jolly and optimistic, and when you look at the nuts and bolts of it, there isn't a suggestion there that would gross over twenty thousand. How are we going to live like this, or even faintly like this, on twenty thousand?'

Paula said nothing.

'You haven't got Gavin,' Karen said. 'You don't, probably, even want Gavin now, but you have a gorgeous flat and an allowance for Toby.'

'Are you suggesting I'm only working as self-indulgence?'

'Certainly not. I'm just trying to put things in perspective. I'm just pointing out that Gavin being a priggish pain is hard to bear but you can't blame him for wanting some say in how you and Toby live, because he subsidises it.'

Paula got up abruptly and turned her back on Karen. She was facing one of Lucas's frescoed cupboards. Stuck in neat rows into the central panel of the cupboard door in front of her was a series of family photographs. Directly in front of her was a picture of Lucas sitting on the top bar of a five-barred gate, with a daughter astride the gate either side of him. They were all laughing.

'Was that taken on holiday?'

Karen craned round to see.

'Dorset.'

'He's a fantastic father.'

'Yes,' Karen said.

Paula turned round.

'Doesn't it feed your ego to work?'

'You sound like Blaise.'

'Well, doesn't it?'

'If you want to know,' Karen said, 'one of the reasons I married Lucas was that he wasn't going to compete with me, that he wasn't a conventional hunter-gatherer, that he wasn't going to feel diminished by my achievements. I think he'd be perfectly happy to leave London and live somewhere much cheaper, much more simply, as long as he could paint.'

Paula sat down again, slowly.

'Last night,' Karen said, 'there was an exhibition he wanted us all to go to. It was in a gallery whose owner quite likes how Lucas paints. So we all went, Lucas and me and the girls. And Blaise. I don't quite know why Blaise came, it's not her sort of art, but it was nice of her. I didn't ask her, she just said she would. And we all stood about, or in Poppy's case, ran about, and looked at the pictures and chatted up the owner and I wanted to like it all so much, and

believe in it, and feel involved in it. And I couldn't. I just
thought about all the things I'd got to do when I got home.'

Paula took a swallow of tea.

She said, 'Why are you telling me all this?'

'I don't know,' Karen said. 'Just letting off steam.'

'That's why I came round to see you –'

Karen stood up.

'Come on. Let's go and see if Toby's OK.'

'The match hadn't finished,' Toby said.

Paula leaned across to fasten his seat belt. He didn't
attempt it himself, but simply lay back and let her wrestle
with the clip.

'We couldn't stay –'

'Why couldn't we?' Toby said. 'Why couldn't we stay till
the match had finished?'

Paula considered saying, 'Well, Karen didn't want us,' and
rejected it after a small internal struggle in favour of, 'Karen
was busy.'

Toby, without looking at his mother, took the end of the
seat belt out of her hand, and fastened it.

'Couldn't you have done that in the first place?'

He ignored her.

He said, looking away from her still, 'Where are we
going?'

'To Lindsay's.'

'I don't want to go to Lindsay's.'

'You like going to Lindsay's.'

'I'm always going to Lindsay's. I went to Lindsay's last
night. I don't want to go again, I don't want to go to
Lindsay's.'

Paula buckled her own seat belt, and turned on the engine.

'We're going,' Paula said.

She put the car in gear, and her foot slipped from the
clutch. The car jerked forward. Her boots were too high to

drive in, and they had felt wrong in Karen's kitchen, as wrong as they had abruptly felt when shouting at Gavin. They were not, Paula reflected with a stab of something close to self-pity, the right kind of boots to feel needy in.

'Stupid,' Toby said from the back seat.

Paula put the car in neutral, and turned round.

'Don't speak to me like that.'

'Can't even *drive*,' Toby said.

Paula took a breath, then she turned the engine back on again, and with elaborate care put the car into first gear and released the handbrake. It struck her suddenly, and out of nowhere, that Jackson had neither phoned nor texted since he left that morning. It was quite common for him not to phone after they had been together, but there were times she found she could endure these silences better than others, and this afternoon was not one of them. She glanced in her rear-view mirror, and caught sight of Toby's averted face and felt a pang of guilt at thinking about Jackson with any intensity while Toby was still recovering from the scene with Gavin.

'We won't stay long,' Paula said. 'At Lindsay's, I mean. I just want to talk to her for five minutes. Then we'll go home. Or we'll go and find a pizza. Whatever you like.'

Toby was silent. She thought that the one person he might probably like to see was the same person that she too would very much like to see, but whom she could not, somehow, mention by name to Toby.

She said, 'I'm really sorry it's been such a horrible day.'

Toby went on gazing out of the window.

'Toby,' Paula said, 'I'm sorry. I –' She stopped and then she said, 'I shouldn't burden you with being sorry. None of this should touch you. I should be able to stop it touching you and I –'

'Just drive,' Toby said.

*   *   *

There was no parking space near Lindsay's flat and they had to leave the car two streets away. Before they left it, Paula found a pair of old trainers in the car and put them on instead of her boots. Then she took Toby's inert but unresisting hand and led him along the pavements to Lindsay's block of flats.

They toiled slowly up the scarred staircase together, Toby pulling slightly at her hand.

At the top, Paula paused a little outside Lindsay's front door.

'Just five minutes,' she said. 'Promise.'

She pressed the bell, gripping Toby's hand, arranging her expression to indicate that seeing Lindsay was, at that moment, of consummate importance. There was silence. No one came. Paula pressed the bell again, then she knocked. Still silence.

'They're out,' Toby said.

'They can't be —'

'They were going out. They were seeing Jules, or something.'

'Toby?'

Toby stared at the door.

'Toby, why didn't you say something? Why didn't you tell me?'

Toby sighed.

'You didn't ask.'

'Did I have to ask?'

'I forgot,' Toby said.

Paula let go of his hand and put her own hands over her face.

Then she took them away again and said, in a tone of deliberate warmth, 'Yes. Of course you did.'

Toby wandered away and kicked at the chipped metal banister.

'Can we go?'

'Yes. Yes, of course. Where would you like to go?'

'Home.'

'Are you sure?'

'I want to play with my theatre.'

Paula moved to put her arm round him.

'Then you shall.'

Toby shrugged her off. He squirmed past her and started down the stairs at speed.

As he went, he said, without particular rancour, 'You wear me out.'

Lindsay and Jules and Noah had had an unsatisfactory late lunch in a Lebanese place off the Portobello Road. Lindsay had hoped that the exoticism of the menu would beguile Jules into eating a meal of vegetables, but Jules, pale and picky, merely made a mess of a plateful of aubergine purée and tabbouleh and spiced chick peas, and said she wasn't hungry. Noah allowed Lindsay to feed him various pastes on pieces of unleavened bread, as if he was a baby, and drank orange juice noisily through a straw. Lindsay, eating neatly and sensibly, and trying to make conversation and build bridges, had failed. She had paid the bill – waving away Jules' unenthusiastically proffered ten-pound note – with resignation, and acknowledged silently to herself that this was not an occasion to try and kiss Jules goodbye.

Jules had crouched down to kiss Noah.

'OK, big guy?'

He nodded.

She straightened up and said, 'See you later, Lin,' and went off down the street towards the club. The manager, she had told Lindsay, was allowing her to come in in the afternoons, to get used to the new sound system.

'It's more sensitive to slip-cueing. I have to practise.'

Lindsay had nodded.

'You have to start a record right on the beat.'

'OK,' Lindsay said. Jules had dark circles under her eyes and her skin was terrible. 'I don't like the look of you.'

'I never have,' Jules said. 'Why else d'you think I get off my face?'

Lindsay and Noah took the bus home. They sat on the top deck, as Noah liked to do, and he watched the trees and the clouds while she watched the street. It was one of those Saturdays, she thought, one of those winter Saturday afternoons, when if it wasn't for Noah's presence beside her in his school parka she would have felt that she had become quite invisible, no more than a breath in the air around her.

When they got off the bus in the Fulham Road and began to make their way home, Noah automatically put his hand in hers. It was warm and slightly sticky. She looked down at him, at his smooth dark head and small unreadable face.

'That was nice, seeing Jules, wasn't it?'

Noah glanced up.

'Where's her house?'

'Whose house? Jules' house?'

'Yes.'

'Oh dear,' Lindsay said, 'oh dear. I'm afraid she hasn't got one.'

Noah thought about this.

He said, recalling the bus journey, 'You could sleep in a tree.'

'If you were a bird. Jules isn't a bird, though. Is she?'

They turned the corner into their street. Lindsay stopped abruptly, jerking Noah to a halt. At the far end of the street, just crossing to disappear out of sight to the left, were the unmistakable figures of Paula and Toby. Lindsay didn't move. Neither, obediently, did Noah. They stood there together, hand in hand, Lindsay slightly tensed, until Paula and Toby had vanished out of sight. Then Lindsay's hold on Noah's hand relaxed slightly.

'OK,' she said to him, 'coast clear. Shall we go home?'

CHAPTER THIRTEEN

'Who let you in?' Jules demanded.

Jackson leaned against the wall on the edge of the sound booth.

'The guy on the door. The Indian guy.'

'What did you give him?'

'Enough,' Jackson said.

Jules looked down at the decks in front of her.

'Yeah, yeah. Why do you try to play the hard man?'

Jackson didn't reply. He watched while Jules put headphones on. Then she took them off again.

'What are you doing here?'

Jackson swivelled slightly so that his shoulders were against the wall and he was looking out across the empty, dusty dance floor.

'Interested.'

'In the club?'

'Partly.'

Jules put the headphones on again.

'Don't bother coming on to me.'

Jackson didn't move.

'Paula said to me,' Jules said, 'don't jump my boyfriend. I said are you *joking*?'

Jackson went on staring across the dance floor.

'Or is it the music?' Jules said with heavy sarcasm. 'Shall I teach you about kick drums and snares and hi-hats and reversed cymbal crashes?'

Jackson slowly eased himself upright. He surveyed the space around him, the black walls with their white graphics – 'You cool Brigade', 'Stereototal' – the narrow lines of scarlet strip-lighting in the ceiling, the long bar menu hung prominently above the locked shelves of bottles, 'Caipirinha, Raspberry Breezer £6.50'.

'There's a magnum of Laurent Perrier Rosé there,' he said. 'A hundred and twenty-five quid. Who'll buy that?'

'Plenty,' Jules said. She indicated a dais in one corner, furnished with black-leather sofas. 'The people in the Reserved section.'

Jackson turned to look at her. She was wearing a chiffon minidress over jeans, and chequerboard plimsolls, and big, lilac-tinted glasses.

He pointed to the mixing decks.

'All four-four beat?'

Jules didn't look back.

She said, 'Just like Mozart.'

'And your job is to keep them dancing?'

'If I break a record's phrases,' Jules said, 'if I don't mix smoothly, I'll throw the dancers off.'

'And the management don't like that.'

Jules ignored him.

She said, 'I'm good at cutting. I can drop mix with the best of the garage boys.'

'I'll buy you a coffee,' Jackson said.

Jules pushed one earphone behind her ear.

She said again, 'What are you doing here?'

'Learning.'

'About what?'

Jackson put his hands in his trouser pockets. He jangled his change.

'Women,' he said. 'About all you women.'

Jules chose hot chocolate and a packet of barbecue-flavoured crisps. Jackson had a double espresso. Away from the club, Jules felt slightly less empowered. There was something about the sound booth and the banks of controls that gave her the feeling she imagined guys got when astride a motorbike. Without the sound booth, without the protection of her knowledge and skills, she was glad of the size of her hot-chocolate mug. She crouched behind it, her hands wrapped round it.

'Usually,' she said, 'I only drink tea.'

'OK.'

'I don't like alcohol. Only vodka.'

'Vodka,' Jackson said, 'is alcohol. Forty per cent proof alcohol.'

'I know.'

'Drink your chocolate.'

Jules blew into the thick swirled foam on the top of it.

'When I'm ready.'

Jackson cut the end off a slim paper tube of brown sugar, and slid the contents into his cup.

'Maybe I could help you,' he said.

Jules scowled into her mug.

'I don't need help.'

'Maybe I could –'

'I live my life,' Jules said, 'like I want to live it. I don't want you organising me. If I want it organised, I'll do it. My sister's bad enough. I don't want you butting in.'

Jackson stirred his coffee. Then he put the spoon in the saucer without, Jules noticed, licking it on the way as she would have done. She put her own spoon into her mug and creamed off a cushion of froth.

'I don't care how you live,' Jackson said. 'It doesn't interest me.'

Jules grunted. She took another spoonful of milky foam.

'But I'm interested in the club scene. In club music.'

'You are,' Jules said, 'way, way, *way* too old.'

Jackson took a sip of coffee.

'Not like that. As an investor. I'm an entrepreneur. If you know what that means.'

Jules snorted slightly.

She said, 'Businessman,' in a tone of contempt.

'More than that.'

Jules shrugged. She broke open her packet of crisps.

'It's someone like me,' Jackson said, 'who takes a commercial chance, often at personal financial risk. It's someone who likes owning and managing things. It's someone who likes a challenge.'

Jules crunched a mouthful of crisps.

'So?'

'Suppose I decided I'd like a stake in the club business. Suppose I decided to invest in something like Soundproof.'

'Nobody's stopping you.'

'So you're not interested. You're not interested in my possibly giving you an opportunity no one else will give you?'

Jules laid three crisps carefully on top of one another and put them in her mouth.

Round them, she said indistinctly, 'Of course I'm interested. But I think you're dodgy.'

'Dodgy?'

'Yeah.'

'In what way, dodgy?'

'We don't,' Jules said in elaborate Mockney, 'know nuffing about you.'

He looked directly at her.

'What's not to know?'

Jules finished her mouthful.

'You tell me.'

'I have a good business, no wife, no children I'm aware of, all my own teeth and no debts. I'm looking for another business. Because of Paula, I've met you, and your world interests me. It interests me as a businessman, an entrepreneur, because it's a huge market, and it's a young market. What's dodgy about that?'

Jules drank her chocolate.

Then she put her mug down and said, 'Long speech.'

'I mean it.'

'OK.'

'I'm coming to hear you. I'm coming to watch you in action.'

'I don't,' Jules said, 'play Saturdays.'

'If you worked for me, you could do Saturdays. Fridays *and* Saturdays.'

Jules looked away.

She said, 'I've got my own websites. On MySpace. On Facebook.'

'I know,' he said. 'I looked you up.'

'You what?'

'I looked you up.'

'You spying on me or something?'

'No,' he said. 'Of course not.'

She pushed her mug away.

'Look,' she said, 'I'm just your girlfriend's best friend's kid sister. Leave it at that. OK?'

'Why?'

'Why what?'

'Why,' Jackson said, 'leave it at who you're related to? Why not at least look at the chance I'm offering you?'

Jules hesitated.

'Maybe –'

'Good girl.'

She looked down at the tabletop. She wanted suddenly to be back in the dusty, empty, afternoon darkness of the club, listening and testing and altering the pitches until what she was hearing was, instinctively, what she knew she'd been aiming to hear. In her mind, she saw herself back in the sound booth, moving that pitch control by hair's breadths until it was fine-tuned to absolute perfection. 'Congratulations,' a boy had written on a note to her the other day. 'Pitch perfect. Let me touch your bum.'

She screwed up the crisp packet and pushed it into the mug.

'I'll think about it,' she said. 'But I still think you're dodgy.'

Lucas, balanced on his bicycle in the dark street, watched Eleanor's lit sitting-room window. She had pulled the curtains across, but only approximately, so that there was a space in the centre through which he could see her pottering about, moving books and papers, putting her spectacles on and then taking them off and letting them hang on their scarlet loop, taking mouthfuls of something from a big china mug. He considered going across the street and knocking on her door, and asking if, while he was there, he could do something useful for her as he sometimes did, like changing blown light bulbs or firming up loose hinges and handles. But if he did that he would then have to explain why he was there in the first place, and he found that he didn't really want to explain anything and nor did he want to reveal that he was waiting for Blaise to come home.

It was all an impulse, after all. Karen had come home, as usual, in her tracksuit, with her big work bag, and he had, also as usual, presented her with two children who had been, at least temporarily, fed, and who had, also at least, made a start on their homework (spelling, times tables, reading practice from a book so badly illustrated, to Lucas's eye, that he could hardly bear to see it in Rosie's hands), and then he had said he might just have a few hours in the studio, and

Karen, opening the domestic business mail he never could face, had said OK distractedly and not presented even her cheek for a kiss. So he'd kissed his daughters and told them he wouldn't be long, and put on the duffel coat he'd had since he was a student – so cool and vintage now – and the long black muffler Karen had given him for Christmas last year, and unlocked his cycle from the basement railings, and set off for the studio and Mr Carpenter. And it was only when he was crossing the Munster Road that Blaise came into his head – Blaise in her dark business suit standing so pleasantly and supportively in the crowd at the private view the week before – and he had felt an impulse, an impulse as warm and gratifying as standing under a sudden hot shower, to go and thank her for coming with them and, by doing so, making it possible for Karen to come too without making any kind of deal, or point, about it. He wanted to thank her in a way as straightforward as her presence the other night had been, and then he wanted to cycle off into the night and spend a few hours in the studio priming canvases and rolling the odd spliff, and thinking. Just thinking.

He did not intend, balanced there on his bike with his chin in his muffler, to think about Karen. Or Karen and himself. Or Karen and himself and the children. He had decided that after their last unsatisfactory conversation of any depth. He had decided that nothing was to be gained by weighing in and confronting Karen in her present mood. It would be better to wait. It would be counterproductive in every way to grasp nettles – even if he wasn't completely sure what those nettles were, just at present – and raise the temperature, and cause them both to flounder about in a swamp of ill-defined anger and resentment. No, Lucas thought, with his knowledge of Karen – fifteen years now, at very close quarters – it was better to roll all his thoughts about her, about them, into some kind of large mental ball, and trundle it off into the dark and accommodating spaces at the edges of his mind. It was better, in every way, to concentrate all his creative energies on his work, on gradually allowing the ideas that had been gathering force in his head for many long months to evolve, at their own organic pace, into something that he could – would – translate on to canvas.

He looked across the street again. Eleanor seemed to have settled into her chair under a reading lamp. Her face and shoulders were no longer visible, but the space left between the curtains showed an interesting slice of her hands and book, both brightly lit against a shadowy background. Then a briskly walking dark figure crossed the illuminated slice and halted in front of a door two houses away. Lucas sat upright on the saddle of his bicycle. Blaise rummaged in a shoulder bag for her keys, found them, inserted them into her front door and let herself and her bag and briefcase into the house. Lucas waited, to watch the lights come on. He would give her five minutes and then he would ring her mobile and say he was just passing. 'Not stopping,' he'd say. 'Won't interrupt. Just wanted to thank you for coming, the other night.'

'Would you like a drink?' Blaise said.

Her kitchen was warm and unused. It was decorated in the same colours as her restrained clothes, and all the equipment – coffee maker, blender, toaster – stood on the empty granite counter tops like shining modern sculptures. There was only one splash of colour, a framed Mondrian poster in red and green and yellow. Lucas admired Mondrian but was of the opinion that his work was best suited to impersonal public spaces. Glancing round Blaise's kitchen, brightly lit by a galaxy of little halogen lamps recessed into the ceiling, he reflected that, if this kitchen wasn't exactly a public space, it was certainly impersonal.

'No, thank you. I really am just here for seconds –'

Blaise opened the tall door of her brushed-steel fridge. The interior was virtually empty except for a single white carton of something, a bottle of champagne and another, with a pristine and medical-looking label, that appeared to hold contact-lens solution. Blaise took a half-empty bottle of white wine and a full one of carbonated Italian mineral water out of the door of the fridge, and closed it behind her with her shoulder.

'Sure? I'm going to make a spritzer.'

'Quite sure. Thank you. I'm on my way to the studio.'

Blaise opened a cupboard and took out a large and shining wine glass.

'Is it impertinent to ask if you are painting anything?'

'No it isn't and no I'm not. But I'm going to. Every day, I know more clearly what I'm going to paint.'

Blaise poured a modest measure of white wine into the glass.

'Not being creative, I can't imagine that process.'

Lucas watched her adding water to the wine.

He said, 'Did you like the other night?'

'I liked the occasion,' Blaise said. 'I didn't, to be honest, like the paintings much. They were so angry.'

Lucas unwound his muffler and let it hang to its full length round his neck.

He said, 'It was so nice of you to come.'

Blaise looked down at her wine glass.

'I wanted to.'

'That was nice, too.' He pushed the edges of his coat aside, and put his hands in the pockets of his jeans. 'That's why I came. I wanted to say thank you in person. For coming, for making it possible for –'

Blaise put up a hand, as if to ward him off.

'For Karen to come,' Lucas said.

Blaise picked up her glass and held it up.

'Sure you won't?'

'Sure.'

'I'm very fond of your family. All of you.'

'I know. It's lovely.'

'I don't really have a family. Everyone is dead, or somewhere else. I probably idealise family a bit.'

'And yet –'

Blaise took a sip of her drink and put the glass down again on the table.

'And yet I haven't made one of my own?'

'Yes.'

'My mother,' Blaise said, 'jettisoned her career to raise children. Being her only daughter, I became the resolution of her frustration. She told me I could achieve anything, that I would never need to marry for money, that I was going to have confidence, and a career.'

Lucas took his hands out of his pockets and folded his arms.

'I find such talk very restful.'

'Do you?'

'Of course. You had the focus, and you followed it. You are – you are –' He looked round. 'You have the clean lines of this kitchen.'

Blaise laughed.

Lucas said again, 'It's really restful. Reposeful. There's a freedom from stress about you –'

'Oh no.'

'No?'

'It's just a different preoccupation with me. I may not have to juggle like Karen, but I'm terrified of standing still. I want to push forward all the time and that drives . . .' She stopped and then she said in a different tone, 'I'm very grateful to you all as a family, you know. I mean, I *value* being involved in your family.'

Lucas waited a moment, looking at her, and then he said, 'We value you, too.'

Blaise picked up her glass again.

'I'm going to change out of my uniform, as Karen calls it.

She's right, of course. I couldn't possibly take a meeting in my pyjamas.'

'Nobody could.'

'I hope this evening goes well. And that the cat is good company.'

Lucas moved round the table until he was standing in front of her. He put his hands on her upper arms.

'You're a good friend,' he said, and bent and kissed her, briefly but firmly on the mouth.

The studio was cold. Mr Carpenter had provided two ancient electric fires that spat and crackled alarmingly, but these plainly could not be left on in Lucas's absence, and the only radiator, crouched under the eaves, had no chance of heating a room of this size and height. Lucas pulled the fires out to the length of their frayed cords, and switched both on to full heat. Then he filled his electric kettle – another cast-off from Mr Carpenter, its element caked in lime – and plugged that in too, and arranged himself on the floor between the fires while he waited for it to boil.

Fred the cat had come up the stairs with him. Fred was not a sleek cat, but an old and lumpy one with a big loose coat that appeared to be several sizes too big for him. He padded softly and heavily about the room for a while, investigating things and reminding himself of other things, and then he halted in front of the tin plate the girls had brought for his use, and miaowed imperiously.

Lucas got to his feet. Fred, not moving, stared straight at him and miaowed again.

'All right,' Lucas said, 'all right.'

He opened the cupboard under the stained and chipped Belfast sink. Rosie had made a symmetrical pile of tins of sardines.

Lucas took one out.

'This is what you're after?'

Fred said nothing. He transferred his stare from Lucas to the sardines.

'You're too fat anyway,' Lucas said.

Fred lowered himself on to his cushiony haunches and licked his lips. Lucas peeled off the key to the sardine tin and slowly rolled back the lid. A smell of fish and oil leapt out, so strong it was almost palpable. Lucas bent and tipped the contents of the tin on to Fred's plate. Fred doubled his front paws up under the folds of his chest, and lowered himself to eat, purring thunderously. Lucas licked his fingers and then turned on the tap to wash his hands vigorously. Rosie had left him a tiny cake of pink soap, shaped like a flower. Sometimes the thought of Rosie brought a lump to his throat.

He dried his hands on a piece of rag torn from one of the old shirts he had brought round for the purpose. Then he found a mug, and the jars of instant milk and coffee he had assembled, and spooned the powders – so depressing, these practical, characterless powders – into it and was about to retrieve the kettle from where it was hissing and spluttering on the floor when the doorbell rang.

He looked at his watch. Ten-past eight. The girls would be in bed now, possibly even being read to by Karen. Blaise would be in her leisure clothes, being leisured, in her sitting room. There was no one else who knew where the studio was, no one who would think of looking for him there. The bell rang again. Lucas picked up the telephone intercom that hung on a battered plastic holder by the door and found that, as usual, the line was dead.

Sighing, he opened the studio door and started down the stairs. Mr Carpenter had replaced the broken light bulb halfway down with a blue one, which cast a gaunt and ghastly light on the landing. Lucas went on down to the narrow hall with its floor of brown-and-yellow intarsia tiles, and opened the front door. A slight figure stood outside, apparently a girl, dressed in a kind of shroud of purple knitting and a denim cap.

'Hi there,' Jules said.

Lucas peered under the peak of the cap.

'Jules?'

'Yeah.'

'Jules, what on earth are you doing here?'

'Can I come in?'

'No,' Lucas said. 'Well, yes. How on earth did you –'

Jules slid past him into the hall. She took off the denim cap and held it in her striped mittened hands. She was, he noticed, wearing a small green rucksack with 'The North Face' woven into its triangular label.

'Karen told me,' Jules said. 'Karen said you wouldn't mind.'

'Wouldn't mind what?'

'Wouldn't mind if I came round.' She glanced about her, at the dimness and the bleakness and the brown-grained doors. 'Cool place.'

Lucas closed the front door.

'You'd better come up.'

He led the way back upstairs, through the eerie bath of blue light, and into the lit and now lukewarm studio. Jules shrugged off her rucksack and dropped it, with her cap, on the floor.

'Wow,' she said, 'wicked. How wicked is this?'

'It's a studio,' Lucas said. 'It's where I come to think and work and paint.'

'Sure.'

'I don't want to be unwelcoming, but it's not really for company.'

Jules spotted Fred and made her way towards him, crouching down and putting her hand on his deep, warm fur back.

'It's just for tonight,' she said.

'What is?'

Jules didn't look back at him.

'Karen said you wouldn't mind if I stayed here just tonight.'

Lucas came to stand close to Jules.

'Would you get up?'

She stood up slowly and, even more slowly, looked up at him.

'What is going on?' Lucas said.

'I've got nowhere to stay tonight,' Jules said.

'You have a sister –'

Jules shrugged.

'What about Lindsay?' Lucas said.

'I can't,' Jules said. 'Not just now. I don't want to ask Eleanor. I can't ask Blaise. Paula's busy. Karen said – well, Karen said you wouldn't mind –' She looked round her. 'Here.'

'I do mind,' Lucas said.

Jules waited.

Lucas said, 'What's going on? Has something happened to you?'

Jules shook her head.

'No more than usual.'

'What does that mean?'

'I can't,' Jules said, 'go where I usually go. Not tonight.'

'Why not?'

'Just can't,' Jules said.

'And if I say no?'

Jules glanced at the space around her, at the divan bed in the corner.

'Why would you?'

'Because I don't want you here. I don't want anyone here. Because if I let you stay, you'll exploit me.'

Jules let a beat fall and then she said, 'You're not working.'

'It would be a waste of breath,' Lucas said, 'to try and

explain to you the nature and manifestation of the work of painting.'

Jules stepped back.

She said, 'I won't exploit you. Let me stay tonight, and I'll go. Promise I will.'

Lucas lowered himself into one of the canvas garden chairs he had acquired at a local Homebase.

'When you saw Karen,' he said, 'what was she doing?'

'Paperwork.'

'In the kitchen?'

'Yes.'

'What did you say to her?'

'I said could I stay and she said no, she didn't want any more interruptions, and then she was why don't you try Lucas, he isn't doing any –' Jules stopped, and then she said, 'And she asked me if Jackson had been to the club again and I said yeah.'

'Jackson?'

'Yeah.'

'Why did Karen ask you about Jackson?'

'Everybody,' Jules said, 'asks about Jackson. He's thinking of buying a club and he says I can DJ in it.'

'Don't.'

'Why not?'

'Just don't.'

'D'you think he's dodgy?'

'No,' Lucas said, 'no. Not exactly. I just think he's an unsettling influence.'

'Can I stay?'

Lucas sighed.

'I suppose so. Just tonight.'

Jules folded herself up on to the floor.

'Can I watch you?'

'No.'

'Aren't you doing anything?'

'Now you're here, no.'

'What'll you do then?'

Lucas got to his feet.

'Leave.'

'OK then,' Jules said. 'Can I have a key?'

'Certainly not.' He looked down at her. 'There's a kettle and coffee and several tins of sardines.'

'Hate sardines.'

Lucas crossed the room and picked his coat and scarf off the divan. He looked back at Jules, still sitting on the floor in her purple knitting.

He said, taking pity, 'I think there are some biscuits too, somewhere.'

She turned her head.

'I'm not hungry. It's nice here.'

Lucas put his coat on.

'I'll be back in the morning. Lavatory next floor down.'

'I like this cat.'

Lucas put his hand on the door.

'Don't touch anything.'

She waved an arm.

'Nothing to touch.'

'Night, Jules.'

'Night,' she said.

He looked back at her, at the fire and the cat and his painting table and the easel. It was strangely hard to leave it.

'Thanks,' Jules said.

Outside the front door, Lucas unlocked his cycle from the drainpipe to which he habitually chained it. The thoughts of Karen, those thoughts that he had earlier rolled away to the edges of his mind, had, in the last half-hour, unrolled themselves, and spread themselves out across the very centre of his preoccupations. They were not, however, coherent thoughts, but instead random impulses of anger and incomprehension and hurt. Whatever lay behind Jules' appearance at his door, whatever chaos or confusion she was dealing with or fleeing from, hardly interested him beyond a common humanitarian instinct to help. But what had impelled Karen to offload Jules on to him was quite another matter, and he could feel turbulent energies rising in him as he considered it.

He wheeled the cycle out into the road. The girls, especially Rosie, were persistently anxious that he never fail to wear his cycling helmet. But they were not here now to upset, and to try and cram a helmet on top of the cauldron of his present feelings was too much to ask of even the most conscientious of fathers. He swung himself, bareheaded, into the saddle. He was going to ride home like the wind, and when he got there he was going to ask – no, *demand* – to know exactly what the hell Karen thought she was playing at.

CHAPTER FOURTEEN

When Eleanor fell, it seemed to her that it was happening in slow motion. One moment she was unevenly but, it felt, quite steadily crossing her sitting-room floor, and then her foot caught in something – an inexplicably rural image of a bramble across a dark woodland path flashed across her brain – and, with the silent slowness of a piece of dropped paper coming to earth, she fell down between her accustomed chair and the table behind it, and struck her head at the left temple, sharply on a table leg.

For some moments she lay still, waiting for her mind to catch up with her fallen body. She looked, with a sort of detached interest, at the sitting room viewed along the carpet (strangely littered with shreds and bits of this and that) through the table legs. And then slowly it came to her that she was on the carpet because she had fallen there, and that there was some unexpected and uncomfortable pressure at one side of her forehead, and that, although not exactly shocked or frightened, she felt distinctly disconcerted to find herself there.

Gingerly, she tested her arms and legs to see if they would move. They would, if only slightly, and one hip was not just painful but felt as if it could not at all be relied upon. The sensation in her head was most peculiar. She put up an unsteady hand and touched her forehead. It was warm and wet. She brought her hand down to the level of her eyes and found it bloody. When she raised her head, with difficulty, and looked down at the patch of carpet on which it had rested, the carpet was bloody too.

'Damn,' Eleanor said out loud. '*Damn*. I have fallen and cut my head and hurt my bad hip. I have done what people who live alone should categorically *not* do, I have tripped and fallen over.'

She put a hand out and grasped the nearest table leg, and slowly pulled herself upright. The blood from her forehead redirected itself and began to run quietly down beside her eye. Her hip, on moving, was abruptly so sharply painful that it brought tears to her eyes, mingling with the blood. With infinite, painstaking, teeth-clenched slowness, Eleanor reversed out of the chasm between furniture into which she had fallen and dragged herself, half crawling, across the sitting room and into the hall where the telephone sat on the base to which, thankfully, she had for once remembered to return it.

Lindsay brought artificial chrysanthemums. Only after she had bought them – thinking yellow was cheerful and spring-like in winter – did she remember Eleanor telling her once about their association, in Chinese culture, with death. She laid them, diffidently, on Eleanor's hospital bed.

'I shouldn't think you'd want these – but hospitals won't allow fresh ones.'

Eleanor, half lying against the angled metal headboard of her bed, said, 'Oh I do.'

Lindsay put her hand in her coat pocket and took out a matchbox. She held it out.

'And this is from Noah. He made it.'

'What is it?'

'I don't know. He wouldn't let me see.'

Eleanor slid the matchbox open. Inside was a button and a

cotton-wool ball and a small plastic snake, patterned in brown and yellow. Eleanor took the snake out and looked at it. It was crudely made and coloured, but it had emerald-green eyes and a definite forked tongue.

'It's very kind of him. Do you think it's symbolic?'

Lindsay sat down in the vinyl-covered chair next to Eleanor's bed.

'I don't know. He spent ages choosing the button. He tipped all my odd buttons out on the floor.'

Eleanor put the snake back and picked out the button. It was made of darkish metal, vaguely military in appearance.

'Handsome.'

'I had it on a jacket once, when – well, before.'

'That's a good present,' Eleanor said. She laid the button on the cotton-wool ball, and slid the box shut again. 'And thank you for the flowers.'

Lindsay looked at her.

'We were all so worried when we heard. I couldn't believe it, I couldn't believe you'd got to the phone –'

Eleanor waved a hand. She was wearing a serviceable blue nightgown with a collar and long sleeves, the kind of night-gown, Lindsay thought, that you ordered from mail-order companies in the North of England who advertised in the backs of Sunday supplements. Mail-order companies who still made long johns, and vests with sleeves, and flannelette sheets.

'The only surprising thing,' Eleanor said, 'was that it hadn't happened before. I've lived with a gammy hip and knee, and rucked carpets and trailing cables, for as long as I can remember, and why, I wonder, didn't I fall over before?'

'You should have rung me,' Lindsay said. 'You should have rung. I'd have been round in a flash –'

'So, surprisingly, was an ambulance,' Eleanor said. She lifted the bunch of chrysanthemums off the bedspread and laid it on her bedside locker. 'It took me for ever to get to the

215

telephone, but once I'd rung, I only had to wait twenty minutes.' She raised a hand and touched the big white dressing on her head. 'Quite a bloody twenty minutes, I have to say. Rather a trail of gore, I must have left . . .'

Lindsay leant forward.

'I'll clean that up!'

'My dear –'

'I'd like to,' Lindsay said, 'I'd like to do something. I feel so bad I didn't know – I feel awful I didn't come straight round.'

Eleanor patted her nearest hand.

'I've been here under twenty-four hours.'

'But if Blaise hadn't noticed. I mean, if she hadn't seen that there were no lights on –'

'But she did. And here you are.'

Lindsay blotted her eyes briefly with the backs of her hands.

'Sorry. I go all to bits when something happens to someone I –'

'I'm fine,' Eleanor said. 'I'm here for a few days for observation, but nothing's broken. Nothing's even cracked. I just shook my heavy old self up a bit. There now. That's *all*.'

Lindsay sniffed. She glanced down the ward at the double row of beds, almost all occupied by women much older than Eleanor.

'You shouldn't be in here.'

'Why not?'

'Well, look at them.'

Eleanor turned her head.

'I'm just grateful there are no men.'

Lindsay said, 'It's depressing.'

'Well,' Eleanor said, 'it isn't very jolly, but then it's a hospital. They were grim when I was growing up, and then they got better while I was working, and now they are grim again. I do wonder why. I saw my old job – well, the new version of my old job – advertised the other day with a salary of a hundred and twenty thousand pounds.'

'What did the doctors say?' Lindsay said.

'About me?'

'Yes.'

'They said rest and then go home and rest some more. Just what I expected them to say.'

Lindsay put her hand on Eleanor's brushed-cotton sleeve.

'I'll come and look after you.'

'No, you won't.'

'Yes, I –'

'Lindsay,' Eleanor said, shaking off her hand, 'you have a child and a job and a life. I won't allow it.'

'But I want –'

'Tell me about work,' Eleanor said. 'I don't want to talk about me. Tell me what's going on.'

Lindsay looked away. She swallowed on something.

'Well?'

Lindsay looked back.

'Well, there's a new boss –'

'At your building society?'

'Yes.'

'And?'

'I don't really know him,' Lindsay said, 'but he seems better than the old one. Younger, anyway.' She paused and then she said, 'Better-looking.'

'With a family?'

'I don't know.'

'If he has a family,' Eleanor said, 'he is likely to be more sympathetic to employees who have families.'

Lindsay plucked at the folds of Eleanor's blue-and-white hospital bedcover.

'He was really nice about my coming to see you. He looked as if he knew I was worried.'

'What,' Eleanor said, with affectionate exasperation, 'are we going to do about you?'

Lindsay gave Eleanor a quick smile.

'Just try not to worry about me.'

Karen had left Workwell's monthly spreadsheets printed out for Blaise to see. She might work in a tracksuit, Blaise thought, but nobody could fault Karen for meticulous presentation of anything to do with work; those beautifully laid-out sheets of figures and statistics, in pristine, clear-plastic envelopes and folders. Karen had left the information out along Blaise's desk with the precision of a table laid for a banquet at Windsor Castle.

Nursing a large cardboard cup of coffee, Blaise sat down in front of Karen's efforts. It was impressive. Turnover was on target, interest-rate rises had been accommodated and the projection for the year ahead was the best since they had started the company. Blaise put her coffee down and put both hands flat either side of the projection file. If they pulled that off, if they managed to increase the business by the projected percentage in the next twelve months, then the turnover would go up by ten to twelve per cent. And if that were to happen, Blaise would be dealing with the workplace problems of eighteen or twenty companies rather than the twelve or so currently on their books. If she were to take on twenty companies, she would have to work twenty-four hours a day and find the kind of energy that powered a whole football team, never mind cope with the inevitable concern of not performing to the best of her abilities at all – or even most – times.

She stood up and picked up her coffee and carried it to the window. It was lunchtime, and Karen had gone grocery shopping and to buy fruit to take to Eleanor later in the day. Blaise had known that Karen would not be in the office, and that it was just one of those things, that her rare opportunity to come back to the office at lunchtime should coincide with a day when Karen had to shop for food for her family.

'I'll leave you the figures,' Karen said. 'They're good. You'll see. What shall I get Eleanor that isn't too messy to eat in bed and isn't grapes either?'

Blaise looked out of the window. There was no view, just a section of brick wall eight feet away, and a dripping gutter and a section of slated roof. Above the roof, the winter sky was pale greyish-blue and damp-looking. Blaise took a long swallow of her coffee and said out loud to the space beyond the window, 'I can't charge more per hour than I'm charging,' and then, 'I can't find more hours than I'm finding,' and then, after a short pause, 'We need to expand.'

In the sky above the slate roof, a small flock of birds wheeled to the left, took an instinctive and sudden collective decision, and wheeled back the way that they had come, without changing a millimetre of their formation. No one, Blaise thought, gazing at the sky where they had been only seconds before, knew how or why they did this, any more than anyone knew why human beings were at one moment almost tribally communal in their desires and decisions and, quite randomly at another, completely independent, even to a point of anarchy. She and Karen had dreamed this company up, discussed it with commitment and shared vision, set it up using – mostly harmoniously – their complementary talents, and run it, for over five years, with just enough mutual tension to give impetus and energy. But now, that satisfactory combination of dynamics was not, somehow, producing the same drive. What was different in their approaches and attitudes to work seemed to be pulling them apart rather than fusing them together. And as Karen appeared to become ever more – well, distracted was the word really, Blaise could feel herself becoming ever more focused, by contrast.

A soft thudding up the stairs behind the closed office door heralded Karen's return. Blaise turned from the window, balancing on her heels, holding her coffee mug in front of her with both hands. The door banged open, revealing Karen stooping to retrieve the handles of half a dozen thinly stretched supermarket bags. Blaise watched while Karen struggled into the room and dumped the bags against the nearest wall.

She said crossly, 'Thanks for helping.'

'It doesn't have to be like this.'

Karen kicked the door shut, and then kicked off her sheepskin boots.

'So you haven't read the figures.'

'I have,' Blaise said steadily, 'read the figures.'

Karen padded across the little room in her socks and looked down at her handiwork on Blaise's desk.

'I thought,' she said, 'I'd get a heroine's welcome. Champagne and let's buy a new computer.'

Blaise moved to stand beside her.

'The figures are fantastic. And beautifully, clearly presented. We hardly need an accountant, the way you keep an eye on things.'

Karen said, with a hint of pride, 'We were one pound seventy-six out this month. I couldn't find it, I simply could *not* find it –'

'Did it matter?'

Karen sighed theatrically.

'Of course it mattered. If it doesn't add up, it doesn't add up, no matter by how much, and it means I've made a mistake and I don't like that. I finally found it. It was on a payment that was scheduled to go out on a Friday, but didn't actually, till a Monday, so it earned one seventy-six in interest, while it sat there.'

Blaise said, not looking at her, still looking down at the spreadsheets, 'Karen.'

'Yes.'

'Karen, this is silly.'

'What is silly?'

Blaise indicated the bags stacked against the office wall.

'You spending a precious lunch hour trailing round a supermarket buying yoghurts and sausages and whatever. I thought Lucas –'

'Not,' Karen said, interrupting, 'not – just now.'

'Well, do it online.'

'I can't.'

'What d'you mean, can't?'

'Well, you can do stuff like washing powder online but you can't choose apples and cheese and which bit of haddock.'

Blaise sighed.

She said resolutely, 'This is not a cottage industry.'

'Oh?'

'Look at our turnover. Look what we've come from. We borrowed five thousand pounds five years ago and *look* at us.'

Karen said nothing.

'But,' said Blaise, 'we can't stand still. We can't go from being a service, however good, to a *brand*, unless we think of growing, of hiring more people, of – of getting ourselves off the kitchen table.'

'A brand?'

'Yes,' Blaise said, 'a brand. A well-known, leading brand in the field of business performance. And we can't do that until we assess, yet again, our own motivation.' She glanced at the bags again. 'And that has to be more than being able to pay for all that stuff.'

Karen went on staring at the spreadsheets. Then she pulled down the hem of her tracksuit top, and sauntered over to her computer.

She leaned forward and moved the mouse on its mat, and

from that position, apparently staring intently at the screen, she said, 'Oh, by the way, I bought Eleanor a pineapple.'

'Well,' Eleanor said, 'it's very kind of you. But I can't quite see how I'm going to eat it.'

Karen looked at the pineapple. It sat on the bed, leaning against Eleanor's legs and exuding its sweet, slightly synthetic smell.

'I forgot that. It just looked theatrical and unhospitalish compared to all the other fruit.'

Eleanor laid a tentative finger on one of the pineapple's stiff, thick, greyish leaves.

'I shall take it home with me.'

Karen crossed her legs and leaned back in the vinyl chair. She looked, Eleanor thought, very tired.

'When will that be?'

'As soon as possible. Naturally, nobody can tell me because nobody knows. But I shall go on asking until I get an answer.'

Karen closed her eyes.

'The girls did you some drawings. And I forgot them.'

'It doesn't matter.'

'Poppy drew a dragon.' She opened her eyes again. 'And Rosie drew you, in a bed in a field of flowers. Very tidy flowers. Daisies and things.'

'I look forward to them,' Eleanor said.

Karen rolled her head sideways.

'Are you really OK?'

Eleanor leaned sideways. She reached down and gave Karen's hand, lying on the arm of the vinyl chair, a brief pat.

'I am. I broke nothing. It will teach me to be more careful. You shouldn't have come.'

'Why not?'

'Because,' Eleanor said, 'you are exhausted.'

Karen rolled her head back. She gave Eleanor a small, weary smile.

'Yup.'

'Well,' Eleanor said, 'more exhausted than usual?'

'Seem to be –'

Eleanor leaned forward and picked up the pineapple. She held it in both hands and studied it.

'If you want to tell me why,' Eleanor said, 'I am very happy to listen.' She glanced about her. 'I am hardly in a hurry to do anything else, after all.'

'We had a row,' Karen said.

Eleanor twisted sideways with difficulty, and put the pineapple on her locker beside Lindsay's chrysanthemums.

'Who did?'

'Lucas and me. Blaise and me.'

'Lucas *and* Blaise?'

'Well,' Karen said, 'Blaise and I had quite a quiet, polite one. And Lucas and I did the full-on yelling kind.'

'Ah,' Eleanor said.

'I am sick of Lucas earning no money,' Karen said, 'and I am sick of Blaise wanting to push the business, just when it gets manageable.'

'Manageable?'

'I mean,' Karen said, 'I can manage *this* level of working, and *this* level of motherhood, and *this* level of family administration, but I really will disintegrate if I'm required to manage more.'

'Lucas did not appear to feature in that list.'

Karen yawned.

She said tiredly, 'He doesn't.'

'Ah,' Eleanor said again.

'He doesn't think money matters. He is *above* money. All he thinks matters are his children and being allowed to take not less than for bloody *ever* to work out how he's going to paint something that nobody is ever likely to buy.'

Eleanor inspected the cuffs of her blue nightgown.

'Jules appeared the other night,' Karen went on. 'I don't know what was the matter, I was too busy and tired to ask her, to care, but she's hardly speaking to Lindsay, and she had nowhere to sleep. And Lucas was in his studio doing, yet again, the square root of damn all, as far as I could see, and I had just had *enough*, just absolutely completely had enough, and there were all these bills to pay, and forms to fill in, and I just suddenly couldn't stand it, keeping everything going, day in, day out, week after week, and I just thought, *Luke* can cope with this, Luke can bloody well pull his idle artistic finger out and *do* something for someone at least, so I sent her round there, to ask him if she could spend the night in his studio. I mean, there's no one there at night, though I wouldn't be at all surprised if there soon is, the way we're going on – and it can't hurt him to have Jules there for just one night. But no. Oh no. He was back in under an hour, guns blazing. He was absolutely incoherent with rage. I'm amazed we didn't wake the children.'

Eleanor stopped looking at her cuffs, and transferred her gaze to the woman in the bed opposite, who lay slumped with her mouth open and no apparent sign of life.

She said, 'Do you suppose she's dead?'

Karen turned her head.

'She's breathing.' She turned her head back. 'You don't want to hear me moaning on. I shouldn't have told you.'

'I'm assimilating it,' Eleanor said. 'I'm visualising the pressure you're under.'

'We've made money,' Karen said. 'We've done well. I run it and Blaise fronts it and we do *fine*. We do better than fine, in fact. But Blaise wants us to do more.'

'Yes,' Eleanor said, 'she would. And Lucas probably wants you to do less.'

'I don't think he cares.'

'I doubt that.'

'Don't defend him,' Karen said. 'I haven't the energy to fight back.'

'You would,' Eleanor said reasonably, 'if you weren't fighting *him*.'

Karen said nothing.

She stared at the ceiling for a while and then she said, 'I just wish he had some *money*.'

Eleanor nodded.

'Always useful –'

'I just *wish*,' Karen said with sudden energy, 'he had some get up and go, some *purpose*, some forcefulness. I wish – I wish he was more like Jackson Miller.'

'It's the biggest there was,' Toby said.

He had laid on Eleanor's knees a monster bar of Toblerone. Eleanor regarded it respectfully.

'It's magnificent –'

'And,' Toby said, 'these.' He rustled in a carrier bag and produced a tattered pile of football magazines.

'Well,' Eleanor said, 'those will certainly keep me occupied.'

'Sorry,' Paula said.

'No. No, don't be sorry. I've neglected my homework just recently. And they will make a nice change from the crossword.'

Toby said, 'I've cut quite a lot of pictures out. But I don't expect you'll mind.'

Paula settled herself in the vinyl chair.

'You look tired.'

Eleanor, leaning back on the pillows, turned to smile at her.

'I've had several visitors. I've been very lucky.'

'Lindsay came?'

'And Karen. And Blaise is coming tomorrow.'

Toby leaned on the bed, and eyed the chocolate.

'I suppose we couldn't open that?'

'Toby!'

'We certainly could,' Eleanor said. 'Much easier to eat than a pineapple.'

'No,' Paula said, 'no. It's for you –'

'It would take me months to eat that. And anyway I am resolved to live on celery and water for a while, so that when I next crash over there will be very much less of me to do it.'

'Great,' Toby said, picking up the Toblerone.

Paula reached across the bed and seized his wrist.

'Stop it!'

'She *said* –'

'Put it down!'

'No, she –'

'Have you,' Eleanor said loudly, 'have you seen Jackson recently?'

Paula let go of Toby's wrist. He shot Eleanor a grateful look.

'Open it,' she said.

'No,' said Paula.

'No?'

'Well, not for a few days. He's so busy.'

'A man of enterprise –'

'That's what he says.'

Eleanor watched Toby pick at the end of the Toblerone box.

'A good quality in a man.'

'Yes,' said Paula, 'as long as he has his priorities straight.'

Toby jerked his head towards the pile of magazines.

'He bought me those.'

Paula looked at Toby.

She said, asserting it, 'You get on well with Jackson, don't you?'

Toby upended the Toblerone box and allowed the huge, silver-wrapped bar to slide out on to Eleanor's bed.

He said to her, ignoring his mother, 'Mega *wow*.'

'You like –' Paula began.

'Yes!' Toby said loudly. He folded back the foil and revealed the long toast-rack of chocolate.

Eleanor said, 'I never saw such a thing.'

'Of course,' Paula said restlessly, 'Gavin hates it, Gavin's still threatening all kinds of things.'

Toby went very still.

'Why don't you break me a piece,' Eleanor said, 'and one for your mother. And two for yourself.'

'It isn't as if he's affected,' Paula said. 'It isn't as if Jackson has moved in or anything. In fact, I wish he'd –'

'Ker*chunk*,' Toby said. He held out a ragged triangle of chocolate towards Eleanor.

'That,' said Eleanor, 'isn't exactly going to get me thinner. Is it?'

Paula was sitting very still. She looked down at her hands.

She said, 'I just wish I knew where I was.'

'You're in the hospital,' Toby said. 'You're sitting next to Eleanor.'

Paula didn't look up.

'I don't mean literally,' she said. 'I mean with Jackson.' She looked up suddenly at Eleanor. 'You can't stand still in relationships. Can you?'

Eleanor was dreaming. She was moving swiftly and smoothly down some bright corridor, and somehow her legs were not involved in her progress – it was more as if she was on wheels. It was a pleasurable sensation, a feeling of speed without noise or wind, and there was, even more intense than the lit corridor, a light at the end which was very inviting and towards which she was inexorably moving and would, indeed, have been moving faster if she hadn't been impeded by something pulling at her shoulder.

'Wake up, dear,' a nurse was saying. 'Wake up.'

Eleanor opened her eyes. There was the hospital ceiling and an unattractive strip-light and, slightly to one side, the small oriental face of a nurse she had never seen before.

'Wakey, wakey,' the nurse said. 'Your granddaughter's here.'

Eleanor thought a moment.

'I haven't got a granddaughter.'

'Well,' the nurse said, 'she's here. You don't want to upset her, do you?'

Eleanor said nothing. Her mind's eye was still preoccupied with the bright, enticing corridor. The nurse's neat little face vanished from her line of sight, and was replaced with another one, which looked at once familiar and unplaceable.

'It's me,' Jules said.

Eleanor blinked.

'Lindsay told me,' Jules said. 'She texted me.'

Eleanor tried to picture this.

Jules said, 'Have you broken anything?'

'Jules,' Eleanor said suddenly, remembering.

Jules nodded. She was smiling.

'What were you doing, falling over?'

'I tripped,' Eleanor said. 'I went down like a tree across a railway line.'

'And hit your head.'

'On the table leg. Rather a mess. I don't mind other people's blood but I do *not* care for my own.'

Jules put a hand out and touched the dressing on Eleanor's head.

'Does it hurt?'

'Not now.'

'What hurts?'

'My hip. A bit. And my knee. And my feelings.'

Jules grinned.

'Nobody saw you, though.'

Eleanor grunted.

'It's not easy, somehow, being beholden to a service you used to help run.'

'I don't get that.'

'It means,' Eleanor said, 'that I don't like being in here.'

Jules looked round her. She shuddered slightly.

'Don't blame you.'

'The decay of the flesh is bad enough in the specific but far worse in the general.'

Jules eyed the bar of Toblerone.

'Can I have some of that?'

'All of it. Except the box. I must keep the box to show Toby my appreciation.'

Jules broke off a chunk of chocolate, and put it in her mouth.

'When'll you go home?'

'As soon as possible.'

Jules chewed for a while.

Then she said, 'Stairs'll be difficult.'

'I'll sleep on the sofa.'

'OK.'

'I'll sleep on the sofa and wash in the sink and eat whatever I don't have to cook.'

Jules broke off more chocolate.

'I'll come.'

'Come where?'

'I'll come to yours,' Jules said. 'I can buy food and stuff.'

Eleanor looked at her for a moment.

She said, 'There's no need to do that.'

Jules put the chocolate in her mouth.

'It'd suit me.'

'What, looking after an unsteady old heap like me?'

Jules regarded her.

'Yeah. Anyway, it wouldn't be looking after. I'd just put stuff where you could reach it.'

'Now that,' Eleanor said, 'I think I could bear.'

Jules said again and indistinctly, 'It'd suit me.'

'How?'

'I need somewhere,' Jules said more clearly. 'While all this new stuff happens.'

'What new stuff?'

Jules looked away.

'I may be changing clubs.'

'But I thought you were doing well at whatever you do, at *this* club.'

'I am,' Jules said. She stretched. 'I'm worth having.'

'Well, then?'

'I've been made an offer,' Jules said. 'I've been made a good offer. But while it all works out a bit, it would be good to be somewhere for a while. Somewhere to sort my head out.'

Eleanor looked at her.

'Am I up for this, I wonder?'

'No drugs,' Jules said, 'no trouble. Promise.'

'I could always throw you out –'

Jules looked away.

Then she turned her head back and said with uncharacteristic pleading, 'Please.'

'Mmm,' Eleanor said. She closed her eyes a moment. Then she opened them and said, 'Would this arrangement be largely for my benefit or for yours?'

'Nobody ever lets me look after anything,' Jules said.

'No. I suppose we are rather influenced by the way you fail, by any conventional standards, to look after yourself.'

'I can change.'

Eleanor heaved herself a little more upright.

'Talking of change, what is this change you are talking about so mysteriously?'

Jules said airily, 'It's a new project. A new club. Maybe.'

'Maybe?'

'No, more than maybe. This guy gets things done.'

'What guy?'

Jules grinned at her again.

'So funny, hearing you say "guy" like that –'

Eleanor folded her hands in her lap.

She said firmly, 'What guy?'

Jules leaned forward and picked up the Toblerone bar again.

'Jackson,' she said.

CHAPTER FIFTEEN

Lindsay had broken Noah's construction. She hadn't intended to – indeed, had spent the weeks since it appeared taking great care not to – but she had been vacuuming, just before she went to bed, and had inadvertently allowed the cable to flick across the space between the sofa and the armchair, and in so doing had swept the knights and the plastic cups clean off the board and into a small chaos on the carpet.

When she realised what she had done, she had switched off the hoover at once and stood very still, hand to mouth, regarding the fallen figures and cups. She knelt down. Her first instinct was to – quietly, even furtively – restore everything to roughly the places where Noah had originally put them. But her second was to leave everything as it was and to confess. She wouldn't touch the wreckage: she would wait until the morning and then she would say to Noah, before he went into the sitting room and saw, 'I'm so sorry but by mistake I broke your – your – what you made,' and then try and gauge what to do next from Noah's reaction.

She thought he would probably cry. He didn't cry out of rage, as Toby was inclined to do, but he cried when he was tired, or frightened, or sad, and she was very much afraid that what she had done would make him sad and also, obscurely and worryingly, frightened. But he didn't cry. She made her sorry speech to him, and he walked into the sitting room, and surveyed the scene, and then he picked up his two knights from the carpet, and carried them into his bedroom.

Lindsay followed him.

'Is it OK? Don't you mind?'

'It's broken,' Noah said. He crouched down beside his cardboard castle and laid the knights still on horseback down on their sides.

'I'm so sorry –'

'They're sleeping,' Noah said. He picked his red-fleece dressing gown off the end of his bed and draped it over the castle. 'It's dark now.'

'Perhaps,' Lindsay said, 'we could make you something else?'

Noah thought about this.

He said, 'Oh no.'

Lindsay knelt down by him.

'I really am sorry. You know that, don't you? I didn't do it on purpose, I didn't mean to do it.'

Noah looked at her.

He leaned forward and said, very loudly and clearly, as if speaking to someone hard of hearing, 'It's broken.'

It would have been nice, Lindsay thought later that day, to have talked to someone about Noah. It would have been nice to be able to explain how unfathomable someone so small could be, and to have another person say, Oh that's perfectly normal, or, My goodness, Lindsay, you're such a one for making mountains out of molehills, or even just, You ought to get out more, Lindsay, you really should. She could, of course, say these things to herself, but they were hard to believe unless authenticated by another human being. And the other human beings who might have uttered consoling versions of these things – Jules, Paula, Eleanor – were, for various reasons, not current possibilities for reassurance. So there was nothing to be done, but sit in the call-centre section of her building society office and listen to people worrying about interest-rate rises affecting their mortgages, and try to persuade herself that these telephone problems had both more reality and more validity than her anxiety about possibly having hurt Noah in a way he couldn't explain, but which was, somehow, damaging to his developing personality.

There was, after all, no one at work she found particularly sympathetic. Perhaps it was the very nature of building societies, but her fellow employees seemed to want to do what they were paid to do between nine and five-thirty and then vanish into the life that was paid for by work, but kept resolutely separate. There was an office tradition – obligation, really – of buying cakes for everyone on birthdays, but nobody had ever suggested to Lindsay that they might have a drink together after work, or introduce their children to one another, or even share a sandwich at lunchtime. Borrowing a collapsible umbrella in a cloudburst once had been the closest Lindsay had ever got to sharing anything with anyone at work, but the money was reasonable, and the place was clean, and she wasn't required to deal with abusive members of the public face to face, and the hours suited her, and anyway what else was she fit for? She pushed thoughts of Noah to the back of her mind and concentrated on explaining to a querulous-sounding man from Brentford that his grievance about deciding against a fixed-rate mortgage five years ago was not one she could do very much about five years on.

A shadow fell across her desk. She glanced up. The new manager, who was called Derek Sherlock, was standing looking down at her. He didn't seem in the least threatening, but it flustered her all the same to have him listening to her trying to be patient with the man in Brentford. She even said, 'I'm sorry, sir,' to conclude the call, which they were not supposed to say when the customer was very evidently in the wrong. They were not, ever, supposed to say anything that might implicate the building society in the faintest possibility of unwarranted responsibility.

Lindsay looked up at Derek Sherlock.

'Sorry –'

He smiled at her.

'One of those?'

She nodded. She smiled back.

She said, 'He just wished he had a fixed-rate mortgage –'

'They all wish that,' Derek Sherlock said, 'when the rates go up. And wish the opposite when it goes down. Human nature.'

She nodded again.

'I suppose so –'

He folded his arms. He was, Lindsay noticed, wearing a nice suit. It fitted him properly, and the cuffs of his shirt were ironed properly too. He was obviously the kind of man whose wife paid attention to the details, to haircuts and cuff-ironing and brushed shoulders and . . .

'Are you OK?' Derek Sherlock said.

Lindsay blinked.

'I'm – I'm fine –'

'I've noticed,' he said, 'that you are an excellent time-keeper, that you are never late and that you don't clock-watch like some of them. But you look under strain some-times. You look as if you had something on your mind.'

Lindsay glanced round her. Nobody had ever spoken to her like this in all her working life, and she was afraid that some of the other girls could hear and would think that she had somehow invited, encouraged, Derek Sherlock to single her out and be nice to her. But everyone else, headphones on, was engaged with their own man from Brentford, and no-body was looking her way. She tried to look at Derek again but failed somehow, and looked back at her computer screen.

'How's your friend?'

'My friend –'

'Your friend in hospital. The friend who had a fall.'

Lindsay recovered herself.

'Oh, she's fine, thank you. She's back at home now. She's – well, she's being looked after by my sister –'

'That's nice.'

Lindsay swallowed.

'You haven't seen my sister.'

'I'd like to,' Derek said. 'I'd like to see your sister.'

Lindsay looked up at him again.

She said, suddenly losing her awkwardness, 'You don't know what you're asking.'

He laughed. He put his head back and laughed.

Lindsay said, without meaning to, 'She's one of the things I worry about.'

Derek Sherlock stopped laughing. He looked down at Lindsay. He was very good-looking, Lindsay thought abruptly, very good-looking in a tidy way, a kind of controlled, ordered way that Paula wouldn't have liked but which she, Lindsay, found really rather . . .

'Good,' Derek said. 'That's more like it. Now we're getting somewhere.'

If Paula had known the letter was from Gavin she probably would never have opened it. With its blandly typed envelope and Central London postmark, it might well have been perfectly harmless. But it wasn't. It was an unpleasantly formal letter from Gavin saying that he was about to take legal action to gain greater and more regular access to his son.

'And as I have, by steady and generous payments, and by frequent visits, demonstrated my commitment to the responsibilities of fatherhood, I am reliably advised that I have a strong case to make and an excellent chance of prevailing.'

There had been letters in Paula's life which had, frankly, frightened her very badly, letters about tax, letters about unpaid bills, letters about eviction and credit withdrawal and dismissal. But this letter, she thought, staring at it as it lay in a pool of light on the breakfast bar among the rest of the scattered envelopes that had arrived in the mail that day, was the most truly menacing she had ever received because it managed, somehow, to deprive her of all initiative. Gavin was not suggesting that there was a problem, as far as he was concerned, with her relationship with Jackson, and thus with Toby, that might be resolved by discussion and compromise; he was simply, baldly, saying that, as he didn't like her choice, he was going to punish her for both making it and persisting in it.

She took a step or two away from the breakfast bar to the sink, and ran water into a tumbler. It was hard to swallow. She stood there, holding the glass and trying to breathe in the deep, steadying manner she had once been taught in long-ago yoga classes. She put her other hand on to the edge of the sink and gripped it. One, two, she said to herself, three, breathe, four, breathe, he can't do this, five, he's just trying to frighten me, breathe, six, he's using Toby to deal with the fact that, breathe, he can't cope, seven, with my . . .

'What're you doing?' Toby said.

He was standing by the breakfast bar, holding the photo-copied sheet of paper of his nightly spellings.

Paula let her breath go.

'Breathing.'

Toby flapped his paper.

'Will you test me on my plurals?'

Paula nodded.

'In a minute –'

'You always say that,' Toby said. 'Always, always.' He imitated her voice, shriller and sillier than she ever sounded:

'Can you stop me falling out of this window? In a minute. Can you stop this terrorist shooting me? In a minute. Can you stop this gangster cutting my head off with an axe? In a minute.'

Paula whirled round.

'Shut up!'

Toby took a step back. He flapped his paper again.

'Keep your hair on –'

Paula swooped towards the breakfast bar and seized Gavin's letter. She brandished it at Toby.

'D'you know what this is?'

He shrugged.

'No, I –'

'It's a letter,' Paula said furiously. 'It's a letter from – from your father. It's a letter full of threats, it's a letter accusing me of being a bad mo –'

Toby slapped his hands over his ears.

'Stop it!'

Paula threw the letter into the fruit bowl. She put her hands flat on the breakfast bar, hunching her shoulders, her head bent, breathing deeply.

'Don't talk about it,' Toby said.

The intercom sounded.

'You go,' Paula said, not moving, still breathing hard.

Toby shuffled across to the tiny lit screen of the intercom. He said flatly, 'It's Jackson.'

Paula began to cry.

'Let him in –'

Toby did not pick up the interconnecting telephone, he simply pressed the button that opened the building's exterior door four floors below. And then he waited, still holding his spelling list, staring at the floor.

When the lift doors on the landing outside the flat clunked open, Toby put a hand out, and opened the front door just wide enough for Jackson to walk in. As usual, he carried nothing more than his laptop case and, in the other hand, a paper cone of dark-purple freesias. He halted just inside the door and glanced from Toby to Paula.

'You two had a row?'

Toby said nothing. He took two steps backwards and then turned and scuffed his way across the floor, past the sofas and the zebra rug to the ladder that led up to his bed platform.

Jackson dropped his laptop case on the floor and went across to Paula. He put the freesias down on the pile of half-opened mail.

'What's going on?'

Paula wheeled round and flung herself at him, winding her arms round his neck. He put both hands up and disengaged her.

'Start at the beginning,' Jackson said. 'What's happened?'

Paula reached across to the fruit bowl and whipped out the letter.

'Look!'

Jackson took the letter in one hand and put the other arm lightly round Paula. He read the letter through quickly and then he put it down on the breakfast bar.

'Not for me, babe.'

'What d'you mean?'

'I mean,' Jackson said, 'that I don't get involved in stuff like that.'

'But –'

'Look,' Jackson said, 'look. The guy's probably bluffing.'

'He wants custody of Toby!'

'No, he doesn't.'

'He does, he does! That's what he's threatening!'

'It's what,' Jackson said, 'he wants you to *think* he's threatening.'

Paula glanced at the letter.

'Really?'

'Really.'

Paula bent her head.

'Sorry.'

Jackson grunted.

'Sorry,' Paula said, 'sorry. He just makes me so wild, he just knows exactly which buttons to press.'

Jackson took his arm away and picked up the freesias.

'Maybe I do too.'

Paula gave a little giggle.

She said, 'If you'd come earlier, this wouldn't have happened. If you'd been here when I opened the letter, I wouldn't have lost it.'

Jackson held the flowers out.

'I was on a mercy mission.'

'Lovely,' Paula said. She held the cone of flowers up to her nose and closed her eyes. 'Lovely.'

Jackson leaned back against the breakfast bar. He folded his arms.

'Yes,' he said, 'an SOS and no one to answer it but me. Your friend Karen.'

Paula's head jerked up.

'Karen!'

'Why not?'

'But why should Karen send you an SOS?'

'Her systems had crashed. Why do people ever send me an SOS? All the boys were out so round I went. Odd little set-up.'

Paula said, 'You went round to Karen's office?'

'Yes,' Jackson said reasonably. 'That's where the computers are. I thought my offices were small but that one is seriously –'

Paula looked away as if she was battling something inwardly, and then she said brightly, 'They make a lot of money –'

Jackson said nothing. He looked past Paula for a while, as

if he was contemplating something, and then he looked back at her. He smiled.

He said with real engagement in his tone, 'Do they?'

When Lindsay rang, Eleanor was propped against the kitchen table, eating scrambled egg out of the saucepan with the wooden spoon she had used to stir it. When she had asked Jules to buy eggs, she had assumed that Jules would return with a standard carton of six. But Jules had come back with two dozen. She had also bought a bale of lavatory paper designed for a family of six, and mere twos and threes of the fruit and vegetables Eleanor had listed. Two potatoes seemed particularly bizarre.

'I shall have to specify,' she said to Jules.

Jules, dazed by the effort of even semi-conventional shopping, shook her head. 'Whatever.'

'Are you all right?' Lindsay said.

Eleanor put the spoon back in the pan.

'Over-egged but fine otherwise.'

'Is Jules –' She stopped.

Eleanor looked round the kitchen. It looked no more streamlined than usual, but if there was more muddle, which there seemed to be, it was not a worse muddle.

'It is all very manageable –'

'I'm afraid,' Lindsay said, 'that she eats such awful rubbish.'

Eleanor began to manoeuvre herself round the table towards a chair.

'Well,' she said, 'I take no responsibility for that. I have wondered whether she has any idea what a knife and fork are for, but then' – she paused a moment, lowering herself into a chair and glancing at the spoon sticking out of the egg pan – 'I am in no position, sometimes, to comment on her habits.'

'I just – I just don't want her to annoy you.'

'No,' Eleanor said, 'nor do I.'

'I mean coming in late and being untidy and not washing up –'

'She does all those things,' Eleanor said. 'But then, those were things I was prepared for her to do.'

'I don't,' Lindsay said, 'want her to take *advantage* of you.'

Eleanor shifted in her chair.

'She won't.'

'But –'

'Lindsay,' Eleanor said, 'dear, kind, anxious Lindsay, we have made an arrangement.'

'An arrangement?'

'Yes,' Eleanor said, 'I am charging her for living here. Not much, but I am charging her.'

There was a silence the other end of the telephone.

'You disapprove,' Eleanor said.

'No, I – well, I suppose I just always think of her as my little sister –'

'Well, she isn't *my* little sister,' Eleanor said. 'We have a somewhat unorthodox friendship but it *is* a friendship, and in order to retain its value and dignity, it's important we don't allow it to slide into the wrong kind of dependencies. So we sat down with paper and pen – no simple task, as you of all people will appreciate – and we made at least a guess at what Jules earns each week and agreed that out of that amount Jules should give me a small proportion.'

There was another silence. Eleanor picked up a pen and drew a neat grid on the blank margin of a nearby newspaper.

Then Lindsay said, 'How much?'

Eleanor added some dots to alternate spaces in her grid.

She said, pleasantly, 'None of your business.'

'No,' Lindsay said, 'sorry.'

'I am not in need of funds,' Eleanor said. 'I live quite frugally, because I always have. But Jules won't mature unless she begins to understand that the world – especially the working world – is a practical place.'

'I've tried so hard,' Lindsay said.

Eleanor put her pen down. She looked up at the wall opposite, where, long, long ago, she had hung a small watercolour of the Lion Court in the Alhambra, in Granada, a watercolour now so familiar to her that she hardly saw it any more.

'Lindsay,' Eleanor said, 'this isn't about you. You have been a splendid sister against appalling odds, you will always be her sister. But you can't keep her a child. She *is* childish, in too many ways, but we'll see if she can, somehow, improve on that. If she can't, if I find the way in which she insists on living her life intolerable, then I shall ask her to go.'

'OK,' Lindsay said, and then, after a pause, 'I wish I had your strength.'

Eleanor picked up her pen again and crossed out the grid she had drawn.

'You know I can't manage it when conversations get maudlin –'

'Sorry, but I –'

'Tell me,' Eleanor said, interrupting, 'tell me how Noah is.'

There was a beat the other end of the line.

'Well,' Lindsay said, 'that was the one reason that I rang you.'

When the call was over Eleanor heaved herself to her feet, and carried the saucepan over to the kitchen bin, and scraped the congealed contents into it. Then she put the pan into the sink among the mugs and bowls and spoons already there, and ran water into it. Then she put the newspaper under her arm, took the disagreeably invalidish walking stick she had been issued with in her free hand, and made her way back to her sitting room.

The room looked familiar, but at the same time slightly distorted. Jules was not the only innovation in Eleanor's life since her fall and her subsequent physical tentativeness had made her realise that it made sense to have a cleaner. A cleaner would not only have some effect on the state of the carpets, which had been something of a surprise to her when she had seen their condition at floor-level, but would also be a human presence in the house periodically, valuable for both physical and psychological reasons. And so, after enquiries made in the corner shop, she had acquired Athina. Athina had been born in Athens, over fifty years before, and had, despite marriage to an Englishman and two children, clung defiantly to her Greekness. She was plump and dark and voluble and clattering with gold jewellery and, if her capacities as a cleaner were more dramatic than effective, she left behind her in the atmosphere a vibrating energy that sustained Eleanor for hours afterwards.

She had tried to rearrange the sitting room, but Eleanor had demurred. Everything was in the comfortable if unsymmetrical places that Eleanor had chosen, but the books were now in stacks, and the rugs smoothed out, and the blurring of dust that had filmed the most obvious surfaces removed. Athina had also added to the windowsill some cuttings of strange flowering cacti from her own plants, which Eleanor assumed she would simply get used to in time. Their unlovable presence was, she reflected, a small price to pay for Athina's enlivening visits. Just as towels stained with hair dye and other undomesticated habits were an equally small price to pay for Jules' presence.

If she had been a houseproud woman, Eleanor thought, if she had been the kind of woman who saw herself validated by, reflected in, the appearance and condition of her house, then no doubt trying to live under the same roof as Jules would be impossible. By the same token, if she had been possessed of a strong sense of her own entitlement – such a very modern preoccupation, this insistence on female entitlement – then she might have found Jules' self-absorption unendurable. But as it was, as she noticed the disorder and the thoughtlessness and the infantile obsession with the moment but couldn't somehow resent them, the signs of Jules' occupation of the house were secretly welcome. She would not admit it to Lindsay – probably would never admit it to anyone – but in the privacy of her own sitting room, she could confess to herself, with relief and a kind of quiet joy, that it was just wonderful to have another human being in her daily life.

She lowered herself into her accustomed chair. The day was bright and the sun shone through the windows that Athina had, at least approximately, cleaned. She had a new crossword to do, sitting here in a familiar chair in a familiar room with the unimagined luxury of Jules asleep upstairs in Eleanor's hitherto unused second bedroom. Jules had come in at four in the morning and had been asleep ever since. Eleanor looked at her watch. It was one-thirty. She would make a start on the crossword, and then she would, as was now their arrangement, telephone Jules on her mobile to wake her. And when she came downstairs, Eleanor would tell her that on Friday night – an evening that had a peculiar emptiness now that the habitual arrangement had become so fragmented – Noah was going to come round for a couple of hours to be looked after while his mother went out on a date.

Toby woke, as usual, in the dark. He lay for a while, waiting for his mind to swim unsteadily to the surface, and then he rolled over in bed and looked at the illuminated face of his bedside clock. It said ten-past seven. He raised his head off the pillow and listened. The flat was very quiet, almost spookily quiet. Usually, by seven o'clock on school mornings, Paula was at the foot of his ladder telling him to get up, hurry up, not to forget his field kit, not to put on yesterday's socks.

He sat up. There was a light shining from the kitchen area. Perhaps Paula had forgotten to turn the lights off the night before. Perhaps she was already up. He pushed the duvet back and put his feet on the floor. Then he padded across the platform and shinned down his ladder in the practised manner he always visualised being admiringly filmed.

In the kitchen, Jackson was standing gazing out into the black early morning, his back to Toby, waiting for the kettle to boil. He was in jeans and the rest of him was naked. He didn't turn. Toby wanted suddenly to say, 'Fuck you,' to his naked back, but there was something about the sight of it, something animal and powerful and alarming, that stayed his tongue.

He turned away and crept quietly back across the living space. He paused by his mother's bedroom door and looked in. One lamp was on, and by its light he could see that Paula was still in bed, lying there in so relaxed a manner that the shape of her body looked as if it had been poured there.

She smiled at Toby, slow and sleepy.

'Hello, darling.'

Something sour and hot rose into his mouth.

'Fuck *you*,' Toby said.

CHAPTER SIXTEEN

Paula stood on the pavement outside Workwell's office building. The ground floor was occupied by a dry-cleaning company, whose huge, sleek Italian machine occupied a prominent central position, almost in the window, as if it were being proudly shown off, like a sculpture. Beside the window was a narrow door, painted black, and on the lintel beside it, a brushed-steel plate with 'Workwell' engraved on it in capital letters and, underneath in lower case, 'First floor. Please ring.'

Paula put her finger on the buzzer, and took it away again. She glanced behind her. Nobody was watching, and anyway what could it possibly matter to her if they were? She swallowed and adjusted her sunglasses. She put her finger on the button again and pressed.

There was silence. Paula waited, staring at the Workwell plate, hardly breathing. Then Karen's voice said, 'Workwell. Can I help you?'

'It's Paula,' Paula said.

'Oh. Is it?'

'Can – can I come up?'

There was another short pause and then a buzzer sounded and the door latch released. Paula pushed it open, and stepped inside.

A steep stair, painted white and carpeted in charcoal-grey,

rose up in front of her. The air smelled faintly and headily of dry-cleaning fluid. Paula went up the stairs, head bent, at a pace she hoped would induce steadiness of purpose, and found the door to the office at the top open, and Karen back at her desk. She turned as Paula came in and laid an arm across the back of her chair.

She said, with a dangerous kind of relaxedness, 'Well, this is a surprise.'

Paula looked round her.

'I've never been here before.'

Karen smiled.

'Impressive, huh?'

Paula took her sunglasses off.

'Very.'

'Coffee?' Karen said.

'No, thanks.'

'Well,' Karen said, 'perhaps you'd like a seat? At least?'

Paula looked at the second chair. It struck her that to be at the same level as Karen would somehow put her at a disadvantage. She moved across the floor and leaned against the workspace to the right of Karen's chair. Then she crossed her arms.

'Oh, wow,' Karen said, smiling.

Paula looked at her feet. She crossed her ankles.

She said, not looking at Karen, 'Funny, really. I always thought it would be Jules.'

'Jules?' Karen said. 'What would be Jules?'

Paula looked up.

'That it would be Jules who tried to jump Jackson.'

Karen stared. She opened her eyes as widely as they would go.

'What *are* you on about?'

'You know,' Paula said.

'I do not –'

Paula unfolded her arms and leaned forward. She gripped the edge of the desk either side of her.

'Oh yes you do.'

'Look,' Karen said, 'I don't –'

'You can give me all the excuses in the world,' Paula said, 'but you fancy him, don't you?'

'No,' Karen said.

'I don't check up on him,' Paula said. 'It's not like that, it's not that kind of relationship. But I can't help noticing things, I can't help noticing when I'm left out, when there are these little meetings. I can't help thinking that this, Karen, is not what friends are *for*.'

'I couldn't agree more –'

'Your loyalty,' Paula said fiercely, 'is supposed to be to *me*.'

'It is.'

'Then why are you behaving like this? What's with all the secrecy and the games?'

Karen's gaze didn't waver.

'No secrecy. No games.'

'There is!' Paula shouted. 'There is, there *is*!'

Karen leaned back a little.

She said, 'I can't help your jealousy, you know.'

'Jealousy!'

'I mean,' Karen said, 'I wouldn't have thought possessiveness went down very well with a man like that.'

'I'm not possessive –'

'Oh?'

'I just want,' Paula said, 'to be able to rely on my *friends*.'

'You can.'

Paula said nothing. She relaxed her grip on the desk edge and stood up.

'There is nothing going on,' Karen said.

Paula took her sunglasses out of her bag and put them on again.

'OK.'

'Nothing,' Karen said. 'He's just been round with Toby and the girls sometimes. Kids' stuff. Some business stuff. Nothing.'

Paula went slowly towards the door.

'OK.'

Karen turned back to her desk.

She waited until she heard the door being unlatched, then she said, 'See you,' as if nothing had happened.

It had been a surprisingly good day. Blaise had been summoned by the chief executive of a marketing company she had been working with for some months, who had then told her that he was unhappy with the criticisms implied by some of her retraining methods, and that he felt she misunderstood the company ethic. He then leaned back, and said, in exactly the same tone of justifiable injury, that the implementation of some of her key ideas – such as fewer meetings and fewer absurd and alarming lists of required competencies – did seem, however, to be improving staff morale and consequent commitment to the tasks in hand.

Blaise, seated the far side of his desk with her knees together and a notebook in her hand, waited politely.

'So you'll be pleased, I think,' said the chief executive, with the air of one waiting to be thanked for an act of magnanimity.

'I would be,' Blaise said, 'if I was certain of your decision.'

'My decision?'

Blaise regarded him.

'I am not at all certain,' she said, 'whether your objections to my strategies and what you seem to see as my non-approval of the basic work ethics of your company amount to this conversation being not only our last, but also constituting my dismissal. Or not.'

The chief executive swung his leather swivel chair to an abrupt halt.

'Good God, no,' he said. 'I want to renew your contract. How on earth could you have thought otherwise?'

Leaving the company's offices, Blaise considered taking the underground back to West London, and decided she was going to indulge herself with a taxi. Karen never took taxis, but then Karen didn't buy business suits or see regular haircuts as part of professional self-respect. In fact, Karen took an almost perverse pleasure in taking her striking looks for granted, as if they were remarkable enough to withstand – or even, strangely, to be enhanced by – being treated with elaborate carelessness. There was something about Karen's looks, something about her slouching, sinewy grace that made you wonder interestedly and appreciatively what she would look like naked.

Blaise, in the back of a taxi with her briefcase on the floor and her bag on the seat beside her, reflected that the difference – well, one of the many differences – between them was that Karen played herself, and only herself, in all her life roles and she, Blaise, presented different facets of herself, depending upon the role required of her. It wasn't that she was ever untrue to herself, but more that she changed the emphasis, depending upon whether she was persuading a company to revolutionise its business practices or sitting in Eleanor's kitchen. In fact, she thought, gazing out of the taxi's window at the crowded pavements of early-evening High Holborn – what wonderful opportunities travel provided sometimes just to gaze mindlessly and some-how re-boot the brain – she wasn't sure she would like, could even cope with, the self-reliance of not working in an office environment, let alone the isolation and lack of variety it would mean. Working from home might be held up as a life-enhancing solution to the need to earn and fulfil oneself being nicely balanced with the demands of family life, but where, Blaise wondered, even without a family requiring fairy cakes and participation in dinosaur games, was one to find the self-esteem and self-discipline gained from working with other people? Karen might – indeed, was beginning to hint that she would – prefer to exchange their tiny but businesslike space for a converted box room behind the girls' bedroom, but could she, Blaise, now cope with the idea of Workwell being run from a place where domestic life unquestionably predominated?

I can, Blaise thought, take myself out of the office. But I can't take the office out of me. And it's not because, as Karen hints, I like artificial constructions where I don't have to engage, because I don't think offices *are* artificial places, I think they are what evolves when people get together in a common work cause. And I like that. I like people and I like the way they behave when they are doing something like working together, and I think it's OK for work to be lucrative and I think it's more than OK for work to be meaningful. And I'm not a sad spinster trying to make work fill the space left by the absence of a man and children because although the right man – oh for heaven's sake, what on earth *is* the right man anyway? – would be wonderful, I don't feel in the least diminished or incomplete because I don't have one. And what's more, surely you can be allowed to like children very much without wanting to have some of your own? Especially if you knew, just knew, somewhere in the depths of your being where instincts and the unbidden impulses lurked, that work was going to give you something that nothing else – nothing – could possibly provide.

What had Eleanor said, suddenly from her hospital bed, describing Toby's visit, describing Lindsay's perpetual fretting over Noah?

'You know,' she'd said, looking at Blaise with an earnestness she was seldom prepared to display openly, 'I like children. I like them very much, and some I am even prepared to love. But I decided not to have any of my own because I don't believe that you can give yourself properly to work and to family. And I do believe that children should never be sacrificed.'

From the bag beside Blaise in the taxi came the abrupt and increasingly insistent sound of her mobile phone ringing. It would be Karen, calling to commiserate about the ending of the contract. Blaise took the telephone out of her bag and, without looking to see who the caller was, said into it, 'You'll never believe this, but he wants more!'

'It's Lucas,' Lucas said.

'Goodness, I –'

'You were expecting Kay,' Lucas said, 'weren't you?'

'Of course,' Blaise said. 'We were expecting rejection today and got the opposite.'

'Well,' Lucas said, 'that must be lovely. Not a feeling, I have to say, that I'm very familiar with.'

Blaise looked out of the window again. The taxi was now beginning on the Fulham Road, on the grand, stuccoed, stately end of it where even a hospital looked authoritative rather than intimidating.

She said carefully, 'Is everything OK, Luke?'

'In what way?'

'I mean Karen, the girls –'

'Oh yes,' he said, 'yes, they're fine. Fine. I just rang on impulse. I wonder – I wonder if I could show you some-thing?'

Blaise hesitated. That kiss in her kitchen – brief, com-petent, possible to dismiss as firmly friendly – had never been alluded to by either of them again, but it had happened. And the trouble with anything like a kiss or a confidence happen-ing between a man and a woman who were not in a position to act unilaterally was that you couldn't unhappen it. Lucas had kissed her, even if she hadn't invited him to by any word or gesture, and she had not slapped him or remonstrated with him. She had been taken by surprise, and by the time she had collected her wits, he'd gone.

'What kind of thing?' Blaise said.

There was a pause.

Lucas said quietly, 'A painting.'

'A painting! What kind of painting?'

'A painting, painted by me. Or at least, started by me.'

'Well,' Blaise said, 'that's wonderful. Has Karen seen it?'

'No.'

'Does Karen know about it?'

'No.'

'Then why are you asking me?'

'Because,' Lucas said, 'I need to show it to someone before I show it to Karen.'

Blaise said, 'I'm on my way home.'

'Via my studio.'

'But –'

'Please,' Lucas said. 'Please. Five minutes.'

'There,' Lucas said.

He was standing several feet from her, his hair tied back becomingly, and wearing a faded plaid-wool shirt and jeans and sneakers in a way, Blaise thought, that managed to look both appropriate and unaffected. She folded her arms across her black work-suit jacket, and looked obediently in the direction of Lucas's gesture. A large canvas was propped on the easel, its surface shimmering with a series of undulating lines in greys and blues.

'Help me,' Blaise said.

'In what way?'

'What am I looking at?'

Lucas crossed his own arms.

'It's a harbour.'

'Oh, I –'

'It's a study, an abstraction, if you like, of water in a harbour. Perhaps St Ives. I like the harbour in St Ives.'

'Is that what you'll call it?'

'I'm not,' Lucas said, 'calling it anything yet.'

Blaise took a step forward and peered at the canvas. Then she took several steps back.

She said, 'I think it's very, very clever.'

'Clever —'

'Yes. It's wet and it's full of light.'

Lucas went on looking at his painting.

He said, under his breath, 'Oh, good.'

'You shouldn't listen to me,' Blaise said. 'I don't know anything.'

Lucas didn't turn to look at her.

He said, 'Oh yes you do.'

'Well, I like some things because of their shapes and colours and I don't like others for the same reason. I mean, I like this, I *really* like this, because it looks to me like the essence of water and I like the colours and I like the calmness.' She gave him a quick look. 'But I don't think you need me to tell you that it's good.'

He smiled.

He said, 'Need, maybe not, but I wanted you to.'

Blaise said nothing.

Lucas went on, still looking at his canvas, 'It's the first thing I've painted for ages. Two years, maybe.'

Blaise looked at the floor.

'Yes.'

'Blaise,' Lucas said, 'you know what I'm going through.'

She waited.

'I think,' he said, turning towards her, 'that you're the one person who does see, who does understand —'

'I may see,' Blaise said, 'I may understand. But I see and understand both sides, don't forget.'

Lucas raised his hands in the air and then let them fall again.

He said loudly, 'Blaise, I'm so *lonely*.' He took a step towards her. 'I know you can see that, I know you know why. No one else can know it like you do because no one knows Karen as well as you do, besides me.'

'No,' Blaise said.

'What d'you mean, no?'

'I mean, I'm not having this conversation with you.'

Lucas took a step or two back again and leaned against the sink.

He said lightly, 'I'm not going to kiss you again. I'd love to, but I'm not going to.'

Blaise gave the floor a half-smile.

'But,' Lucas said, 'I am going to tell you that I love your company. I love it when you're near. I love the feeling of being inside a ring of still water. It is so precious when everything else is so uncertain, so turbulent, so changeable.'

Blaise raised her head.

She said, 'We're all in turbulence just now. It's not only you. Everything's changing. I'm not the answer –'

'Because of all this sisterhood stuff with Karen.'

Blaise closed her eyes briefly.

She said, 'I'm not the answer even if I look as if I am. I may look it, because I'm not doing the traditional-woman stuff, I haven't got family clutter, I look more sorted, simply by contrast.'

'So you're rejecting me.'

'I'm behaving,' Blaise said, 'as if you had never said what you said.'

Lucas considered a moment, and then he said, 'Why haven't you married?'

Blaise laughed.

'Oh that. Well, Luke, it just, somehow, was never my highest aim.'

'But you must want –'

'What?'

'Well,' he said, 'you must want love, sex, companionship –'

'Oh I do. But not above all else. Not at any price.'

'A fear of the orthodox union –'

'A fear of losing independence, more like.'

'Karen –'

'Karen,' Blaise said loudly, 'has a lot to look after, a lot to be responsible for, a lot to maintain.'

'She sets her own standards –'

'And you set yours.'

'Goodness,' Lucas said. 'Are we having a row?'

'You brought me here,' Blaise said crossly, 'on false pretences. You said it was to look at a painting and actually, it was just to – to bleat at me.'

'Wow,' Lucas said admiringly. 'No wonder strong men sign your contracts.'

Blaise looked at the canvas again.

'Let's go back to the beginning. That's going to be a terrific painting.'

'I know.'

'And it will sell.'

'Yes,' Lucas said, 'I think it will.'

Blaise turned to look full at him.

'Then what was all this about?'

'This?'

'All this sob stuff?'

Lucas relaxed against the sink. He put his hands either side of him on the rim, and returned Blaise's look.

'Well,' he said, 'everything I've said tonight I meant. You are all the things I told you you were. I would like to kiss you even if I know you won't let me. But the thing that's most on my mind, the thing that's nagging away there while I'm painting, the thing that I suppose really got me fired up enough to paint again is –' He stopped.

Blaise leaned forward.

'What?'

'Jackson.'

*   *   *

Rosie sat very still. She had learned to do this in response to realising that a) Poppy was always going to hold centre stage whatever else was going on and b) that there was a lot in life that, if it didn't require actual worrying about, certainly needed keeping an eye on. And this situation at the kitchen table, with her mother and the Jackson man, and the bottle of wine, and Poppy skirmishing about in her new ballet leotard and Rosie's swimming goggles, definitely needed watching. And so, with her very dull, and in her opinion unrealistic, French homework about a family going shopping on, apparently, another planet (*la boucherie, la droguerie, la boulangerie, la pâtisserie* – where was Sainsbury's, for goodness sake?) Rosie was keeping very still, and very quiet, and with her head bent was writing very slowly and carefully in a way that would make Mrs Roberts of year four write, 'Very nice, Rose,' in fine-nibbed red rollerball pen at the bottom of the exercise.

Karen was wearing earrings. Usually – it was the kind of thing Rose noticed – she only wore earrings when she wasn't wearing a tracksuit and she was going out somewhere and had her hair loose. Today she was in a tracksuit – it was the new one, black velvety stuff and the trousers were really quite tight – and she had her hair sort of half loose and half skewered up in a red clip with cherries on it that Rose had given her on Mothering Sunday, and these dangly, swingy earrings that caught the light and sent little sparkles flying about like sequins. Rose felt mistrustful of the earrings. She also felt mistrustful of her mother – too much laughing, too much leaning languidly back in her chair – and of Poppy's capacity to take sides in the right way and not sidle up to Jackson now and then and lean on him and whisper urgently from behind the swimming goggles. She thought – and not for the first time – that she could have done with a pet, a dog or a cat to keep her company when she got lonely inside her family, when she couldn't be certain that they weren't going to do something destructive or dangerous. She put her non-writing hand into her lap and imagined stroking fat Fred from her father's studio. To have Fred, warm and reverberating, on her lap would have been a real comfort.

To be fair to Jackson – Rose preferred to be fair if it was at all possible – he wasn't also laughing and being languid. He seemed extremely relaxed and he was being perfectly pleasant and friendly, but he didn't seem to be at all mesmerised by the earrings. He was, of course, Paula's boyfriend and, equally of course, it was very wrong to behave in an excited, over-belonging way to someone if you were anyone else's special friend – this was painfully familiar to Rose from the school playground – so there was that to remember, and factor in, but then grown-ups often appeared to be very certain of how to behave until circumstances actually required them to behave like that, whereupon they seemed to think it was perfectly OK to make new rules, just for them.

Rose sighed. She wrote, '*Un chou-fleur, un kilo de carottes et deux melons.*' She said '*melons*' the French way, to herself, under her breath, several times. Poppy bumped against her and hissed, 'Poo bum.' Rose took no notice. Poppy had pulled her leotard on over her vest and knickers and the edges of her knickers showed under the edges of her leotard and the look was not professional. '*Des fraises,*' Rose wrote, '*un concombre, quelques oignons.*'

'Poo bum,' Poppy said in a louder whisper.

Jackson looked at her. He raised his eyebrows.

'Enough,' Karen said indifferently.

Poppy struck a pose.

'To think,' Jackson said, 'that I thought I'd like a daughter.'

Karen laughed. She leaned across the table and poured wine into Jackson's glass (he had hardly drunk any of it, Rose noticed) and then refilled her own.

She said, 'I can't believe this. What am I doing, having time off?'

Jackson looked at her. He gave a half-smile.

He said, 'Just that.'

Karen wound a long curl of hair round a finger.

She said, not looking at him, 'All your fault.'

Poppy hopped round the table until she was next to her mother. She thrust her goggled face into Karen's.

'I need to do a poo.'

'Don't be a baby,' Karen said. 'Go and do one.'

Poppy bounced a little beside her, not obeying.

'Go,' Karen said.

Rose lifted her head from Madame Duvalier's cornucopia of fruit and vegetables and looked at Poppy. Very slowly, Poppy walked backwards away from the table and out of the room, shutting the door behind her with a crash. Karen got up and went over to the door, past Jackson – very closely, past Jackson – and opened the door again. Then she came back to the table and perched on the edge of it, near Jackson. '*Un ananas*,' wrote Rose. '*Un chou. Des artichau . . .*' She stopped. What happened to them in the plural? Was it an 's'?

'You know how it is,' Karen said. 'You built up your own business. It doesn't leave you much slack.'

Jackson leaned back and put his hands in his pockets.

'I don't know what to do with slack,' he said. 'I like business. I always have.'

'But you don't get deflected –'

'Nope.'

'And you aren't distracted by – other responsibilities –'

'Nope.'

'And you still have time to sit here with me, on a Friday afternoon, and drink wine.'

There was a pause. It was not a peaceful pause. Rose wracked her brain for more fruits and could only think, for some bizarre reason, of the French for toothbrush.

Jackson said in a low, private voice, 'I am interested in your business. In your and Blaise's business.'

From upstairs came a bang and a thud and then a shriek. Rose dropped her pen.

Karen raised her head and looked at Rose.

'Be a love,' she said. 'Go and see.'

Rose said sturdily, 'She'll be fine.'

There was a further thud and a wail.

'Please,' Karen said. 'Go. Just go.'

Rose got off her chair reluctantly and went out of the room and up the stairs to the bathroom. Lucas had painted the bathroom blue and white, to be like the seaside, with garlands of fish round the window and the mirror above the basin, and a whale spouting water behind the shower head. Poppy was on the floor, in a tumble of rolls of lavatory paper, beside a fallen tower of stools and a chair and an upturned wastebin.

'I *fell*,' Poppy whispered furiously. She had stripped off everything except her vest. 'There was no loo paper and I couldn't reach the new one and I *fell*.'

Rose looked round the room.

She said tiredly, 'D'you want me to kiss it?'

Poppy hugged one leg defiantly.

'No. Why didn't Mummy come?'

Rose bent and began to stack the paper rolls in a tower.

'You know that chair's wobbly.'

Poppy let go of her leg and retrieved her leotard.

She said, 'Go away.'

Rose stopped piling. Poppy was struggling back into her leotard. The goggles were round her neck, causing her to hold her chin unnaturally high.

'OK.'

'I don't want you here,' Poppy whispered. 'I don't want you. I don't want Mummy. I want Daddy.'

Rose stood up.

'He'd say you were daft,' Rose said.

Poppy flipped over and turned her back, wrenching her arms into the leotard. Rose looked at her and then she turned and went out of the room and down the steep stairs to the hall. It was quiet down there, so quiet that she felt impelled to tiptoe, to tiptoe across the hall and halt in the kitchen doorway.

Karen had been bending over Jackson. She was straightening up as Rose appeared in the doorway, and Jackson was saying something. He was saying, quite clearly, quite calmly, 'Sorry, lady, but I'm not up for this,' and Karen was looking as if she'd walked into a wall by mistake.

She stared at Rose.

'How's Poppy?'

Rose stared back.

'Fine,' she said.

When Jules opened Eleanor's front door to Blaise, Blaise gazed at her as if she couldn't quite remember who she was, and said, 'Oh!'

Jules relaxed on to one hip, holding the door in her left hand.

'Forgotten I live here? Or something?'

'Sorry,' Blaise said, as if regaining some kind of consciousness. 'Sorry – yes, I –'

'Well,' Jules said, not moving, 'I do. I've been here for two weeks.' She leaned forward and said in an elaborately toff accent, 'Eleanor and I are having supp*ah*.'

Blaise regarded her. She was wearing some kind of glitter vest under a short black jacket and, apparently, striped pyjama bottoms. Her feet were thrust into red canvas boots with the laces undone.

Blaise said, 'Can I come in?'

Jules stood back, still holding the door.

'Sure,' she said.

Blaise went past her into the hall. She took her raincoat off and hung it on the hall stand, on the mound of other coats already hanging there.

She said to Jules without turning, 'Sorry to be a bit spaced. It's been rather a day.'

'OK,' Jules said.

Blaise went ahead of her into the kitchen. The strip-light, whose ugliness had never seemed to trouble Eleanor, had not been switched on, and the room was instead illuminated by a couple of mismatched lamps and a cluster of candles stuck into jam jars. At the table, her stick propped companionably beside her, sat Eleanor in front of a large plate of something unrecognisable. Her face by candlelight looked interestingly unlike its everyday self.

'Blaise!'

'I'm so sorry just to land myself –'

'No,' Eleanor said, putting her fork down. 'No. Sit down. Jules dear, find her a chair. Find her a plate. Sit down.' She peered at her in the flickering light. 'You look exhausted.'

Blaise grimaced.

'Long day –'

Jules scraped a chair along the floor towards her.

'It's chilli,' Jules said. 'Want some?'

'No, I –'

'It's quite good,' Eleanor said. 'In fact, it's very good.'

'We made it,' Jules said.

Blaise looked at the chair.

'I'm interrupting –'

'Sit down,' Jules said.

Blaise sat.

'Well?' Eleanor said.

Blaise glanced at Jules.

Jules said to Eleanor, 'She doesn't want to say, in front of me.'

'Oh come –'

'I do,' Blaise said, 'I will.'

'OK,' Jules said, 'who's died then?'

Blaise shook her head. She was half smiling.

'I'll make you tea,' Jules said.

Eleanor pushed her plate aside.

She said, 'Since Jules came, I've never drunk so much tea in my life.'

Jules switched the kettle on. Then she went to stand beside Eleanor.

'Well?' Eleanor said.

'I don't know what's going on,' Blaise said.

Jules inspected her fingernails.

Eleanor put a hand out and grasped her stick.

She said, 'In what way?'

'All of us,' Blaise said.

'My sister,' Jules said, 'has a fella.'

'I know,' Blaise said, 'I'm glad.'

Eleanor glanced at Jules.

'Mugs,' she said, 'mugs for tea.'

Jules moved back a step.

Eleanor said to Blaise, 'Perhaps just start at the beginning?'

Blaise hesitated.

She said, 'Karen and Lucas.'

Jules opened a wall cupboard and took out three mugs. She lined them up beside the kettle.

'You know about Lucas's studio. You know about him not painting for ages.'

'Yes.'

'Well, he is painting again. He has started something. He's started something rather good. He showed it to me.'

'Did he?' Eleanor said.

The kettle gave a small scream, and switched itself off. Jules went to pick it up.

She said over her shoulder, 'Did he come on to you?'

'Not really.'

'Ah,' Eleanor said.

'What's ah?'

'Well,' Eleanor said, 'you probably look stable to him.'

'Yes.'

'And?'

'And especially,' Blaise said, 'when Karen is being de-stabilised. A bit.'

Jules was ripping tea bags apart.

She said, 'What by?'

'Guess,' Blaise said.

Jules turned round, a tea bag in each hand.

'Surprise me.'

'Jackson,' Blaise said.

'Or,' said Eleanor, 'a fantasy of Jackson.'

'Lucas knows this,' Blaise said. 'Lucas knows and doesn't know what to do and he's painting as – as a kind of *competition*.'

Jules poured water into the mugs and carried them over to the table.

She said carelessly, 'Jackson is not interested in her.'

Blaise looked at the swollen tea bags bobbing on the surface of the water.

'No, I don't think he is.'

Eleanor glanced up. She took her hand off the top of her stick and put both hands on the table.

'I'd just got home,' Blaise said, 'from Lucas's studio, from looking at Lucas's painting, and the doorbell rang. And – well, it was Jackson.'

'Jackson?'

Jules was quite still. She stood a little apart from them, holding a milk carton. The room was too shadowy to see her face clearly.

'I don't really know him,' Blaise said. 'I mean, I've met him a few times and you always feel you know your girlfriends' boyfriends, somehow, don't you, you sort of feel predisposed to –'

Jules moved forward and put the milk on the table.

'What did he want?'

'I didn't know,' Blaise said. 'I couldn't tell. He didn't want a coffee or a drink or anything, he seemed quite OK just to stand in the sitting room.'

'Did he mention Karen?' Eleanor said. 'Or Paula?'

Blaise shook her head.

Jules leaned across the table and began to squeeze the tea bags against the side of the mugs with a knife handle.

She said again, 'What did he want?'

Blaise looked down.

'He wanted to talk business.'

'Business?'

'He wanted to talk,' Blaise said, 'about buying into the business. About buying Karen's half, about buying her out of our business.'

Jules gave a little yelp. She spun round with the knife in her hand and flicked a sodden tea bag across the kitchen.

'I'll kill him,' Jules said.

Eleanor looked at Blaise.

'And what,' she said, 'did you tell him?'

'I said no. I said of course not.'

'Good.'

Blaise leaned forward a little.

She said, her gaze directed at the tabletop, at the mugs of tea, 'I said no. But it's started me thinking.'

Jules flung the knife after the tea bag, with a clatter.

'And what,' she shouted, 'about *me*?'

CHAPTER SEVENTEEN

N
o man had ever sent Lindsay flowers before. She'd had flowers from Paula, and occasionally a supermarket bunch in apology for something from Jules, but never, ever from a man. When she opened the door on Saturday morning to a florist delivery boy and saw the flowers in his arms, her first thought had been that they must be meant for someone else in the flats.

'They won't be for me.'

The delivery boy, tall and skinny and black with a blazing white smile, was used to this kind of reaction in women.

He said teasingly, 'They's from your mum, yeah?'

'Oh no,' Lindsay said. 'Not *my* mother.'

He put a delicate black hand into the flowers and pulled out a plastic card-holder with a tiny white envelope fixed in it.

'That your name, yeah?'

Lindsay peered.

'Well, yes.'

He adjusted the flowers so that she could take them.

'There you go, then.'

Lindsay took the flowers as reverentially as if they were a baby.

'Can't believe it.'

'Somebody loves you,' the boy said.

Lindsay blushed into the flowers.

The boy held out a delivery confirmation pad.

'You sign here.'

Awkwardly, round the flowers, Lindsay signed her name.

'You have a nice day,' the boy said. 'You have a nice *life*, while you're about it, yeah?'

He gave Lindsay a last brilliant smile and loped away from her across the landing and down the staircase. He was whistling.

'What you got?' Noah said.

Lindsay turned round. Noah was standing in his bedroom doorway, wearing socks and the top half of his pyjamas.

'Look,' Lindsay said.

She knelt on the floor. Noah came over and looked at the flowers appraisingly, as if he were an expert.

'See that little envelope?'

Noah peered.

'Yes.'

'You want to open it?'

Noah took the envelope out of the bunch and sat on the floor beside Lindsay. She reached out and pushed the front door shut. Noah looked at the envelope and then he turned it over and looked at the back. Lindsay watched him. There was no hurry. There was no hurry at all. In fact, the longer this delicious moment could be prolonged, the better.

'Can I rip it?' Noah said.

Lindsay nodded.

Noah looked at the envelope front again.

'That's your name.'

'Yes.'

Noah glanced at the flowers.

'Is it a present?'

'Yes.'

'Have I got one?'

'Not this time.'

'Oh, well,' Noah said.

He took a corner of the envelope and twisted it. It tore raggedly, tearing the card inside at the same time. Lindsay made herself sit still. Noah tore on doggedly, then he held the two pieces of envelope out to Lindsay.

'Nothing inside.'

'There is,' Lindsay said. 'There's a card in there. It's stuck inside.'

Noah dropped one half of the torn envelope on the floor and investigated the other one. He extracted with difficulty a small piece of white card with a flower printed in the corner.

'And the other half,' Lindsay said. Her head felt full of light.

Noah repeated the process and held the second piece of card out to Lindsay.

'Put them together,' Lindsay said. 'Put them on the floor together, like a jigsaw.'

'OK,' Noah said.

He put the two pieces on the floor, blank side upwards.

'Daftie,' Lindsay said. 'Turn them over.'

Noah turned the pieces over, very slowly. He laid them side by side.

'What does it say?'

Noah bent.

'T,' Noah said.

'After that?'

'Don't know.'

Lindsay crouched beside him.

'It says,' Lindsay said, ' "Thanks for a great evening." '

Noah got up.

'Can I have cereal?'

'They're from Derek,' Lindsay said, conscious that she wanted to say his name, even to Noah. 'Derek Sherlock. You remember Derek?'

Noah thought.

'Yes.'

'Did you like him? Did you like Derek?'

Noah thought some more. Derek had sat on his bedroom floor and allowed him to show him his knights and his fort without needing to ask him anything. Noah had appreciated that. The rest of his life seemed permanently occupied by people asking him things.

'Yes,' Noah said.

'He liked you,' Lindsay said. Her voice sounded ridiculously happy to her. 'He likes me. That's why he sent me these flowers.'

'OK,' Noah said.

'He wants to take us out. He wants to take us to Legoland.'

Slowly, Noah smiled. His smile grew enormous. He nodded vigorously.

'You know,' Lindsay said, looking adoringly at her flowers, 'I want to tell everyone. I want to ring everyone I know and tell them that Derek sent me flowers and wants to see me again. And again after that.'

'And me,' Noah said.

Lindsay turned to look at him.

'And you. Thank goodness there's you to tell, at least. Thank goodness for that.'

Noah said unexpectedly, 'Ring Paula.'

Lindsay smiled at him.

'You're a poppet. But I can't really. Not at the moment.'

Noah hopped a little, on one foot. He was getting the hang of this.

He said, almost excitedly, 'Ring Toby!'

Lindsay laughed. She began to scramble up off her knees, clutching the flowers.

'Why Toby?'

Noah seized her free hand. An image came into his mind of Toby's toy theatre, of his computer, of the exoticism of the

270

ladder going up to his bed platform. He began to jump on the spot, pumping Lindsay's hand.

'Ring Toby! Ring Toby! Tell him we're going to Lego-land!'

Lindsay looked down at his bobbing head.

'Aren't we lucky? Oh Noah, aren't we just – *lucky*?'

Paula lay on her sofa. It was tempting to lie face down and even bite one of her orange cushions, but she was not going to permit herself to do that. Lying down was enough, and she must lie face upwards, and breathe, and breathe, and tell herself that this was not the end of the world. It was not even necessarily the end of anything. Not if Jackson was to be believed. Not if she were to take, at face value and as meant, what Jackson had said, how Jackson had left her.

She picked up one of the orange cushions and placed it on her chest, and held it there with both arms. It was strangely steadying, despite being only a cushion and not a body, and absurdly she felt a kind of gratitude to it, some connection, as if the cushion had mysterious capacities for reassurance in its feathered depths. She turned her head sideways and looked across the dusky space towards Toby's ladder. His light was out: there was no sound. He was either asleep or wishing to be thought so. Whatever he had heard – what had he heard? – he was now either digesting or ignoring in his preferred way. If he had wanted to let her know how he was feeling, Paula knew, he would have done so, even if it just meant hurling clothes and football magazines off his plat-form on to the floor below. But he had hurled nothing and there was no sound.

Paula raised her head an inch.

'Toby?'

Silence. Paula waited.

She said again, slightly louder, 'Toby? You OK?'

No sound. Paula let her head fall back. She raised her left arm and looked at her watch. It was nine-fifteen. Jackson had been gone twenty minutes. She knew that because she had, for some reason, looked at the kitchen clock the moment the door had closed behind him, and then she had tipped the wine he hadn't drunk into the sink, and the pizza he hadn't eaten into the bin, and put the glass and the plate into the dishwasher, and banged the door shut, with finality. And then she had taken her own glass of wine and a tumbler of water, and put them down on the coffee table, and lain down on the sofa and stared upwards at the shadowy spaces of the ceiling, which could seem wonderful or rather awful, entirely depending upon one's mood.

She hadn't really been expecting Jackson that evening. One of her most recent resolutions, with reference to Jackson, was to try not to notice whether she knew where he was or not, to try just to appreciate him when he was around, to try and see her own life as being as independently absorbing to her as his plainly was to him. These were noble aims, such resolutions, but implementing them she found took more will power than natural inclination. She had to rearrange her actions, her reactions, all the time, in order not to ask him – and not to respond badly when he told her – where he'd been, if he'd seen Karen again, why he wanted to see Blaise. It was hard work on a daily basis, and on days like today, when she seemed to have enough natural optimism to buffer her against persistent small anxieties, she felt not just relief, but a degree of self-congratulation. And so, when she had managed to persuade Toby to go to bed, and was standing in front of the fridge thinking that perhaps a supper of leftover cooked chicken, half a pot of guacamole and the remains of a tin of creamed sweetcorn had distinct appeal, it was a glorious reward for the rigours of emotional self-restraint for the doorbell to ring and Jackson to announce himself.

He was carrying a pizza box, a bottle of wine and a single white rose in a long cellophane tube. He seemed cheerful, if a little breezy, and let his hand rest, in a pleasingly proprietorial way, on her bottom when he kissed her.

'Toby's in bed,' Paula said.

Jackson was opening a drawer in search of a corkscrew. 'Fine.'

'Had a good day?'

'Fine,' Jackson said, in the same tone of voice. Then he applied himself to taking the cork out of the wine bottle and, as he passed her, carrying the wine, on his way to the cupboard where the glasses were kept, he said casually, 'You look good.'

Paula felt the usual surrendering small leap of inward pleasure.

'Thank you.'

Jackson grunted. He took the wine and the glasses to the coffee table and sat down on the sofa, knees spread, leaning forward to pour. Paula followed him, with the pizza on a wooden board, and two plates. She sat down on the sofa, at a distance she judged unremarkable and not open to misinterpretation or pressure. She began, neatly, with a special roller cutter Toby had brought back from one of his afternoons with Gavin, to slice the pizza.

'To what,' she said, looking steadily at the pizza, 'do we owe this honour?'

Jackson stopped pouring and looked at her.

'Come again?'

'I didn't think you were coming. I didn't know you were coming. It's lovely to see you, but it's a surprise.'

Jackson turned back to the wine.

'I wanted to make sure you were OK.'

'OK?'

'Yes,' Jackson said. 'After Gavin's letter.'

Paula levered out a wedge of pizza and put it on a plate.

'You told me not to worry. So I haven't.'

'Good.'

'I mean,' Paula said, 'I've thought about it a lot, and when Gavin came to collect Toby last week, I just stayed in my bedroom till they'd gone. But I don't feel frightened now.'

Jackson turned and put a glass of wine in front of her and then he put a hand on her knee.

'Good,' he said again.

Paula looked at his hand. It was, still, extremely disconcerting to react so strongly every time a particular person touched you, but there it was: she just did.

She swallowed. She took a breath.

'Jackson –'

'Yup?' He took his hand away.

'Jackson, the letter did make me think –'

He gave a little snort.

'That you're well out of that one.'

'Well, yes. Yes, of course. But I've probably known that for some time. No, the letter made me think more about now. About my life. About – about the future.'

Jackson leaned back into the sofa. He folded his arms. He looked very comfortable, very easy. He also looked – it was one of the things that made him exciting to Paula – as if there was a lot of contained energy in him, ticking quietly away there, until the time should come for him to use it.

Paula found her hands were together in her lap, tightly twisted. She relaxed them and pulled them apart and then clasped them again, deliberately loosely. She glanced at Jackson. She remembered the hand on her bottom, the single white rose, the hand on her knee. 'I wanted to make sure you were OK,' he'd said.

'Gavin was angry,' Paula said, and then she stopped. 'I mean,' she said, 'that one of the things Gavin *said* he was angry about was you living here, you being a substitute father to Toby. Well, you aren't, in either case. You don't live here, do you? And you've taken Toby to one football game, haven't you?'

She paused.

Jackson looked at her, almost serenely, and said, 'There'll be others.'

'Other what?'

'Other football games.'

'Oh,' Paula said.

'He'll get to go again,' Jackson said. 'Course he will. Don't worry.'

Paula relaxed her hands again.

'I'm not worrying. I'm – I'm just thinking. I'm just thinking about – how things are, and – and how they might be. I'm just saying that you don't live here now, that you don't do much with Toby now, but – but, that you *could*.'

'Could?' he said.

'Live here,' Paula said. 'Move on. Move in with me.'

Jackson sighed. He unfolded his arms and leaned forward. He said, in a perfectly friendly voice, 'Don't do this.'

'Don't –'

'Don't ask this. Don't try and make something happen that can't.'

'Why can't it?'

He half turned and put his hand back on her knee.

'I don't do this, babe. I don't do this regular-guy stuff.'

Paula, despite her best efforts, felt her voice rise uncontrollably.

'Then why are you here? Why are you with me?'

He squeezed her knee and let go.

'You know why I'm with you. Would I be here now, otherwise?'

'But we've got to move *on*,' Paula cried. 'We've been like this for *months*. Relationships don't stay the same, they can't, they can't just go on being like they are at the beginning, they *die*.'

Jackson said nothing. He looked disconcerted but not angry, not sad.

Paula said in a fierce, half-tearful whisper, 'I love you. I want to live with you. I want us to be a *couple*.'

Jackson sighed again.

He said, staring straight ahead, 'This *is* together. For me. This is how I do together. I'll go on doing this, but I can't do more.'

She said, staring at her lap, 'D'you want us to stop?'

He glanced round.

'No. Why should I?'

'But you won't live with me. You won't let me live with you.'

'That's right.'

'Suppose,' Paula said, 'suppose I can't stand that?'

'You'll tell me.'

'And if I did, what would you do?'

Very slowly, Jackson stood up. He looked down at her. 'I'll wait till that happens.'

'Maybe it's happening now –'

'I'll wait,' Jackson said, 'until it happens when you're not upset.'

Paula thrust her clenched fists between her knees.

'You are so *frustrating*. I'd like to hit you.'

'Don't,' Jackson said.

There was a silence. Out of the corner of her eye, Paula could see his trousered leg, his hand hanging loosely. She felt suspended, poised on the edge of something, like those childhood holidays with her father on the north Cornish coast, standing in the sea with her surfboard poised, waiting for the next wave to rear and curl and crash-carry her back to the beach.

'Can I ask you something?' Paula said.

'Of course,' Jackson said.

His tone was friendly.

'Has – has this got anything to do with Karen?'

There was a beat, and then Jackson said calmly, 'Absolutely bloody nothing.'

'You sure?'

'Quite sure. This is me, babe. This is me. OK?'

'Go away,' Paula said tiredly.

'Yup.'

'Now.'

Jackson moved. He took a step closer and bent over Paula and dropped the lightest of kisses on the back of her bent neck.

'See you,' Jackson said. And then he picked up his jacket and went lightly across to the door and let himself out.

Paula stood up at once, picked up his glass and plate and marched to the kitchen with them. The clock on the wall above the fridge said eight-fifty-five.

Paula sat up slowly now, still clutching the cushion. She wondered why she wasn't crying. She felt full of tears, full of the urge, the need, to cry, but she wasn't crying. She stood up unsteadily. She had asked Jackson to live with her and he had turned her down. She had summoned all her courage in order to ask him and he had not, in any way, indicated that he had noticed this bravery, been aware what it had cost her. Perhaps that was because he really meant that he didn't want it to end, that he – and somehow, she – could just go on dating and texting and talking on the phone and having sex and not knowing, not being sure, not advancing, for ever and ever.

Paula bent down and put the cushion back among the others. Then she carried her wine glass back to the kitchen sink, as she had done with Jackson's. Then she went back into the sitting area and across the zebra rug to the dark space at the bottom of Toby's ladder. She looked upwards. It was quite quiet and the only light was the tiny green eye of Toby's computer monitor.

She leaned her hands on the sides of the ladder and craned upwards.

'Toby?'

Silence. She pushed herself upright, and closed her eyes. It would be such a relief, such a comfort, such a validation of what she had tried to do, to be able to telephone someone, to ring Lindsay. But she could not, just now, ring Lindsay. And nor, for a whole host of different reasons, could she ring Karen or Blaise or Eleanor. She thought of Eleanor, Eleanor and Jules, the oddest of couples, and a pang of unbidden, unwanted, misplaced jealousy went through her like a cheesewire.

Oh God, Paula thought. Oh God. I'm going to cry.

Joel perched himself on the edge of Paula's desk. He was carrying three flat cardboard boxes with 'Lacquer tray – blk' printed on white labels stuck to their sides. When Joel wanted to talk to Paula, he always came carrying something, so that she could never accuse him of stopping work to gossip.

Paula was gazing at her computer screen. On it was a printout of soft-furnishing stocks in the warehouse and it might as well have been the lyrics to a nursery rhyme for all the significance it had for her that morning. She was, she knew, just going through the motions, as she had with getting up and getting breakfast and getting Toby to school. She was not surprised to feel like this. Feeling like this was, after all, what happened when you had spent the whole night awake, gingerly probing to see how badly your heart was broken.

'What?' Paula said without inflection, staring at the screen.

'I saw your friend Lindsay,' Joel said.

'Oh, good.'

Joel adjusted the boxes in his grasp a little.

'Saturday night. I was out for a meal and so was she.'
Paula sighed.
'I know.'
'She looked good,' Joel said. 'Really good.'
'Mmm.'
'With,' Joel said, his eye on Paula, 'this gorgeous guy.'
'And you're the judge?'
'Of guys, I am,' Joel said. 'And this one was really fit. A real loss to the cause.'

Paula said nothing. She kept her hands on the keyboard in case they shook, even a little.

'And your friend Lindsay was having a lovely time. You could see that, right across the restaurant. Of course, she didn't see me. Far too busy to see me.'

Paula said steadily, 'I hope *you* were having a lovely time.'
Joel eased himself upright.
He said as usual, 'You wouldn't want to know about that.'
'No, I wouldn't.'
'But I thought you'd like to know that your friend Lindsay had one hot date.'
'Thank you, Joel.'
'Any time, Paula, any time.'

He moved away from her desk and down the polished stairs to the shop floor. Paula listened to his light, designer-trainered tread, and then to him greeting a customer he'd found waiting, one of those women, no doubt, who had days to fill spending money someone else had earned. Paula gave her left wrist a light slap. It was mean to think that way, just as it was mean to react to the news of Lindsay's happy evening with anything other than unaffected pleasure. But, Paula thought, bending forward as if to engage better with the information on the screen, disappointment makes us mean, disappointment in ourselves, disappointment, especially, in other people.

Joel's feet came rapidly back up the stairs.
'Can you come a minute?'

Paula looked up.

'A problem?'

'No,' he said. He looked unnaturally alert. 'No. Just someone to see you.'

'A rep –'

'No,' Joel said. 'Someone else. Come on.'

Paula stood up and reached for her jacket. It was all very well for Joel, in his trim black T-shirt and jeans, to dress informally for customers, but something in Paula wanted – needed – to assert her managerial status. She put on her jacket and found a lipgloss in the pocket.

'It's not a man,' Joel said.

Paula ignored him. She dropped the lipgloss on her desk and went past him and down the stairs. At the far end of the main display space, contemplating a greenish lacquered cupboard, hinged and bound in brass, stood a small woman, in a long dark overcoat, with fair hair to her shoulders.

At the sound of Paula's approach, she turned and waited until Paula was quite close, and then she said, 'You won't have been expecting me.'

Paula looked at her enquiringly.

The fair woman said composedly, 'I'm Fiona.'

'Fiona –'

'Yes,' she said, 'Fiona. Gavin's wife.'

'Oh –'

'You never thought you'd see me, did you?'

'No, I –'

'Well,' Fiona said, 'I decided just to come. I decided to grasp the nettle and come. I've wanted to kill you for years, but time changes most things, and now I rather want to kill Gavin. D'you know the feeling?'

Paula nodded. She kept her gaze fixed on Fiona's small, pretty, apparently unremarkable face.

'This letter he's sent you,' Fiona said, 'these threats. It's all about *him*, as usual.'

Two other customers, a middle-aged man and a girl carrying a baby strapped to her front in a canvas sling, were walking slowly across the floor towards them. The man, although gazing at the objects as he passed them, had a piece of paper in his hand, and a piece of paper usually meant a specific request or complaint.

'I'm so sorry,' Paula said, 'but I can't talk now, I can't –'

'I didn't mean you to,' Fiona said. 'I didn't intend that. I just wanted to make a start. Break the ice.'

'I can't even react,' Paula said, 'I'm too –'

Fiona made a brusque little gesture. She put her hand in her coat pocket and pulled out a card. She held it out.

'My mobile number.'

The middle-aged man was six feet away. He was looking directly at Paula.

Paula said uncertainly, 'Thank you –'

'Ring me.'

'Excuse me,' the man said, 'but I was hoping to speak to the manager?'

Paula turned.

She said, in the voice she kept for customers who looked like trouble, 'How may I help you, sir?'

Fiona didn't move.

She raised her head, and very slightly her voice, and she said extremely clearly, 'Look. We have something in common, don't we? After all, we both fell for Gavin. Didn't we?'

CHAPTER EIGHTEEN

At first, Lindsay didn't see Jules at the school gates. She was focused – as she always was, the dash from work to be punctual being regularly preoccupying – on being in place, and evidently waiting, by the time Noah drifted out in his panda backpack, usually holding some strange and fragile artefact he had made, in honour of a festival, or a religion, of which he had no concept except as yet another arbitrary punctuation mark in the inevitable sequence of his days. So she was startled, to the point of jumping a little and saying, 'Oh!' when Jules said, from only inches away, 'It's me.'

'You shouldn't have –'

'What d'you want me to do?' Jules demanded. 'Wave a placard saying here I am, it's Jules, remember me?'

'No,' Lindsay said crossly. 'No. Course not. No, I just –' She stopped and put her arms round Jules. 'Course not,' she said. 'I'm glad to see you. Relieved.' She tightened her arms. 'Glad, Jules. Glad.'

'OK,' Jules said.

Lindsay let go. She held Jules at arm's length and studied her.

'Where've you been?'

'You know where I've been.'

'You look better.'

'Fatter,' Jules said. She pulled a face.

'You could do with it, being fatter.'

'Look who's talking –'

'I missed you,' Lindsay said. 'I know you've been OK with Eleanor. But I've missed you.'

Jules looked away, at the playground. Noah was coming towards them, very slowly, his anorak off one shoulder, towing his backpack.

'Noah's coming.'

Lindsay turned.

'Look at him. Just look at him. In another world –'

'What about your world?'

Lindsay smiled.

'Good.'

'So I hear.'

Lindsay said quickly, 'It's early days, Jules. I'm not keeping anything from you, I'm not hiding anything –'

'Didn't think you were.'

'He's lovely,' Lindsay said.

'He better be.'

Noah reached the school gate and the teacher, waiting to see him safely escorted home.

'Goodbye, Noah.'

Noah looked up at her. He nodded.

She said again, 'Goodbye, Noah. Goodbye, Mrs Brownhill.'

'Bye,' Noah said.

He moved forward and stopped in front of his mother and his aunt.

He glanced up at Jules.

'You got your music?'

'No,' Jules said. 'You want music?'

Noah nodded again.

Lindsay bent down to rearrange his anorak.

'Isn't it lovely to see Jules again?'

Noah thought.

He said, 'I need to see a dinosaur.'

'Well,' Lindsay said, 'not today. Another day we can see a dinosaur. After Legoland.'

'You going to Legoland?'

Lindsay took Noah's hand.

She said with a small air of pride, 'Derek's taking us to Legoland. On Saturday.'

Jules went round to the other side of Noah and took his other hand.

'Can I come?'

'To Legoland? With us?'

'Yeah.'

'D'you want to?'

'Would I ask,' Jules said, 'if I didn't?'

Lindsay gave Jules a quick look across Noah's head.

'What's happened?'

Jules began to walk, pulling Noah and her sister along with her.

'Nothing.'

'Then why have you turned up all of a sudden, after all this time? Why d'you want to spend Saturday at Legoland with Derek and me and Noah?'

Jules walked on in silence.

'Jules?'

'Perhaps,' Noah said, 'there'll be a dinosaur at Legoland.'

'Jules?'

'He didn't mean it,' Jules said.

They all paused at the edge of the pavement.

'What?'

'He didn't mean it,' Jules said again. 'About the club.'

'You mean Jackson?'

'He didn't mean to help me. It was just a line. He just shoots lines.'

'But you didn't believe him, you never really thought –'

They began to cross the road, linked together.

'I did,' Jules said. 'I said I didn't, but I did. I wanted to. I wanted someone to show me what to do next.'

'Oh, Jules –'

'It's OK.'

Lindsay stopped walking. She disengaged Noah's hand and transferred him to her far side so that she was in the centre. She took Jules' hand and squeezed it.

'What a rotten trick.'

'I'm the fool,' Jules said. 'I should have known better.'

'I don't know,' Lindsay said. 'We can't go round suspecting everyone. You have to hope, don't you, that most people mean what they say? Maybe he even did, when he said it.'

'You defending him?'

'Well –'

'Because of Paula? You still want to defend him because of her?'

Lindsay squeezed her hand again.

'No. No, I don't want to defend him. Even for Paula.'

'Well,' Jules said, 'you'd be wasting your time.'

'What?'

'It's over,' Jules said. 'Him and Paula.'

Lindsay stopped again.

'Oh my God.'

'He's just doing the rounds. Coming on to Karen, sucking up to Blaise, leaving me to find out he's not interested in buying a club, telling Paula he's not moving in with her.'

Noah, at the end of the line, began to pull in a half-circle towards a nearby baker's window. It was an old-fashioned baker's, displaying glossy yellow and brown cakes and pastries, iced in blinding white.

'Oh, poor Paula,' Lindsay said. 'Poor, poor Paula. Is she OK?'

'Can I have one of those?' Noah said.

'I dunno –' Jules said to her sister.

'With the cherry?'

'I feel awful,' Lindsay said. 'I feel terrible. I should have been there, I should have known. I should have been there, for both of you.'

'Can I?' Noah said. 'Can I? Can I?'

Lindsay looked down. Noah's finger was pressed against the glass, above a Bakewell tart the size of a saucer.

'Can I?'

'No,' Lindsay said.

Karen switched off the computer. The heating in the office, programmed for a regular working day, had gone off some two hours ago, and she had been working in her padded jacket and the brightly coloured woven hat, made in the Andes, that Poppy had insisted she buy at the last school fund-raising sale. She had considered turning the override on the heating on again, but then something, no doubt due to the strained and unresolved difficulties between her and Blaise just now, had made her think again, and she had put her jacket on. Once, she thought, once upon a time, and not so long a time ago as all that, I would have defiantly done what made me comfortable. Today, defiance isn't how I'm feeling. I don't seem to have the energy – or the taste – for it.

She went round the small room ordering things, papers in wire baskets, clips and pens in pots, rubbish in the bin. On Blaise's stretch of desk she left the usual plastic folders containing the week's figures but without the usual review of the past week or projection for the next. Somehow, like defiance, she had no heart for it tonight. The past seemed oddly reproachful in its settledness: the future without much attraction, certainly not enough to contemplate it in terms of goals and targets. She gathered up her bags, her work bag and two unwieldy supermarket bags, one already pierced in several places by the corners of boxes inside, and gave a last look round. Then she closed the door, dialled the security code for the lock, and manoeuvred her burdens down to the street.

The queue at the bus stop looked as dispirited as she felt. Everyone seemed to be carrying too much and, regardless of that, still trying to read the evening paper by the light of the newsagent's by the bus stop, or talk on the telephone. Karen leaned against the pavement ticket machine and felt the handles of the supermarket bags pull themselves into agonising plastic strings against her fingers, and the strap of her work bag grind into her shoulder, and reflected that her immediate situation, there at the bus stop weighed down by bags, was a metaphor moment, a point of time that symbolised not just the major aspects of her life but the way they had come to oppress her and unbalance her and cause her to feel that, however hard she tried, however fast she ran, she was not capable of regaining even a measure of control.

The bus, when it came, was full. She stood on the lower deck, wedged in against a handrail. All the faces round her, in the harshly lit interior, looked as if painted by Toulouse-Lautrec in a seedy Parisian bar. Karen closed her eyes. The girls would be at home. So would Lucas. Lucas had agreed to collect the girls and to make supper for them. Then he was, he said, going back to his studio. It would have been much easier, Karen thought, if he had left for his studio before she got home, if she did not have to present herself to him in the stumbling, haphazard condition she presently found herself in. But he would be there, because the girls could not be left alone, and would be able, after years of practice, to read every nuance of her mood and she was going to have to endure, quite simply, letting him.

She noticed, as she approached the house, that every floor was glowing. It looked welcoming and wonderful, and all she could think was, Who pays the electricity bills? She dumped her bags on the doorstep and put her key in the lock. When the door swung open, she was aware that she always, at this point, called out, 'Hi, guys!' and that this evening she couldn't.

Rose appeared in the kitchen doorway. She was in her school uniform and it had a long smear of green paint or chalk down the front.

'Hi, pumpkin,' Karen said tiredly.

Rose said, 'I've got a project on windmills.'

'Windmills?'

'And wind farms. Anything windy.'

'Oh good,' Karen said.

Rose went back into the kitchen. Karen followed her. Lucas and Poppy were sitting at the kitchen table eating spaghetti off the same plate. Rose's plate was almost empty. The air smelled of toast.

'Hi,' Karen said.

Lucas got up. He came round the table and took the bags out of Karen's hands.

Poppy said in her hoarse whisper, 'I'm the dancing queen.'

'In her form play,' Rose said. 'They've all got a part. To be fair.'

'Darling, that's great.'

'I know,' Poppy said. She put her fork down and slid off her chair. 'I've had enough.'

'Back,' Lucas said.

'But I –'

'*Back*,' Lucas said. '*On* your chair.'

He put the bags on the counter top.

He said, without looking at Karen, 'Tea?'

She went slowly across to the table and pulled out a chair and sat down heavily.

'Don't bother. You get off.'

'Tea?' Lucas said again. 'Or whisky?'

'There isn't any. It's fine. You go.'

Rose, standing behind her chair, was watching.

'I'm full,' Poppy said. 'Full *up*.'

Lucas didn't look at her.

'Three more bites. Don't argue either.'

Poppy picked up her fork.

'Really,' Karen said. 'You go.'

Lucas opened a cupboard and took out an almost empty bottle. He tilted it and the tea-coloured liquid inside formed a small triangle at the bottom.

'Just enough,' Lucas said. 'And I'm not going.'

'Not –'

'No.'

'Why not?'

'Because,' Lucas said, 'I want to talk to you.'

Rose gripped the back of her chair.

She said, 'I don't want you to argue.'

'We won't,' Lucas said.

Poppy said with her mouth full, 'Finished!'

Lucas was pouring the whisky into a tumbler.

'Don't move.'

'But, Daddy, I –'

'Don't move,' Lucas said, 'until your mouth is quite empty. Then scrape your plate into the bin and put it in the dishwasher. You too, Rose.'

'I didn't *do* anything,' Rose said.

Lucas put the tumbler down in front of Karen.

'Water?'

'Please.'

She watched while both girls took their plates across to the kitchen bin.

'I'm not cross,' she said, 'nor's Dad. Nobody is.'

'I hate it,' Rose said, 'when it's like this.'

'Upstairs,' Lucas said.

'But I –'

'Go upstairs,' Lucas said. 'You can do what you like. I'll be up later.'

'No,' Poppy said.

Lucas crossed the kitchen and put his hands on Poppy's shoulders and propelled her from the room.

He turned to Rose.

'You too.'

Karen tried to catch Rose's eye, but she wasn't looking. The door closed behind them. Karen stayed where she was, her Andean hat still on, and looked at her whisky.

Lucas opened the fridge and took out a bottle of beer. He flipped the top and sat down with it at the table.

He said indifferently, 'I've sold a painting.'

Karen gave a little jerk.

'Luke!'

'Fifteen hundred pounds.'

'That's wonderful!' Karen said. 'Congratulations. That's – that's wonderful.'

He took a swallow from the bottle.

'You think so?'

'Of course I do!'

'I sold it to the gallery we went to the other day, even though I haven't finished it. A Japanese buyer. He wants another.'

'Luke, I am so pleased.'

He looked straight ahead.

'Good.'

'It – it's fantastic that you're working again.'

'Yes.'

Karen bent over her whisky.

'Luke?'

'Yes?'

'I don't want to rain on your parade, I really don't want to spoil this, but – but I don't think I can go on.'

He turned to look at her.

'Not go on?'

'No,' Karen said. She raised her head. 'I'm exhausted and frustrated and I can't go on working like this just to pay the bills.'

He said, 'Please take that hat off.'

Karen pulled off the Andean hat and dropped it on the floor.

'Is that why you work?' Lucas said. 'To pay the bills?'

Karen gave a little snort.

'What do you think?'

'I thought you worked because you liked it. I thought it gave you satisfaction.'

'Not any more,' Karen said.

'Which justifies you kissing someone who you suppose might provide the life of leisure you imagine to be preferable?'

There was a silence.

Then Karen said, 'I didn't kiss him.'

'Oh,' Lucas said. 'Oh really?'

Karen put her face in her hands.

From behind them, she said, 'I tried to kiss him, but he wouldn't let me. He didn't want me to. He said, "I'm not up for this." He said it quite loudly. I think Rosie heard.'

'She did.'

'And yes, I did try to kiss him because there was a kind of relief in being with someone I'm not – I'm not –'

'Propping up?'

Karen took her hands away.

'Yes.'

Lucas looked at her tumbler.

'Drink your whisky.'

'I'm too tired.'

'For God's sake,' Lucas said. 'First the children, now you. *Drink* it!'

Karen picked up the tumbler and took a sip.

'You think,' Lucas said, 'that you want to stop working. Is that what you think?'

Karen nodded.

She said, 'Luke, I don't know –'

He turned towards her.

'I can get a job. I can get a teaching job. I expect I can get a teaching job quite easily. But that isn't the point, is it? I can't make the money you make and, even if I could, that still isn't the point, is it?'

'I don't know –'

'The point is that you like working, that you are good at working, that working, for all the fuss you make about it, suits you. Doesn't it?'

Karen watched him. She was beginning to feel, obscurely, that she would like him to get up and come round the table, and hold her.

'Do you,' Lucas said with energy, 'really want to give up? Don't you want Rosie and Poppy to see you working? Don't you want them to see what women can *do*? Do you really want to give up that achievement, that independence?'

Karen sniffed. She picked up the whisky glass and gulped.

'Maybe I can do more,' Lucas said. 'Maybe I can do more and you can do less. Maybe we can think about living differently. Maybe you should be employed rather than self-employed. It doesn't really matter what we do except that we, and you especially, do *something*.'

Karen pulled a tissue out of her pocket and blew her nose.

'Sorry.'

'Sorry about what? Kissing that wanker?'

'I didn't –'

Lucas raised his hands in the air and brought them down on to the table with a slam.

'OK. OK. And I didn't get anywhere with Blaise, even though I half wanted to.'

'*What*?'

'You heard me.'

'*Blaise*?'

Lucas turned to look at her.

'I was in a twitch about everything, you, me, painting,

292

Jackson, everything. Blaise just looked so sorted. And she is. She told me where to get off.'

Karen began to cry.

'Don't cry,' Lucas said. 'It isn't worth it. We've made fools of ourselves and that's not worth crying over.'

'No.'

'Blaise is on your side.'

Karen said in a whisper, 'I kind of hate her.'

'Because she's behaved well?'

Karen nodded.

'Unfair, don't you think?' Lucas said.

Karen nodded again.

'Kay,' Lucas said, leaning forward, 'if you squander your abilities, I'll throttle you. With my bare hands.'

She looked up at him. Her nose was red. He slid a hand along the table and grasped her nearest one. Then he got up and walked to the kitchen door and pulled it open. Rose and Poppy were sitting on the hall floor, just outside, wrapped in a blanket. They looked up at him, like a pair of chastised puppies.

'All over,' Lucas said. 'You want to come in?'

'There,' Fiona said.

She laid three photographs out in front of Toby on Paula's coffee table.

'Elizabeth, Sarah and Jane. Jane is good at sport. Very good.'

Paula waited for Toby to leap up and dash away to his bedroom. But he didn't. He was visibly tense but he stayed where he was, looking at the photographs.

'Of course,' Fiona said, 'you always knew about them. Didn't you? But it's different when they don't have pictures and names. You can pretend they aren't real when you don't take in their names. Now you have. Elizabeth and Sarah are older, of course, but Jane's about your age.'

Toby bent forward. Jane was wearing dungaree shorts and a T-shirt. She was scowling slightly at the camera.

'She hates being photographed,' Fiona said.

Toby muttered.

'What?'

'Me too,' Toby said.

Fiona put another photograph down.

'That's our house.'

Toby looked at it intently.

Fiona said, 'There's a pool.'

'Don't do this,' Paula said sharply.

Fiona glanced up at her.

'Don't – *bribe* him,' Paula said.

Fiona waited a moment, and then she said, 'It's not just him. I'm trying to bribe you, too.'

'Why?'

'It's time,' Fiona said.

Toby picked up the photograph of the house and began to move his forefinger along the façade, counting windows under his breath.

Paula said, 'I don't know what you're talking about.'

'Well,' Fiona said, 'I'm feeling my way, rather.' She looked round. She said, in a voice with a hint of surprise in it, 'It's nice here.'

Paula flung herself back in the sofa.

'For God's sake! What did you expect? Why are you so bloody patronising?'

Toby didn't look up.

He said very clearly to his mother, 'Don't swear.'

'Excuse me?'

'Don't swear,' Toby said.

'Can I start again,' Fiona said. 'Can I go out and come in again?'

Paula looked away.

She said wearily, 'I don't really know why you're here.'

'You rang me.'

'You asked me to ring you.'

Toby said, 'Is she a sister?'

'Who?'

'Jane.'

'You know that,' Paula said exasperatedly. 'You knew Jane was one of your half-sisters. You've known that all along.'

'Yes,' Fiona said to Toby. 'A half-sister. Same father, different mother. But a sister.'

'Did you just want,' Paula said, 'to see what Gavin spends some of his money on?'

Fiona looked at Toby.

'No,' she said.

Toby put the house picture down and picked up Jane's. He looked slightly sideways at the photographs of the older girls lying on the table.

'I don't quite know how to put this,' Fiona said, 'but I just got to the point of not wanting us to be fantasy figures of hate to one another any more. I just thought, Hang on, there's children here, there's four children who are related by no action of their own. And I thought – well' – she glanced quickly at Toby – 'I thought it was only fair to tell you that – that men who stray don't usually stop straying. If you get me.'

Paula waited.

'I mean,' said Fiona carefully, 'that you were not alone. No more babies, but other – other interests.'

Toby looked up.

He said, 'Are you talking about Gavin?'

'Yes.'

'Well, don't,' Toby said.

Paula sat forward.

She said sadly, 'I don't know if that makes me feel better or worse.'

'Better, I hope. You're the only one I wanted to see, the only one I've made an effort about.'

'Because of Toby?'

'Partly.'

Paula looked at her and then looked away.

'Hard for you –'

'Hard,' Fiona said, 'for all of us.'

Paula stood up.

'I'll make some coffee.'

'I'm going soon –'

'Why,' Paula said suddenly, 'why d'you stay?'

Fiona looked down at her lap.

She said steadily to it, 'Because the alternative is so much worse.'

'Can you mean that?'

'I can. You work, you see.'

'I thought you –'

'I stopped. I'd have to retrain. I might retrain.' She looked up at Paula. Her manner was quite changed. She said, 'Confidence goes, you see. You can look so capable, so certain, in your own world, in the world that requires some incredible talents but doesn't actually ask you to get out there and graft with everyone else. People think that if you can run a house and a family you can run anything. Well, maybe you can, but the world out there doesn't think so.'

In Paula's mind there arose a spontaneous image of the showroom, of her small white office up its staircase, of Joel's spare, black-clad figure padding silently about, his arms full of cushions.

She said rather uncertainly, 'Work isn't everything –'

Fiona briefly twisted her wedding ring.

'From where I'm sitting, it looks like quite a lot.'

Paula sat down again. She looked at Toby. He was leaning back, still holding the photograph, but staring past it to the rattan chest by the window where Gavin's picture lay, as he had left it, on its face.

Paula said very directly to Fiona, 'We aren't a project for you, you know.'

'No.'

'We aren't something just to fill a gap. I can't gang up with you, whatever I feel about Gavin. I can't let Toby be part of some kind of game.'

'I know. I didn't intend any of that. I just thought we'd all got stuck, and then that letter to you kind of – kind of *galvanised* me.'

'OK.'

Fiona said, 'The way I see it, you just have to work out what you can live with, and what you can't, and some kinds of pain are better than others. It seemed to me that not trying, as far as you're concerned, was worse than trying and getting my head bitten off. So bite away. If that's what you want.'

'I want to go,' Toby said suddenly. He spun Jane's photograph across the table.

'Go?' Paula said.

'Yes.'

'Go where?'

Toby roused himself from the depths of the sofa. He flicked a casual hand in the direction of the picture of the house.

'There,' he said.

Toby leaned in Paula's bedroom doorway. She was looking out of the window. She was extremely still, her hands resting on the windowsill. She had been standing like that for ten minutes or so, the ten minutes that had elapsed since he saw her put the telephone down.

Toby had no qualms about eavesdropping. Quite apart from its being a natural consequence of living in a loft, it had become quite clear to him in the last few weeks that, if he didn't know what was going on, he would have no chance at all of influencing events in a way that was acceptable to him. He had spent years avoiding being told anything, in case knowledge led to unwanted and disagreeable involvement, but it had recently struck him that, if he was going to behave like a human parcel, he would be treated like one. It was amazing – and faintly alarming – to him to discover that you could have your say by – well, by saying it.

At the same time as discovering this potential for at least the beginnings of power, Toby retained, quite firmly, a lot of his old habits of deliberate ignorance. Pain, discomfort even, were best dealt with by distance in many cases, as much distance as possible. One of these cases, right now, was Jackson. Toby preferred, in self-defence, not to think about Jackson. Adults, it seemed, could be as unreliable (Jackson) as they could also be trustworthy (Eleanor) and the misery inflicted by the former quality was best dealt with by deletion. He would not, of course, give up his enthusiasm for and loyalty to Chelsea Football Club – that would have seemed to him both wrong and unthinkable – but he would somehow exorcise the means and the man that had introduced him to it.

Which was, as a plan, all very well, except for his mother. For Paula, Jackson did not seem, despite the fact that he hardly appeared any more, to be as easy to eliminate from her daily consciousness as Toby was determined to find it. He had no intention of asking her anything directly, but at the same time he was aware that a miasma of unhappiness hung in the flat like a melancholy mist, and that he had been relieved, earlier in the day, to see her getting quite shirty with Fiona. On the subject of Fiona, and Jane and – and the others – Toby was not going to venture just yet. It was enough to have won his small victory. It was enough that he was going, next weekend, to see the swimming pool at his father's house.

He had thought, when he heard Paula on the telephone, that she was talking to Lindsay. He would rather have liked her to have been talking to Lindsay, which might, in turn, have enabled him to indicate something of the swimming pool to Noah. But it became apparent, quite quickly, that Paula was not talking to Lindsay, she was talking to Jackson, and then, when he was right outside the door and openly listening, that she was talking to Jackson's answering machine.

She did not sound angry, talking to a machine. She did not sound, even, and although he'd heard her crying recently quite a lot, as if she wanted to cry. She just said, in a flat kind of voice, that she had decided that where they'd got to (what?) wasn't where she wanted to be and it wasn't making her happy, in fact it was making her anxious and strung out, and that she understood that he couldn't change, wouldn't change, and so really she had decided to break off everything after this call and that's why she was ringing and he should know that she was miserable and that she loved him. And then – by then, Toby was in the doorway, watching her bent back as she sat on the edge of the bed – she stopped talking, and just held the phone for a bit, and then she clicked it off and chucked it towards the pillows, and got up and put her hands on the windowsill and stood there, looking out.

Toby waited. He waited for what seemed to him like hours and hours, watching the digital-radio clock by the bed click from one oblong green number to the next. Occasionally he looked at Paula's phone, lying in a little dent it had made when it fell on the pillow. The sight of it filled him with relief and, at the same time, anxiety and disappointment. He also felt, disturbingly but excitingly, a growing sense of anger. He was aware, very keenly, who he was angry with, he just wasn't going to name him. As Fiona had said, if you didn't name things, you didn't have to acknowledge that they were real. Well, up to a point, anyway, and that point would do fine for Toby just now.

He picked a small flake of white paint off the door jamb, and inspected it closely. Then he flicked it to the floor and trod on it.

He said to Paula's back, his eyes still on the floor, in a clumsy rush, 'There's still me.'

CHAPTER NINETEEN

B laise went up the stairs to Workwell's office, carrying her laptop, her briefcase, and a plastic carrier bag containing a bottle of white wine that had spent five minutes in the rapid chiller at the supermarket. In her briefcase were her notes on the day's meetings – three satisfactory, out of five – and an estate agent's valuation on her house. That, too, was satisfactory. In fact, very satisfactory. There was something enormously contenting about seeing the manifestation of five years' effort and earning in something as incontrovertibly solid as a house. Perhaps that explained the British passion for house-ownership. Perhaps possessing a house was the modern equivalent of a bound chest full of medieval gold. And why gold, in the first place? Who was it who had decided that gold was so significant?

Karen, not in a tracksuit, was, as usual, at her computer. There were papers on the surfaces around her and papers strewn on the floor and two drawers of the tall filing cabinet were half open. Blaise stepped into the room, put down her briefcase, and slid both drawers shut with a bang.

Karen didn't look round.

She said, 'I was in the middle of filing.'

'So I see.'

Karen made an embracing gesture with both arms towards the scattered papers.

'This is all filing.'

Blaise took the bottle out of its bag, and reached on to a shelf for a stack of disposable tumblers.

'You shouldn't be doing this.'

There was a tiny pause, and then Karen turned round.

'Shouldn't be doing what?'

'Filing.'

'Excuse me, but I have always done the filing. Maybe you haven't noticed, flashing about here and there in your business suit. But it's been going on, day in, day out, for five years and in any case if I don't, who will? Hardly you –'

Blaise unscrewed the wine-bottle cap.

'No,' she said, 'hardly me.'

Karen looked at the wine.

'What's that for?'

'Drinking.'

Karen stood up. She was wearing black trousers and a cherry-red polo-necked sweater and her hair was held up haphazardly in a red plastic clip.

'What's going on?'

Blaise poured wine into two plastic glasses and held one out.

'I've got something to tell you.'

Karen took the glass and stepped back to lean against the desk edge.

She said, 'Are you going to complete my humiliation by telling me you think Jackson would seriously make a useful business partner?'

Blaise looked at her. Then she sat down in the chair nearest to her and took a swallow of wine.

'No,' Blaise said.

'No?'

'No, of course not.'

'Weren't you tempted?'

Blaise looked at her.

'Not by him.'

'And not,' Karen said boldly, 'by Lucas?'

Blaise looked away.

She said, 'I always thought, if I ever were to marry, that one of the kindest things I could do for my husband was *not* to tell him absolutely everything.'

'OK, Miss Perfect,' Karen said, 'but *we* don't work like that, Lucas and me.'

Blaise transferred her gaze to Karen's face.

She said with some emphasis, 'No, I was *not* tempted.'

'Really?'

'Really.'

'Lucas is very attractive –'

'Kay,' Blaise said, 'don't bait me. Don't take your state of mind out on me.'

'I'm fine,' Karen said defiantly.

Blaise said nothing. She looked at the wine in her tumbler.

After a pause she said, 'I said you shouldn't be filing because you are too able to be doing the filing.'

'I've done it for five years,' Karen said again.

'I know. Brilliantly. You have run the business brilliantly.'

Karen put her tumbler down. She leaned forward.

'What do you want to tell me?'

Blaise bent down and retrieved her briefcase from the floor. She balanced it on her knee, and extracted a slim sheaf of papers in a plastic wallet. There was a photograph on the top sheet, visible through the wallet. She held it out to Karen.

Karen looked at the photograph.

'That's your house!'

'Yes,' Blaise said. 'I've had an agent round. I've had it valued. It's worth a lot.'

Karen was still looking at the photograph in her hand.

She said slightly abstractedly, 'You're selling your house, you're putting your house on the market –'

'Yes,' Blaise said.

Karen threw the plastic folder on to the floor.

She said a little wildly, 'But what about *me*?'

Blaise stretched out and picked up Karen's wine and held it out to her.

'That's why I'm telling you.'

'But what –'

'I'm telling you I'm selling up,' Blaise said, 'because it'll help you. It'll help you to make up your mind.'

'How can that help?' Karen said. 'How can you destabilising everything possibly help?'

Blaise looked at the folder on the floor.

'Think,' she said. 'Just *think*.'

'I don't wish to seem sarcastic,' Eleanor said, 'but I had almost forgotten what you looked like.'

Karen was leaning against the tall cupboard in which Eleanor kept her broom and the ironing board. She had her hair on her shoulders and she was wearing a skirt. Eleanor wasn't sure she had ever seen Karen's legs before, in all the years they had known one another. They were, Eleanor thought, rather good legs. She waved a hand, holding a teaspoon.

'Why don't you sit down?'

Karen detached herself from the cupboard and sank into the nearest chair. She picked up a paperclip lying on the table among the papers and cereal boxes and jars of this and that, and fiddled with it.

'Where are the girls?' Eleanor said.

'At school –'

'Usually,' Eleanor said in the deliberate tone of voice her former colleagues would have labelled 'pleasant', 'when the girls are at school, you are at work.'

'Not today,' Karen said. She pulled one side of the paperclip open and regarded the wire prong she had made.

She said without looking at Eleanor, 'How are you?'

'Well,' Eleanor said. 'As the Australians would say, I'm good.'

'Living with Jules –'

'Strangely successful.'

'You *look* well.'

'So, I believe,' Eleanor said, 'does she.'

Karen leaned forward and punched a periodical cover neatly with the wire prong, in a pattern of tiny holes.

'I haven't seen her.'

'No.'

'I haven't seen her, or Paula, or Lindsay, or anyone. Not for ages.'

'Tea?' Eleanor said. 'Coffee? Jules drinks more tea than you would believe possible. And she has become rather arcane about it and wants to make it with loose tea, in a pot.'

Karen dropped the paperclip and folded her hands firmly together, as if to keep them still.

'Coffee, please.'

'Sometimes,' Eleanor said, 'a stage of life becomes almost obsessively preoccupying. In itself.'

'Why do you say that?'

Eleanor turned round, holding a packet of coffee in the hand that wasn't holding the teaspoon.

'In response to your saying that you hadn't managed to see any of your friends recently.'

Karen said quickly, 'I've just been so busy –'

Eleanor spooned coffee, tiny spoonful after spoonful, into an earthenware jug.

She said, 'You all are.'

'Sometimes,' Karen said, staring at her hands, 'being busy means you don't have to think too much. You don't have to decide things.'

'Certainly.'

'I wanted to see you,' Karen said with force. 'I wanted to talk to you –'

Eleanor poured boiling water into the jug and began to stir it in a leisurely manner with a carving fork.

'Here I am.'

'Blaise –' Karen said, and stopped.

Eleanor laid the fork on the counter and brought the jug over to the table. She set it down on the nearest pile of newspapers.

'Yes,' she said, 'Blaise. And Lucas. And the mysterious Jackson. Open the drawer next to you, would you, and find a strainer.'

Karen rocked back in her chair in order to pull out a shallow drawer in the table in front of her. Its contents reminded her of her childhood, a comfortingly old-fashioned jumble of pickle forks and primitive can-openers and the reddish rubber rings for Kilner jars. She extracted a small dented tea strainer, and held it out.

'That do?'

'The very thing.'

'You know – about Jackson, about –'

Eleanor limped back to the kitchen counter and unhooked two mugs from hooks on the wall.

'I know enough.'

'I expect you think we're all pathetic, me and Paula especially –'

Eleanor came back and lowered herself carefully into a chair.

She said, 'He's very personable. And very enigmatic. A powerful combination.'

'And a liar.'

'No,' Eleanor said, 'not really. An encourager of illusion, possibly. But not a liar in the sense of being a pathological fraudster. But certainly –' She stopped.

'Certainly what?'

'Certainly a catalyst.'

'Oh, *thank* you –'

Eleanor began pouring coffee through the strainer into mugs. 'And maybe what you all needed.'

Karen watched the coffee grounds building up in the strainer.

'D'you need a plate?'

'Please.'

Karen got up and retrieved a plate from the rack by the sink. She put it down near the jug and waited while Eleanor tapped the contents of the strainer on to it. Some of the grounds sprayed on to the papers near by. Eleanor took no notice.

Karen said, 'You know he wanted to buy into Workwell –'

'I know he suggested it.'

'And now –'

Eleanor stopped pouring.

'Now what?'

Karen looked suddenly distraught.

She said in a rush, 'Now Blaise is selling her house in order to buy me out, and move on herself in some new arrangement with one of our clients.'

'Ah.'

'What's ah?'

'I thought that might happen,' Eleanor said. She pushed one coffee mug towards Karen.

Karen gazed at her. She looked as if she might cry.

'What am I supposed to do?'

'Do?'

'Yes,' Karen said. 'There's me to consider. Can you imagine what it's like, after everything else, just to be summarily *dumped*, by your business partner?'

Eleanor indicated the end of the table.

'The milk is there somewhere. Maybe behind the corn-flakes.'

Karen moved the cereal box and found a carton of milk. She said angrily, 'She said it would set me free.'

'Yes.'

'And Lucas thinks it's wonderful and wants to sell our house too and move out of London and start again with a completely different kind of life.'

'Yes.'

'He says if I don't go on working, he'll strangle me. But I can't. I can't go on in all this confusion and exhaustion and having no initiative because everyone's snatched it from me. I was *managing*, Eleanor, I really was. Six months ago, I was tired but I knew where I was, I could control things. I know I told Blaise I didn't want us to expand, but that was just while I caught my breath. I didn't mean *never* expand, I just meant give me a break, just for a few years. And now this. Luke sells a painting, *one* painting, and thinks everything'll be solved, and different, and Blaise offers me all this money and tells me, slam, bang, thank you, ma'am, that our partnership is over and that she is doing me a bloody *favour*.'

Eleanor poured milk into her coffee.

She said, 'He's right.'

'What?'

'Lucas is right. About you working.'

'I was working. I've always worked. I was working fine.'

'Possibly,' Eleanor said, 'possibly. But you weren't stretched.'

'I was,' Karen said, 'I *was*. I was stretched almost to breaking point –'

Eleanor took a sip of coffee and made a face.

'Not a success –'

'I couldn't have been stretched further –'

'Administratively no, probably not. But you weren't using all your capabilities.'

'Lucas thinks that. Blaise said that.'

'Mmm.'

'Eleanor, I feel like the washing in the drum. On the spin cycle.'

Eleanor pushed her mug away, and folded her arms on the table.

'This business of work –'

'Yes?'

'For us women,' Eleanor said, 'it has always seemed to me to fulfil two functions. It can enable us to become our most genuine and complete selves – as men know perfectly well – and it can protect us from the fickleness of fortune. The latter appears to me especially important if you have children.'

'I'm hardly economically dependent.'

Eleanor glanced up.

She said sharply, 'How about bringing those little girls up on your own?'

Karen said nothing. She picked up her mug and took a long swallow of coffee seemingly without noticing its taste.

She said unsteadily, 'I don't think – Lucas would leave me –'

'He might die,' Eleanor said.

'Don't say that!'

Eleanor stretched out one hand and gripped Karen's nearest arm.

'Well, think.'

'People keep saying that –'

'Karen,' Eleanor said, 'why should this not be the chance to improve your life in many ways?'

Karen turned to look at her, eyes wide.

'You want us to leave?'

Eleanor took her hand away.

'Don't be childish.'

'But –'

'I want you to see,' Eleanor said vehemently, 'that if you can't seize the chance to make yourself independent nobody can seize it for you.'

'I *was* independent, working with Blaise –'

'Were you?'

'Yes!'

'Then why did you drag your heels? Why didn't you want the company to grow?'

Karen muttered something.

'What?'

'I said,' Karen said tiredly, 'I said OK.'

'It seems to me,' Eleanor said, 'you can either start something else on your own and view it as an exciting challenge and not merely as a meal ticket, or you can work for someone else and devote all your energies to the job rather than running the job.'

Karen picked up her mug again.

'Don't drink it,' Eleanor said, 'it's filthy. It's just as well that the modern cult of fulfilment through domesticity was never an option for me.'

Karen put her mug down. She put her own hand out and took Eleanor's.

She said, 'Would you have liked it to be?'

Eleanor gave her hand a squeeze and withdrew her own. She shook her head.

'No, my dear.'

'But now –'

'Now is different.'

'And it suits you, with Jules –'

'Thus far.'

Karen leaned back in her chair. She regarded Eleanor, the fuzz of whitish hair, the strong features, the bulky clothes.

She said with sudden warmth, 'I'll miss you.'

Jules was carrying a bag, very carefully. It was a canvas bag, designed as a nonchalant kind of briefcase, and inside it, cushioned in bubblewrap, were two promotional vinyls that Jules had persuaded the current disc jockey at Soundproof to lend her. He had been rather reluctant, suspicious of her enthusiasm.

'What you want them for?'

'I like them –'

'Nobody,' he said, gesturing dismissively, 'knows about these geezers. No one's heard of them. What you gonna do with them?'

Jules looked at the records.

She said, 'You want them?'

He shrugged.

'I get promos all the time –'

'So you don't want them.'

He leaned forward.

'That does not mean I want you to have them.'

Jules looked at him blandly.

'What can I do with them? A couple of decks in my bedroom –'

He took out his Rizlas and a black pouch of tobacco. 'Take 'em.'

'Really?'

'Yeah,' he said. He ran the tip of his tongue along a sheet of Rizla. 'Just remember who gave them to you. Right?'

She picked up the records. She gave him a quick glance. He was a gross-looking guy, but when he got playing he was magic.

'I won't forget,' Jules said.

She had played the records in her bedroom at Eleanor's house. She had arranged her decks inside the wardrobe, having removed her clothes, and discovered that, if she climbed inside with the music, she could play it much louder than would have been possible otherwise, and also strangely but exhilaratingly absorb it better. There was something wonderful about crouching in that wooden box absolutely filled with sound, with the beat magnified into something almost completely physical, and it was while she was in there one day, arms round her knees, eyes closed, quite lost and taken over by the music, that it had come to her that, rather than go on trying to be a top-rank DJ, she might instead become a producer. After all, she was good at sound-engineering, she liked it, she understood it, and when she thought about finding undiscovered music and putting it together and recording it she wondered, with something close to amazement, why she hadn't thought of it before.

She had taken the vinyls, and her ideas to D'Arblay Street. Benny had been as encouraging as his laid-back profession-alism would permit. He told her he knew of a group of boys in Croydon whom he rated – he even said 'really rated' – who were looking for the next step, the way forward from playing together in a workshop somewhere that belonged to the uncle of one of them. They'd managed to scrape together about five hundred pounds, for half a dozen guitars and some percussion. He said he'd put Jules in touch with them. He flicked the record covers with his fingernails.

'Good choice.'

Jules came back to West London glowing. She felt as she used to feel when she first discovered music, except better, because she knew more now, she understood more, because the hits on her website were so steadily numerous now that she knew that she was communicating, that the message was out. Shielding her canvas bag from the crush of people on the tube, she realised that, if she went on DJ-ing, she couldn't, as a girl, go on and on until she was ancient, like thirty or something, and that producers could be any age, that in fact producers could only get better the more they knew, the more experience they had.

She emerged into the daylight in a spirit of enthusiasm and generosity. She thought that she might go and find Lindsay, and tell her what had come to her, and then she remembered that Lindsay would still be at work, and that work inevitably included Derek, and that, although Derek might prove himself to be all the admirable and reliable things Lindsay assured Jules he was, Jules was not ready, yet, either to accept anything about him she hadn't seen for herself, or – more significantly – not to begrudge him a share of Lindsay's preoccupations. Sharing Lindsay with Noah was one thing – sharing Lindsay with Derek and his unimpeachable appearance was quite another. Especially as – and she couldn't fool herself about this – she was going to have to.

Jules paused on the pavement and looked about her. She was possessed by the energy of excitement and relief, and the accompanying wish to share it. She could, of course, go home to Eleanor, but she was rather saving Eleanor for later, for one of those weird sessions she had somehow come to depend upon, late at night in Eleanor's sitting room, with only Eleanor's reading lamp on, and maybe the telly on too but with the sound off, and the teapot. Jules would lie on the sofa, under the grossly coloured crocheted blanket that Toby used to lie under, and kind of ramble round her thoughts to Eleanor, out loud. She couldn't believe how much she talked then. She couldn't believe the things she told Eleanor. Once she said, 'Aren't you shocked?' and Eleanor, not looking up from her polygon word puzzle, said, 'I'm almost unshockable, I think. Rather as I believe nuns are reputed to be.'

Jules slung the canvas bag on her shoulder, and put her right arm protectively over it, holding it close to her side. She didn't somehow want to shock Eleanor. She didn't, in fact, want to do anything that might upset or displease Eleanor because Eleanor, while never – thank *goodness* – saying anything openly warm or affectionate, always seemed to have time for her. Lindsay had always *made* time, but that was different. The difference was the effort it cost Lindsay, and the fact that that effort was visible to Jules and often uncomfortably visible. But Eleanor was just there. Apart from going, slowly, to the corner shop, Eleanor was steadily, peacefully, reliably there, and Jules wasn't about to jeopardise that dependable source of solace for the sake of some careless impulse. She looked up briefly at the raggedly cloudy

London sky and was aware of another impulse, quite unbidden and obscure in either origin or purpose, an impulse to
go and see Paula. She glanced at the traffic, spotted a gap
between a bus and a van, dodged with agility across the
road. Even if Paula was, for some reason, not in the shop, she
could expend some of her energy in winding up Joel.

'What's happened?' Paula said.

She was at the computer in her office, which was stacked
almost completely with unopened boxes.

'Nothing,' Jules said.

'Is Lindsay –'

'She's fine.'

Paula got up from her swivel chair and moved a box or
two to make seating space.

'Joel's got to unpack all this. We can't move for stock. I
suppose you want lunch.'

'Had it,' Jules said.

She perched on the space Paula had made for her. Paula, in
jeans and trainers, looked tired and thinner.

'You OK?' Jules said.

Paula shrugged. There was a black fleece hanging on the
back of her chair instead of the usual jacket.

Paula said without inflection, 'Well, what do you think.'

Jules slid the bag off her shoulder and propped it against
the wall of boxes beside her.

'That shit.'

'It doesn't help,' Paula said flatly, 'to think like that.'

Jules said, 'I'm better angry than sad.'

Paula nodded.

'It's easier.'

'Toby OK?'

Paula sat down sideways in her swivel chair.

'Oh yes. He has a new project.'

'Not footie any more?'

'Oh, the footie goes on,' Paula said. 'This is in addition. He's adding family to footie.'

'Family.'

Paula looked at her. She gave a half-smile.

She said, 'Gavin's family.'

'Wow –'

'We're going there. We're going at the weekend. We're going to admire the swimming pool and the double garage and the American fridge. We're going to meet Toby's half-sisters. He's got the photograph of one of them under his bed.'

'How d'you know?'

'I looked,' Paula said.

Jules watched her.

'Does Lindsay know?'

'Nope.'

'Why not?'

'Because,' Paula said, linking her hands around one knee, 'I haven't told her.'

'You're still not speaking?'

'She's busy –'

'She's always,' Jules said vehemently, 'got time for you.'

Paula sighed. She unlinked her hands and reached across the desk for a tube of peppermints. She held it out to Jules. Jules shook her head.

'It's full-time work,' Paula said, 'being happy, like she is just now.'

Jules said, 'She knows about you. She knows about you and Jackson.'

'She hasn't been near me –'

'Have you been near her?'

Paula studied her feet.

She said, 'Don't lecture me.'

'It's not always about *you*,' Jules said.

Paula raised her head, and looked at Jules.

315

'It's not always about you when you're happy,' Jules said. 'It's not always about you when you're sad.'

'Oh, go away,' Paula said.

'Ring her.'

'I can't –'

'Ring her,' Jules said.

Paula said nothing.

'I'm going out at the weekend too,' Jules said. 'I'm going to Legoland with Lindsay and Toby and Derek.'

Paula stared.

'Are you?'

'Yup.'

'D'you want to?'

Jules stared back.

'Don't know.'

'Why are you going?'

'You know why,' Jules said. 'For Noah. For Lindsay.'

'And you?'

Jules shrugged.

'Maybe. Like you.'

'Like *me*?'

'You're not going to Gavin's house just for Toby. Are you?'

Paula stood up.

She said, 'I'm not going to turn into Fiona's new best friend. Don't think that.'

Jules waited a moment, then she said again, 'Ring Lindsay. Ring her.'

Paula looked at her reflection in the flower-shop window. The sight was not encouraging. Her jeans were some she had bought when fatter and they hung on her in a way which was far from streetwise, and merely depressing. Her trainers, for some reason, looked larger than usual, clumsy and bulbous, and the fleece was – well, it was the sartorial equivalent of huddling under a blanket because anything else was just too much effort. Even reflected darkly like this, it was plain that her hair spelled the same kind of defeat as the rest of her. Well, she thought, this is how I started the day and this is how I'll have to stay as I continue it. At least Toby should be pleased. At least Toby has got a mother looking like he thinks normal mothers should look. He hadn't actually commented at breakfast, however. In fact, when she thought about it, he'd behaved as if she wasn't there, as if she had all the presence and vitality of the microwave, or the fridge.

The flower shop was dank, and smelled of river water. Paula chose three bunches of white freesias, the flowers still tightly, greenishly budded, and asked for them to be wrapped in a single bouquet. The girl in the flower shop slapped the three individually tied bunches on to a single sheet of florist's paper, and sighed.

'No,' Paula said. 'I mean can you undo all three bunches and put them together again, as one.'

The girl sighed again. She took scissors out of her apron pocket, and snipped the elastic bands round the freesias. Then she slapped them down on the sheet of paper.

'Careful,' Paula said.

The girl froze.

She said, her eyes on the flowers, 'You want to do my job for me?'

'No,' Paula said, unaccountably suddenly altogether more energised and engaged, 'but I want you to do it properly and not waste my money.'

With elaborate slowness, the girl picked up the freesias and began to lay them, one by one, on the sheet of paper. Then she rolled the paper up, with exaggerated care, and tied it with some strands of raffia. Then, eyes averted, she held the bunch out to Paula as if the entire shop had suddenly been filled with an unbearable stench.

'There,' Paula said cheerfully. 'That wasn't so hard, was it?'

The girl turned her head, and surveyed Paula inch by inch, head to toe. She allowed her gaze to rest, for a fraction too long, on the worn toes of Paula's trainers.

She said, in fair imitation of Paula's tone, 'Nine seventy-five, madam. *If* you'd be so kind.'

Out on the street, the day seemed rather brighter. Paula rummaged in her bag as she walked, and found a folding plastic hairbrush that had been given away with a magazine, and pulled it, with satisfaction, through her hair. She had told Joel she was going out for forty minutes and he had looked straight at her head and said, 'Going for a blow-dry?' and she hadn't even had the spirit then to pull a face at him, or make the obvious rejoinder.

Outside Lindsay's building society she paused for a moment. She had always teased Lindsay about her place of work, about its appearance, its employees, its particular language and clientele. It was a far cry, she'd always implied, from clacking about the polished floors of a sophisticated and slightly mysterious oriental trading emporium, and dealing with the customers who could afford to obey whim rather than necessity. She wasn't, she thought, peering through the poster-plastered glass – 'We'll lend you five times your salary! (Terms and Conditions apply)' – about to withdraw such comparisons, but she was, she reflected with some irony, perfectly dressed that day to pass without notice among the people sitting at blue-and-white plastic desks inside, being instructed by Lindsay's colleagues in their blue-uniform suits and conspicuous name badges.

Paula pushed the door open, and went in. Nobody looked up. She walked across the floor to the huge glass wall that divided the public space from the workings of the actual office, as if those seeking a mortgage needed to see those providing it actually in operation, like a visible kitchen in a restaurant. At the back was a kind of large cubicle, with conventional-length windows and an open door, in which Paula could see a tall dark man in a suit, standing up, as if better to survey his kingdom, and talking on the telephone. That, Paula thought, must be Derek, Lindsay's Derek. She looked at him with interest and, to her surprise, with some respect. That was Lindsay's Derek, who was taking her, and Noah, and even Jules, on a Saturday outing to Legoland.

Three desks away from the cubicle sat Lindsay. She too was in a blue-uniform suit, but she seemed to be wearing it better than anyone else. Or maybe it was her hair, which was looking much improved on its usual self, shinier, richer. Had Lindsay, who never spent money on herself that might more honourably be spent on Noah, or her home, actually had her hair treated? Coloured? Paula put her face close to the glass and willed Lindsay to look up and notice her.

Lindsay went on typing. She was sitting very upright, and typing as if she had plenty of appetite for it, as if it was not in fact some kind of repetitive chore in which any sort of individual creativity was instructed to be repressed. After a moment or two, Derek left his cubicle, said something to the middle-aged woman at the nearest desk (she looked up at him, and smiled) and then moved across to stand beside Lindsay. He said something, Lindsay smiled, but she did not look up and she did not stop typing. Derek bent a little – he's tall, Paula thought, really tall – and said something else, and the way he was bending, the attitude of his head and shoulders, suddenly made Paula's heart turn over in a sharp unwanted recollection. She blinked.

Lindsay laughed. Derek's hand hovered above her shoulder for a second, and pulled back. He was smiling. Lindsay's hands slowed on the keyboard, and she looked up, not at Derek, but straight across the office, straight at Paula, standing there the other side of the glass.

Lindsay went quite still. Derek stopped looking down at her, and let his gaze follow hers. Paula stood there, watched by both of them, in her jeans and trainers and her big black fleece. She tried to smile but nothing much happened. Lindsay gave a tiny, jerky movement, like the beginning of a wave. Paula let her bag fall to her feet and, with both hands, lifted the paper cone of flowers, so that Lindsay could see. She did not care, for that moment, that both her gesture and her expression were beseeching.

CHAPTER TWENTY

On the counter in the kitchen, Paula had left a bottle of wine. It was greenish and translucent and on the label it said 'Sancerre Terre de Maimbray'. Toby inspected it and observed that it had a cork. He also observed that Paula had left two glasses beside it, while she went off to have a shower, and a stiff cellophane packet of something called seaweed rice crackers. Toby shook his head. The things Paula chose to buy, when you thought of what she *might* have bought, were unfathomably peculiar.

Toby sighed. He was aware that this was not his habitual sigh of incipient despair at having to live with the arbitrary decisions and actions of adults, but rather a sigh of happy exasperation. He supposed, looking at the wine and looking at the glasses, that it ought to be opened. And it also, being white wine (why was it called white, when it was always yellow?) ought to be in the fridge.

He opened a drawer and extracted Paula's fish-shaped corkscrew, and applied it to the bottle. The top of the bottle was encased in thick metal foil. Toby laid the corkscrew on the counter, prised the foil off with a kitchen knife and threw it, accurately, towards the kitchen bin, which it hit, and then fell on the floor. Toby picked up the corkscrew again, fitted it over the bottle neck and, with an ease that he was sorry no one was there to witness, expertly pulled out the cork. Then he opened the fridge and stored the bottle in a rack in the door, and banged it shut again with a complacent sense of accomplishment.

There were only two glasses, of course, because only Eleanor was coming. Paula had said, before she disappeared into the bathroom, that she was sorry that no children were coming, that it would be pretty tedious for Toby, but Toby didn't really mind. To be honest, he'd always found Noah a bit of a baby, and although Poppy was OK, Rose was the kind of girl that gave girls a bad name in Toby's view, the kind of girl who always seemed to be waiting for you to upset her, or say or do something she disapproved of. And she was not, definitely, interested in sport. Rose liked sitting at tables, with adults not very far away, doing all this neat drawing and stuff. You couldn't imagine Rose running, or throwing anything, or liking going fast. Not having Rose too much in his life any more was not, Toby thought, going to leave an exactly big black hole.

He sauntered out of the kitchen and into the living space. Paula had changed the orange cushions for lime-green ones, a colour Toby considered completely gross, but if she liked it then in his present mood of remarkable benevolence he supposed he'd go along with it for the moment until he felt it was only fair to point out that he lived here too, and he'd like blue cushions. Chelsea-blue cushions. And some white ones, maybe. Paula had lit some of her tea-light candles. Toby had no objection to those; they were really quite pretty, he supposed, even if pretty was a word he'd rather only use as a qualifying adverb than as an adjective.

He walked straight across the zebra rug and flung himself on the sofa. There was a lot to tell Eleanor when she came, and he was going to stick around while Paula had her say to make sure that she didn't kind of twist things around the way she was inclined to. Toby wanted Eleanor to know that they were going to Gavin's house in a completely *normal* way, that Gavin's house was also his house, since Gavin was his father, and that there was a family in that house whose father he was too, which meant that Toby was somehow much better furnished with people in his life – family people – than he had ever thought he was. And if Eleanor said, 'Well, you never wanted to know about them before,' he'd say, 'I didn't know what was OK to know, did I? I didn't remember their names,' and if Eleanor said, 'You didn't *want* to remember their names,' he'd say, 'I didn't know it would be like this, did I?' Which was true. It was also true that he was a bit nervous, but he wasn't going to let Paula see that in case it was catching and made her more nervous than she already was. It was amazing really that he could control things this way. He thought that piloting a plane might feel like this, not a huge plane with banks of computers to fly it, but a little plane, with a joystick, that you could actually kind of *steer*. He moved his hands in the air above him, guiding the plane called Paula down through the clouds, and the bumpy patches of turbulence, and landed her smoothly in the centre of the zebra rug.

Paula came out of the bathroom in a robe, brushing her hair.

'Would you do me a favour?'

Toby made goggles out of his fists and peered at her through them.

'Maybe.'

'Could you take the cork out of the wine for me?'

Toby flipped over on to his back again, and goggled up towards the faraway ceiling.

'Done it.'

Paula went over to the kitchen. He heard her move the corkscrew and then open the fridge.

'Wow,' Paula said.

Toby went on goggling.

'That's amazing,' Paula said. 'You just *did* that?'

323

'Yup.'

'Well,' Paula said, 'thank you.'

Toby took his hands away from his face.

'You really going to eat those seaweed things?'

'D'you think we shouldn't?'

'I think,' Toby said, 'they look dire.'

Paula sat down beside him.

'I shouldn't buy stuff unless I'm feeling happy –'

Toby tensed slightly. He might be feeling better, but he couldn't risk letting Paula slide back into this weepy, mushy stuff. Especially not with tomorrow coming.

He said, in a voice whose heartiness surprised him, 'What about cheese?'

Paula laughed. She gave Toby a nudge.

'Eleanor likes cheese,' Toby said.

'It'll be odd, just having Eleanor,' Paula said. 'Lindsay was going to come, but Jules persuaded her to take Derek to the club tonight. They'll be the oldest there by miles. Jules wanted them to see her in action. Try *not* to be a DJ when you grow up?'

Toby picked up the nearest lime-green cushion and flung it as high into the air as he could.

'No *fear*.'

In her sitting room, Eleanor waited for a minicab from Murphy's. She sat peacefully, but carefully, in her usual chair because today had been one of Athina's days, and after one of her visits Eleanor had the sense that both she and the house had to make more effort, had to try somehow to live up to Athina's energetic standards. All Eleanor's papers and books were in recognisable piles, the carpet was swirled with the sweeping strokes of the hoover, the air was synthetically fragrant with all the sprays and polishes that Athina used with such lavish enthusiasm. She had brought Eleanor a new and monstrous cactus with improbable purple flowers on the edges of its fat leaves, and Jules a box of baklava. Eleanor had had to remind her not to touch Jules' dirty washing or ironing.

'Ironing?' Jules said, eating baklava out of the box with her fingers. 'Never heard of it.'

In the bag on her knee, Eleanor had her spectacles, money for the minicab and a book for Toby called *Chelsea, by the Fans* which Jules had ordered for her on the Internet. By the same means, Jules had acquired for Eleanor a new electric blanket, a biography of Alexander the Great, a subscription to *Prospect* magazine and a case of Cabernet Sauvignon at twenty per cent off. These things had been silently ordered in Jules' bedroom, and had then magically – and almost immediately – arrived at Eleanor's door. It was, Eleanor reflected, a wonderful way of benefiting from progress without having to involve oneself in its mechanisms. It was a way of enjoying change because change, in this form, seemed only acceptable.

Other changes were, however, going to be harder. Other changes were going to require adjustments in what she had come to rely on, not least the reining in of the comfortable exercise of affection of the last few years. Starting, of course, with the children. You could tell yourself, as Eleanor often had done, that you genuinely did not regret not having had your own children, but that did not mean that your life was not considerably enhanced by having other people's children in it. And half the children who had run so easily in and out of her life for the last five years were leaving. Rose and Poppy were leaving London. They were leaving London and going to live in Dorset, where Lucas was going to teach art, at a fashionably liberal private school, and Karen was going to – well, Karen was going to see what she felt like doing once the sensation of being on the spin cycle had receded.

'Don't worry,' Karen had said to Eleanor. 'Don't worry. I'll work. I'll work at something.'

Rose and Poppy were both alarmed and excited about going. Rose, in particular, was distressed about abandoning familiarity, about the disloyalty of leaving their London house, their London bedroom, their school, Mr Carpenter's cat Fred. But they were going to have a house with a garden, and a swing and perhaps a donkey. They were going to a village school, on bicycles.

'I hope they won't be bored,' Karen said. 'Oh, God, I hope they won't be bored.'

Eleanor had looked at her.

She looked back.

She said, half laughing, 'I hope I won't be bored.'

'You can always come back.'

Karen put a hand out and gripped Eleanor's arm.

'You can't, you know.'

'Correction,' Eleanor said. 'I'll put it better. You can regard this as a period of transition, not as a final destination.'

I have, she thought now, to make my own transition. I have to get used to us all moving round in the dance, to some leaving the circle, to some, like Lindsay's Derek, joining it. I have to get used to Blaise not being two doors away but instead in a rented flat in Charterhouse Square, within walking distance of the new office she is setting up somewhere off Holborn, in partnership with an Englishman and a Dutchman who have been impressed by the effect she has had on their company. She says she will come and visit me and I believe her. But I also know that she is moving into a different life, a different set of connections, and her visits to Fulham, and her promised visits to Dorset, will be conscientiously made, but from a new perspective. And this is particularly painful for me because I understand it so well, I understand what Blaise is doing because it is what I, in her place, in this day and age, and with the present opportunities, would do myself. I would do it, even knowing, as I do now, what lies ahead, when work is over. Paula and Karen and Jules are women who fling themselves into their particular emotions, Lindsay flings herself into the lives of others – and Blaise and I are women who fling ourselves into work. And none of these passions are, in the end, very different from one another in the effect they have on us all, and certainly not in their intensity, nor in their subjection to the passage of time. Children grow up and leave, relationships founder, work ends. But if you hold back from plunging in, while anything enriching is on offer, then the alternative seems to me to be no more than dust and ashes, and a criminal squandering of being alive. That is what I said to Blaise when she came to tell me about her future. That is what I shall say to Paula tonight, because that is what I feel, and I feel it as urgently in my seventies as I felt it in my teens and oh Lord, Eleanor thought, scrabbling suddenly for tissues in the nearest of Athina's piles, oh Lord, I am becoming quite emotional.

From the street outside, a car horn sounded twice. Murphy's drivers, with whom she could now readily talk football, felt familiar enough with her not to bestir themselves from the driving seat on arrival in order to ring her doorbell. They were helpful men on the whole, and she could see that the horn tooting was almost a mark of affection, often confirmed, at the sight of her fumbling to lock her door while encumbered with sticks and bags, by them springing out of the car, after all, to assist her. She blew her nose with decision, hung her bag round her neck – a contemptible habit, but practical – and struggled to her feet. She paused for a moment, straightening and steadying herself, and then, grasping her stick, moved purposefully across the sitting room, and into the hall ahead.

When she opened the front door, the driver was already half out of his door and waiting. Eleanor gave him a wave and set about locking the door behind her.

'You OK?' the driver called.

'Fine,' Eleanor said. 'I'm fine.'

She pulled the key out of the lock and gave the door a final testing thump. Who knew what lay ahead? Who knew how all their lives would develop, what people and situations all these tentative new connections might bring? She began to negotiate her way between the cars parked at the kerb towards the taxi, and the driver came forward and put a hand under her elbow to steady her.

'Thank you,' Eleanor said.

'No problem –'

'We're not going far, just down towards the river –'

'Somewhere nice?'

Eleanor heaved herself into the back seat, grasping her stick.

'Oh yes –'

'That's the ticket,' the driver said. 'Innit? That's what you want, on a Friday night.'

ACKNOWLEDGEMENTS

The research for this book has been some of the most purely engaging that I've ever been lucky enough to undertake. It involved a number of extraordinarily generous and enthusiastic people, whom I would like to thank, most warmly, for introducing me to – for me! – two completely new worlds.

The first is that of clubbing and house music. I am so very grateful to Emma Feline for introducing me so vividly to the life and aspirations of a girl disc jockey, and for sending me to Uptown Records, in D'Arblay Street, Soho, where Joel Chapman, recognising an eager but utter novice, instructed me about house music, and the abiding life of the vinyl record. He then passed me on to the Neighbourhood club, in Ladbroke Grove, specialists in house, who could not – and nor could their clientele – have been more welcoming to a novelist with a notebook . . . And I would also like to thank Jason Kouchak, very much, for being both escort and – frequently – interpreter, on this exhilarating musical journey.

The second new world is football, and this, I think, looks like a permanent fixture in my life. Bradley Rose, of Transworld, took me to Stamford Bridge (he has been going since he was seven . . .) for my first ever live Premiership game and that was it, a coup de foudre (and in particular, for that *beau garçon*, Didier Drogba). Brad then took me a second time, which confirmed my commitment, and on both occasions, my seat was that usually occupied by his brother, David, who gave it up for me . . . I don't know how you thank a man adequately for such gallantry, but THANK YOU, DAVID.

I am also indebted to Piers Presdee, of Harcourt Chambers in Oxford, who wrote *A Football Guide for the Thinking Woman* especially for me. Clear, energetic, comprehensive and funny (although he is more frustrated by Drogba's volatility than I am . . .), it deserves to be a best-seller in its own right.

A NOTE ON THE AUTHOR

The author of eagerly awaited and sparklingly readable fiction often centred around the domestic nuances and dilemmas of life in contemporary England, Joanna Trollope has also written a number of historical novels and *Britannia's Daughters*, a study of women in the British Empire. In 1988 she wrote her first contemporary novel, *The Choir*, and this was followed by *A Village Affair*, *A Passionate Man*, *The Rector's Wife*, *The Men and the Girls*, *A Spanish Lover*, *The Best of Friends*, *Next of Kin*, *Other People's Children*, *Marrying the Mistress*, *Girl From the South*, *Brother and Sister* and, most recently, *Second Honeymoon*. She lives in London.

A NOTE ON THE TYPE

The text of this book is set in Linotype Sabon, named after the type founder, Jacques Sabon. It was designed by Jan Tschichold and jointly developed by Linotype, Monotype and Stempel, in response to a need for a typeface to be available in identical form for mechanical hot metal composition and hand composition using foundry type.

Tschichold based his design for Sabon roman on a fount engraved by Garamond, and Sabon italic on a fount by Granjon. It was first used in 1966 and has proved an enduring modern classic.